MULTIVERSE OF MYSTERY

A Holmes and Watson Anthology

Sponsored by the International Association of Media Tie-In Writers

Edited by Carrie Harris
Project Managed by Robert Greenberger

For Tina Good and Paul Simpson
With gratitude

MULTIVERSE OF MYSTERY
Edited by Carrie Harris
Project Managed by Robert Greenberger
IAMTW President Jonathan Maberry, Executive Vice President D.J. Stevenson

Publication Design by Aaron Rosenberg
Cover design by Abdullah Bukhari of Book Cover Hub
ISBN 978-1-7362524-6-8 – ISBN 978-1-7362524-5-1 (pbk.)

First edition

Contents

Introduction

This anthology would not exist if not for the International Association of Media Tie-In Writers (IAMTW). The IAMTW is a professional organization for tie-in writers; our membership includes writers of novelizations and original tie-ins based on popular franchises such as *Star Trek*, *Doctor Who*, *Star Wars*, Marvel, *Minecraft*, and Disney, to name just a few. Tie-in writing is a craft all its own, and one that is often misunderstood and underestimated. It needs to work within the framework of the existing material while delivering something new to casual readers and die-hard fans. Doing that well is quite a challenge.

Every story in this anthology is written by IAMTW members who are arguably experts in the field. Their takes on Sir Arthur Conan Doyle's detecting duo transport these familiar characters throughout the multiverse from the far reaches of space to the here and now. They re-envision the characters themselves as time-traveling simian detectives, teenage girls, or Pinkertons. In the process, they explore exactly what makes Sherlock Holmes and Dr. John Watson so compelling.

This project would not be possible without the expertise of the following IAMTW members:

Carrie Harris, editor
Robert Greenberger, project manager
Keith R.A. DeCandido, anthology consultant
Aaron Rosenberg, KS graphics and layout
D.J. Stevenson, finances and fulfillment
Jonathan Maberry, IAMTW President

Special thanks go to proofreader David McDonnell and cover designer Abdullah Bukhari of Book Cover Hub.

The Adventure of the Lioness's Mane

by

Diane Duane

It was early autumn of the year 1895 when Holmes and I, having been caught up in that spring's events surrounding the return of the abominable giant "rats" of Sumatra III, were at last able to return from deep space to the familiar environs of Baker Street. After months of headlong flight among too many planets of five systems, being caught up in not merely one or two but *three* major on- and off-planet engagements, and pursuing (or being pursued by) malefactors and their minions through the unexplored catacombs of an anciently abandoned alien city, the prospect of resuming something like normal routine came as a great relief.

Our exertions on behalf of our nonhuman allies had won us "mentions in dispatches" from the High Guard and the interstellar Alliance. They had also left me with greatly upgraded service kit, and freer access to it than would normally have been allowed to a soldier invalided out in circumstances like mine.

Things had seemed to be quieting down... until the morning of September 28th. Dawn had barely broken when, just past seven, the in-House annunciator system murmured into my implant: *Watson, get up and get dressed. We've a guest coming.*

I groaned... not that it would help in the slightest. "High Guard day blacks," I said to the House after a moment. "Rank flashes only. No medals." *Because whoever they are, they can't expect formals at* this *hour!*

The House laid out the uniform over the end of my bed before I even had time to sit up. "And coffee," I muttered, trying not to make it sound like an imprecation.

When I made my way downstairs, Holmes was sitting by the fire, well-dressed for so early in the day—shirt and tie, and his datavest on—frowning at his hard-paper reader's display. "Ah, Watson," he said, not looking up, "good morning. I heard your coffee arrive."

"One for you as well?" I said, heading into the kitchen.

"Mmnh," said Holmes.

I opened the House's kitchen provisioning box and saw my coffee and one of his: black, two sugars. The cups were two of our good porcelain ones. My eyebrows went up. "Who *is* this new arrival? Someone we know?"

"No," he said, tossing his reader aside. "And yes."

When Holmes was this uncommunicative, it could mean either extreme boredom or great concern. The second seeming more likely, I drank my coffee as quickly as possible. And sure enough, by the time I finished it Holmes was standing by the front windows, gazing downward. "Here they come..."

I joined him there, seeing only Baker Street's normal early traffic: pedestrians, tradesmen's hovs, robocabs passing through. But Holmes's own implant kept him constantly intertwined with the House's data resources, themselves always rooted in London's... so there was no cause for surprise when a handsome streetcraft slid silently up outside 221 and settled down onto its impellers. It was sleek and dark, a custom coachbuild with no external markings.

I whistled softly. "Goodness gracious . . ."

"There's either money or politics in this, Watson," Holmes said. "Possibly both." He pointed at my chair. "Sit!"

I settled myself. A moment later, the front door's knocker rapped.

"Let them in," Holmes said softly to the House. "Direct them upstairs. Then make all secure."

The door opened and shut. Then I heard through my augmentations the quiet hum of the House's anti-surveillance defenses going live.

I glanced at Holmes. He did not often invoke such protections before even speaking to a visitor. But his attention was on the stair.

Our sitting room door slid open, and a tall slim figure veiled in a dark ripple of opaque concealment shields crossed the threshold, pausing there. "Mr. Sherlock Holmes?" she said.

"I am he," Holmes said as the door closed. "And this is my friend and companion, Doctor and Captain John Watson. You are welcome, mistress—?"

"My name is not important." She moved a few steps into the room, looking about; and her carriage and kinesics immediately said to me, *Nonhuman.*

"Very well," Holmes said. "Pray take a seat, Madam, and tell us what brings you here."

The lady's veiled head turned toward Holmes. "I appear to have lost my contact with the Outernet," she said, that low throaty voice sounding suspicious.

"That would be our House's privacy shielding," Holmes said, "which you may have desired to test." He smiled. "No government sited in this city—local, planetary, or interplanetary—can overhear what happens within these walls."

"Excellent," the lady said.

"However, if we are to be of any use to you, it would assist us to see your face."

She hesitated; then waved her veiling away.

Beneath it was a woman of the Mau-t people—a bipedal hominid, furred and leonine of face, with a short mane bound back in rope-plaits entwined with gold wire. Her dress was unremarkable: bodice, leggings and boots in a somber dark blue, a long overskirt of the same, and a darker waist-length cloak pushed back over her shoulders.

"Thank you, Madam," Holmes said. "Sit now and say how we may assist you."

I rose to give her my seat across the fire from Holmes's; then stood behind his chair.

"Mr. Holmes," she said, "the business I must communicate to you may, if it comes to pass, have significant effects on the Alliance."

He nodded. "You may count on our discretion. What is the nature of the expected event?"

"An assassination."

Holmes's eyebrows went up. "Ah. Then I perceive that though you have borrowed one of your household staff's livery-habits today, you are no mere messenger. You are yourself the intended victim; to wit, her Excellency the High Commissioner for Alliance Hearth-world Affairs, Madam Enauheh hsh Hwúnhirh, the senior hereditary pride-queen of Mau-t'Gebh."

Her golden eyes blinked in surprise. "You are correct," said the

Alliance High Commissioner for our entire solar system. "But how ever did you know I had borrowed my clothes?"

Holmes leaned back in his chair. "I did not know. I *saw*. I applaud your Excellency's attempt at anonymity. But as your staff manage your garments' rigging, you have too little experience with setting an intelliraiment-wearable to adjust itself for your height." He gestured at the lady's skirt. "Your hemline had trouble dealing with our stairs. On reaching the landing the skirt tried repeatedly to readjust itself toward someone else's default settings, changing length three times. Between that and your conveyance—the home garaging of which our House tells me is across from the Embassy—your identity was no great reach."

The High Commissioner laughed a Mau-t's growling laugh. "Mr. Holmes, I apologize for my stratagem's ineffectiveness."

Holmes waved this away. "No matter, Madam. You are welcome. May we offer some refreshment?"

"I should not take the time," Madam Enauheh said. "But thank you."

She sighed. "Mr. Holmes, naturally our whole world knows of your and Doctor Watson's services to us and the Alliance during the subspace-Rats' irruption. Since on Friday next we are holding a garden party to celebrate the victory, coming dressed as a courier delivering invitations seemed apt. Yet I cannot help but feel my own business rather more urgent."

"Your forthcoming assassination," Holmes said.

She nodded. "Our system-intelligence service has seen an uptick in chatter on the shadownets about my impending removal from office 'with extreme prejudice.' "

Her casual tone seemed odd to me. "Has your Excellency any known enemies who would be behind such a move?"

She laughed. "Doctor, how does one work in politics without acquiring enemies? But mine have normally been located on Mau-t'Gebh. Now, though, some have relocated here." She lifted her hands, let them fall; her sharp gilded claws flashed in the firelight. "And my intelligence chief, a trusty associate who came up through the civil service with me, informs me that one of the current crop of would-be assassins is located inside the Embassy itself."

I sucked in a shocked breath. "You have no doubts about this?"

"None. 'Dummy' data on my movements that I directed my intelligence chief to plant in our network has appeared on the Shadownet. One of our staff is leaking Alliance-critical information to bad actors. I have, however, delayed opening any internal investigation."

"Fearing such might tip off the mole, impelling them or their co-conspirators to move prematurely," Holmes said. "I think your caution is well-advised."

"The Embassy's extraterritorial—indeed, extraterrestrial—legal status is complex," the High Commissioner said. "We rely on t'Gebh-originated in-house security... but this also may have been compromised. So I have come to you."

Holmes frowned. "Well, we cannot permit the loss of an Alliance High Commissioner to murder."

Astonishingly, Madam Enauheh laughed. "'Loss?'" she said. "Mr. Holmes, don't be overly concerned about that! This has happened to me before. I'm on my third life, with two standby clones in secure storage on t'Gebh. My consciousness backs up to them via hyperspace link every sleep cycle. For me an assassination is a painful but brief inconvenience." She shrugged. "My planetary government's concern is for the perception of political instability that would follow. An indicator that our two worlds' 'special relationship' is not as special as it seems."

Holmes considered. "Tell us how you would like us to proceed."

"You both would naturally be expected at the celebration next week," Madam Enauheh said. "To be subjected to some... I think the word is 'lionization?'"

Holmes's smile was as dry as hers.

"But before then I would ask you to examine our internal data systems, with an eye to ascertaining the identity of our mole."

Holmes glanced at me. I nodded. "Gladly," Holmes said. "All we require is a list of what embassy employees normally have system access, and a way in."

The High Commissioner reached into a hyperinclusion pocket in her robes, withdrew a coin-shaped data tab, and passed it to Holmes. "This contains back-door passwords and the staff access lists."

Madam Enauheh stood, gathering her skirts about her—then

laughed, dropping them as they tried to adjust themselves to the previous defaults. "Mr. Holmes, Doctor—my thanks."

"And ours to you, Excellency," Holmes said as we rose, "for your trust. We will share our findings with you on Friday evening."

She gestured her forceveiling back into existence and went down the stairs.

"A pretty problem," Holmes said, dropping into his seat as the House closed up. "And unfortunately, we must assume that—disguises aside—notice has been taken. We must discover who noticed, and how they react."

He flipped the data-wafer to me; I caught it. "Holmes, what are we dealing with here? Earth-based anti-Alliance insurrectionists? I thought we were years done with such."

Holmes shook his head. "I will not extrapolate ahead of data. But—" He looked exasperated. "There are always people who wish 1690 had never happened; who think we'd be better off alone among worlds and 'free.' However *that* would have looked after the Rats were done with Earth and its inhabitants."

"Indeed. Thank heavens for Sir Isaac Newton!"

"Quite. Meanwhile, whatever fools think, the Alliance's friendship saved our world. Newton being beyond our reach, it's the Mau-t to whom we owe that debt."

"Time to repay a bit of it, then."

Holmes's eyes closed as he sat with fingers once more steepled. The subsurface-jacquarded circuitry of his datavest was shimmering in the morning light as Holmes slipped into the House's data storage to prepare for the work ahead. "This case's waters are already deep," he murmured. "But we face the same old question: *who benefits?*"

"We'll soon find out," I said . . . hoping that that was true.

In the following days, I had little leisure to move away from the data-displays and input portals normally hidden inside the old Chippendale breakfront by the sitting room door. At least I was on familiar ground, for networks were part of my stock in trade: no battle armor functions long without them. And always nearby in the virtual landscape, glimpsed through the glowing underbrush of code-lines, was Holmes, carving his own pathways through the thorny tangle of interrelationships and holographic imageries.

The analysis spilled over into the reality of the sitting room. Endless documents and virtual objects cluttered the air, connected by an ever-more complex web of bright charactery. Holmes sat for hours in a nest of cushions at its heart, classifying what we found... laying the groundwork for the minute observations and deductions only he could make.

The sheer amount of data rendered the task daunting. Every imaginable kind of information from the Embassy had been made available to us, including some that didn't much please me.

"Personal diaries?" I growled to Holmes late Sunday night, sitting on the floor by his cushion-pile while scrolling down one of many lists. "*Medical records?* I don't care for this."

"Nor I," Holmes said. "But there's no telling what we might find that will prevent a murder." He shot me a worried look. "One less reversible than the High Commissioner believes."

"What?"

"Her neurosomatic backups, she says, are backed up every night. But, Watson, where *to?*" Holmes was scowling. "They are being sent out, right enough. But I am not seeing acknowledgement codes that correctly complete the sequences. *Where* are those data packets arriving? And into whose hands?"

That unnerved me. "Perhaps I should cancel this week's appointments and assist you instead . . ."

"By no means! Attend your engagements as scheduled. If our quarry realizes your habits have suddenly changed, our work may become more complicated."

I saw his point and did not like it, but agreed. Unable to set aside my concerns about Madam Enauheh, I went back to examining medical data, hoping clues to her backups' whereabouts might be buried there.

Yet inevitably I was distracted by detail. "Surprising how many of the Embassy's Mau-t staff are female. The ratio is easily four to one . . ."

Holmes nodded. "A working-through of their ancient matriarchal hunting efficiencies into the social and political realms. They do seem to be slowly overcoming a perception of male Mau-t being less capable of producing effective work results than females."

"Except on the battlefield, as we saw."

"Yes; there is more equality there. Elsewhere, less martial social mores are shifting to reflect the change. More gradually, I'm sure, than some would like . . ."

I glanced over some other records. "I suppose there was no reason for her Excellency to mention her pride-family connections in the Embassy."

Holmes raised eyebrows in brief interest. "Are there many?"

"A son and a daughter, both on staff. The daughter works as principal personal assistant; the son supports her." I scrolled idly through the routine medical records attached to their profiles... then paused.

Holmes noticed. "What?"

"Nothing really," I said, still reading. "Their neurochemical and hormonal balances can look peculiar sometimes. The daughter's levels are slightly jagged. Stress, perhaps. She might want to see a Mau-t endocrinologist . . ." I went on to the next batch of documents.

"It's her dam's continued health I'm worried about right now," Holmes said.

"I too. I begin to wonder whether this event will be entirely trouble-free..."

Holmes leaned toward me and gave my arm a conspiratorial squeeze. "Best make sure to bring along your medical kit then, Doctor," he said, launching himself out of the cushions, up to his feet and down toward his room.

On Monday morning I went to the Chelsea Pensioners' Hospital for a long day's physio work on former brothers-in-arms. But returning, I kept getting a sense of being watched; of bright blank glassy gazes just at the edge of my vision. Whenever I looked, they were gone.

It was easy to blame this on the stress of our research—late hours, early mornings. On Tuesday morning I made my way to Baker Street Tube to connect to a jumper for the High Guard orbital installation, there to consult on the servomotor issues plaguing the new Ddraig Goch armor models. And there it was again: the sunlight-glint off some watcher's optics. Finally, I stopped looking—but could not rid myself of an itching sensation between my shoulder blades.

Once planetside I caught a hovcab home, climbed the 17 steps to our flat, and found Holmes in his cushion-nest. He looked up at me and immediately said, "You're troubled."

There was no hiding anything from him, damn it. "Surveillance," I muttered, dropping into my chair, "always bothers me."

"Well, of course you were being watched. That was my intent."

"Holmes!" I said. "What have you been up to?"

"I had a word with the Irregulars."

I concealed a smile. Mechanical creation had become sufficiently advanced for many everyday dronebots and mobiles to unexpectedly surpass the basic synapse number required for sentience. The growing negative reaction to such beings' enslavement finally manifested itself in the Cybernetic Emancipation Act of 1883.

This, however, had left floating or rolling about the city a sad residue of the broken and abandoned—beings whose contracts had run out and who had no one to maintain them. Holmes, though, had seen in these beings' plight an opportunity of sorts, and began funding warehousing and service for a quietly-salvaged flock of them. The day I suggested he was doing this not entirely out of clever practicality, but partly for sentiment's sake, he refused to speak to me for hours . . . as if that was any less revealing a response than straightforward denial. I knew my Holmes.

"I could not have managed this myself," he said. "But I needed to see who might be watching *you*."

"And I was being followed by someone *besides* our own small friends."

Holmes looked grim. "Yes indeed. And where do you think the other watchers were coming from?"

"Perhaps the Alliance Embassy?"

"Exactly! And an Irregular also tracked a non-liveried drone making pickup from a compounding pharmacy *not* used by the Embassy."

"Someone desires to keep their drug purchases off the Embassy's records." My eyes widened. "Holmes! Those hormonal fluctuations I mentioned—"

"Exactly." He gave me a wicked look. "One is tempted to consider some breaking and entering."

"What, of the pharmacy?"

"Pharmacies. The Embassy's onsite purchase records are likely already being altered by the guilty parties—"

"But they'll have no access to those *offsite.*" I leaned back in my chair, cracking my knuckles. "Might be wisest to break into *both* pharmacies, then. If going in through the Alliance Health Service prescriptions system counts as a break-in..."

Holmes chuckled. *"Watson!* Your medical ethics—"

"Primum non nocere, Holmes," I said, grinning. "We're preventing harm. Come lend a hand."

And then it was Friday.

"A fine pair of peacocks we look," I muttered as we got out of the cab in Pepys Street, outside the Alliance's World Embassy.

"I look well enough," Holmes said. On *that* count he was right. Black tie suited him, and it was unfair how much taller the top hat made him seem.

"And *you,* in black and scarlet, look a bit dangerous," Holmes said. "It hints at that other article of clothing..." His gaze dropped to the mess jacket's lapel, and the inside pocket beneath it.

"All's present and correct," I said. "Do you really believe it will be needed?"

"I hope it will not. But . . ." He turned away.

While the molecule-thick synchsuit under my formals was already warning me about my adrenaline levels, I needed no sensors to tell me Holmes's state. "You're nervous."

He scowled. "I fear I may yet be missing something vital, Watson. Deducing Mau-t is not like deducing humans. This evening will make our case or break it."

"Holmes... trust your instincts. Off planet, they served you well. On your own turf, I have no fears. You'll solve this in two shakes of a lion's tail."

He did smile, if tensely; then glanced downhill toward the Tower. "Did you know there was once a zoo down there, Watson? People came from far and near to look at the lions . . ."

"No change, then," I murmured as the Embassy gates opened to reveal their greeter, a broad-shouldered, magnificently maned Mau-t in a coat of gilded brocade. We followed him up the walk into the main building, an arched echoing expanse of amber marble.

Madam Enauheh, also robed in gold, greeted us with a courteous and expert simulation of "we have never met." She led us out a rear door to the famous garden with its unusual surface: a daisy-starred chamomile lawn like the one behind Buck House. It had been a gift from the Royals after the Battle of the Great Repulse near Mars, so that Mau-t'Gebh would have for its own a little spot that was forever England.

The herby turf sent up a sweet sharp scent when trodden on, and was now doing so most emphatically with the crowd of people tucked into that small square plot. Mau-t were roughly equaled in numbers by Earth-humans and nonhumans of the Alliance, and the hedge-bounded space was full of dulcet autotranslation overlaying the growls and trills and melodious shrieks of guests. In the center was a ring-shaped table laden with food and drink, where mechaservitors hovered with drinks trays.

Holmes gazed around with a thoughtful smile, handing his top hat to a passing helper drone. "What now, Holmes?" I said. "Champagne?"

"Not just yet. But shortly, I hope."

He moved off, his gaze roving everywhere in his version of pre-engagement targeting. I made my way to the buffet table and asked for a glass of heqet. "Beer" the Mau-t might call the beverage, treating it as a working-class intoxicant . . . but that was due to the way their metabolisms handled saccharides. It was a safe way for me to avoid alcohol on occasions when I might later be driving.

I spared a few moments to look around at the more nonhuman nonhumans, interested despite myself in the gaggle of Mehretek in their waist-high mobile refrigeration units. But my attention was mostly on the Mau-t. I felt certain that the months spent among them had taught me and Holmes far more than most Earth-humans understood about their expressions and movement.

Holmes, quietly, was making sure. He made the rounds of the Mau-t functionaries and staff in the gathering, being unusually pleasant with them, watching their responses—particularly the Mau-t jaw-dropped "smile" and hissing laughter.

He was certainly getting those, and not just from the Mau-t.

Repeatedly, he was surrounded by beings eager to meet either the hero of the Irruption, or the world's first consulting detective. Each time he had enough of a crowd, Holmes began deducing details about them, one after another, with a sort of merciless good cheer.

Eventually, I joined one such group, accepted some embarrassing adulation, and waited for a moment when I could take my friend's elbow and steer him away.

"Did I seem to need rescuing, Watson?" he said, amused. "Or did you need escape?"

I smiled. "No indeed. But the High Commissioner has been trying to get your attention. I think she has an introduction to make."

He followed me to where she stood with two young Mau-t. "Mr. Holmes," said Madam Enauheh, "Doctor Watson: I present my pride-son Ahauti and pride-daughter Nefer. Nefer is my assistant and attaché in training."

Both wore formal embassy livery. The daughter had her mother's height and cast of face; the son's muzzle was broader and his mane darker, shorn to the length of his sister's. "Master Ahauti," Holmes said, "Madam Nefer—"

He broke off, regarding Nefer closely. "...Madam, I hope you are finding London to your liking."

Small talk was odd for Holmes—but his widened eyes suggested he had seen something alarming. Madam Nefer looked at him curiously. "Very much so, Mr. Holmes!" she said. "It is my favorite city on Earth. Possibly because we have spent more time here than anywhere else . . ."

A little more desultory conversation ensued before the littermates, perhaps reading some signal from their mother, made a courteous excuse and strolled away. Madam Enauheh, meanwhile, regarded Holmes with slight perplexity. "Mr. Holmes—?"

"Your Excellency," Holmes said quietly, "I would ask you to laugh at a joke I have not just made. You too, Watson. Then turn away from the crowd and move toward the hedge."

The High Commissioner immediately threw her head back and hissed like a suit's pressure valve about to fail. So unexpected was the sound that I had no trouble laughing too. Smiling, Holmes reached out to take her sleeve and mine, and led us away.

When no one could see our faces, Holmes eyed Madam Enauheh sidewise, smile quite gone. "Madam, you were not sufficiently open with me last weekend. *Why* did you not tell me about your daughter's mane?"

She blinked. "What? That she *has* one?" She shook hers, its braids' beading clinking. "Mr. Holmes, surely you saw on t'Gebh that females of our class wear manes when in public office. Once manes were rigorously gender-linked, but over centuries they became merely a symbol of authority." She waved at Holmes's throat. "Along the lines of gentlemen's neckties here."

Holmes scowled. "Madam, of *course* it is not that your daughter wears a mane! It is that it is *coming out.*"

The High Commissioner stared.

"You have not noticed?" Holmes said. "Yes, her hairdresser is skilled. But no amount of product or styling can conceal what is happening if one knows what to look for. *Her mane is thinning!* In places the follicles have visibly ceased functioning. Someone has been tampering with her hormones without her knowledge. Someone wants her so ill she must leave her position here."

"Mr. Holmes," the High Commissioner said, very soft, very shocked. "*Who* would—"

"That I hope to tell you within minutes. I believe someone in this garden is associated with the planned attempt on your life, and has been tampering with your somatic backups so that they arrive on Mau-t'Gebh too corrupt to restore your clones."

Her ears went flat. "I will go downstairs to the secure refuge—"

"No," Holmes said. "I beg your Excellency to remain here. If we hold our nerve, we can force the plotter's hand tonight, rendering them harmless."

The High Commissioner hesitated—then said, "I have trusted you thus far. What next?"

"Merely continue circulating among your guests . . . and stay away from *me.* If the Embassy staffer involved with your intended murderers *is* here, it remains only to provoke them into revealing themselves."

She nodded. Holmes nodded back, and turning, wandered off.

The Ambassador glanced at me. "Doctor Watson . . . what do you make of this?"

"Holmes's behavior?" I shook my head. "Standard operating procedure, Madam. But take him at his word—stay well clear."

She nodded to me in turn and moved away.

I was considering another heqet when Holmes reappeared at my elbow. "They are exactly where required to start the drama moving," he said. "Look there—"

Master Ahauti and Madam Nefer had moved apart from the crowd and stood side by side, heads close together as they talked. As we watched, each idly laid their tail across the other's back. Master Ahauti's shoulders shook, and even here one could hear his sister's hiss of laughter.

"The lion's *tail,*" Holmes said softly. "Look at their body language! Even for us, their mutual affection is unmistakable. And as for others, who might for some reason be offended by it—?"

Holmes was tense now, a predator preparing to spring. "There is something I must see before they move."

"Can I help?"

"Stay near, but out of view. I am about to set the scene. *You* be ready to make one." He meandered away in the general direction of the Commissioner's son and daughter.

Holmes paused by the central table, seemingly considering the refreshments. But I saw how, after another glance at Ahauti and Nefer, he began idly turning on the spot so as to take in everyone in the garden.

Then Holmes stopped, sighting something. His eyes narrowed.

I knew that look. I had no clear view of his sightline, but I backed behind a large ornamental planter and moved along the nearby hedge, hoping I was sufficiently out of sight . . . while making sure I did not lose sight of *him.*

Having acquired a glass of champagne, Holmes went sauntering toward one of the small tables standing about the lawn where people could gather and rest their glasses. Carefully, I worked my way along the hedge until I could see both Holmes and, leaning at one table, a tallish young Mau-t in Embassy livery. He was lean, with a long dark mane, nursing a tall mixed drink of some kind.

Holmes wandered up with his glass of champagne and nodded in a friendly way. "May I?"

"Of course."

He peered at the name showing breast-high in the fabric of the being's intelliraiment. "Master–Isfet, is it?"

"That's right, Mr. Holmes. A pleasure to meet you!"

"Diplomatic staff?" Holmes said.

"Oh no," Master Isfet said. "I work in IT."

"Fascinating work," Holmes said, all admiration. "Do you mind answering a question?"

"Of course not," Isfet said. "Anything for the human who helped win the Battle of the Irruption!"

"You're very kind," Holmes said. "Master Isfet—why the Mefilistenone?"

The Mau-t stared. "I beg your pardon?"

"You started poisoning her with Emitramib first," Holmes said, glancing over his shoulder at Madam Nefer. "But then you changed your mind—or the pliable doctor assisting you did—and began using Mefilistenone instead." Holmes was gradually raising his voice. "Were symptoms manifesting before your associates were ready to act against the High Commissioner?"

Heads turned. Master Isfet bristled visibly. "I don't know what you're—"

"The change of medications seems to have helped for the moment. But it will still be just a matter of days before Madam Nefer winds up in hospital with seriously damaged hormonal and brain chemistry."

Isfet stared at Holmes. I kept moving through the shadows, along the hedge.

"They'll not be able to do much for her, of course. She will be shipped back to Mau-t'Gebh for treatment that will be too little, too late... and will depart the diplomatic service with not just her career, but her health destroyed."

Everyone in the garden was staring now. "I'm sure you think Master Ahauti will move right into his poor pride-sister's position," Holmes said. "The one he deserves, if you're someone who believes your species' males are badly treated for this day and age, and change isn't happening fast enough. But those far above you who sold you this idea were using you to further far deadlier intentions."

Master Isfet lowered his head and began to growl.

"Oh come now," Holmes said, "you never fancied yourself their *equal*, did you?" He laughed. "You were a tool. And such easy prey! All those nights spent down in the designer sugar bars in Soho, hmm? All those conversations with people who bought you drinks to loosen your tongue. People who suggested you could help Master Ahauti into a position of power... whether the 'help' was legal or not. But they didn't really care about your little in-house power play. What they wanted *you* for was access to the High Commissioner's backups."

The young Mau-t began to bend into a crouch over the table, so that his face, wrinkling into a snarl, was almost on a level with Holmes's.

Holmes's eyes narrowed. "Don't delude yourself, Master Isfet. With control of Madam Enauheh's backup data and her clones, those people intended to blackmail her into supporting their own positions on the Alliance's affiliation with Earth. If she refused, she'd have an 'accident' from which her backups could not restore her. And *you,* who'd panic and spill everything under questioning, would quickly have an accident too. Or did you truly not think that far ahead? *Pitiful.*"

Isfet's growl grew louder. I slipped closer, sliding my hand into the inclusion pocket inside my mess jacket's breast and feeling for the expansion actuator.

"Anyway, using your palmprint to pick up those replacement drugs was idiotic," Holmes said. "Naturally the pharmacies stored that record. That didn't occur to you either? You're really not cut out for this kind of thing."

One of Isfet's hands had slipped out of sight, into his intelliraiment. *The Embassy will have its normal weapons damper field operational for this event,* I thought, as the actuator stud vibrated under my fingers to let me know my equipage was ready for release. *Let's hope the field's settings haven't been tampered with—*

"In any case," Holmes said, leaning forward until he was practically nose-to-muzzle with Isfet, "the evidence of your signature at the pharmacy was not *quite* enough to raise you above the level of deluded stooge."

All down my back, under my mess jacket, the synchsuit vibrated—hooking not-yet-deployed weaponry into my nerves as I initiated preliminary target acquisition. The in-eyes display glowed softly in my field of vision, identifying the lifeform signatures gathered before me and highlighting the two that were of the greatest interest—

"What *I* needed," Holmes said, "was to see how you looked at Madam Nefer and Master Ahauti when they were together. And to see you *hating* how content they were with their present relative positions at the Embassy, and with each other, *just as they were*—"

Master Isfet kicked the table aside, grabbed Holmes around the body from behind, and pressed a blaster into his side.

I stepped out of the shadows, hit my equipage's actuator, and spread my arms.

The first time people see the quick-rig basic High Guard armor deploy itself, they usually say, "It seemed like it was alive." And when in synch with a trained armorist in his synsuit, it *is* alive. In barely a breath's time the compressed matter of the structure pulls itself out of abeyance-space, expands into a sudden hard-shelled flower of metal, enfolds the limbs, encases the head, builds out its weaponry, and hums its readiness.

That hum pulled all eyes away from Holmes and Isfet and over to me. A man in a mostly-black uniform had been standing there. In his place was a darkly gleaming blank-helmed metal statue plated in the Royal Armoured Medical Corps' blood-crimson and ebony, with the glowing telltales of primed weapons running up and down its back and chest and arms.

"Drop that," I said through the suit's audio.

Master Isfet immediately made the mistake others have made. He turned his weapon toward *me*, thinking me equipped with something too clumsy and undiscriminating to use in a crowd.

In speed-augmented time the armor noted Isfet's finger tightening on the blaster's trigger, analyzed its speed and pressure, and listed useful options.

Nonlethal 2, I told the suit.

From the faired-in shoulder rack, the armor fired a single shining smart round that in midair broadcast-damped the blaster's pulse coil, extruded a four-pronged claw, snatched the blaster from Isfet's fingers, arced back toward me while crushing the weapon into a useless lump, and dropped it at my feet. Then the round perched on my shoulder like a bird of prey ready to fly again.

Isfet staggered—then grabbed at Holmes once more, got him in a hammerlock, and dug his claws into the side of his neck. "Get back, or I'll rip his throat out!"

But the Mau-t had made another common mistake: thinking my friend's great brain was all the defense he had. Holmes instantly tossed the contents of his champagne glass over his shoulder into Isfet's eyes. Then while the Mau-t tried to shake his vision clear, Holmes threw the glass aside, took a two-handed hold of the arm across his throat, bent forward, and flung the Mau-t hard over his head.

Holmes was already on his feet again even as Isfet hit the ground and began trying to scramble back up once more.

"Stay right where you are," I said. "I wouldn't care to set fire to you—"

He glared at me. "I'm a Mau-t citizen on Mau-t soil, you're *bluffing—!*"

Isfet froze as my right-arm pulsers lanced out in needle-thin lines, annihilating the air they pierced through and stitching a red-hot arc exactly half a meter around him. A second later, when the smoke cleared, everyone stared at the ground around the Mau-t, and the tiny spots that (having moments before been daisies) were *all* that was burning.

"I wouldn't have liked to hurt the chamomile," I said. "Which as it happens is on Terran soil. The dirt came from Buckingham Palace, with the plants. But as for you? Stay down... or who knows? The burning might spread."

Like everyone else, Isfet could hear my armor's servos making the adjustments needed to fire again—

Snarling, Isfet collapsed to a defeated hands-and-haunches crouch on the chamomile lawn.

Holmes stepped nearer, gazing down at him in chilly disdain. "Planetary and Alliance Intelligence now have a full record of what you tried to do. The police will shortly collect you and the Embassy's security video . . . which should prove most edifying, once coordinated with our report—"

From the front of the Embassy came a sudden humming chorus of impellers as a crowd of Met vehicles began to land. This was swiftly followed by the commotion of a swarm of recording drones and uniformed officers piling through the garden door.

I had other concerns as the constabulary took Isfet away. Having told my armor to fold itself away, and with its mass collapsed and stowed back into its inclusion pocket, I went to Holmes. "Let me see your throat."

He scowled affectionately at me. "Doctor, don't fuss, it's merely a scratch!"

"You will kindly let *me* be the judge of that," I muttered, reaching into my mess jacket's pocket and pulling out a dermafuser.

The High Commissioner hurried over. "Mr. Holmes! Are you quite all right?"

"He will be in about 30 seconds," I said. "Sherlock, hold *still!*"

Holmes threw her a look of helpless amusement. "And you, Madam?"

"Shaken," Madam Enauheh said. "Both by the threat to my children—which I never imagined—and seeing it so emphatically removed."

"Understandable," Holmes said as I turned him loose. "Meanwhile, once the video gets out—for easily half your guests were camming what occurred—the criminals of London may allow Doctor Watson and myself *some* peace before becoming bumptious again."

"One can only hope," I said.

"Meanwhile," said Holmes, "I am glad to leave to your Excellency's own intelligence services the business of tracking these plotters back to their lairs on Mau-t. I am sure ours will cooperate in whatever way you ask."

"Speaking for Mau-t, I can safely say that our world is grateful for Earth's partnership," Madam Enauheh said. "As for you and the Doctor, Mr. Holmes—how are we to thank *you* properly?"

Holmes glanced at me. "Madam," I said, "perhaps we can discuss that after the weekend. Our own needs are small... but our House can always use more server space."

"And beyond that," Holmes said, dusting off his tails, ". . . for now, I think I should like another champagne."

The Curious Incident of the Blog in the Night-time

by

Marshella Rockwell

"Pinkerton? Those are still a thing?" asked Adina Solomon, my newest client, her blonde brows arching in surprise.

Here we go again, I thought, my perfunctory smile turning plastic.

"Yes, though that whole Wild West, union-busting thing isn't really our schtick anymore," I replied, adopting my best bored tour-guide tone, hoping to hurry things along. Scuffed boots, jeans, and pearl snaps on my shirt notwithstanding, we truly weren't the same company Allan Pinkerton had created back in the 1800s, not since my great-something aunt, Danita Warne—the granddaughter of Kate Warne, America's first female detective and one of Pinkerton's pre-eminent spies—had purchased the company outright in the early twentieth century. But Allan Pinkerton cast a long, dark shadow that we still languished beneath. "We mostly focus on personal security and investigations these days. I do the latter. I'm just a regular old private investigator."

Well, not *quite* regular. Which was supposedly why I was here.

"Oh," Solomon replied, seemingly disappointed. They always were, though for the life of me, I'd never understand why. The Pinkertons had done some nasty shit on ole AP's watch, leaving us with a legacy that should by rights be more con than pro, but somehow never was.

"Speaking of which, can you give me a little more information about your case? All the office told me was there were horses involved."

Not exactly true, but most clients were eager to fill in any details they thought "the office" might have left out of my briefing.

"*A* horse," Solomon corrected. "A thoroughbred. My Derby hopeful, Rapid Ash. He's gone missing."

Great. A missing Pokémon case. Aunt Helena must still be pissed at me after I'd bungled the Morrison job. But her ire didn't explain why I'd been assigned this particular case. My branch of the Pinkertons didn't do run-of-the-mill investigations; not unless those mills were haunted. We focused on what some would call the paranormal—cases that actually wound up having a perfectly rational explanation 99.99% of the time. The other 0.01%, they were filed under "God Only Knows and He/She Ain't Talking" and quickly hushed up.

But since I was pretty sure I wasn't looking for an actual Pokémon, I needed a *bit* more information to go on.

"Gone missing . . . ?" I repeated encouragingly.

"Yes," Solomon replied, waving a diamond-bedecked hand at me. "Talk to his trainer, Jimmy Cadotte. He's down at the stables. He was there; he can tell you everything."

I wrote down "Pokémon trainer Cadotte" in my battered Moleskine before pushing up the glasses that had begun their inevitable slide down my perennially sweaty nose. As I turned to leave, Solomon tacked on one last caveat. Though honestly, it sounded more like a threat.

"Oh, and Ms. Adler-Watson?" she added, rather rudely omitting my honorific, which was just as hard-earned as that of any medical doctor, if somewhat more esoteric. "Rapid Ash is the favorite to win the Derby and take the Triple Crown. No one can know he's missing. The oddsmakers in Vegas would lose their minds."

Nothing compared to what you'd lose, I thought, but wisely refrained from saying, as I saw myself out.

A young woman in a red ribbon skirt and a much older man stood waiting for me in front of Ash's stall, watching silently as I approached. The man had skin like bark, silver hair, and eyes as dark as a moonless night. The woman was shorter, with black hair worn in two long braids, beaded earrings that hung to her collarbone, and those same dark eyes that pierced and engulfed, all at once.

"Jimmy Cadotte," the man said, holding out his hand to me, which I grudgingly tore my eyes away from his companion to accept. "This here's my niece, Shirley Bagakaabi Holmes. She's from the—"

"—the rez, Uncle, just like you," Shirley interrupted smoothly, giving her uncle the side-eye while she held out her own hand. Her grip was strong, but her hand was nowhere near as calloused as her uncle's.

Hmm. Probably a college girl. Who doesn't want me to know where she landed after or what she's doing here. Interesting.

"From the rez, huh?" I replied, giving her hand a firm shake before releasing it more reluctantly than I would have liked. "Which one?"

"Shirley's people are Little Shell, from over in Montana," her uncle replied. "Also Métis, from the Red River, up Manitoba way. Me, I'm Mille Lacs."

"I'm Reena Adler-Watson," I said. "Ms. Solomon hired my firm to find out what happened to her Poké—err, her stallion. She said Mr. Cadotte was here the night Ash disappeared and could fill me in?"

Cadotte snorted.

"Not much to tell. Least not in Ms. Solomon's version."

"Uncle . . ." Shirley began, but I just smiled benignly at Cadotte.

"I'd very much like to hear your version, if you don't mind," I said, pulling out my much-abused notebook.

"Okay, well, I don't like to work my horses too hard before a race, so I took Ash for a nice, easy ride through the woods there," Jimmy began, gesturing to the wall of pines that marked the Superior National Forest. "Only supposed to keep horses on the roads, least accordin' to the Rangers. But my people knew this country long before it was a 'park.' Ain't nobody tellin' me how to handle my horse *here*."

"Of course not," I agreed quickly, trying to head off a rant about the evils of the US government and settler-colonialism in general. Not that I didn't agree; I just didn't have time for it. I had a missing Pokémon to find. "But I'm assuming that's not when Ash disappeared?"

Cadotte snorted. Okay, it *had* been a dumb thing to say. But it got the story moving again, so I wasn't particularly embarrassed about it.

Then I noticed the corner of Holmes's mouth twitching.

Well, *now* I was particularly embarrassed.

"No, but you wanted me to tell you what happened that night, so I'm tellin' ya," Cadotte replied, a little huffily. "Anyway, ride was pretty peaceful; not a lot of folks in the forest that time of night. I did run into David and Gretchen Springer comin' back from the Bee Dub. That's the Boundary Waters Canoe Area Wilderness, where they go for material for their nightly stargazin' blog. Good night for it, too—clear, bit nippy. Place is a designated dark sky sanctuary, you know."

I did not, but I nodded anyway, jotting down the Springers' names and the words "stargazin' blog," "clear," and "nippy" in my notebook before squinching my nose to push my glasses back up.

"Anyway, they didn't stop for their usual chat—Gretchen looked a little pale, so I figured her mornin' sickness was actin' up, or she was bushed from that heavy pack she's always carryin'—so me and Ash just went on our merry way, takin' a quick loop through the pines before headin' back to the stables."

Solomon Equestrian Farms was located in northern Minnesota; a strange place to raise thoroughbreds. Or maybe not so strange, considering Solomon got a significant tax break from her good buddy, Governor Bobby Joe.

"Was this a route you normally took with Ash?" I asked, pulling my thought-train back onto the tracks and making a mental note to ask my doc about upping my ADHD meds. "And was anyone else privy to it?"

"Yes and no," Cadotte replied. "Yes, because it's safe—clear of roots or hidden gullies just waitin' to trip up a horse. No, because Ms. Solomon knows winnin', but she don't know horses. Not when it comes to handlin' them with respect."

I jotted down "safe path" and "no respect."

"Okay, so the ride was uneventful," I prodded. "What happened when you got back?"

"I brought Ash into his stall, brushed him down, made sure he had enough feed and water, gave him some sugar as a treat. Then I closed the stall up behind me and left for the night. That was the last time I saw him."

"No security cameras in the stable?" I asked. Seemed like a no-brainer for a place housing a Derby contender.

Cadotte shook his head.

"Not since Mr. Solomon caught Ms. Solomon on tape makin' hay with a stable hand. She had them all taken out the day the property was signed over to her in the divorce."

Unfortunate for both Mr. Solomon and myself.

"So, what do you think happened to Ash?" I asked Cadotte, pen at the ready.

The old man shrugged.

"I think Mishipeshu got him."

"Mishi-*what*-now?" I asked, pen hovering uncertainly.

"Mishipeshu. The great underwater panther who guards our waterways." Ahh. A possible cryptid. *That's* why I'd been assigned this case. "There've been sightings."

"Uncle—" Holmes started again in that same warning tone, but Cadotte cut her off as I scribbled down "M.P." and "sightings."

"No, Shirley," he said with a sharp shake of his head. "You may have gotten yourself a degree from a fancy school and a job with the Feds, but you don't know everything."

Ooh, interesting. I'd gotten the college student part right, but hadn't clocked her as a suit. To be fair, she wasn't *wearing* a suit. And even if she had a job with an alphabet agency, it could just as easily be the BIA or IRS as the FBI or CIA. Still . . . would an accountant have come to investigate a racehorse "gotten" by a cryptid? Seemed unlikely.

". . . are reasons our Anishinaabe ancestors passed these tales down from generation to generation," Jimmy was saying, "and it's not because they had nothin' better to do on cold winter nights. It's because these stories contain knowledge that kept them alive. Knowledge we'd do well to heed if we want to be here to pass it down to the generations to follow."

Cadotte turned to me, his face grim.

"Mark my words. There is somethin' in those woods makin' Mishipeshu unhappy. Poor Ash was just collateral damage."

With that, Cadotte excused himself to tend to some of the other horses while I wrote down "collateral damage" in my notebook. When I looked up, Holmes was staring at me.

"You didn't even crack a smile when Uncle declared that a creature out of Anishinaabe legend was the culprit behind Ash's disappearance. Why is that, I wonder, Ms. Adler-Watson?"

I shrugged, a little uncomfortable at her scrutiny.

"There are more things in heaven and earth than are dreamt of in my philosophy. I try to keep an open mind."

"Or, more accurately, you get paid to," she replied, those dark eyes narrowing.

I didn't see any point in denying it. But it made me more certain than ever that she was no bean counter; the fact that the Pinkertons dabbled in paranormal investigations was not public knowledge.

"I get paid to investigate lots of things, Ms. Holmes, just like you do." It was a shot in the dark, but I didn't think I was too far off target. Folks like Jimmy Cadotte reserved a particular tone for the word "Fed," and there were only a few agencies that merited that sharp blend of distrust and contempt due to their mistreatment of Native Americans over the course of the country's history. Of the four most frequent offenders I'd already narrowed it down to, only two would know about the Pinkerton Agency's extracurriculars, and only one would be interested in said activities on American soil.

Shirley Holmes was a Feeb.

To my surprise, her expression lightened and she laughed.

"Nicely done," she said, sticking her hand out again. "I think we got off on the wrong foot. Hi, I'm Shirley."

Chuckling myself, I took the proffered hand.

"Reena. It's a pleasure."

Then she released my hand and her face turned serious again.

"I may be a 'Fed,' as Uncle likes to say, but I'm not here in an official capacity, and even if I were, I'm definitely more Scully than Mulder. I don't believe Mishipeshu is roaming the Superior National Forest gobbling up thoroughbreds, and I don't think Adina Solomon does, either. I think they're going to try to pin Ash's disappearance on Uncle Jimmy, if for no other reason than because he's brown. And I'm here to make sure that doesn't happen."

I nodded. Cadotte *was* the most likely suspect, whether he'd acted out of greed, malice, or sheer inattention. But I didn't think it was him.

Aunt Helena had sent me the financials on Solomon, Cadotte, and a handful of others who might have some interest in either selling, ransoming, or making an insurance claim on Ash, and Cadotte's hadn't raised any red flags.

That was part of the problem. *No one's* had.

"No reason we can't work together," I said, then immediately felt my cheeks burning, though I wasn't sure why. "If you're amenable, that is."

"Sure. Six eyes are better than two," she said, winking—I assume to show she was joking and not because she was flirting—before turning to Ash's stall.

"I did take the liberty of examining the stall before you arrived," she admitted. I wasn't surprised; I'd've done the same. "No indication Ash was drugged, no signs of a struggle. You're welcome to look yourself."

She opened the door and stood to one side, but having been in a stable only a handful of times before, I motioned for Holmes—err, Shirley to take the lead. I followed her in and the stall door swung closed automatically behind me, latch clicking into place.

I was unprepared for the overwhelming stew of odors that immediately assaulted my unsuspecting nostrils. I'd smelled both compost piles and sewage ponds before, and this was like they'd had a gassy—and possibly demonic—baby. I knew these stables were pristine by most standards, but my nose was unusually sensitive when it came to certain scents, and apparently *parfum d'écurie* was one of them. Trying not to gag, I gave the stall the most cursory of glances, noted the absence of both blood and ransom demands, and pushed my way back out again as quickly as I could. It was only after the door had swung closed behind Shirley and latched again that I realized how odd that was.

"Isn't the latch supposed to keep things *inside* the stall?" I asked when I could breathe.

Shirley looked at me sharply, then went over to pull on the stall door. The latch held firmly. She went back inside, waited for it to close behind her, then pushed on the door.

It opened right up.

"Well, I guess now we know there's a good chance Ash escaped, as opposed to being Pokémon-napped," I quipped as I made note of the latch's defect in my Moleskine. "Now we just have to figure out where he wandered off to."

"Or was lured to," Shirley added.

"Or that," I agreed, a bit dubiously. "Though I'm sure you have someone back at Quantico watching the financials of everyone even tangentially related to this case, just like we do. You'd know by now if money had changed hands."

"I like to keep an open mind," she replied with a quick grin, and I couldn't help but smile back at her. Then her expression grew thoughtful, which I found equally mesmerizing. "If Ash did get out, he would have gone somewhere familiar. But he's not anywhere on the grounds, or they would have found him by now. So he most likely retraced the route he was on last."

I nodded. That tracked.

"Let's go find Uncle Jimmy," I said.

Cadotte took us out into the woods, albeit begrudgingly.

"I already looked all along our regular path," he protested. "He ain't here, and even if he had somehow wandered out this far, he'd have come home by now. For the food, if nothin' else. He doesn't like pine needles."

I didn't blame him. The forest smelled like Christmas on steroids and was already giving me a headache.

"We know, Uncle," Shirley said placatingly. "We're just looking for clues. Any little thing might hold the key, even if it seemed insignificant at the time. Like where you crossed paths with the Springers, for instance."

"Oh, them? Ran into 'em just over by that log. But they didn't have anythin' to do with Ash's disappearance!" Cadotte exclaimed, obviously affronted.

"Of course not, Uncle," Shirley said, her tone remaining respectful and conciliatory. "We're just trying to find him, that's all."

While they argued, I surreptitiously pulled out my phone and Googled "Mishipeshu." To my surprise, in addition to watching over the multitudinous lakes and waterways in the Great Lakes area, the great underwater panther was also credited with fiercely guarding the area's copper deposits, and not reacting kindly to those who mined them without permission.

Which made me wonder why Mishipeshu would bother going after a stallion when there were plenty of mining operations around to harass, with new ones popping up every few months. Maybe Ash had just been a midnight snack?

Cadotte's huffing subsided as we approached the log. Shirley leaned over to examine the ground, motioning for me and her uncle to stay back, presumably so as not to disturb any tracks where the path Ash and Cadotte had taken and the one the Springers had followed intersected.

As she inspected the ground—which just looked like a carpet of pine needles indistinguishable from any other part of the forest floor to me—I exchanged my phone for my notebook and turned to Cadotte.

"What can you tell me about the Mishipeshu sightings?"

Cadotte eyed me for a moment, as if gauging whether or not I was making fun of him. Apparently deciding I was in earnest, he spilled all the great underwater panther tea.

"The legends say Mishipeshu has the body of a great cat, the horns of the bison, the tail of a dragon, and is covered in scales. His eyes glow red like the fires used to smelt copper and his voice is the voice of the storm."

"What do the people who claim to have seen him today say? Do their descriptions match those of the legends?"

"Eh," he replied, his tone suddenly dismissive, as if the legends were to be believed unequivocally, but the modern-day accounts might be a different matter. "Depends on the people, I'd say."

My pen hovered.

"Care to clarify?"

"Sometimes you hear rumors through the telegraph—" he began.

"Telegraph?" I interrupted, unsure if this warranted a note.

"The moccasin telegraph. The Indian grapevine. They talk mostly about a warnin' presence dartin' through the trees, too fast to be seen, only felt. Or a sudden wind roarin' across the shore, even though the skies are clear and water's calm. Those I believe.

"The ones from that website? Red eyes and growls and giant pawprints? Those, not so much."

"Website?" I repeated, writing the word down, leaving my pen on the paper to record its name, should Cadotte deign to share it.

"Minnesota Monster Mapper."

"Does it have a record of the sightings? Any times when they are more likely to occur, any detectable pattern to them? If so, would Ash's disappearance fit into one of those timeframes?"

Cadotte held up a hand as if to ward off my barrage of questions.

"Slow your roll there, cowgirl," he cautioned, shaking his head at my enthusiasm. Or maybe at my irritation quotient. My ADHD often made those two things indistinguishable, at least for people who weren't me. "I wouldn't know. Never seen the damned thing myself."

I highly doubted that, given his familiarity with its contents, but Shirley returned at that precise moment, so I left the comment unchallenged as I dutifully noted the information down.

"It rained the day after Ash's disappearance," she said, brushing pine needles and dirt off her ribbon skirt. "I've been able to make out his hoofprints on the trail every so often, and I can see where two sets of footprints I presume belong to the Springers join them, right where Uncle said. But once you get off the trail, there's no sign of any of them."

She paused for a moment, gazing thoughtfully at nothing in particular.

"It is interesting, though."

"What is?" I asked.

"The Springers' prints appear to overlap Ash's. Which shouldn't be the case if they left *before* Ash and Uncle Jimmy did."

I jotted down "overlap" and "left first" before looking up to meet her gaze.

"Time to visit the Springers?"

She nodded.

"Time to visit the Springers."

After agreeing to meet Shirley at the Springers' place the next morning, I headed back to my hotel room, where I perused the website Cadotte had mentioned over a dinner of too-spicy Chinese takeout. Minnesota was apparently home to Bigfoot, multiple lake monsters, something called the Minnesota Iceman that may or may not have been a hoax, and a homegrown werewolf known as the Duluth Dogman, among others. Mishipeshu had his own page complete with known "sightings" going back years, as contributed by various "witnesses" who left their rambling, misspelled, and poorly punctuated tales in the comments section, along with their screen names.

Interestingly, the most recent sighting had happened the same night Ash had disappeared, and in somewhat the same vicinity. As Cadotte had intimated, the garbled tale spoke of flaming red eyes and roars so loud they made the ears bleed, with a mysterious fog that rolled in from nowhere thrown in for good measure. This entry into the region's cryptid folklore had been authored by someone going by the moniker of SLaDe. Upon further investigation, SLaDe appeared to have been the lucky winner of several terrifying near brushes with the great underwater panther, all within the past five years. Seeing as the rest of the entries were from people with different handles and writing styles—some who even knew how to properly use an Oxford comma—I noted SLaDe's encounter dates in particular down in my notebook and texted the links to Shirley, just in case she could suss out some other pattern that I wasn't seeing.

I was about to plug my phone in for the night when a local news notification popped up about PolyMet Mining having filed permits for a new proposed copper mine just outside the Boundary Waters Canoe Area Wilderness. Apparently, Adina Solomon's pocket wasn't the only one the governor resided in. Shaking my head at corporate greed and wondering again why Mishipeshu didn't go hunt down *those* guys, I dismissed the notification without reading the article and went to bed.

The next morning, Shirley and I met at the turnoff leading to the Springers' home. Being someone who investigated things that went bump in the night, I wasn't as accustomed to the early hour as she was, and it showed.

"You look tired," she said by way of greeting, to which I responded with an indecipherable grunt, proving her point.

The Springers lived in a two-story house on five acres of land a few miles from Solomon Equestrian Farms. The property had once been a working farm, as evidenced by a dilapidated barn visible beyond the house, but was clearly so no longer. The fields had gone to seed, weeds grew high and rampant, and limp strips of faded blue exterior paint hung from the house, flayed from the wood by the unforgiving elements. The porch stairs creaked in protest as we made our way up to the door, though their complaints could not be heard over the clanging of multiple rusted windchimes.

The porch itself housed an impressive collection of large geodes, stacks of soil sieves, and what looked like core samples with the labels mostly worn away—I could just make out a "NOCU" on one and what might be "YME" on another, both of which I quickly jotted down on the off chance they might prove to be important. The whole assortment of rocks and equipment seemed more fitting for the home of a geologist than that of two astronomers.

Shirley and I exchanged silent glances before she knocked loudly on the screen door.

A dingy curtain in the window next to the door twitched almost imperceptibly, but I'd had a feeling we were being watched long before now. I doubt the Springers knew what to make of us, though, a Native woman in a ribbon skirt and blazer and a white woman in flannel and jeans.

Or maybe they knew exactly what to make of us, and that's why they hadn't answered the door.

Shirley had just raised her fist to knock again when the interior door opened to reveal a very pregnant woman standing in the shadows.

"Can I help you?"

"Mrs. Springer?" Shirley asked, pulling her badge from inside her jacket and flashing it at the startled woman on the other side of the screen. "I'm Special Agent Holmes and this is my associate, Dr. Adler-Watson." I blinked in momentary surprise, since I'd never shared my title with her. Shirley had been doing some research of her own last night.

"May we come in?" she continued, pocketing her ID. "We have a few questions for you and your husband about the disappearance of Rapid Ash from Solomon Farms."

"Oh, but we don't know anything about that!" Mrs. Springer protested, one hand flying up to cover her mouth. "We'd never hurt Ash!"

"Of course not," Shirley said, using that same conciliatory tone she'd used on her uncle earlier. "No one is suggesting that. We just want to ask you a few questions. People often have information that seems inconsequential, but turns out to be very important."

"I—I suppose so," Mrs. Springer replied in a deflated tone, opening the screen door and waving us inside. "Though I'm surprised the FBI would care about a missing horse."

The FBI would be surprised, too, considering Shirley's presence here was personal, not professional, but I certainly wasn't going to rat her out. I figured the intergenerational trauma visited on her people by the federal government gave her pretty wide leeway when it came to using that same government's resources to help her family. And if those resources also helped me crack this case and get paid? Win-win.

Mrs. Springer led us down a gloomy corridor lined with framed newspaper articles featuring pictures of her and a bespectacled man I presumed was Mr. Springer. We were walking too quickly for me to process any of the headlines except one: "U of M Astrogeology Professor and Several Native American Activists Arrested at Line 3 Protest." It was an odd thing to display on your wall. Springer was either proud of his activism or had a giant chip on his shoulder.

Then we were being ushered into a small living room that was only slightly less dim than the hallway had been; the curtains were all drawn and there was only one lamp lit, on a side table forming the corner angle between a mismatched green couch and loveseat. Mrs. Springer sat on the loveseat while gesturing for us to sit on the couch.

"I apologize for the lighting," she said as Shirley and I settled as best we could onto the lumpy couch. "I've been having a lot of migraines, and sunlight has become my nemesis. I'm only teaching night classes now."

"I'm so sorry," Shirley said sympathetically. "Chronic migraines are the worst."

"I appreciate that," Mrs. Springer replied with a tight smile. "But you said you were here about Ash?"

As she spoke, the bespectacled man from the newspaper articles entered the room. He reeked of bourbon and cigarette smoke.

"Don't get up," he said as he walked over to shake our hands, though neither Shirley nor I had made a move to do so. "Professor David Springer. And you are?"

My attention drifted while Shirley explained why we were here again. Scientific journals and parenting magazines littered the coffee table, while the stone fireplace was flanked by tall bookcases overstuffed with a mix of academic texts, art books, and other volumes I couldn't identify from where I sat. Several framed licenses and diplomas hung over the mantle, some bearing Mrs. Springer's maiden name—Gretchen Marie Williams—and some bearing that of her odorific husband, David Lee Springer.

". . . run a stargazing blog?" Shirley was asking when I reined my focus back in, though something about the sheepskins on the wall tickled at the back of my brain.

"Dark Skies Over Dark Waters," Springer said guardedly. "What's that got to do with Solomon's missing horse?"

"You update it regularly?" Shirley pressed, ignoring his question.

"Pretty much every night, unless we're both travelling or too sick to go out to the Bee Dub. We're kinda sticklers about it, since it's linked to Gretchen's teaching stipend," Springer replied, his eyes narrowing. Mrs. Springer was chewing nervously at the remains of a nailbed, eyes darting back and forth between the two verbal combatants.

"In point of fact, you failed to update your blog 15 times over the course of the past five years," Shirley said, her eyes shining brightly in the dim room, like a bloodhound that had caught the scent of her quarry. I leaned forward, eager to see how she'd connected what to me were still just scattered dots.

"If you say so," Springer responded, "but I still fail to see what that has to do with Ash."

"It has everything to do with him. Or, rather, with the date on which he disappeared."

"What are you *talking* about?" Springer demanded, clearly angry now.

"I'm talking about the date in question and the curious incident of the blog in the night-time."

"But, wait. There *was* no blog entry for that night," I pointed out, now as confused as Springer.

"*That* was the curious incident."

"*Enough!* Stop speaking in riddles and just tell us what you think we did!" We all turned in surprise to look at Mrs. Springer. "I simply *cannot* handle more stress."

"My apologies, Mrs. Springer," Shirley replied, inclining her head to the other woman. "I'll speak plainly."

She turned back to Mr. Springer.

"Mr. Cadotte has already told us that he encountered you in the forest returning from the 'Bee Dub' when he was riding Ash in the forest the night the stallion disappeared. But if you had indeed returned home after that chance meeting with Mr. Cadotte, you would have had plenty of time to make a blog entry. And your footprints would not have been found on top of Ash's hoofprints on the trail."

Mrs. Springer had gone back to biting her nails, her face pale, while Mr. Springer's complexion was getting redder by the moment. Shirley ignored the man's mounting ire, continuing calmly.

"You clearly came back to the forest after that encounter with Mr. Cadotte and Ash, presumably to return to the place where you've been doing illegal core sampling for PolyMet Mining." Mrs. Springer and I both gasped at the same time, while Mr. Springer opened his mouth to protest, but Shirley just kept going. "Maybe you forgot some equipment, or couldn't pack it all out in one trip. Whatever the reason, you encountered Ash when you returned to the trail. You couldn't take him back to Solomon Farms, because that would raise questions about why you'd been out in the woods again at that hour. And you couldn't just leave him there, because there *are* dangerous things in the forest, your fake Mishipeshu sightings notwithstanding. So you stowed him in your barn, where I imagine he's still waiting right now while you try to figure out a way out of this mess you've gotten yourselves into."

"Ohmygod, ohmygod, ohmygod . . . ," Mrs. Springer began murmuring, rocking back and forth on the loveseat and hugging herself. The cuticles of several nails were bleeding.

"You can't prove any of this," Springer said, taking a threatening step toward Shirley.

At which point I stood up and inserted myself between them. I had gauged correctly when Springer first entered the room; I had a good two inches on him. And though he probably outweighed me by 20 pounds, his glasses were quite a bit thicker than mine and I suspected he might be a bit drunk. I was pretty sure I could take him, if it came to that.

"Actually, we can," I said quietly. "All we have to do is check your barn."

"Not without a warrant!" he growled in my face. I felt Shirley stand up behind me as I shrugged.

"We could come back with one. And if you tried to move him in the interim, you'd just be compounding your troubles."

"David, listen to her!" Mrs. Springer said suddenly, pleadingly. "Think of the baby. Think of *me!* I can't deal with you in jail again."

With that, all the defiance drained out of Springer. He walked over to sit down by his wife, who took his hand and clasped it tightly in both of her own.

"How did you figure it out?" he asked, defeated.

"IP addresses are easy to trace these days, even without a warrant. 'SLaDe' being your initials in reverse was also a pretty big clue," Shirley replied, shifting so that she was standing beside me instead of behind me. I noticed she'd taken the opportunity while momentarily hidden by my larger frame to pull her phone out—getting ready to call 911?—but now she put it away again.

"I wasn't certain about the PolyMet link until I saw the discarded core samples on your porch that had failed to detect copper in the desired amounts. But it was the news about the company's expedited permit application filing the day after Ash's disappearance that really tipped me off. The money my office just informed me was deposited in your checking account this morning from a Swiss bank confirmed my suspicion."

"It's understandable, considering," I said, trying on Shirley's conciliatory tone for size and finding it an uncomfortable fit. I barreled on, regardless. "Your wife's pregnant, you've got mounting medical bills, and your arrest record means you can't get back on the tenure track. You're hurting for money, so when someone from PolyMet who knows there's copper in them thar woods showed up with an offer you couldn't refuse...you didn't."

Springer nodded while his wife began to weep softly.

"Pretty much," he admitted.

"But why involve Mishipeshu?" I asked, truly curious.

"I'd heard about the legend during the Line 3 protests," Springer said, his eyes growing furtive and his voice becoming a whisper. "And I saw him once. For real."

My ears pricked up at that.

"I was canoeing alone out in the middle of the Bee Dub when I heard a woman yelling for help. I rounded a bend and saw her fighting a man with a knife. There'd been a string of disappearances—mostly Indigenous women, so of course it wasn't making news, but I still had connections in the activist community, so I'd heard some things. I had a feeling this guy might've been behind the disappearances, so I shouted at him to get away from her and started paddling as fast as I could. But before I'd gone more than a few feet, something erupted out of the water in front of me, nearly capsizing my canoe. It moved so fast it was basically a blur, but I remember horns and a long, scaled tail. It snatched the guy, then splashed back down into the water and disappeared, man and all. The woman took off into the woods. And I got really, really drunk.

"But the disappearances ended. Those ones, anyway."

Would that Mishipeshu was around to solve all the missing and murdered Indigenous women cases in this country. Or at least avenge them.

"Maybe I watched too many cartoon dogs as a kid, but when I realized the copper connection, it seemed like Mishipeshu would be the perfect cover to keep people away. Worked, too."

"Actually," Shirley replied dryly, "I think the high fire danger and subsequent park closures had more to do with that than your tabloid tales."

Springer looked sheepish.

"So . . . are you going to turn me in?"

Shirley and I exchanged a wordless glance.

"Right now, all we care about is getting Ash back home," she said. "We can say we found him wandering in your fields. No one has to know you were involved at all."

Mrs. Springer looked up, her tear-filled eyes hopeful.

"You—you'd do that for us?"

"In exchange for a couple of things," Shirley replied.

"Like what?" Springer asked, guarded again.

"First, that 'SLaDe' retract all his ridiculous lies about Mishipeshu from that website and apologize on the forums there for disrespecting Anishinaabe beliefs."

"Done."

"Second, that you stop doing sampling for PolyMet, no matter what they offer you in the future."

"Also done," Springer replied easily, almost with relief. "What else?"

"Lastly, while I would never expect you to testify against PolyMet, I will need copies of everything you have from them—emails, texts, whatever. We may not be after them now, but that doesn't mean we won't be in the future."

Springer nodded silently. He seemed less sure of this condition, but also seemed to understand just how lightly he and his wife were getting off.

"Do you want me to take you to Ash?" he asked, but Shirley shook her head.

"It's better if your involvement with him ends now." She smiled at Mrs. Springer. "Good luck with your pregnancy. I will put tobacco down for an easy birth and a healthy child."

"Thank you," Mrs. Springer said, and everyone in the room understood she was thanking Shirley for more than just her prayers.

Once outside the house, I turned to Shirley.

"Are we really going to let PolyMet get away with illegal sampling and what have to be, at the very least, irregular procedures with respect to the environmental permitting process?"

"We?" she asked, her tone teasing. At least, I thought it was teasing.

"Sure. We made a pretty good team, don't you think?"

She smiled, and I felt a little jolt of something bright and sweet in my heart.

"But there's nothing paranormal about PolyMet's case."

I shrugged.

"Maybe not yet, but if Mishipeshu's going to punish anyone around here for stealing copper, it's going to be them, right? Unless we beat him to it, that is."

"Now you're making me not *want* to chase the case," she laughed. "But you're right, we did work well together, and I can see us doing so again in the future—unofficially, of course. Officially, the Bureau doesn't believe in the paranormal."

I snorted.

"That's okay. Officially, neither do the Pinkertons."

Shirley laughed again, a joyful sound made even more melodious when contrasted to the awful din of the Springers' windchimes, thankfully fading into the distance now as we walked toward the barn.

"Then it's settled," I declared, grinning myself now. "First, we get this Pokémon back to its trainer. Then there's only one thing left to do after that."

"What's that?" Shirley asked warily.

"Gotta catch 'em all!"

She groaned and punched me in the arm—hard—and I knew right then and there we were going to be working together for a long time to come.

Threads of Deceit

by

Ammar Habib

The fog rolled in like a silent specter through the streets of Delhi, its tendrils creeping and curling with an almost sentient touch. Shahid Hafiz's heart pounded a frantic rhythm as he waded through the cloying mist, his voice hoarse from calling out his daughter's name.

"Aminah!"

The sound of his voice was swallowed by the impenetrable gray.

His hands groped blindly before him, desperate to find something, anything, that would lead him to her. The air was thick, laden with an ominous chill that seeped into his bones.

A frail cry echoed in the distance, "Father . . ."

It cleaved through the haze. He lunged forward, his feet stumbling over unseen obstacles.

"Where are you?" he pleaded, his voice splintering into the void.

Laughter, cold and mocking, cut through the tenebrous shroud, tightening its noose around his heart. It spoke of lost time, of ghosts that lingered just beyond the veil of reality. His breath came in ragged gasps as the laughter crescendoed into a cacophony of scornful mirth.

Shahid's eyes snapped open, the remnants of the dream clinging to him like cobwebs. The laughter faded into the quietude of dawn, leaving behind the bitter aftertaste of dread. He lay there for a moment, allowing the stillness to calm his racing pulse.

Rising from his disheveled cot, he moved with slow deliberation, the weight of solitude bowing his tall frame. His once meticulous attire hung loosely on his lean physique, threads of despair woven into the very fabric. The piercing eyes that had scrutinized countless truths were now dulled by the shadows of his relentless grief.

Outside, the nascent sun cast a mournful glow upon the twin graves—one weathered and one fresh—that lay in the shadow of the family home. Here, where memories whispered through the leaves, Shahid stood motionless. An amulet—a delicate piece filigreed with care—rested cold in his trembling hand. It had graced Aminah's neck in days of laughter, now a talisman of perpetual sorrow.

"Shahid," came a gentle voice, its timbre imbued with a warmth that seemed alien amidst the chill of loss.

Jamil Waqar approached, his sturdy build moving with purpose through the courtyard. The soft concern etched on his features was a stark contrast to Shahid's haggard countenance. In his compassionate gaze, one could read the unwavering loyalty of a companion who had weathered storms beside his friend.

"Jamil," Shahid acknowledged, his voice a low murmur while his focus remained on the twin tombstones.

"We have been summoned," Jamil said, his words deliberate, mindful of the gravity they carried. "The Sultan's court beckons."

The message hung in the air, a portent laden with unspoken urgency. Shahid's fingers tightened around the amulet, the metal biting into his skin—a reminder of the daughter he could not save, now propelling him toward a duty he could no longer ignore.

"Lead on, then," Shahid replied. He tore his heavy gaze from the graves and followed Jamil, each step a measured tread on the path of a man who had buried pieces of his soul beneath the earth.

The opulent tapestries of the Sultan's court hung heavily, their intricate patterns a stark testament to a glory that seemed distant amidst the prevailing gloom. Shahid and Jamil crossed the threshold into the cavernous chamber, their footsteps resounding softly against the marble floor, as though wary of disturbing the sanctity of the court's silence.

Sultana Yasmin stood apart from the whispered congregation, a solitary figure enrobed in sorrow. Her presence commanded attention, not through ostentation but by the sheer gravity of her plight. As Shahid approached, he was struck by the resemblance in her eyes to those of his late wife—pools of profound grief veiled behind a stoic resolve.

"Detective Shahid," she began, her voice laced with an urgency that betrayed her composed exterior. "Delhi is besieged by shadows that threaten to engulf us all."

Shahid remained silent, his gaze never leaving the Sultana's face, as if reading the chapters of agony inscribed there.

"Your acumen is the beacon we seek in these stormy seas," she continued. "My husband, our beloved Sultan, languishes from a vile poison, and my daughter . . . my sweet Alia . . . has vanished like a mirage at dawn."

The air grew thick with the weight of her words, each syllable imbued with the desperation of a mother who had tasted the bile of dread. It echoed within Shahid, resonating with the hollow space where his own heartache dwelled.

"I know you have been marred by grief," Sultana Yasmin said. "Your wife's passing last year from the illness that swept the city many seasons ago . . . and then your sweet child . . . her disappearance never solved."

"Many moons have passed since I last donned the mantle of a seeker of truths," Shahid's response finally came, measured and heavy with the dust of his soul's recesses. The memory of his daughter's unsolved fate clung to his words, a silent specter in the chamber.

The Sultana remained silent.

"Yet . . ." he added. The amulet concealed beneath his garments burned against his skin—a quiet reminder of the bond between parent and child, unbroken even by death's cruel hand. "How can one so marred by loss refuse the plea of another whose heart is similarly besieged?"

The Sultana's eyes glistened, a glimmer of hope amidst the desolation that sought to claim her spirit. "Your empathy is the balm for our affliction, Detective Shahid."

"Empathy," Shahid echoed quietly, almost to himself, his mind's eye tracing the lines of sorrow that ran parallel in both their lives. In that moment, bound by the shared language of loss, he knew his retreat from the world could no longer shield him from duty's call. "Then let us unearth the venom that festers in the heart of Delhi."

Sultana Yasmin nodded, her gratitude a silent prayer that fluttered in the space between them, and Shahid steeled himself for the journey ahead. In searching for another's lost light, perhaps he might find a glint of solace for his own enduring night.

Amid the labyrinth of spice bazaars, beneath the shadow of the minarets and the suffocating heat of Delhi, Shahid Hafiz's keen eyes were fixed upon a handful of saffron threads. They lay innocuously on a slab of marble, their crimson hue a mocking semblance of vitality. Beside him, Jamil Waqar held a vial to the light in his gloved hand, the liquid within shimmering with a sinister iridescence.

"Deadlier than the cobra's kiss," Shahid murmured, his voice a whisper, as if afraid to disturb the silent poison that had wrought such havoc. The rare toxin, known only to those well-versed in the arcane arts, was a testament to the malevolence that had seeped into the Sultan's palace. "This is the only evidence they found after the Sultan's poisoning."

Jamil nodded solemnly, his warm smile lost amidst the gravity of their finding. "This points towards one direction alone—Viceroy Karim."

Shahid listened to Jamil's theory.

"The viceroy's fascination with dark magic is no secret. His family's fortune originates from spice traders. And then there is his access to the palace. He can come and go at will. The idea of him slipping the poison into the Sultan's food and abducting the princess is not far-fetched. It has been rumored that he has explored dark magic to find ways to communicate with his deceased son."

"Or perhaps someone using the viceroy," Shahid replied.

"Yes . . . perhaps."

Shahid's gaze lingered on the vial, his mind's eye seeing not the poison but the visage of his daughter, another innocent claimed by the shadows of this city. He veiled his emotions, turning his focus back to the task at hand.

"Yet we tread on delicate ground," he said. "We must seek counsel before wandering into the serpent's lair."

"You summoned us?" Shahid Hafiz asked, his eyes fixated on a palace servant—a young lady—before him and Jamil.

"I did," she replied.

"What is your name?"

"Laila."

"Laila," Shahid repeated, noticing her foreign accent. Her eyes held the depth of the ocean—secrets brimming just beneath the surface.

"Speak, child," Jamil urged, breaking the silence that enfolded them in the servant's quarters. "What whispers have flitted past your ears?"

"Viceroy Karim has been restless of late," Laila began, her voice a delicate thread weaving through the tension of the room. "Nightly rendezvous shrouded in secrecy, visitors cloaked in darkness . . . and talk of a shipment, one that arrived just before the . . . incident."

"Can you ascertain the nature of this shipment?" Shahid asked, noticing the ashes clinging to her fingertips

"Only that it was not of this land and precious enough to be guarded by sorcery," she replied, the unease in her tone painting vivid images of nefarious dealings under the cover of night.

"Thank you," Shahid said. With a nod to Jamil, he signaled their departure, each step away from Laila heavy with the burden of untold stories and unspoken tragedies.

The sun beat down mercilessly upon the crowded bazaar of Delhi, a relentless force that seemed to slow time itself. Shahid Hafiz's gaze cut through the throng like a scimitar through silk, his keen eyes fixed on the figure weaving ahead—a merchant whose allegiance to Viceroy Karim was as certain as the shadows that clung to him.

Through narrow alleys and over-brimming market squares, Shahid and Jamil trailed their quarry with the stealth of panthers. The air was thick with the cloying scent of spices and the clamor of commerce, an orchestra of human endeavor in which every vendor played for survival.

They came upon a secluded courtyard, where the shade provided a scant reprieve from the oppressive heat. Here, the merchant halted and, after a furtive glance over his shoulder, engaged in hushed discourse with another—a compatriot cloaked in the guise of respectability.

Shahid's eyes narrowed as he observed their secret meeting from the concealment of a timeworn archway. His mind smelted fragments of gestures and half-caught phrases. Each movement of the merchants' lips, each exchange of parchment or coin, was a tesseract in the mosaic of conspiracy.

"Dark dealings are afoot," murmured Jamil. "Two serpents entwined in their venomous dance."

"Indeed," Shahid replied, the word a mere exhalation, as if speaking louder might shatter the fragile web of evidence they witnessed. As they watched the merchant and his contact disperse, Shahid turned toward Jamil. "Patience. The truth shall emerge as the lotus from the mire."

With measured steps, they retreated from the scene. As the sun began its descent, casting elongated shadows across the city of Delhi, Shahid could not help but feel the darkness grow within him as well—a reflection of the night that was encroaching upon the soul of the land he vowed to protect.

Shahid's breath came in ragged gasps as he stumbled through the thick, oppressive fog that swathed the landscape like a suffocating veil. Unseen hands seemed to claw at him from the mists, each step forward an act of defiance against the dread that clutched his heart.

His daughter's voice, distant and desperate, pierced the gloom, "Father!"

Yet, no matter how fervently he strained his ears, her cries became echoes lost in the ether.

The ground beneath his feet shifted from the familiar gravel of the roads he knew so well to a cold, slick marble that gleamed an ominous crimson underfoot. Blood—his mind recoiled at the sight, but the liquid horror spread inexorably, staining his shoes, seeping between his toes. The metallic tang of it filled the air, suffusing the fog with its acrid scent.

A malevolent presence shadowed his every move, lurking just beyond the periphery of his vision—a sinister whisper in the void, a chilling breath upon his neck. It was the embodiment of his deepest fears, a specter of despair that had haunted him since the day his world had been torn asunder.

With dogged determination, he pressed on, driven by the single, unyielding thought of finding his beloved child. The spectral landscape yielded to the softer contours of grassy fields—the very ones that bordered his own abode, where laughter once blossomed like the sweetest of blooms. Yellow flowers with a golden hint painted the field.

It was here, in this place of now-muted joys, that he last saw her, her innocent smile etching itself into his memory before she vanished into the unknown.

And then, with the abruptness of a candle snuffed out by a cruel gust, the dream shattered, leaving only the stinging residue of his anguished soul.

Shahid's eyes snapped open, the remnants of terror clinging to him like cobwebs as he lay disoriented in the darkness of his room. His chest heaved with the effort to dispel the lingering phantoms of sleep as he sought to reacquaint himself with reality. Moonlight filtered through the window, casting angular shadows that played upon the walls like silent specters from his nightmare.

Drawing a shuddering breath, he anchored himself in the present moment, pushing aside the tendrils of fear with the force of his will. It was then, in the quiet aftermath of his torment, that a singular thought took root in his mind—a thought as sharp and penetrating as a blade crossed his mind.

The flowers in his dream . . .

Those yellow flowers were not a memory. They were a sign. A clue from his subconscious.

"I must go to the saffron warehouse," he murmured to the empty room, the words a lifeline cast into the mire of uncertainty.

As if guided by the hand of fate, his dream had led him there. With a resolve that was both his curse and his salvation, Shahid Hafiz rose from the depths of his bed, his tall, lean frame a silhouette against the pale light. The detective within flared to life, igniting the embers of a hope that refused to be extinguished.

He would return to the warehouse; he would follow this ethereal thread woven by his subconscious, for it was all he had left to cling to in a world bereft of answers.

The pungent aroma of saffron hung heavily in the stale air. Shahid's piercing eyes scanned the dimly lit expanse of the warehouse, each overturned crate and scattered spice heap a testament to the chaos that had recently unfolded there. The ghosts of bygone prosperity were all that remained, and they watched as Shahid's lean figure maneuvered through the dereliction with deliberate steps.

"Nothing but dust," Jamil muttered, his voice a warm ember in the cold gloom. He swept his hand across an ancient wooden beam, watching the grime of ages dance in the sliver of light that pierced the shadows.

"Look at this," Shahid called out suddenly, his tone betraying a hint of urgency.

Jamil approached and saw what Shahid held: gravel.

"Gravel from the north part of Delhi," Shahid said.

"How can you be sure?"

Ignoring Jamil's question, Shahid motioned for Jamil to place his hand near a crack in the wall. Jamil did so.

"What do you feel?" Shahid asked.

"...air," Jamil replied, realization dawning like the first light of dawn upon a desolate landscape.

"Old catacombs run underneath this part of the city," Shahid murmured, more to himself than to Jamil. The revelation seemed to pull him deeper into his own mind, where memories lay coiled like serpents in wait. "Once used for smuggling."

They found a loose brick. Pushing it, the wall moved, grinding against the ground with a screech. When the movement stopped, a passage waited before them.

"We must be cautious," Shahid whispered.

In the oppressive darkness, the torch in Shahid's hand was a lone star battling the night. The flickering flame cast dancing shadows upon the walls as they moved cautiously, the somber echo of their footsteps a drumbeat to the rhythm of their search.

Shahid's senses caught the subtlest whisper of air stirring against the stillness. A hidden chamber, its secrets sealed behind stone and silence, beckoned to him with an almost magnetic pull. With careful fingers, he traced the outline of the passage until the wall yielded, revealing the chamber within.

Inside, the evidence of illicit wares lay bare beneath their scrutiny. Vials of poison glinted malevolently, the residue of death's tender caresses staining each glass container. The trade of such nefarious concoctions spoke of a malice that ran deeper than mere greed—it whispered of power and influence wielded without conscience.

And then, amidst the chaos of corruption, Shahid's gaze fell upon the coded messages. The script was meticulous, the language of deception elegantly scribed.

"A coded message . . . their scheme," Jamil whispered. "Can you understand it?"

"Ahmed," Shahid breathed.

"Ahmed?"

"That name is the cipher key to this code. It is the name of Viceroy Karim's son . . . one who drowned when they were children. If he is involved, that name is the key."

"How can you be certain?"

"Because no matter the soul, the loss of a child is one that is forever etched in one's heart . . . and it is stained into the subconscious."

Together, they decoded the words that spelled out treachery and transactions of great magnitude.

"The Serpent's Kiss," Shahid read aloud, the name a sinister invocation that curled around them, a tangible presence in the room. Money and murder entwined in a deadly dance, orchestrated by hands that once played in innocent mud by the riverbank.

"Removing the Sultan and his heir to create a power vacuum . . ." Jamil muttered. "That is their scheme."

"But who?" Shahid asked. "Who wishes to create a void so that they can fill it?"

Shahid tucked the incriminating evidence into his coat. Jamil's hand rested on his shoulder, a silent signal that it was time to depart the clandestine chamber. With measured steps, they retraced their path toward the secret passageway, the torch casting elongated shadows against the damp walls.

A sudden rush of movement shattered the sepulchral silence. From the peripheries of the flickering light, figures cloaked in obscurity launched themselves at the investigators. Steel glinted, a harbinger of death as it sought out flesh in the darkness.

"Down!" Shahid barked.

They dropped to the ground, the whistle of blades slicing mere inches above them. The somber rhythm of their escape now punctuated by the cacophony of deadly intent.

Jamil grappled with an assailant, the sound of fist against bone resounding through the chamber. Shahid rolled away, feeling the keen edge of a blade graze his sleeve. His mind raced, dissecting each move of their attackers with cold precision, seeking an advantage where none seemed to exist.

Shahid and Jamil moved as one, an orchestrated defiance against the assassins who sought to silence their discovery.

A sharp pain seared across Shahid's arm—a souvenir from the grim dance. He stifled a groan, his focus unyielding as he parried another strike. The stench of sweat and malice filled his nostrils.

"Go, Shahid! Left passage!" Jamil urged, his warm smile replaced by a snarl of determination as he shielded Shahid from another onslaught.

"Keep moving," Shahid replied, his words sparse. They navigated the labyrinthine catacombs, their breaths ragged symphonies accompanying the drumming of their hearts.

They burst forth from the catacombs' mouth, the night air a harsh gasp in their lungs. Behind them, the echo of their pursuers faded into the bowels of the earth, swallowed by the very shadows that had birthed them.

On the cobblestone street, beneath the indifferent gaze of the stars, Shahid and Jamil stood side by side—two souls weathered by tribulation, yet unbroken. They had escaped with the fragile thread of life still intact, the weight of "The Serpent's Kiss" a tangible burden upon their shoulders, whispering of battles yet to be waged and truths yet to be unearthed.

The moon, a mere sliver in the heavens, cast faint shadows across Shahid Hafiz's face as he applied pressure to the gash on his arm. The crimson stain seeping through the makeshift bandage was a stark contrast to the pale light. Silently, he acknowledged the pain, not as an affliction but as a grim companion to his relentless pursuit of truth.

His eyes, those piercing orbs dulled by countless sleepless nights, drifted towards the amulet resting on a nearby table. It was hers—his daughter's, a memory frozen in time, her laughter now a ghostly echo in the recesses of his mind.

As he bound his wound tighter, he whispered a solemn oath over her image, "For you, and for the princess, I will unearth what's been buried in shadow."

Jamil watched his friend with a steady gaze, empathy etched into his weathered features. "Shahid," Jamil began, his voice a low hum, "the daggers, they were not local make—too ornate, the craftsmanship foreign."

Shahid met his gaze, a glimmer of intrigue cutting through the fog of his thoughts. "Iranian," he murmured, as if the word itself conjured images of distant lands and their veiled secrets.

"Indeed. And it's no coincidence that such blades find themselves here, now." Jamil's words hung between them, laden with implication.

"Meet me at the darkest hour of the night," Shahid instructed, his tone leaving no room for argument, "near the palace grounds. There is a pattern emerging from the chaos, one I intend to trace to its source."

Jamil nodded once, a silent accord sealed between them. They understood the stakes, the tendrils of conspiracy that seemed to entangle ever tighter around the heart of the kingdom. With each revelation, the shadows grew denser, yet their resolve only solidified.

In the quietude that followed, Shahid turned his attention back to the dark window, where the night whispered its secrets to those willing to listen. His mind, a labyrinth of logic and intuition, began to piece together the fractured mosaic of their case.

Shahid Hafiz's silhouette melded with the shadows as he and Jamil Waqar navigated the palace's corridors, guided by nothing but the faint glimmer of the moon seeping through crevices. The air hung heavy with an anticipation that clung to their skin like a shroud. With measured steps, Shahid led them to an unassuming tapestry depicting the grandeur of bygone eras—a facade for the secrets it veiled.

With a deft movement, Shahid swept the fabric aside, revealing the outline of a door. It yielded to his touch, silent hinges betraying no hint of the passage of time. They slipped through, and Shahid secured the entrance behind them. The chamber that welcomed them was a stark contrast to the palace's opulence—bereft of light, save for the ghostly glow of moonlight that painted an eerie tableau.

The remnants of a black magic ritual lay scattered about—a circle of salt, charred bones, and half-melted candles forming an arcane pattern on the floor. The stench of sulfur lingered in the air, its acrid bite a testament to forbidden incantations recently uttered.

"By the heavens," Jamil murmured, "what manner of sorcery has been practiced here?"

"Darkness, old as time itself, festers in this room," Shahid replied, his eyes tracing the detritus of the ritual. "And Laila is at its heart."

Jamil turned sharply, his countenance etched with disbelief. "Laila? The servant girl we spoke to?"

Shahid nodded.

"But how can you be certain?"

"Recall her fingertips," Shahid replied, his voice a low rumble of conviction. "They bore the ash of otherworldly fires. Her tongue, too, carried the cadence of Iranian speech—indicators not to be overlooked."

"Such traits alone cannot condemn her," Jamil protested, yet uncertainty flickered across his features.

"Consider Viceroy Karim," Shahid countered, his gaze piercing the gloom. "For a crime this large, he is too obvious a suspect. Yes, he possesses interest in the dark arts, but he has no experience in them . . . not enough for what we've seen."

Jamil listened.

"Perhaps, as he reached into the dark arts, something reached back . . . something took a hold of him . . . something controlled him . . . *someone* took control of him." Shahid paused. "Controlled him to use his influence to enact the plan of the puppeteer, and the one pulling the strings is somebody from a land where the dark arts are prevalent. Someone in the palace who is always present but never seen. Someone who has every reason to hate the Sultan but no reason to ever be a suspect."

"A palace servant. From Iran . . ." Jamil whispered.

"Laila," Shahid finished.

"Then her motive?" Jamil pressed, seeking the final piece to complete the grim mosaic before them. "If you claim that Karim is under her spell."

As if summoned by the question itself, the air grew taut, and from the deeper recesses of the chamber emerged figures cloaked in darkness. Laila, flanked by assassins whose Iranian daggers glinted with malevolent intent, fixed her gaze upon them.

"Bravo, Shahid Hafiz," she intoned, her voice a silken threat. "You have unearthed what many have failed to see. Regrettably, your discovery is where our tale must end."

"Your vengeance runs deep, Laila," Shahid spoke, unflinching before the encroaching peril. "A prisoner of war. That's what you once were when you came here. However, no longer are you confined by chains . . . instead, it is hatred that binds you."

"Indeed," Laila acknowledged, her eyes alight with the fire of retribution. "I once watched my mother and father murdered at the hands of the Sultan's soldiers. I was left enslaved . . . until I came here."

They watched her eyes turn dark.

"I have woven myself into the fabric of this court," she continued, "waiting for the moment to unravel it all. And now, with the kingdom teetering on the brink, my purpose is nearly fulfilled."

A pause . . .

"Assassins!" she commanded, her voice slicing through the tension. "Eliminate them."

The hush of impending doom hung heavy in the air as the assassins closed in, their blades hungry for blood. Just as the first strike was to be dealt, a clamor arose from beyond the chamber walls—a harbinger of salvation or another twist of fate?

"Stay your hand!" The command boomed through the chamber, authoritative and unyielding. Sultana Yasmin, resplendent in her royal garb yet wearing the countenance of a mother scorned, stood flanked by palace guards. The torchlight flickered across her face, illuminating the resolve etched into her features.

"Your treachery has reached its end, Laila," Shahid said, his voice steady. He nodded towards the Sultana, revealing the final gambit in this deadly game. "Sultana Yasmin was privy to your confession."

Laila's countenance faltered, caught in the snare of her own machinations.

With a gesture from the Sultana, the guards apprehended her and the assassins.

When Laila disappeared from sight, Shahid turned to the Sultana, his eyes softening with the promise of hope. "Your Highness, follow me."

Together, they traversed the labyrinthine corridors to Laila's chambers. A silence settled between them, each step a drumbeat in the somber march.

"Do you know where Alia is?" the Sultana asked.

"I believe Alia was not taken from the palace. Rather, she was hidden. If Laila was the culprit, then your Alia will not be far."

In Laila's chambers, Shahid paused before a wall that seemed indifferent to the untrained eye as he held his lantern's light against it.

"What is it?" the Sultana asked.

"Iranians are known for their fascination for hidden labyrinths. But every passageway—no matter how secret—needs a key."

He produced an Iranian dagger, the same blade that had cut him in the catacombs.

"And I believe we have that," he finished.

With a precise movement, he plunged it into an inconspicuous crevice. A muted click heralded the release of ancient mechanisms. The wall yielded, revealing a hidden chamber veiled in shadows.

Seeing what lay on the other side of the wall, Shahid breathed in relief.

"Princess Alia," breathed Sultana Yasmin.

There, upon a solitary cot, lay the Princess, her visage the very image of innocence besieged by darkness. A spectral pallor clung to her skin, a testament to the poison coursing through her veins.

"Her slumber is not natural," Shahid said, his gaze never leaving the stricken princess. "It is the work of Laila's foul sorcery. But where there is malice, there lies a path to redemption. I shall devote my acumen to reverse-engineering the curse and restoring her to the living."

Yasmin's hand trembled as she reached out to her daughter, her touch a tender caress against the chill of enchanted sleep. Her voice wavered, a fragile thread of maternal longing. "Can it truly be done?"

"By my honor, I will leave no stone unturned," Shahid vowed. In his heart, the specter of his own loss loomed large, fueling his determination to spare another parent the agony of an unanswered fate.

Sunlight filtered through the latticed windows, casting a warm glow on the pale face of Princess Alia as she stirred from her unnatural slumber. Shahid stood vigil at her bedside, his keen eyes softening when they caught the hesitant flutter of her lashes.

"Where am I?" Her voice was frail, confusion etched upon her delicate features as she took in the opulent chamber around her.

"Safe," Shahid assured. "You are safe within the walls of your father's palace."

Recognition dawned in her eyes, widening with the awareness of his identity. "Detective Shahid Hafiz . . . the one they speak of?"

"None other," he replied, a wry smile touching his lips. He observed her closely, noting the resilience beneath her bewilderment. In her gaze—an intense cerulean that mirrored the skies above Delhi—he saw the reflection of a soul that echoed his own daughter's spirited curiosity.

"Did you rescue me?" she asked, her words a whisper.

Shahid nodded.

"Thank you," the Princess said, her gratitude resonating like a solemn vow.

Shahid's throat tightened, an unbidden sorrow threading through the sinews of his heart. From the pocket of his vest, he withdrew a small, intricately carved amulet.

"This belonged to my daughter," he said, the words imbued with a quiet strength as he placed the heirloom in the Princess's palm. "I ask that you guard it well."

"Your loss..." Alia began, empathy coloring her tone, but Shahid raised a hand to forestall further words.

"Your life is a testament to hope restored," he said, his resolve a bulwark against the tides of grief. "Let this be a symbol of new beginnings."

As he left and stepped into the palace's corridor, he found Jamil waiting for him. "Shahid," he said. "This has arrived for you."

Shahid paused, his silhouette framed by the doorway as he took the letter from Jamil's hands. "A beckoning from a distant land?" he asked.

"Will you answer the call?" Jamil replied, watching as Shahid traced the seal with a thoughtful finger.

A smile, rare and enigmatic, curved Shahid's lips as he stepped beyond the threshold and patted his friend's shoulder. In the halting gait of a man who had traversed the chasm of despair, yet emerged unbowed, Shahid walked on. With each step, the shadows of loss receded, giving way to the undimmed light of purpose.

A Study in Alchemy

by

Scott Pearson

An incessant pounding woke John Watson from much needed sleep; he'd had three surgeries that day and was dead tired. When a glance at his bedside clock indicated it was two in the morning, he decided to ignore the knocking, certain it was someone in his cups at the wrong door. He pulled a pillow over his head.

Unfortunately, the pounding had already awakened the patients boarding with him, and they expressed their anger in loud barks and howls. Clearly, getting back to sleep was not an immediately available option. It would likely take an hour to quiet the recuperating canines after chasing the drunkard off his stoop. It had taken him long enough to settle in a particularly nervous Corgi who had already awakened him once just a couple hours earlier. Throwing off the covers, he donned his slippers, grabbed his dressing gown, and made his way downstairs, grumbling as he went, pausing only to turn up the gaslight in the hallway.

He'd worked himself up into a right strop by the time he threw wide his front door, ready to give a verbal lashing to whomever he discovered there. But, taken aback by the gentlemen before him, softly lit by the light from inside and the street lamp on the corner, Watson found himself at a loss for words. He'd expected someone aged beyond their years by the ravages of drink, or whatever drugs they abused to get through a dreary existence in Mile End. Instead, he saw a slim man of more than six feet, wearing a black homburg and ulster, appearing about his own age, late twenties. The man had piercing gray eyes, a hawk-like nose, and an intelligent countenance that would have made a good impression on Watson under different circumstances.

"I apologize for the hour," the stranger said, speaking loudly over the barking in the background, "but needs must. You are Doctor Watson?"

"*Mister* Watson," Watson said sharply. It was right there on the sign beside the door: MILE END INFIRMARY FOR HORSES, DOGS, &C, MR JOHN H WATSON, VETERINARY SURGEON. "Practitioners of veterinary medicine are not accorded that title." It was a sore point and a reminder of his difficult past. "What do you want?" He purposefully left off *sir*. The man actually seemed to smirk, however fleetingly, at Watson's anger, further incensing him. Watson pulled his dressing gown tighter against the chill, damp London air.

"Again, I apologize for waking you, especially after you've already been up with a nervous Corgi. However—"

"How could you possibly know that?" Watson interrupted, angrier still at the possibility that this man had somehow been watching him in his duties.

That needling glimmer of amusement returned briefly to the man's thin face and was gone as quickly as it had appeared. "Quite simple, actually. I discern the distinctive yipping of the breed among the canine chorus within; a Pembroke, I'd wager, due to the timbre of the bark suggesting the smaller breed. Also, Corgis are well-known for shedding, and your dressing gown is rather covered with white and fawn fur. From those points of fact, it's elementary to deduce that you were already up at least once trying to quiet the little beast. That you were asleep already, and not just in your nightclothes before bed, I surmised simply by the—how to describe it?—*riotous* state of your hair."

"Well, I . . . erm." His anger slightly abated by his astonishment at the man's clever reasoning, Watson once again found himself uncertain what to say. His testiness at being up at two in the morning soon won out, and, as he tried to smooth down his hair with his hands, he blurted, "Who are you and what's all this about then?"

"I may need your ministrations—"

"Is that meant to be a joke?" The man again seemed to be purposefully galling him regarding the unfortunate circumstances that led him to his profession. Unless . . . Watson peered around the man to see if he had a horse somewhere in the shadows.

"Not at all. You may be uniquely qualified to assess my injuries. My name is Sherlock Holmes."

And with that pronouncement, the man stumbled forward, passing out in Watson's arms.

Watson had dragged the stranger through to his sitting room, maneuvering him into a chair near the fire, which he had stoked with a fresh log. It had been relatively easy; the slim man was nothing compared to some of the four-legged patients Watson had to move about during examinations. The man—Sherlock Holmes, he'd said his name was—had a strong and steady pulse, deep, regular breathing, responsive pupils, good color in his cheeks, no sign of any head wound . . . in short, no obvious reasons to lose consciousness.

Just as Watson sat on the edge of a chair across from Holmes to contemplate his next move, grateful that the dogs had quieted down on their own, the man sat up straight, removed his hat, and said, "Sorry for the ruse, but it got us inside quickly. Best not to draw attention to my presence."

Watson leaped to his feet, unsure if he was more startled or angry. "Now see here, I want you out of my house."

"If you would hear me out, Mr. Watson, before you throw me out?"

Watson stood silently dumbfounded by the man's casual behavior but finally grunted an assent, annoyed at being curious about what brought this infuriating man to his stoop. Feeling Holmes's sharp gaze on him, he retrieved his cigarettes from the mantel, sat back down, and lit one.

With a nod, Holmes then continued, "As I said outside, I sought you for your unique qualifications. They may prove key to my current investigation."

"Investigation? You're with the police, then? Scotland Yard?"

"Certainly not." Holmes waved a hand dismissively. "I am a consulting detective; I am called upon when the police are out of their depth, which is more often than not. As they are now."

Fancies himself Poe's Dupin, Watson thought, wondering if the man suffered from delusions, though he had to admit the business about the Corgi was well reasoned. "But what's this to do with me? What 'unique qualifications' could I have related to your investigation?"

Holmes leaned forward, focusing his unblinking gaze on Watson. "My fainting may have been feigned, but my injuries are not. If you would examine them . . ."

Exasperated, Watson stood and made his way to the sideboard to pour himself a brandy. "Need I remind you I am a *veterinary* surgeon?" He glanced back at Holmes. With a subtle smirk, his uninvited guest nodded toward the decanter in Watson's hand. Sighing, Watson poured another brandy, which he delivered to Holmes before sitting down with his own.

Holmes took a sip of the brandy, then set the glass down on the table beside his chair. He stood and removed his ulster, draping it over the back of his chair. Watson, resigned to the idea that Holmes expected an examination, took a healthy drink and watched as Holmes removed his suit coat and undid the buttons of his waistcoat and shirt. When Holmes lifted his undershirt, exposing the injury, Watson got to his feet.

"Whatever caused this?" Watson said, stepping closer. There was a reddened and bruised band across the skin of Holmes's abdomen, perhaps four inches wide, with odd, circular mottles or welts unevenly distributed throughout the band.

"I had hoped to hear what you think caused it."

As Watson leaned over to peer more closely at the circles, he noticed the band extended around Holmes's ribs. "How far . . . ?" Watson trailed off as Holmes pulled his garments further up and slowly turned; the spotted band wrapped entirely around him.

After completing his rotation, Holmes began tucking and rebuttoning his attire. He put his suit coat back on, leaving it unbuttoned, and sat down, looking at Watson expectantly.

Watson returned to his seat as well and took a nip of brandy before furrowing his brow and saying, "How is it you have this injury without knowing what caused it?"

"That is indeed the question."

"It seems rather to be but one of many questions," Watson said, frustrated by Holmes's deliberate obtuseness. "More to the point, you've yet to explain what this has to do with your investigation, and how either could possibly have any connection to me."

Holmes stared appraisingly at Watson. "If you would first indulge me with your diagnosis, I will then explain what has brought me here."

"Very well, but I better get some answers in return. It looks like a wide strap, canvas or leather, was wrapped around your torso and tightened, painfully so. If the strap had several large metal grommets along its length, that could explain the circular welts. But if such violence was done against you, surely you would be aware of it?"

Holmes nodded appreciatively. "A well-deduced, prosaic theory, which pleases me to hear."

"Well, what did you expect?"

"Mrs. Hudson, my landlady, who is far more superstitious than I previously realized, swears that it was"—Holmes slipped into a mild Scottish brogue—" 'black magic, and no mistake.' "

Watson placed his cigarette on the ashtray before it dropped from his trembling hand. He quickly clasped his hands tightly together in his lap, but he could tell that Holmes had noticed his reaction from the look of disdain that crossed the detective's face. But Watson didn't care, because surely this was what had brought Holmes to his door, no matter what the detective believed—or didn't believe.

His hands had steadied, so Watson had another drink of brandy, forcing himself not to down the rest in a shot. Folding his arms across his chest, he tried to return Holmes's penetrating stare. "Perhaps it's time you just tell me what you're investigating."

That seemed to earn an approving glance before Holmes's expression turned unreadable again. "Inspector Lestrade of the Yard brought me three cases linked only—or so he thought—by their seeming impossibility. In each case, there was only one individual with an apparent motive for committing the crime—and each of the three gentlemen had unassailable reputations as well as unquestionable alibis. Suspecting these upstanding members of society, all three doctors of renown"—Watson couldn't fail to notice that Holmes watched him closely as he divulged that—"was inconceivable to the blinkered thinking the Yard favors and encourages."

Ignoring Holmes's scornful asides—and the troubling implication of the look attached to his mention of the doctors—Watson said, "What were the crimes?"

Holmes's eyes gleamed as he warmed to his tale. "On the surface, offenses that would have drawn little interest and less effort if perpetrated against the average, hard-working Londoner. But since the victims were of such stature that they could afford to replace tenfold what had been stolen, all the resources of Scotland Yard—such as they are—were brought to bear. And when that yielded nothing, the Yard knocked on my door."

"What exactly was stolen? And from whom?"

Holmes withdrew a pipe and tobacco pouch from his jacket. "Inconsequential details of no interest to me in this case." He added a pinch of tobacco to the bowl, tamped the tobacco lightly with his thumb, took a test draw through the pipe, and continued filling the bowl while he talked. "What drew my attention were the suspected thieves whom Lestrade refused to suspect. I quickly discovered what Lestrade should have—all three were connected, a coincidence too unlikely to be ignored."

Watson picked up his cigarette, realized it had gone out, and relit it. He hoped it might settle his stomach. There seemed to be only one place all this could lead—somewhere he had hoped to never revisit.

"Although these three doctors have their own specialties, their own practices spread comfortably across Belgravia, Kensington, and Mayfair, a decade ago they were all studying medicine at the University of London: Michael Villacrusis, Paul Simpson, and Ian McCormack."

Watson went still, except for his heart, which beat faster and louder than seemed possible. He watched unblinking as smoke rose from the tip of his cigarette in his outstretched hand, filling the air between himself and Holmes, who took a moment to light his pipe before continuing.

"They had a fourth in a study group they formed, a promising young student by the name of John H. Watson."

This time Watson did finish his brandy in a single gulp, then walked shakily to the sideboard to bring the decanter back to his chair. He sat back down and refilled his glass. Holmes's eyes remained focused on him the whole time, but Watson said nothing.

With a tilt of his head, Holmes continued. "Within the year, however, Watson abruptly left university and the medical profession—for humans, at least. There are no records of expulsion, and no one willing to discuss what happened. And now three of the group are wealthy physicians no one dares to suspect for their indulgences, and the fourth is a veterinary surgeon living and working between an empty storefront and a doss-house." Holmes leaned back in his chair and puffed on his pipe. "So I'll ask again, Mr. Watson—what do *you* think caused my injury?"

Watson felt he was being dared to give the answer that Holmes, for all the detective's railings against blinkered thinking, would find immediately unacceptable, just as unacceptable as Scotland Yard found the idea of suspecting the doctors. Watson took a different tack.

"I presume in these crimes that it seemed impossible for there to have been an intruder . . . but for the fact that an item *was* stolen."

Holmes gave an almost imperceptible nod; clearly it pained him to admit he didn't know how it was done.

"And these are the same circumstances under which you suffered the injury to your torso?"

Again the begrudging subtle nod, this time accompanied by a large exhalation of smoke.

"I see." Watson reciprocated Holmes's posture by leaning back in his own chair and puffing on his cigarette. "Then I must recommend you listen to your landlady."

Holmes's frown was immediate, and he sat up rigidly. "I approach my trade scientifically, and I would have expected the same of a man of medicine, whether his patients arrive on two legs or four."

Watson's free hand tightened on the arm of his chair. "Yet here you are, in the middle of the night, desperate for my answer, yet expecting to not like it." Watson leaned forward, and he could feel the fear he tried to hide within spreading across his face. "Scoffing at superstitions is easy, but I tell you that lurking beneath them is a dark science we do not understand, and that I'd rather not understand. Once learned it lingers, like a scar always reminding you of a terrible accident you'd sooner forget."

The two men stared across at each other for a time that seemed to stretch on for minutes. Holmes finally relaxed, slumping deeper into his chair. Was there again a hint of amusement scurrying across his narrow face before it faded behind an undecipherable mask? Watson wasn't sure; he simply couldn't tell how much of Holmes's behavior was genuine and how much was calculated to elicit whatever reaction he wanted.

"Nevertheless," said Holmes softly, "perhaps it's time you told me what happened in that study group."

After another drink, Watson said, "I won't willingly speak of everything that happened. I see certain events from those days too often in nightmares to want to bolster the memories by voicing the details." He shook his head and took a drag of his cigarette. "But I will tell you enough for you to understand my viewpoint, which you are free to heed—or discount. I feel no obligation to convince you; I know what happened, and that is all that matters to me."

Holmes nodded. "Fair enough, Mr. Watson."

Watson stood, stepped over to the fireplace, and added a log. He remained standing at the hearth as the fresh wood caught flame. "I was an eager student, desperate to excel in all my studies and lab work. That drive caught the attention of Villacrusis, two years ahead of me. He invited me to join his study group." He glanced over at Holmes. "I was . . . flattered, I guess, to be noticed by the older students." Watson grabbed the poker and adjusted the logs in the grate, then returned to his chair.

"I threw myself into the work, and at first the group was quite helpful. The late hours we put in improved my test results. But soon Villacrusis expanded the focus of the group. It became clear that that had always been his intention, as his knowledge of the recondite subjects he introduced was beyond that of a novice.

"Still, in those first weeks, it appeared appropriate if unorthodox. He framed his unusual interests as for the good of our future patients; why limit ourselves to the approved textbooks when there were other schools of thought to draw upon? It was all rather worldly, appealing to our youthful overconfidence and the urge to show up the stodgy know-it-all professors.

"If it had gone no further than that . . ." Watson paused, taking a sip of brandy, then settled back in his chair and shook his head. "But Villacrusis always took it further. I began to think our future patients were not foremost on his mind. His drive to prolong life—at any cost, with no ethical boundaries—was becoming an obsession. When I casually brought it up to Simpson and McCormack, they were defensive and dismissive; they were too devoted to Villacrusis. Outwardly, I shrugged away my concern, but inwardly my worries grew. Next Villacrusis delved into methods of resuscitation, advocating that life could be revived much later than commonly accepted—more like the reanimation of Shelley's *Frankenstein*.

"That was troubling enough, but the methods he advocated veered away from scientific medical experiments, becoming rather rituals most succinctly described as satanic—" Watson flinched at the sudden, sharp rapping of Holmes's pipe on an ashtray as the detective emptied it.

"Excuse me," Holmes said. "But surely you speak metaphorically . . ."

Watson chuckled without amusement as he stared at the flames in the fireplace. "I do not. We would not be in our present circumstances if I did. The hermetic rituals became increasingly distasteful, with little connection to patient treatment. Each meeting of the group—now conducted only in dank, forgotten cellars—felt steeped in a miasma of fear. Fear of the results, and fear of Villacrusis himself; he grew bolder, stronger, drawing on preternatural energies, attempting to summon otherworldly creatures to his will. The others, cowed by their sycophancy, would brook no discussion of my concerns, but I could not allow it to continue. I went to the vice-chancellor of the university, divulging in full all our transgressions." Watson turned away from the fire, looking directly at Holmes. "You know the outcome of that."

"You were forced out."

Watson nodded. "The Villacrusis family had great influence at university and in society, as did, to a lesser degree, the Simpsons and McCormacks. And we were all exemplary students, on our way to becoming renowned doctors who would reflect well on the medical school. Such heinous events as I confessed being a party to simply could not be true; they would besmirch the fine reputations of all involved, as would documenting the accusations, no matter that they'd already been fully discredited by the authorities. Not that even the most cursory investigation was conducted into my accusations. I was unceremoniously shown to the pavement, blackballed, whispered about behind closed doors. No medical school would accept me; not for human medicine, that is. Meanwhile, the remaining three continued their rise, their unholy pursuits unhindered as they received the accolades of the medical community. And now, beyond whatever other malefactions they've committed in the years since, it seems they're using their arcane powers for selfish enrichment."

Watson raised his glass, as if toasting their success, and downed it. He waited for some response, but Holmes sat there without speaking, his faraway gaze indicating a man deep in thought.

When Watson could no longer stand the silence, he said, "So, Mr. Holmes, I have shared all I know. Perhaps now you could explain your injuries?"

Holmes slowly turned his gaze upon Watson, his thoughtful expression replaced by one of concern. "I was in bed by ten p.m., though I had some difficulty falling asleep as I turned the details of the case over and over in my mind. Within an hour, I finally nodded off, but around midnight I awoke from a nightmare the details of which rapidly evaporated from my consciousness. All I remember was the feeling of something constricting about my torso, squeezing me, as if the viselike grip of a giant constrictor were crushing my ribs. I tumbled from my bed with a shout that eventually brought Mrs. Hudson to my rooms to check on me. She noticed me wincing; merely breathing was painful. Upon examination of my injury, she made her diagnosis. I shooed her away.

"I commenced an examination of my rooms, bringing all my skills to bear. Nothing was out of place. All locks and latches were fastened. Mrs. Hudson had had to use her key when she came upstairs. Delicate experiments set upon my kitchen table were undisturbed. Rugs showed nothing beyond my ordinary foot traffic. All my files were in order. In short, there was not an iota of evidence—beyond my singular injury, of course—that anyone had entered, nor was anything missing. There was no rational thread of evidence by which to connect the thefts and the apparent assault—and yet . . .

"It was maddening, and returning to sleep was out of the question. Coming to your door was as close to a whim as I have ever allowed myself, and even after hearing your sincere recounting of the events of a decade ago, I am reluctant to—" Holmes stopped at the sound of the dogs whimpering in their kennel, a strange keening

Watson had never before heard a dog make.

Watson's eyes widened as the room seemed to dim, though the fire and lights remained bright as ever, as if some darkness had infused the very air.

"What is this?" Holmes said, rising from his seat.

"Surely you've surmised the answer." Watson also stood, struggling to keep his voice steady. "Though you've avoided admitting it."

Holmes nodded, a pained expression on his face. "Impossible thefts, the investigator impossibly injured—the latter was a warning."

"Which you didn't heed, bringing your investigation to me—and I answered your questions. Over the years, though prepared, I never truly expected reprisal; it seemed enough that I hadn't been believed and was expelled, my career ruined. But now . . ." Watson gestured around the room.

The darkness in the air seemed to be thickening. There were hints of movement, dim currents flowing around the room. The whimpering of the dogs stopped abruptly. Holmes took a step as if to see what had quieted them, but Watson grabbed his arm.

"Whatever happens, stay here. Don't step off the rug."

Holmes looked baffled by Watson's instruction but said nothing. Watson muttered words under his breath; he'd wondered if he'd be able to recall them after ten long years, but they came easily to his lips, disturbingly so.

"There's something in the room," Holmes said, his voice hollow and awestruck.

Indeed, the coagulating undulations in the air were taking on visible form, as of great tentacles writhing and coiling about. Watson's fear from those abandoned cellars of old resurfaced from where it had been buried, a dark stain upon his soul.

"Watson . . . ?" There was so much implied in the one-word question.

Watson held up a hand requesting silence as he quietly continued an ancient mystical chant; focus was more important than volume. Meanwhile, other sounds arose, gurgling exhalations as the thick tentacles gained substance and weight, slapping wetly against the floor and walls, knocking down pictures, swiping knickknacks off the mantel, stretching over the men, knocking against the ceiling. Watson could no longer see beyond the tentacles coiled tightly around them.

Suddenly, all the tentacles constricted inward, closing like a giant fist. Holmes ducked, raising his arms above this head— but the tentacles were held back, their circular suckers pressed flat as if against a glass dome arching over the two men. As the tentacles clenched and strained against the invisible barrier, a low, angry moaning reverberated through the room, growing louder and louder until Watson could feel it in his chest. Holmes wrapped his arms around his bruised ribs, falling to his knees. Through gritted teeth Watson still repeated the chant in its forgotten tongue, though it felt as if the deep thrumming against his sternum would keep him from drawing another breath.

Just when he feared he could go on no longer, he heard Holmes taking up the chant, mimicking the words though the detective had no understanding of their meaning. The support brought him a second wind, and Watson pressed on, Holmes keeping up with him as he increased the pace—

And abruptly the tentacles were gone. There was a great outward rush of air, the flames flaring in the fireplace, the tables beside their chairs tipping over, loose papers fluttering about, and the men staggered as if aboard a rolling ship. After but a moment of silence, the dogs erupted in a cacophony of barks and howls.

It took Watson a while to calm the dogs, finally resorting to giving them treats usually reserved for good behavior. By the time he returned to the sitting room, Holmes had restored a semblance of order, righting the tables and gathering the papers, rehanging pictures and replacing items on the mantel. Watson noticed that every item was exactly where it had been, a testament to the detective's observational skills and memory, even under unprecedented circumstances.

Holmes poured them both a brandy, and they sat down. Watson had a sip and waited, watching Holmes repeat the slow, methodical ritual of preparing his pipe. Only after several long puffs and the comfort of a cloud of smoke gathering around him, did Holmes speak.

"It would be of great interest to me to hear your explanation of what just happened."

The tone was straightforward, as if he were simply enquiring of a child how a vase came to be knocked over and broken. Watson smiled, chuckled, then broke into laughter so expressive he had to put down his glass for fear of spilling.

Holmes kept a straight face for a while, though there was a twinkle in his eye, then he joined in the laughter, a well-needed release of tension, though it wasn't long before seriousness returned to both men.

"Easier to show you," Watson said as he stood. "If you'd assist me?" As Watson moved his chair and end table off the rug, Holmes followed his lead and did the same with his chair and table. Then Watson got to his hands and knees and rolled the rug aside. The hardwood floor beneath was inlaid with two large concentric circles, between which were arcane symbols and inscriptions. Within the inner circle was inscribed a pentagram, with more symbols at its points and within its geometries.

Watson stood back up as Holmes took it all in. "I said I'd been prepared for reprisals. These are all protective wards from various occult traditions. The longer the dark energies directed at us strained against them, the more they were pushed back. I'd not be surprised if our three adversaries were seriously injured—perhaps even killed, though that wasn't my intention—when their attack was finally repulsed, and all that built-up energy blew back at them."

Holmes nodded thoughtfully. "When the Yard investigates what happened to the doctors, perhaps they'll find the stolen items, so they can be returned to their owners, though no one will really understand what happened."

"Except for us."

Holmes nodded. "Except for us." He drained his glass and stood, retrieving his ulster and homburg. "I need to alert Lestrade."

"Of course."

Watson walked Holmes to the door, still in his dressing gown. Holmes opened the door and stepped outside. A sickle moon hung low in the sky over London, above the earliest hints of the coming sunrise. The detective turned back to Watson.

"May I consult with you again if ever I encounter similar . . . circumstances?"

Watson was taken aback. It was clear how uncomfortable Holmes was with the occult encroaching upon his rational worldview. And Watson had spent a decade putting that all behind him. He couldn't deny, however, that the morning's events, although dangerous and frightening, had been a healthy change of pace from his veterinary practice—and an invigorating victory over his past. After a moment's further hesitation, Watson shrugged and, still a little surprised at his response, said, "You may."

Holmes nodded, drawing a card from within his ulster and handing it to Watson. As Watson glanced at the address—221b Baker Street—the dogs began barking again. Holmes, with a slight smirk, said, "I also have a spare room, if ever you need a break from your vociferous patients."

Watson chuckled. "Thank you."

"Well, until then. Good morning, Doctor."

"I told you, I'm not—"

Holmes didn't let him finish. "Considering you saved my life this morning, the title seems apt. It is what I shall continue to call you. Please call soon, Doctor Watson." Then Sherlock Holmes touched the brim of his hat and made his way down the steps, again leaving Watson at a loss for words.

The Adventure of the Greenwoods Bandit

by

John Peel

It was early in the morning in the Year of Our Lord 1292 when a messenger from Hugh, High Sheriff of Nottingham, arrived, summoning Sir Locke to the Castle within the week. Sir Locke observed the man depart with his reply that he would attend as soon as was convenient.

"Well, John," he murmured. "What do you make of that?"

"Dashed impertinent, if you ask me," I replied honestly. "Giving you orders like that."

He smiled slightly. "Hugh *is* the High Sheriff," Sir Locke pointed out, "which does give him the authority to order me to appear. But—what for, eh?" He steepled his fingers and glanced at me over them.

"He didn't have the grace to say," I complained. "Just snapped his fingers and told you to come a-running."

"Well, I think we can deduce that he doesn't intend to arrest me, at any rate. Had he wished that—for whatever reason—those armed men would have been more than sufficient to affect my capture."

"Well, that's a relief," I commented. "With Hugh, you can never tell."

"I must confess to feeling intrigued," he observed. There was actually a sparkle in his eye. "Life has been dull recently—perhaps this will enliven it." He gave orders to his manservant to ready two horses. Sir Locke's small estate lies in Holme Pierrepont, some six miles southeast of Nottingham, and on the very edge of the forest of Sherwood. It would be a ride of no more than an hour or so, so we would have little excuse for a delay. Unless . . .

"Are there any reports of bandits about?" I asked him, as we readied ourselves for travel.

"My dear John, there are *always* reports of bandits about," he replied. "The Law these days creates a good number of outlaws, and all of them have to be *somewhere*."

"Will we be safe, then?" I asked apprehensively.

He laughed, and slapped me on the upper arm. "Two strapping men armed with swords would hardly be a tempting target, now would they?"

"Depends on how many of them there are. It would have been polite of the High Sheriff to have left us an escort."

He chuckled. "It's not often one hears the words *polite* and *High Sheriff* connected. Now, stop worrying and let us be off. I'm getting more curious about the reason for this summons every minute, and you know how cranky my unanswered curiosity makes me."

My fears proved unfounded, and the ride was without incident. However, I can never pass so close to Sherwood without apprehension. The shadows of the trees hid many secrets—and almost as many outlaws and wolfsheads. Bands of rogues and vagabonds roamed the greenwood, and even the Sheriff's men hesitated to ride the trails within. I was glad our business kept us reasonably far from those haunted trees.

We made good time, and the guards at the gate—Goose Gate, I believe it was called—recognized us and waved us through, pushing the various merchants and peasants out of our way. We took the road up to the Castle, and we were allowed to pass again. I find castles to be heavy, gloomy places, but they always have the best of views, for obvious reasons. The meadows below led the way to the River Trent beyond. There was even the relatively recently-built Trip to Jerusalem Inn at the foot of Castle Rock, named to celebrate the departed King Richard's Crusade.

We were led into the main hall, where the seneschal announced our arrival: "Sir Locke of Holme Pierrepont and his apothecary, John, son of Wat." Hugh, seated in his high chair which he clearly thought should be a throne, beckoned us forward. Standing at his right hand was none other than that schemer, Sir Guy of Gisbourne. We had never met either man before, but both had their unsavory reputations. Of course, so did almost every noble in the land, and there were even people who spoke ill of Sir Locke. However, they were still the duly appointed authorities, and had to be treated as such—whether we approved or not.

"Gentlemen," the High Sheriff said (with what he clearly believed was a friendly smile), "I bid you welcome."

"I am honored—and intrigued—to be summoned," Sir Locke replied. "Is there some small service that I can perform for you?"

"Indeed there is," Hugh agreed. "Your reputation precedes you; you are rumored to be among the best investigators in the country."

"*Among*?" Sir Locke asked, clearly offended. Then, remembering whose presence he was in, added: "I'm touched that you have heard so flatteringly of me. I take it, then, that you have a problem that you hope I can help you with?"

"Quite so," Hugh agreed. "Have you heard of the outlaw known as Rob in the Hood?"

Sir Locke chuckled. "Who has not? They've made up plenty of ditties about him. He sounds quite the . . . scoundrel."

"He's worse than that," Sir Guy growled. "He's like a thorn branch to the backside. He needs hanging."

"I gather you've not had very much luck with that so far," Sir Locke observed, drily.

"He has proved . . . elusive," the High Sheriff admitted. "I want your assistance in capturing the felon."

"Mine?" My friend was taken aback. "My Lord, there are just the two of us—what can we do that your own much larger forces have not?"

Hugh leaned forward, gripping the arms of his chair as if he was attempting to strangle them. "I'm not asking you to charge into Sherwood after him," he replied. "If such a tactic worked, Gisbourne or I would have hung him by now. No, he knows the byways and hidden trails too well to ever be captured in such a fashion." I didn't think it politic to mention that he'd already tried—and failed—at that often in the past. "The way to capture him is through subterfuge."

Sir Locke snorted. "I wouldn't *think* of going into Sherwood after him. He's probably got men behind every greenwood tree. We have to make him come to us here in Nottingham."

Guy laughed derisively. "And how are you going to do *that*?" He gave a mock bow. "Please, Mister Robin, come and visit us at the castle. You'll be most welcome."

My friend gave a slight smile. "I doubt that would be very effective. What we need is the right bait to lure him into your clutches. Gold isn't his only weakness."

"And, pray tell me, what is?" the Sheriff asked, curiously.

"His vanity. He boasts that he's the best archer in all of England." Sir Locke smiled conspiratorially. "Why don't we give him the chance to prove it?"

"Go on," the Sheriff urged.

"It's the annual Goose Fair next week. Why not announce an archery competition to discover the best archer in England? His egotism wouldn't allow him to miss such an event. Especially if there is a special prize announced."

Guy sighed. "He'd never be so stupid as to fall for that."

"No," the Sheriff said, waving his hand and showing interest. "I can see that he might. He does so love making us look like idiots. Remember what he did to your man Giles."

"Giles?" Sir Locke queried.

"Giles!" Guy called loudly. One of his retainers came forward. He was a large man, dressed in Gisbourne's livery. Part of his face was obscured by a scarf. "Show Sir Locke your face." The retainer hesitated and gave a sort of strangled grunt. Guy scowled. "Come on, man—don't act like a bashful bride on her wedding night—show him your scar."

The man unwound the scarf from his lower face. I gave an involuntary gasp as he showed his mutilation. He'd clearly lost a sword fight, the final blow of which must have nearly killed him. The resulting scar ran down his left cheek, across his mouth and partially down his throat. He was amazingly fortunate to have survived the blow—and the medical treatment he'd received afterwards. Even now, the wound was red and swollen. I had to confess that whoever had attended him had been a superb craftsman, though I couldn't help but wonder how much constant pain and shame Giles was forced to endure.

"How does he eat?" I asked, awed.

"Badly," Gisbourne replied. "He doesn't get invited to meals."

"And the Hooded Man did this?" Sir Locke asked.

"Yes. The outlaw interfered when Giles was . . . persuading a farmer to pay his taxes." Knowing Gisbourne's reputation, I could well imagine what form of persuasion this Giles must have been employing. Were I a fighting man and not an apothecary, I might have been tempted into striking him myself. Guy growled: "Cover it up, man. None of us wants to see more." As the retainer did as he was told, Gisbourne turned to Sir Locke. "He saw this Hooded Man close-up, and if you can get the robber here, Giles will identify him."

"I'm sure he will," my friend murmured. He glanced at the Sheriff. "Now all we need is the appropriate bait."

Hugh nodded. "I'll offer a purse of 50 gold pieces to the winner," he said.

Sir Locke shook his head. "The outlaw can get that on a good day in Sherwood," he replied. "As you well know. No, we need something *unusual.* Something that no other man will have. *That* would tempt the wolfshead out of his leafy retreat. Something he could crow about. It doesn't even have to be terribly valuable—it merely has to say that whoever has it is an exceptional man. The best archer in Nottingham . . ."

"An arrow?" I suggested. Seeing the Sheriff scowl, I added: "A *special* arrow. One that would immediately demonstrate uniqueness."

Sir Locke clapped me on the back. "That's it, John—an arrow . . . made of *gold.* Something absolutely without peer."

Hugh's scowl turned into a wide grin. "By the Lord, I like it! Yes, this scoundrel is so vain that he would *have* to possess it."

"He's hardly likely to show his face, though," Gisbourne complained. "He'll know that it's bound to be a trap."

"Which would make it all the more fun for the man," my friend pointed out. "He's bound to show, but he'll be in disguise, of course. He's bound to realize Giles will be there, and looking for him, but he won't be able to resist the chance to thumb his nose at all of us." He thought for a moment. "Well—if he can disguise himself, why can't we?"

Gisbourne looked at Giles and scowled. "There's not much disguising *him,*" he pointed out.

"And we wouldn't want him disguised anyway—this Robin will expect to see him, so we must make certain he'll see him." He grinned. "What sort of an archer is your man?"

Guy looked puzzled. "He's very good—one of my best, in fact."

"Splendid!" Sir Locke exclaimed. "Then *he* will enter the contest—can't get more visible than that, can he?" He dug his elbow into the retainer's ribs. "Maybe you'll be able to beat this outlaw as well as capture him." Giles gave an enthusiastic grunt, clearly liking the idea. "And I'll compete as well, in my own disguise." He laughed. "With Giles and myself in the competition, we should be able to seize this scoundrel without any trouble."

Everyone in Nottingham loves a good fair, and the best is always the Goose Fair, held in the first week of October. There are almost as many geese as attendees, though the geese are destined for the cooking fires. It's a time of merry-making, of competitions, games and sports. And food and drink, of course. Merchants set up booths and sell their wares, each insisting that they have the best pies, ale, or sweetmeats. It's boisterous, noisy and a time and place for the population and visitors to enjoy themselves and join in fun-filled activities.

And this year was to be even better—announcements had gone out to three counties touting the archery contest and its unique prize. More travelers than ever turned up—most to watch, but many to compete. There are laws, of course, compelling all able-bodied males to practice their skills, as there is always need of skilled archers, either for the latest Crusade or any of the inevitable wars in France. So, many men felt they had a good chance of winning the prize, and were determined to prove that they were the champion archer of all England. Or, at least, of the parts of England to which the news had traveled.

I had to confess that I wasn't entirely in accord with what my friend had set into motion. True, the bandit *was* a wanted man, and it was undeniable that the man was a thief of long standing. But I knew from my rounds of my patients that this Rob in the Hood was popular with the populace, and not without reason. It was rumored that he gave a large portion of what he stole to help the poor and down-trodden. These men and women would not turn in the outlaw, no matter what reward the High Sheriff had offered. I wondered what might happen if the wolfshead were to be captured today. Perhaps there might even be an uprising? There were plenty armed men about, and a general blood-letting of a far worse kind than I was used to seeing with my leeches might yet occur. I wondered if these thoughts had occurred to Sir Locke. After all, he seemed to be strangely keen on helping capture the villain. I had tried to raise my concerns with him, but he had dismissed them casually. "I am certain all will go as planned," he assured me, and refused to listen to my worries and fears. As undeniably brilliant as his mind was, I have noted occasions when he seemed oblivious to the obvious. Still, he was my friend, and—however hesitant I felt, I knew my duty was to support him.

Gisbourne and the High Sheriff had set their men to regulating the contest, with the straw targets set up in public. The public were confined behind rope barriers—close enough to watch, and far enough away to avoid the most potentially dangerous spots. I had been included in the party that was ostensibly there merely to do the judging—though we were all rather too-well armed for merely that. The first task of the day was to winnow down the contestants, of whom there were well over a hundred present. Twenty straw-stuffed targets had been set up, and so twenty competitors could compete at once.

It was actually quite an impressive sight, as a score of men lined up, each with five arrows, and then on command they loosed their shots at the targets. The crowd—already rather well lubricated and enthusiastic—cheered before any results could even be announced, and they continued roaring their approval as the flights of arrows whistled through the air—most of them toward the targets. Even at this hour, there were some men so drunk that they couldn't have hit the target if they were standing six inches from it and holding an arrow in each hand. Thankfully, any such were quickly eliminated from the contest—either by being escorted off the field, or by disqualifying themselves by falling over and having to be dragged off. Meanwhile, the judges tapped the successful candidates and sent the rest off. Then it was the chance for the second score of men.

The elimination rounds took up the entire morning, by which time the entrants had been whittled down to a final twenty. I had not been paying overmuch attention so far, knowing that if this Hooded Man did show up, he'd certainly have made it through the initial trials. Now, though, I was more attentive. I didn't know how Sir Locke had disguised himself—he liked to be mysterious and playful at times like this—but I was sure he'd have made it through this far also. And I did see Giles, looming darkly and studying the other entrants. He, too, had made the selection.

There was a short break, ostensibly to allow the competitors to rest, but more likely to allow the judges to wet their whistles with a pint of strong ale. Hawkers wandered through the crowd, offering food, drink and entertainment. I saw a couple of cut-purses being hauled off to the castle jail by armed retainers; such thieves always frequented these kinds of events, sadly.

And then, with the arrival of the afternoon, the competition continued. Four times, the would-be winners lined up and fired. Of these twenty, only six managed to score five hits and were advanced to the finals, accompanied by enthusiastic public acclaim. Another target was added to the five, and all were moved back a further five yards. There was dead silence from the crowd at this point, because we all knew that this was at the limit of even a skillful archer's range. These competitors were great to have reached this far, but there was no way they would all get through this next round.

Now the rules were changed slightly; instead of all six firing at once, each man was to take his turn solo. I'm sure that this was simply so that the tension would be maintained longer, and the crowd kept on edge. The six men drew lots for their firing order, and Giles was to go last.

The first man stepped forward. He was a stocky, muscular man, by the name of Edgar of Walesby, we were informed. I could tell by his stance and the way he tested the slight wind that he either was or had been a soldier. Carefully he drew, aimed and loosed his first shot. Nobody even breathed as we watched it fly straight, and then hit the very edge of the target. Swiftly, Edgar plucked up arrow after arrow and loosed them. The judges ran to examine the target, and we heard the call: "Three!" It was a fine performance at such a distance, but I had a presentiment that it wouldn't be enough. From the expression on his face, so, too, did Edgar.

The second man stepped forward, with a slight smile on his face. Clearly, he thought he could do better. Whether he was right or not, we would soon see. He was handsome and on the tall side, the sort of man who felt himself irresistible to the ladies. He sported a small, pointed beard, and bowed to the audience with a flourish. A cheer greeted his histrionics, as he'd clearly expected. He took his time lining his shot, posing for admiration with every move. He was announced as Roderick of Saxonby, and I frankly wished I could kick him all of the way back there. I felt some smug satisfaction when he only scored two hits.

Third was a heavily bearded fellow with a mass of curled hair. He was dressed in an untidy smock, and announced as Hal the Thatcher. He certainly looked the part. With that hair and beard, you couldn't see a lot of his actual face, and it seemed to me that this would have been a perfect disguise for someone who didn't want to be identified. I glanced around, and saw that Gisbourne was staring at the man and stroking his own forked beard. So, Sir Guy was also suspicious of this fellow? Well, we'd have to see how he shot . . .

Four. Four of his arrows went into the target—the best yet. I wasn't *entirely* convinced this was the Hooded Man in one of his disguises, but it certainly looked very possible.

Next up was a tall, slender individual. I blinked in surprise, because he was a man of the cloth. He had on a plain brown robe of some monkish order, bound at his waist, and his hood pulled over his head so that his face was in shadow. I blinked furiously. Could *this* be Robin? Did he have the audacity to show up as an actual hooded man? The scoundrel had a reputation for boldness, but this, surely, was going too far? "Brother Andrew!" the judge called out. I glanced at Gisbourne, who glared furiously at the monk. He was clearly thinking much the same as myself. It looked like he wanted to attack the supposed holy man, but a gesture from the Sheriff forced him to hold his temper in check.

Brother Andrew bowed slightly and held his hands in prayer before crossing himself and then gripping his bow. He took his first arrow, strung it and fired. He had strung his second before the first hit the far-off target. He went through all five arrows in little more than the time the other contestants had loosed but one. Then he stood, waiting, as the judges checked the target.

Four. I didn't know if he was a monk or not, but he was certainly an archer.

The fifth man stepped forward. He, too, tested the wind by throwing a few blades of grass into the air. He was another stout fellow, with a scar across his cheek that seemed relatively fresh. A soldier recently returned from the Crusade, I decided. He was named loudly as Hal the Archer, which confirmed my guess. He stood carefully, his attention focused on the distant target. He fired slowly and deliberately, waiting for his arrow to hit before readying the next. He was good.

But not good enough. He had only three hits.

And last, of course, was Giles. The great ugly brute, his mouth still hidden behind his scarf, stomped forward. He wasn't interested in the response of the crowd, and simply stood there, launching one arrow after another.

And another four. I was surprised—the surly, unlikable fellow was a very decent archer. He gave a grunt, which I assumed was as satisfied as he'd ever sound.

So we had three contestants for the final round. The three losers trooped off, none staying to watch the end. They clearly didn't care who would be the ultimate winner if it wasn't going to be them. I watched as Hal the Thatcher, Brother Andrew and Giles took their places. The target was moved back yet again to what appeared to me to be an astonishing distance. I would honestly be surprised if any of the three managed to hit the target at all.

The High Sheriff was leaning forward in his seat, eager to see who would win, and thus be exposed as the outlaw. Gisbourne could barely restrain his impatience, and gestured to a small group of his retainers who already had their swords drawn and who looked like hounds wanting desperately to have their leashes loosed. As for myself, I was wondering where—and who—my friend might be.

And now, the crux had come. I looked at the three contestants—as different from each other as could be—as they drew lots to determine that order they would shoot in. The crowd, of course, was very excited, and cheered indiscriminately—though I noticed that there was less support for Giles; Gisbourne and his thuggish men were not popular with the populace. The shaggy Hal and the lean Brother Andrew drew rousing cheers, though. The crowd had certainly entered into a merry mood for the finale, no doubted aided by ample supplies of fresh beer.

The order was chosen—Brother Andrew, Hal and then Giles. It was difficult to see how the men took it—the monk behind his voluminous cowl, Hal behind his bushy beard and Giles with the lower half of his face wrapped in his scarf. Presumably one of the men was the outlaw in disguise—certainly Gisbourne and the Sheriff assumed this was the case, as they watched eagerly. Was my friend also one of the three? I knew he'd donned one of his disguises, but he'd deliberately not informed me what it was. I suspected that he was teasing me, challenging me to guess. I confess, I wasn't at all sure. No doubt he'd crow about it at supper that evening. He sometimes enjoyed a rather childish pleasure in beating me. And I knew that he was a more than capable archer, one who practiced frequently, so he was *probably* still one of the competitors. But only probably, for on occasion his plans didn't proceed entirely to his liking. Some of the competitors were still hanging about, eager to see who would carry off the prize that they had all striven for.

Brother Andrew stepped forward to concentrate on the far-off target. He readied himself, four arrows in his quiver and one resting in place as he aimed. The crowd was silent, either because they didn't want to ruin his concentration or—like me—through sheer tension. The first arrow sang towards the target, and, once again, Brother Andrew had reached for the next, and fired it before the first had reached the target. Again and again and again . . . Then he bowed his head and waited for the verdict.

"Three!" the far-off judge called. The crowd cheered heartily. At such a distance, getting *any* in the target was amazing. The monk bowed his head and stepped aside so that Hal could take his turn.

The grizzled archer stood ready, limbered his muscles and spat to test the air. Then he hunched forward slightly and loosed his first shot. He paused and then continued firing. Finally, he stood there, leaning slightly on his bow and waited for the judgment.

"Five!"

The crowd was hushed for a long moment, and then erupted into cheering. *Five*! That was almost unbelievable. Surely there was only one archer in all the land that could have managed that.

But Giles still had his opportunity, and he growled as he shouldered his opponent rudely aside. He took his stance and fired, slowly and carefully. The spectators were dead silent as we all watched those arrows fly toward their target. We could none of us see if they struck or not, and there was hushed expectancy as the judges hurried to their judgement.

"Four!"

There was a second of absolute silence and then the crowd roared its approval as Hal stepped forward, his bow raised in victory. Giles snarled loudly, and then struck out, felling the winner in a daze. Once again, there was silence—this time in shock at this appalling behavior—and then the roar of the spectators changed to anger. Giles grunted and gestured at the fallen man, and Gisbourne's men ran forward, seizing the semi-conscious archer. Guy himself strode along, smiling cruelly.

"Yes," Gisborne said in grim satisfaction. "I do believe that we have our wolfshead, eh?" Giles growled in response. "You've done well, my man."

Giles growled again, and shook his bow, and pointed to the target. I suddenly realized what he was implying.

"I think he wants to be proclaimed the winner," I said, disgustedly. "After all, if you're arresting Hal, then he *was* the second-best." What audacity! How could that be beaten?

Gisbourne laughed and nodded. "Yes, yes, you're quite right—you *are* the winner, my man. Go on, run to the Sheriff for your prize." As Giles ran off, Gisbourne signaled for his men to take the dazed Hal to the cells.

These actions were not popular with the crowd, and there was much muttering and low-voiced complaining. But with both Gisbourne's and the Sheriff's men all over the field, there was no organized protests.

"It's not a popular decision, awarding Giles the prize," I pointed out.

"Bah." Gisbourne growled, almost as animal-like as his mute man. "What do I care for popularity? It's good for them to see that one of my men won." He pointed over to the stands, where the High Sheriff was presenting the golden arrow to Giles. "It will keep the common scum in their places and teach them to fear the authorities. Too many of them try to get away with too much as it is."

Giles held the prize up in the air as he ran off the contest field. Gisbourne's men—knowing what was best for them—cheered his win, but the majority of the crowd remained silent. Then, as Giles reached the edge of the field and the crowds beyond, he suddenly pulled off his scarf, threw it into the air and—in a clear voice, even at this distance—cried: "Thank you for your gift, Sheriff! It will look proud amongst my trophies in Sherwood Forest!" As he disappeared into the fair-goers, he was followed by cheering as everyone suddenly realized who it had been.

If *he* had been Rob in the Hood, then *who* had Gisbourne arrested? The same thought clearly occurred to Gisbourne. He sent a patrol to pursue the fleeing outlaw—though with small chance of catching him in the mass of fair-goers—and yelled to his men dragging his captive off to halt. I hurried with him to where Hal had been dropped onto the ground. Guy tore at the man's clothing. The shaggy hair and beard came free, and beneath them were very familiar features . . .

"Sir Locke!"

My friend smiled wanly. "Indeed. That scoundrel felled me before I could reveal him as a fraud." His voice was shaky, and already there was the beginning of a large bruise on his cheek. "John, I fear I may need some of your invaluable tending."

I immediately bent to examine him, attempting to keep him quiet as Gisbourne fumed. He sent men to search for the real Giles, who was soon discovered shut in a room in the castle, completely naked and hog-tied and gagged. I swear that we could almost hear his howls of fury once he was released, and I imagine that his previous dislike of Robin was multiplied by his imprisonment and humiliation.

And—speaking of humiliation—Sir Locke had hardly covered himself with glory, and Gisbourne let my friend know his opinion of his lack of success. Sir Locke took the man's abuse with an admirable restraint that I didn't feel myself. Still, it wasn't my place to defend my friend's actions to the nobleman—"noble" in name only, though, I should add. Gisbourne ended his diatribe with orders for the pair of us to get out of Nottingham and his sight with the utmost alacrity, which we were more than happy to do.

As we rode back to Holme Pierpont, I allowed myself one small comment. "Hardly your finest hour."

Normally, if he is faced with criticism, Sir Locke tends to get moody and defensive, so I was expecting a stinging rebuttal. For once, though, all he did was smile slightly. "Oh, I don't know, old friend," he commented. "It's all a matter of perspective."

"What do you mean?" I asked.

"He means," a fresh voice broke in, "that I indisputably owe him an apology for striking him so strongly. But it had to look good."

I whirled around so quickly that I almost fell off my steed. We were passing a section of Sherwood Forest, and a tall man in green raiment had stepped out from behind a large oak. He had a broad grin on his face and the golden arrow hanging nonchalantly from his hand.

"Hood!" I exclaimed.

He removed his cap and gave a deep bow. "The same," he agreed, impudently.

I turned to Sir Locke. "Arrest him!" I insisted.

My friend merely smiled and shrugged. "I have no authority to arrest anyone," he pointed out.

I admit that sometimes it takes me a moment or two to catch on, but finally it sank in. I looked from my friend to the grinning outlaw. "You two planned this together," I realized.

"I knew you would get there in the end," Sir Locke said, laughing.

"But he's an outlaw!" I exclaimed.

Rob sighed. "Some laws you have no choice but to be out of," he replied. "Laws that oppress the poor and weak and sustain the strong and merciless. I am proud to be outside of those laws."

"Gisbourne and that brute, Giles, savage the innocent under color of the law, my friend," Sir Locke stated. "I thought it was time that they were humiliated and made to look like fools before the people of Nottingham." He grinned, and then winced. "But your blow, Robin, was a shade *too* authentic, I fear."

The wolfshead laughed unrepentantly. "Next time I shall tone it down a shade."

"I sincerely hope there will not be a next time," my friend replied. "One blow from the greenwoods bandit is sufficient, I believe."

Rob turned his cheek. "You may have a free chance to take your revenge."

Sir Locke shook his head. 'I have . . . other satisfactions from this business." He touched his cap. "Farewell, and stay safe, my friend."

The outlaw smiled. "And you also." He ran off into the forest, his laughter dancing behind him.

Sir Locke glanced at me. "I suspect that you have at least one observation to make," he murmured.

"You helped an outlaw," I pointed out.

"Aye, and proudly," he agreed. "And you know full well that too many laws are used as weapons against the common man. There are laws—and there is justice. *I* serve justice."

I nodded. "And I am glad to be by your side as your friend," I added.

We rode home in a companionable silence.

The Junkyard Dog of the Baskervilles

By

David Avallone

"You realize, of course, that the Berkowitz stories of the talking dog . . . Harvey, right? That's all complete nonsense intended to appeal to the limited imagination and stunted moral sense of a policeman. Surely you see that."

Sherlock Holmes stared at Captain Lestrade in that unblinking, maddening way he has. It is not specifically intended to make the receiver feel like a complete moron, but that is the inevitable response. Lord knows I have had it turned on me often enough. It takes an effort to ignore it, and Lestrade is not the kind of man who is particularly likely to make that effort. I jumped in, trying to salvage the situation.

"Look, Holmes is just saying we should be a little skeptical . . ."

"I am saying no such thing," he interrupted. "I am saying we should reject this pitiful hoax out of hand. He's playing you, just as he played the media and Breslin."

The red flush of rage had made its way from Lestrade's collar all the way to his hairline. I tried again, this time from the other direction.

"C'mon, buddy . . . cool down. This isn't our case. It's not even the Captain's case . . . it's all in the hands of the lawyers now, anyway . . ."

"There's a moral imperative here, Watson. One this oaf doesn't seem to grasp," he pointed at Lestrade, "and neither do you!" The Captain had been watching Holmes rant in silence. Holmes was digging a hole, and Lestrade was building up a head of steam, watching the hole get deeper. Holmes continued to work the shovel.

"We have a responsibility to speak up. This charade, this vaudeville act placing the blame for mass murder on madness or Satan—take your pick—must not cloud the process of justice. And yet this clown . . ."

"Enough!" It was loud. I'm sure they heard it in the squad room. Holmes looked at Lestrade. He even seemed puzzled.

"Enough?"

"Enough. I have had it with you two characters. You're both busted back down to patrol officer. As of now."

It was my turn to get mad, but unlike Holmes, I knew when, and how, to watch my mouth.

"What did I do?"

Lestrade gave a short, barking laugh. "You? If I bust him down and keep you in plainclothes, you'll just drag this bum to every crime scene and hang on his every word. Remember last time? That scandal in the Village? Nah, where he goes, you go with him . . . and he goes back to the street. You keep him out of trouble and out of my sight."

So the next night, as ordered, we were pounding the pavement in our street blues. Holmes never quite fit into his. He looked like a scarecrow designed to discourage jaywalking.

It was night, of course, because Lestrade wanted us on the shit detail. Though to be honest, in New York City, in August 1977, there wasn't any such thing as a non-shit detail. Ask anyone who walked a beat in those bad old days. Still, it was a quiet first night, followed by a quiet first week. The neighborhood wasn't particularly terrible, particularly for that ugly summer. The city was still in shock from the big Blackout, from the Son of Sam, and mostly the citizens were concentrating on the Yankees, their one bright spot. Why think about our crumbling city when you could distract yourself with Reggie Jackson? I was a Mets guy, myself—I prefer underdogs to contemptuous, overpaid god-kings—but my boys weren't having a good year.

Maybe eight nights in, ambling down what the poet called "these mean streets," the quiet streak ended with a woman's scream and a crazy, inhuman howl. A dog, definitely, but like no howl I'd ever heard. Something tortured about it. Holmes and I ran towards the sound. Turning the corner, we found a dead man, and a woman in shock.

The body was even skinnier than Holmes, and a very highly paid tailor had put in some long hours cutting a very expensive suit to make him look like a normal human being. He had failed, but you had to admire the effort. A look at his face and my untrained eye would have told you he had been dead a long while, but there are all sorts of things that make a man rot from the inside, long before he stops moving. The eye sockets were deep-set, the skin was like leather in that specific way you get when you smoke like a chimney for half a century or more. There were no obvious holes in him, though. No puddle of blood. Nothing dramatic, just a well-dressed stiff.

The screaming woman was Kaitlyn Maxwell, nee LeClair, and she was kneeling by the body when we got there. She stood up, and I got her statement, and Holmes listened while checking out the body. Of course I had to needle him for not waiting for the "real" detectives and the crime scene guys, but he ignored me.

Mrs. Maxwell told me the old man had come staggering out of the alley just off to her left, huffing and puffing, and had dropped at her feet. Looking back at the alley, she'd seen the dog. Like it was following him.

She paused, and said, "It glowed. The dog. It was . . . glowing."

"Glowing."

Holmes looked up for a moment. I'm sure he wanted to see the expression on her face.

"I know it sounds crazy. But it glowed. The dog glowed. I screamed when I saw it. It was probably just shock . . . this old man dropping dead, that dog . . . like something out of *The Omen*. Did you see that movie?"

I confessed that I had.

"It was one of those dogs. The devil dogs."

"A Rottweiler? You're sure?"

"Pretty sure. I don't know the name of the breed. I just remember it from the movie. The dog looked at me, looked at him, lying there," she gestured at the body, "and howled that crazy howl."

She took a deep breath. "I felt the old guy's neck, like they do in the movies, but he was already stone cold dead. When I looked again, the dog was gone. It must have gone back up the alley."

I glanced up the alley. It was a reflex, and it felt like a stupid one, but that's reflexes for you. There was no dog now, of course. Just an alley. I noted that it was maybe a little less filthy than most of the alleys I've seen.

"You didn't see where it went after that? The dog?"

"No," she said. "I'm sorry." She shook her head. "I was just on the way to the bodega, you know?"

Holmes stood up, smiled at both of us. "Watson, have you got her statement and her information?"

I waved my notebook at him. "Took care of it all by my lonesome while you overstepped protocol. Did you find any ID?"

"I did, but it wasn't necessary. Do you not recognize him?"

I peered a little closer at the ghastly, skeletal face.

"Only from nightmares."

"That, Watson, is Mister Hugo Baskerville. Surely you've heard of him?"

"Oh, sure. Real estate guy, right?"

Holmes smirked and pointed straight up. The skyscraper we were standing in front of had an enormous sign across the top floor. BASKERVILLE.

"Subtle," I said.

"The Baskervilles are not known for their humility." Holmes turned to Kaitlyn Maxwell. "I believe we have everything we need, Mrs. Maxwell. If you like, I will escort you to the bodega across the street."

In spite of everything, she blushed a little and agreed. "Holmes . . ." I started to ask, but he cut me off, "There's something I want to pick up for myself. Back in a flash."

I watched Holmes and Mrs. Maxwell cross the street as I called it in. He didn't stay long in the bodega. "Bus on its way," I told him as he walked up.

"Follow me, Watson. We'll have this wrapped up before the squad even gets here." Before I could even question that, he was already charging up the alley on a full head of steam.

"Have what wrapped up?" I asked, following with some reluctance. "Old man gets startled by creepy dog. Has heart attack. Maybe all that crazy dog-talk about Berkowitz was on his mind. What's the mystery?"

"That's the story we're being sold . . . by the murderer." He stopped and pointed to the ground. "Look closely, Watson. What do you see?"

Concrete. I saw concrete, and told him so.

"Closely, Watson. Closely."

I got down on one knee. There was something, a shimmer in the concrete, reflecting the streetlights.

"It's been a long time since I've been in a strip joint . . . but is that . . . glitter?"

"Excellent. Yes. And I'll wager there are traces of it all the way to that door."

There was a door on the left side—the Baskerville building side—of the alley. It was unmarked.

"Someone put glitter on a Rottweiler? That's your theory right now? What the Hell . . . ?"

"Get me through that door and we'll find out 'what the Hell' is going on. Perhaps even 'why' while we're at it."

As he'd guessed, the door was locked. Holmes also guessed what I was about to say next. "Probable cause, Watson. A man is dead. We're following a time-sensitive lead."

It was a heavy door, and it opened out. Violence would just get me a sore shoulder. A lock pick was a lot easier, and quieter. I did catch Holmes excitedly tapping his foot while I worked. I ignored it and a few seconds later the door popped open. He rushed past me and I followed, drawing my sidearm.

It was a fluorescent-lit hallway, completely unremarkable and spotless white walls. There was a single elevator door at the end of it.

"Your weapon, Holmes."

He ignored me. He wasn't much for pulling his .38 out unless there were already bullets flying. Drove me crazy, like so many of his other delightful quirks. He pointed down again, and the glitter was even more visible in the well-lit corridor. A very large shoe had picked up some of the glitter and left a partial smudge, but nothing you could use for a print.

"The dog took the private elevator to the Penthouse?"

Holmes snorted. "I have a strong feeling there was someone with a leash, who could reach the buttons. Let me have your lock pick."

I fished it out of my pocket with my left hand and gave it to him as we reached the elevator door. He poked the call button with the point of the lock pick.

"Don't want to smudge a fingerprint?"

Holmes smiled. "You're having a banner night, Watson. I am rubbing off on you."

"Just let me go in first this time, you smug bastard. Let the guy with the gun go first."

Holmes nodded. "I defer to you in matters of combat, Captain."

He calls me Captain when he's trying to get my goat. He knows I was a Lieutenant, back when it was combat all the time for me, in that place I don't name even in the privacy of my own head. I didn't take the bait, and after a few minutes past forever, we heard the "ding" we were waiting for.

The elevator was small. The Penthouse was 42 floors up.

"Just big enough for a couple of millionaires, I guess," I said as we entered. Holmes pushed the Penthouse button with the lock pick and handed it back to me.

"Smell that?" he asked.

"Yeah. Like hairspray?"

"Like hairspray, but specifically spray paint. If I had a guess, I'd say Rust-oleum's specialty glow-in-the-dark spray paint."

"Hell of a thing to do to a dog."

Holmes looked up at the roof of the elevator.

"No security cameras. Bad luck and good. No evidence of who was just in here with the dog . . . but also no warning for him of who's on the way. I hope he's occupied and doesn't notice the elevator coming up."

"He who?" I asked. "You have a suspect?"

"Hugo Baskerville was a horrible man, a crook, a racist, ill-mannered and friendless. Many will read his obituary with pleasure in the morning papers. But as always, who benefits the most?"

"His son. Roger. The heir."

Holmes looked genuinely pleased with me.

"Bravo, Watson. The heir."

I looked at the floor indicator over the door. Just three more to go.

"I've seen stories about Roger in the tabloids. This seems ambitious for him."

"You raise a good point, Watson. He may not be alone in this.

The man with his hand on the dog's leash may have had a leash of his own, held by Roger."

"Or a woman. There's the wife to consider, too."

I pointed the .38 at the door and hoped the damn thing didn't "ding" when we arrived at the penthouse.

Naturally, it did.

I should have expected that the dog would be waiting for us. That was, after all, the weapon of choice for the evening. Roger had no way of knowing who was coming up the elevator, and his dog was still all dressed up to greet trick-or-treaters, even if we were two months too early.

The room was dark, and the dog was, in fact, glowing. Knowing it was spray paint and glitter and backlight did less than you might imagine to blunt the visual impact. Between the surprise, and my overall reluctance to send a .38 caliber slug through the brain of Man's Best Friend, I hesitated just long enough for the Rottweiler to get its jaws around my wrist. The right one. The one holding the gun. It didn't quite snap my hand off, but it growled and tugged and I was, I admit, momentarily hypnotized by just how uncanny the situation was.

Out of the corner of my eye, I saw Holmes reach into his pocket and pull something out. I didn't immediately register what it was, but the Rottweiler immediately let go of my wrist and chomped at Holmes' hand. The growling ceased, and the massive beast trotted away, chewing something.

"The bodega . . . ?" I started.

Holmes held up a couple of those disgusting beef stick things they put out by the register. Not even the brand-name ones. The unpackaged ones, the ones that seem to be mostly bone and horsemeat. He still had a couple, in case our four-legged murder weapon came back.

"How's your wrist?" he asked. I had a feeling he was more interested in my ability to operate the Smith & Wesson Model 19 than in my personal health. I assured him I was fine, as a light went on, and a voice called out to us.

"Cops? What are you guys doing up here?"

With the light on, we could see the elevator opened directly on a lavish living room. Lavish, in the most tasteless way imaginable.

Liberace would have blanched at the level of ostentatious gaudiness. Even the wallpaper was some offensive gold and silver thing that hurt your eyes to look at.

The room's owner stood looking at us. He was big and broad, but the posture made him look a little smaller than he actually was. He was mid-thirties, and the rug on his head did nothing convincing about the early onset male pattern baldness he was desperate to hide. His face was contorted into an aggrieved pout. The gold, starched pajamas were the final, ridiculous touch.

Standing next to him was Beryl Baskerville. I'd seen her in magazines, same as him. His wife had once been very beautiful, but the last plastic surgeon had gone that one step too far and ruined the whole effect. Her gold pajamas were a little less baggy but matched her husband, as did her aggrieved pout. They stood before a giant picture window with an incredible view of the city.

"Put away the bazooka, officer. You're making my wife nervous."

I lowered the .38, but I didn't holster it. I glanced at the dog, who had finished eating and curled up to watch us, like any other dog.

"What the Hell did you do to that dog?" It wasn't the most professional opening line, and Holmes put up a hand before I could continue. Roger Baskerville snorted.

"My dad wants to use the mutt for some promotional thing at his casino. You'd have to ask him. Look, I love the police. Cops love me, and I love cops. But it's late and no one called you. What are you doing in my penthouse?"

Holmes said, "I'm Officer Holmes, and this is my partner, Officer Watson. When was the last time you saw your father, Mr. Baskerville?"

Roger looked at his wife. "What was it, like, an hour ago? We had dinner and he took Adolph—that's the dog—out for a walk."

"Adolph. For real." I was trying to tamp down my anger, but not doing the greatest job.

"Listen, hothead, it was my grandfather's name, okay? Don't get ideas."

Holmes continued, "The dog is back, and your father is not."

Roger's impression of "surprise" was not persuasive. "Isn't he? I thought he was in his room."

"He's on the sidewalk. Dead."

Roger and Beryl both did their best to crank "surprise" up to "shock." Again, nothing that would win you a Tony was happening on their slack mugs.

"Dead? C'mon, that's crazy. How? Dead?"

"Heart attack," said Holmes.

"Get outta here. Shit. I'll get dressed and go down . . ."

Holmes allowed himself a smirk. "Seems like a bother, considering you just changed into those pajamas a minute ago."

"What the Hell does that mean?"

Roger was blustering. I was looking at Beryl, who was silent and watchful. She knew better than to interrupt his act.

"Apparently you send your pajamas to a dry cleaner, who leaves a very elegant crease in them for you. A crease that wouldn't be there if you hadn't taken them out of the box moments before we stepped out of the elevator."

"Crease? Of all the crazy . . . my father is dead, you asshole! I don't have to . . . "

Holmes ignored him, and turned to me. "There's someone else here, Watson." He drew his pistol, finally. "I'll keep them covered. You look . . ."

"No need for that," said a deep voice.

I raised the gun, and turned towards the sound of the voice. So did Adolph, but he remained curled in the corner. I saw an enormous man, in a dark overcoat, holding an ugly shotgun leveled at me and Holmes. I recognized him, too.

"You're a long way from Buffalo, Eric."

"You a fan?"

"Less so every minute."

Holmes was pivoting his gaze between the shotgun man and the Baskervilles.

"You know this man, Watson?"

"Eric Obert. Linebacker for the Bills some time back. Before he let Roger put a leash on him."

"Ouch, my man. Ouch. That's just mean. How about you and your skinny partner put away those guns?"

"Don't see it happening, Eric. Sorry."

Roger stepped forward. You could tell he thought things were now well in hand.

"Guys. Fellas. It doesn't have to go like this. Even before tonight, I was rich as Hell. I have more money than two street cops like you will ever see in your lives. And that's just too bad. Like I said, I love cops. You guys should get paid more, am I right?"

"How much more?" said Holmes, to my surprise.

"The sky is the limit . . . Holmes, was that what you said? This could be your lucky day, Officer Holmes. You and your buddy. You hit the jackpot here."

Holmes chuckled. "The venal can never imagine you don't share their venality. I will say . . . I've been wondering if you remembered to put your father's heart medicine back in the pill bottle, or is it still full of whatever placebo you've had him taking?"

Roger couldn't help it. He shot a nervous look at his wife. She sighed.

Holmes and I burst out laughing. We couldn't help it, either. Whatever the direct opposite of a "poker face" is, that was Roger and Beryl Baskerville. Roger turned bright red. He pointed at Holmes.

"You're a smart boy, huh, Holmes? A lot of smart boys have tried to cross me. The lucky ones just ended up broke losers. The unlucky ones . . ."

Eric obediently chambered a shell in the shotgun. A good henchman, like a comedy club drummer, knows a cue when he hears it. Things were about to get very messy, and I tried to stop it.

"You think you can have a shootout in your penthouse with a couple of cops and get away with it?"

It was Roger's turn to laugh. "Buddy, I could shoot Abe Beame in Madison Square Garden, sell tickets, and get the NYPD to pin a medal on me. Money always wins. Eric?"

Holmes put up a hand.

"Surrendering already?" asked Roger.

"I was wondering if your wife wanted to leave the room before the gunplay breaks out. Unless Eric also has orders regarding her . . ." said Holmes.

I shot a look at Beryl. Maybe the thought had already occurred to her, maybe it hadn't, but she was looking at Roger, and you could see the wheels turning. She knew what he was, and what he was capable of. Holmes turned the screws a little tighter.

"Beryl is your second wife, am I remembering that right, Mr. Baskerville? Is number three to be that actress you were photographed with at the Met Gala? Surely one of the Miss USA finalists you've been seeing would be eager to step in . . ."

Eric tried to interrupt. He took aim directly at my head and said, "Shut up, Holmes, or I'm taking off your pal's head!"

But it was too late. Holmes didn't need to say any more.

"Quiet, Eric." Her first words since we'd entered. She said them softly, then turned back to her husband. Still not raising her voice. "Is this true, Roger? You promised me . . ."

"Beryl, baby . . ." Roger started. "Don't listen to this dumb bastard . . . it's you and me all the way . . ."

"Is that what you said to Wendy while we were dating?"

"It wasn't like that . . . I wouldn't do that to you! I love you!"

Surprising everyone, Beryl moved quickly and got Baskerville between Eric and herself. Roger kept trying to turn around, but he was a lumbering oaf, and she still had the grace and agility of a former ballerina. Roger couldn't get a hand on her.

Holmes chose that moment to take the rest of the meat sticks out of his pocket and toss them at the confused man with the shotgun. Eric had no time to understand what was happening to him, as Adolph launched across the room to get the meat sticks and collided with him. As I feared, the shotgun went off in Eric's fumbling hands. The picture window shattered. A gust of warm, muggy New York air blew into the room. It's windy that many floors up.

Holmes shouted, "Take Eric!" I knew what he meant. Eric was struggling with a hundred pounds of hungry abused dog and trying to chamber another round from his position on the floor. I crossed quickly and stomped on the hand on the shotgun's foregrip. He screamed, and I have to admit it was satisfying to hear a Bills linebacker yelp in pain, particularly for a Giants fan. He let go of the weapon, and I kicked it away from him and pointed my .38 at his head.

"Be smart!" I ordered, and he made the smart choice. He raised his hands.

I couldn't take my eyes off him, so I only heard what happened behind me. I can't say I was surprised, though. A couple of amateurs having a wrestling match in front of a broken picture window, 42 floors up. It was only a question of when, and who.

I have to admit, when I heard Roger scream, that was satisfying, too.

"Holmes?" I yelled.

"I'm fine, Watson, as is Mrs. Baskerville."

"Roger take the high dive?"

"All the way down."

I looked from Eric's face down to his shoes. The soles were covered in glitter.

I knew it would be a messy night after that.

You toss a millionaire out a window in midtown Manhattan, it draws a crowd. Two dead millionaires get an even bigger crowd. Let's just say no one in the crowd looked all that broken up about it.

Lestrade came screeching up in his unmarked sedan and put on a good show in front of the squad. Just the right amount of rage and indignation at Holmes and me. We didn't wait for backup. We didn't wait for the homicide detectives. And we let an angry wife throw a millionaire out a window. But it was very much a show, and I could see he was pleased to have a murder cleared before he even got to the scene.

The news vultures got there pretty fast, too. I have to say Mrs. Beryl Baskerville's acting chops improved markedly when talking to the press. She vividly portrayed loss, shock, and even mustered some outrage for how her husband had abused their poor dog. Her father-in-law barely got a mention, but like they say: know your audience. It was good practice for a woman who was going to have to sell a pretty unlikely story to the DA, and failing that, a judge and jury.

I felt bad for the dog. I wondered what Mrs. Hudson would think if we brought it back to Baker Street. I'd definitely have to get the spray paint off it, first. And rename him.

When Holmes and I were finally alone for a minute, watching the cleanup, waiting to get yelled at one more time by Lestrade, I said, "Good guess about the pills."

"It's not easy to count on killing a man with a heart attack. They had to have been working that angle for a while. I have a feeling that Mr. Berkowitz might have given them the dog idea."

"Or Gregory Peck."

"Gregory Peck?"

"Star of *The Omen*, Holmes. You need to get out and catch a movie sometime."

He grumbled, and I continued, "But imagine my surprise that you read the tabloids."

"Once again, Watson, I don't know what you mean."

"The Met Gala actress, the Miss USA contestants . . ."

Holmes smiled, indulgently. "Those were educated guesses. I have some idea what rich, useless playboys do with their time."

"Still, he didn't contradict you."

"They were excellent educated guesses, naturally."

I conceded they were. I had one more question for him. For my good friend and infuriating partner, Sherlock Holmes.

"You ever consider turning in the badge and going private?"

"Private as in private detective?"

"Sure. Why not? You hate the bureaucracy. You hate answering to Lestrade. We can't solve a major murder every time you get us busted down to patrol."

"Can't we?" he said, with a twinkle in his eye.

"That's not an answer."

"Fair enough, Watson. We've met private eyes, though, haven't we? Greasy little snoops, mostly invading personal lives for profit. It's an ugly business. There's no dignity in it, and no money or honor in vigilantism. For all the frustrations, the New York Police Department is stuck with me."

"Fair enough, Holmes. Now let's find Lestrade and get our detective shields back."

A Study in Vacuum
by
Dayton Ward

One thing I hate more than living inside a tin can on the Moon is walking around outside it. Yet here I was, standing on the lunar surface in an excursion suit. It happened from time to time as part of the job, but that doesn't make it suck any less.

Parched gray soil stretched toward a horizon of utter darkness broken only by the sloping rims of distant craters. With the colony's location on the lunar plains adjacent to the Sverdrup and Henson craters near the Moon's south pole, Earth wasn't visible from my current vantage point. I'd be lying if I said this didn't amplify the sense of isolation that always gripped me whenever circumstances forced me to venture beyond the colony's protective shell. I couldn't deny the view was breathtaking, but that thought seemed rather inappropriate given why I was out here in the first place.

"Agent Watson? I think they're ready for us."

The voice of my new partner, Sergeant Sherilyn Holmes, filtered through my helmet's comm system. Turning away from the unchecked yet mesmerizing desolation, I could see her through her faceplate, and her complexion seemed as ashen as the pallid soil around us.

"You all right?"

Holmes offered a nervous nod. "I think so." She drew a deep breath, and I wondered if she might actually throw up in her helmet. Instead, she said, "I don't have a lot of experience with this sort of thing." Despite her evident discomfort, her crisp British accent remained unbowed. "Not exactly much call for it on Earth, you know."

Prior to graduating from the United Forces Criminal Investigation Division Academy, Holmes had spent the first six years of her uniformed career with the military police. We at least had that in common, owing to my own nine-year stint as an MP, which I suspect had inspired our commanding officer, Colonel Amanda Hawkings, to assign Holmes as my new partner. So, here we were, two "agents away" from Earth assigned to Luna One, the first off-world permanent settlement. Though under military jurisdiction, the colony was home to nearly a third more civilian contractors than UF personnel. It was still our house and our rules, with UFCID carrying investigative authority over the entire population.

Noting Holmes' strained expression, I said, "Try to relax. Breathe normally. We won't be out here that long, and hopefully not doing anything too crazy."

We'd been diverted from the spaceport, where inspectors had found a shipment of crank—a catchall term for various amphetamines and other illicit stims intended for nefarious uses—hidden between the inner and outer hulls of a transport vessel from Earth. I'd only just started interviewing Craig Denham, a maintenance worker assigned to the docking facility whom we believed was the traffickers' point person for delivery and distribution. Now Denham sat in a holding cell, as Colonel Hawkings had made this new case our top priority.

Death before drugs, as it were.

Motioning for Holmes to follow me, we bounded in the one-sixth lunar gravity toward the crime scene. Electronic barricade strips linked four metal poles to form a square extending 20 meters from the maintenance module's still-open outer airlock hatch. Inside that area lay the debris field caused by the airlock's explosive decompression; tools, unworn components of excursion suits, and the three victims. Inside and beyond the perimeter, multiple sets of footprints wandered to and from the module in multiple directions, indicating routine exterior activity. Matching them to anyone would be impossible.

"Based on their supervisor's initial report," said Holmes, "the three workers—two men and a woman—were preparing to work outside."

None of the victims had their helmets on, and the woman's hands were missing their gloves. All three had matching expressions of shock and terror, eyes squeezed shut and mouths frozen open.

Stopping outside the perimeter, I noted the pulsing red endcap on each of the poles forming the cordon. High-resolution cameras built into each stanchion would record everything within the established perimeter, capturing the precise location, measurements, and condition of every item along with its relative distance to other articles. That information would transfer back to our offices to aid in digitally recreating the entire scene inside our forensic imaging lab. There, our investigative team could walk around an entire simulation of the scene and everything it contained.

"We trained with those cameras at the academy," said Holmes. "They're quite something."

I nodded. "Yeah, but still no substitute for getting your own eyes on the actual scene. That first look is critical."

Another suited figure stood beside the body closest to the open airlock. Even from this distance I recognized Eleanor Hill, the civilian pathologist assigned to UFCID as a medical examiner. "Take her, for instance," I said as Ellie, having waited for the evidence cameras to finish their work, began loping toward us. "She's as old fashioned as it gets when it comes to scene investigation."

Ellie stopped on her side of the barricade and I made introductions. Nodding to Holmes, I said, "It's her first time at an exterior scene. Go easy on her."

"First day, Sergeant Holmes? And they shackle you to Jonas?" Ellie smiled. "Are you being punished?"

"Hawking's idea," I said. "She figured a new partner would make my last year more interesting."

Ellie studied me with mock derision. "Still on about retirement?" She waved as if to dismiss the idea. "I don't buy it. Nobody does."

"I guess we'll see what we see." Looking past her, I studied the bodies. "First impressions?"

Shaking her head, Ellie replied, "I won't make any official declarations until after the autopsies, but cause of death seems pretty obvious. It's a good bet their lungs are ruptured, just for starters. Their faces are bruised and swollen, indicating rapid, violent transition of the victims' bodily fluids from liquid to vapor."

"Ebullism," said Holmes.

"You got it." Ellie sighed. "What we don't yet know is why. According to their supervisor, they were prepping to service one of the nearby antenna clusters. They were still suiting up inside the airlock, so the inner hatch was open when the outer one opened. The hatch leading from the adjacent compartment farther into the module was closed, or else it would've vented a much larger section." She gestured to the three bodies. "It's a tragedy for these three, but for an accident it could've been much worse."

"If it was an accident."

Ellie and I both turned to Holmes, whose attention seemed fixed on the open airlock.

"You think it *wasn't* an accident?" I asked.

The young agent frowned. "The outer door can't be opened if the inner door isn't secured or if the airlock itself isn't depressurized."

Ellie pointed to the airlock's open outer door, and a lever pulled from a recessed area at the hatch's center. "Sure, but airlock outer doors include an emergency lock override. For that to be activated, someone has to enter a code to the control pad near the inner hatch, which in turn frees an access panel on the outer hatch which normally covers the lever itself."

"So, someone enters a code," I said, "then crosses to the outer hatch to pull the lever. That releases the hatch's locking pins, interrupting the magnetic seal. If the airlock itself is pressurized when that happens, anything inside would be shot out of there like a cannon." I looked again at the scene before us. "That would explain . . . all of this."

"Were there any cameras inside the airlock?" asked Holmes.

"Video feeds throughout that entire section of the colony were offline." Ellie grimaced. "There was a software upgrade being installed around the same time."

Holmes said, "Convenient."

I was thinking the same thing. Turning to my partner, I noted her contemplative expression. "What?"

Holmes replied, "This wasn't an accident."

She's eager, I thought. *But she's not wrong.*

The interview room at UFCID headquarters was a drab, uninviting affair. Dark walls, no windows, and a single door with no interior opening mechanism was enough to intimidate even the most hardened suspect. Cameras embedded into the walls allowed for remote observation of the proceedings. A gunmetal gray table flanked by two chairs on opposite sides were the room's only furnishings.

I sat facing our second interview subject for this newest case. Patrick Sheehan was slight of build, and the blue coveralls which looked a size too large for him bore the insignia of the Santeri-Braun Corporation, one of three military defense contractor firms assigned to the colony. He looked tired, his black-gray hair and matching beard in need of grooming. In the corner over my left shoulder, Holmes stood with her attention divided between us and the data tablet in her hands.

"Mister Sheehan," I said. "I'm Special Agent Jonas Watson with UFCID." After introducing Holmes, I glanced to my own tablet which displayed my subject's personnel file. "We'd like to ask you some questions. You're not under arrest, so if at any time you wish to end the interview, you're free to leave. If you desire legal counsel, we can stop for that to be arranged. May we proceed?"

Sheehan appeared unconcerned about his present circumstances. Instead, his expression was one of sadness, which I'd expect from someone who'd just lost three co-workers. "Ask me whatever you want. I need to know what happened, too."

"You're the primary maintenance supervisor for Colony Sector Four?" I asked.

"Yeah," he snapped. Then, he seemed to deflate. "I'm sorry. It's been a tough morning."

I replied, "I'm very sorry about your people. Did you know them well?"

Sheehan nodded. "They've been here about a year." He closed his eyes for a moment, releasing a long breath. "They were my friends."

"You were on duty when the mishap occurred?" I asked.

"Yes. I authorized the service order."

"Found it," said Holmes, not looking up from her tablet. "Mister Sheehan, did you also authorize the upgrades to the computer systems overseeing Sector Four?"

Sheehan shook his head. "They're corporate-mandated, since they impact all the colony systems. Everything is pushed out to the different subsystems at their direction." He sighed. "The only thing

I can do is slot it for a time that works with our schedule, but it still has to happen within 24 hours after the order comes down. I try to schedule those updates for the graveyard shift, usually between 0300 and 0500, to impact the least number of people."

Holmes asked, "Were you overseeing the upgrades?"

"Not this time. That was Neal Seigel, the third shift supervisor. He's on from midnight to 0800, but I was there an hour early to oversee the antenna work."

I already knew this from my earlier interview with Seigel. Like Sheehan, he'd also been upset by the tragic news, displaying the expected shock and dismay that something so awful could happen. I didn't know what to think, about him or Sheehan, but we were just getting started.

"According to the system logs," said Holmes, "it was Meredith Yates who entered the override command to access the emergency lever on the airlock's outer door. Her identity code was tagged to the instruction."

"Impossible." Sheehan reached up to wipe his face. "Meredith would never do something so stu—" When he stopped this time, his eyes widened in horror. "Wait. You're saying she did this *on purpose*?"

I watched Sheehan's expression change from confusion to shock and finally disbelief as Holmes stepped toward the table and recited the known facts and as well as our current theory about Yates.

"That's insane." Sheehan grimaced, still fighting apparent incredulity. "Why would she do that?"

It was a valid question. I'd reviewed her medical file and found no evidence of mental health issues. There were no prescribed medications, and neither had Yates even visited the colony's clinic after completing the required physical every colonist received upon arrival. There were no records of her visiting a therapist, and a perusal of message traffic to her Wisconsin home on Earth revealed nothing troubling. By all accounts, she had adapted to life on Luna One with little to no difficulty.

She just doesn't fit the profile for suicide. My simple, unspoken conclusion echoed in my head. That meant it had to be something else. Something worse.

"It's our job to answer that question, Mister Sheehan," I said. "I promise we'll do everything we can."

While I hoped to reassure him, my own words sounded hollow to me.

Crime scene reconstruction and reverse theorizing was one of the things I hated most about this job. It was one thing to examine evidence and bodies during the course of an investigation, but our imaging lab took things to a far more uncomfortable level.

"Everything's loaded, Jonas," said Ellie Hill, stepping away from the terminal set into the lab's forward wall. "The computer's taken everything recorded at the scene and backtracked to the most likely sequence of events, based on the final resting place of each victim and debris, factoring in the full effects of violent decompression along with the lack of atmosphere and the reduced gravity." Around us, the rest of the room was already transformed into a perfect holographic simulation of the mishap scene. The far wall recreated the maintenance module and its closed hatch, away from which stretched an expanse of barren lunar soil already marked with uncounted footprints leading to and from the airlock.

Her features betraying her obvious apprehension, Holmes said, "We didn't get to train on anything like this."

"It can be a little unsettling." Bracing myself for what I knew was coming, I looked to Ellie. "Do it."

The pathologist pressed a key on the computer terminal, initiating a holographic representation of a digital clock in the air above our heads, set to 15 seconds before the accident. It advanced at normal speed until I watched the airlock door swing open, propelled by the atmosphere inside the compartment. As expected, tools, excursion suit components, and the simulated bodies of Valmiki Goswami, Park Ji-hu, and Meredith Yates tumbled onto the recreated lunar soil. Everything scattered toward its final resting place, the debris field forming as the representations of the three maintenance workers suffered through their death throes. Goswami, having exited first, landed the farthest from the airlock, followed by Park and Yates. Once everything settled, the simulation and the clock halted and I read the timestamp: 07:31:20.

"Seventeen point eight three five nine seconds, start to finish," said Ellie. Walking across the simulated crime scene, she knelt beside Yates's now still form and pointed to the woman's bare hands. "She wasn't wearing her gloves, and it's a given all their fingerprints would be on the keypad just from normal use."

Intent on studying the scene and replaying the tragic seconds in my head, I didn't notice Holmes until she passed Ellie on her way to the open airlock. Pausing at the threshold, she inspected the compartment's reconstructed interior.

"Agent Holmes?" prompted Ellie after a moment. "What is it?"

Instead of answering, the young agent turned from the open airlock and moved toward the simulation of Merideth Yates' body before her gaze shifted to those of Park and Goswami.

"Yates was the last to exit the airlock," said Holmes, then pointed to Goswami. "Based on what we think we know about their positions inside the compartment, if Yates was the one to enter the override code before moving to pull the emergency lever on the outer hatch, wouldn't she be the first one pushed out?"

Confused, I turned to study the positions of the three bodies. What Holmes said made sense, and yet the obvious physical evidence belied her observation.

"The computer can't extrapolate from data it doesn't have." Ellie frowned. "So far as it's concerned, what we're seeing is consistent with the data it had when it modeled the simulation."

"But not consistent with what we think happened," I said.

Ellie asked, "We believe Yates entered the override code, because her ID was tagged to it." She pointed to Goswami. "Could it have been him?"

"Possibly," I replied. "But why not use his own code? If he was trying to kill himself, why hide it?" A search of personal belongings had turned up no suicide notes. Goswami's personnel record showed he had no family, and no beneficiaries listed for any payouts in the event of his death.

Holmes added, "It also makes no sense for one person to enter the code while someone else pulled the lever, unless it was an emergency. Even then, none of them were properly suited, and more than one of them contemplating such rash action is highly unlikely." She fixed her gaze on me. "That leaves two plausible explanations: a fault with the system controlling the airlock, or deliberate action by another, as yet unidentified individual."

I took another look at the recreated crime scene, wondering about the secrets it might still hold. "It's a whole new ball game, now."

Though I didn't yet know much about Sherilyn Holmes, her personnel record documented her strengths for criminal investigation. College transcripts and test scores indicated a strong aptitude for information systems, matching her interest in computer forensics. I could make my laptop terminal and even my mobile carry out simple, everyday tasks, but that was my limit. Computers for me had always been useful if occasionally irritating servants. I left it to younger, brighter agents to carry out the almost mystical communing that seemed necessary to extract useful information from the depths of those interminable gadgets.

Holmes, on the other hand, was sitting at her newly assigned desk and showing its accompanying computer terminal who was boss. With her tablet inserted into its docking port, she took advantage of the desk's more expansive setup. Her fingers danced across the membrane of the larger console's backlit keyboard as though of their own volition and in response to her ministrations, rows of information scrolled across three display screens arranged side by side. Standing just behind her, I saw each screen offer its own lists of data. Trying to make sense of it all was impossible.

"You can read all of that?"

Not looking away from the screens, Holmes asked, "Am I going too slow? I can speed it up if I'm taking too long. I just didn't want to risk missing anything." Her tone was not at all mocking, which only served to further sully my pride.

"Do whatever works best for you." I stifled a grunt of resignation as Holmes pressed a key and the data began scrolling even faster.

One year to retirement, I reminded myself. *One lousy year.*

Letting Holmes work, I studied the report sent to my tablet from Ellie Hill. One of her crime scene technicians had found something odd in the form of an emergency excursion suit crammed into a tool locker near the maintenance module's operations center.

"An emergency suit is rather less complicated than a regular one," said Holmes without looking away from her monitors. "At least, that's the intent?"

"Right," I replied. "They're not nearly so fancy or robust. They come in one size, and you pull on a set of built-in cords to fit it to your body, all in 20 to 30 seconds. The idea is you wear it just long enough to make your way to a different module's airlock in the event of a hull breach or some other incident requiring quick evacuation." I'd trained in how to don them a few times, and it was standard procedure to have them staged in lockers throughout the colony.

Holmes said, "I'm guessing there's something suspicious about this particular suit?"

"Yeah." I read the report from my tablet's screen for a second time. "They found it in a locker near the module's computer server room, instead of the office locker where it was supposed to be. Guess who it belongs to?"

"Patrick Sheehan." She glanced at me. "I've already read the report." Before she could elaborate, her console beeped for attention and she resumed watching over the data streaming across the terminal's screens.

"I'm not going to pretend I can keep up with any of that," I said, watching the cascade of information. "Just give me the highlights. What are you looking for?"

Holmes replied, "Every colony control pad or computer station interfaces with the central mainframe. Any command or query made through any of those access points is recorded, along with relevant information pertaining to the resulting action. System logs track everything down to the simplest requests, like the code to open an airlock hatch. I'm searching those logs, looking for anomalous entries which might explain a fault in our airlock's control pad." She grimaced. "So far, I've found nothing out of the ordinary."

The right and left-most screens halted their scrolling, each highlighting a different line of text. Leaning closer, Holmes studied the data for a moment before saying, "Huh."

"Huh, what?" I asked.

She pointed to the left screen. "This section of data is a dump of every command sent or received by the airlock control pad for the past month. The highlighted line is Meredith Yates' override to release the hatch lever."

Moving so I could better read the screen, I noted the string of numbers and letters indicating Yates' identification code as well as what had to be the override sequence, followed by a second stretch of numbers I recognized as a timestamp. The first eight numbers indicated the calendar year, month, and day: 20780613. Twelve additional numbers denoted the time in 24-hour format: 073103048915, with the seconds recorded to six decimal places.

"According to the log," said Holmes, "this is the timestamp when her code was recorded. Yates would've had access to the lever within a few seconds and assuming she pulled it immediately, the door would open and we know what happens after that."

She tapped another control and the display on the console's center monitor changed to a recording of Ellie Hill's imaging lab simulation. In the screen's upper left corner was a digital clock similar to the one running when we reenacted the incident. Holmes replayed the simulation and I watched the recreated forms of Goswami, Park, and Yates make their violent exit from the airlock. When Holmes froze the video, I noted the timestamp: 07:31:03.

"They're the same," I said.

"Not quite." Shifting in her chair, Holmes pointed to the highlighted line of text on the rightmost of her three computer screens, and I read that time code: 073103020015.

"A fraction of a second before the timecode for the override being entered?" I asked. "How?"

"The system log was altered," replied Holmes, tapping the screen. "And that's not the only instance I found." More keystrokes brought up another selection of highlighted text on the two conflicting screens, and she pointed to them. "On the right, what the log shows for what Yates entered. On the left? The actual instruction that was executed."

The code on the right screen was completely different than the one on the left, save for that portion representing Meredith Yates' ID number.

"Don't tell me," I said, not wanting to believe the words coming out of my own mouth. "She entered a proper code, but the computer interpreted it as the override."

Holmes turned from her console. "More accurately, someone deliberately reconfigured the system to accept the code she entered—an instruction to close the airlock's inner hatch—to instead open the outer hatch while overriding the safeguards."

It took me an extra second to put it together. "Wait. You're saying that code triggered the hatch *by itself*?"

"According to the system log," said Holmes, "that's exactly what happened. Someone tried to cover their tracks, but they weren't precise enough. Hence, the log discrepancies."

I said, "That doesn't explain the lever." Then, it hit me. "The suit."

Fragments of thoughts, questions, ideas, and theories swirled in my head as I worked to will it all into something that made sense. "We can definitely call this murder, but we have no idea if one or all of the victims were targeted." I didn't really believe that last part. Instinct told me it was simpler than that.

"I think it was one target," said Holmes. "Yates. The other two provided convenient cover to further the illusion it was an accident."

There you go. Her gut was sounding like mine. "Okay, why?"

Clearing her throat, Holmes said, "The effort to make it look like Yates was responsible. This suggests someone with an axe to grind. A personal issue with another colonist."

I held up my tablet. "Way ahead of you. Ellie sent us a dump of the messages on her tablet and mobile."

Holmes turned back to her console and went to work. Within seconds I saw new streams of text coursing down all three screens.

"Work-related texts and messages," she said after a minute. "Conversations with friends. Meetups for dinner or for a drink. It's all rather boring." She tapped a control and the streams of data slowed. "Invitations from several potential male suitors and a few women, all of which she seemed adept at resisting without prompting more troublesome responses."

"That's the part I found unusual," I said. "This place can make you lonely for home. It has a tendency to breed problematic behavior, if you catch my meaning."

Her attention still on the screens, Holmes grunted. "I do, indeed." With an abrupt movement she stabbed at her console, halting the information flow. "Hang on." Again I saw different versions of what at first appeared to be the same dataset highlighted on two of the screens. "This came from her personal devices?"

I replied, "That's what Ellie said."

"They've been altered." Holmes pointed to the rightmost screen. "This is an extract from the mainframe's master log, where copies of all communications are stored offline." UF policy was to capture all internal and external comm traffic for security purposes, to identify potential risks such as espionage or even physical threats to the colony. All of it was encrypted to keep the average idiot from accessing sensitive data, but none of that seemed capable of stopping Holmes.

"There are additional text messages here that weren't on her tablet or mobile." She entered another command string, and an excerpt from the larger log was highlighted and expanded in size:

I know what I saw

You're confused

I saw you meeting that guy. You'll get caught. Fired. If they find out I know, they'll fire me for not saying anything

Just giving people what they want. Making this dump more bearable. Keep quiet and I'll cut you in for a piece

No thanks. I don't want any part of this

You can't say anything. Not now

I'm not saying anything, but if you get caught you leave me out of it

Not that simple. More than just us. I have to tell Craig

I don't care. I don't know anything

"Wait." I hit the control to freeze the screen. "Craig? I'll be damned."

Holmes said, "Craig Denham? Our suspected drug trafficker?"

I scanned the rest of the log extract. "Why aren't these texts tagged with their senders?"

"That information's encrypted for security purposes," replied Holmes. "We'd need authorization from Colonel Hawkings before—"

I was already moving for the door. "I've got a faster way."

Holmes found me in Denham's holding cell as I threatened him with three counts of conspiracy to commit murder. That and the accompanying death sentence made him fold in what had to be my new personal best record for breaking a suspect. This was enough for Colonel Hawkings to approve decrypting the protected comm logs which in turn generated the necessary arrest warrant authorizations. Then it was a matter of finding the person Denham gave up. My suspect made it easier by meeting his companion in one of the colony bars, perhaps to plot his next move or even his escape back to Earth. It was my job to ruin those plans and also the rest of his life, along with those of anyone else who got in my way.

"Patrick Sheehan," I said, presenting my badge as I approached his table near the bar's far corner. "You're under arrest for the murder of Meredith Yates, Valmiki Goswami, and Park Ji-hu." I was aware of other patrons eyeing us, but I also knew UFCID agents were positioned at every exit.

"What?" To his credit, the haggard-looking maintenance supervisor looked genuinely shocked and even a bit terrified at the accusation. His eyes wide and his jaw slack, Sheehan looked first to me then to his companion at the table, Neal Seigel, his third-shift supervisor. "What the hell are you talking about?"

I placed my tablet so he could see the text messages exchanged with Yates. Now each text was marked by its sender's name. Hers, and Sheehan.

"Mister Sheehan," I said, eyeing the increasingly agitated man. "It seems you had quite the disagreement with one of our victims shortly before her death. Unfortunate timing, since you were also someone who could kill her in a way that looked like an accident."

Standing across from me and closer to Seigel, Holmes said, "Reconfiguring access and command codes and then covering your tracks in the system logs? There's a pretty short list of people with the skillset to pull that off."

"Damned short," I said. "Did I mention the timing and the opportunity? During a software upgrade that deactivated all the cameras in your sector. How many people knew about that maintenance window? People who are still alive, I mean."

Sheehan gestured with both hands to the tablet. "I never sent these messages. This wasn't me!" His eyes had reddened and I could see moisture around the edges, and his hands started to shake.

"Spare me," I said, pressing forward. "We know about your relationship with Craig Denham. You make sure to schedule system upgrades whenever he brings in a crank shipment. Yates found out about your little operation and spooked you."

Sheehan's face was a mask of shocked disbelief. "Meredith knew?" Then, he glared at Seigel. "What the hell is he talking about?"

Unlike Sheehan, Seigel seemed poised, if not a bit put off by the confrontation. He was also a somewhat bigger, more muscled man than his boss, which concerned me. I'd just shoot him, if it came to that.

"Tell him, Neal," I said. "It'll sound better coming from you." That earned me the response I wanted, with Seigel's expression falling. When he said nothing, I looked to Holmes. "Help him out, partner."

Her look told me she was enjoying my banter. "It was quite a technical feat, reconfiguring the airlock command codes to trigger the outer hatch while Yates and the others were inside, and to make it look like she'd entered the override."

"But someone had to come behind them and pull that emergency lever to make it look good when we showed up," I added. "It almost worked. You had me fooled."

Seigel snorted. "Neat story." Even he didn't believe what he was saying, but he had to try. "You can't prove it."

I nodded to Holmes. "She can. Good thing she's smarter than me. And you."

Moving as far from Seigel as he could without bumping into me, Sheehan regarded his colleague with incredulity. "You killed her? You killed *all of them*?"

"The emergency evac suit gave him away," said Holmes, looking at Seigel. "You took it from Sheehan's locker and used it to reach the hatch from outside and pull the lever. No cameras, remember? Yours were just one more set of footprints along with all the others. Easy to get lost in that shuffle, but you sized his suit to fit you, and you left it that way when you shoved it into the tool locker where you knew it'd be found."

I shook my head. "Rookie move. For what it's worth, Denham gave you up. He copped a plea for a lesser sentence in exchange for you and everyone else involved in the crank operation." I smiled. "There's going to be a whole lot of bad people very mad at you. I'd start praying we catch them first, but that's just me."

Sheehan was almost trembling. "You son of a bitch. You killed them and then you made it look like *I did it*?"

I knew Seigel wouldn't go down without one last act of stupidity. Faster than I would've expected, he was pushing himself from his seat, charging at Holmes before I could draw my weapon. Holmes never found her own sidearm, but she didn't need it.

As Seigel reached to push her aside, she grasped his outstretched arm and pivoted into him, using his momentum to pull him across her right hip and down to the floor. The lower gravity certainly helped, but Seigel's own bulk saw to it he landed hard, and I was sure I heard something pop before he screamed in pain. His body went limp and she rolled him onto his stomach, wresting his arms behind him and securing his wrists with a restraint band pulled from her back pocket. For his part, Sheehan watched the entire thing unfold without moving a muscle, silent as Holmes pulled Seigel to his feet and I got my first look at his bent, bloodied nose.

"Ouch," I said.

Pulling a defeated Sheehan from his seat, I restrained his hands behind his back before handing him and Seigel to another pair of agents. Sheehan looked to me, fear in his eyes.

"I swear, I didn't know he was going to do that."

Maybe it was true. I didn't care. Even if he hadn't killed Yates and her companions, I had to wonder how much misery and perhaps even death his crank business had inflicted. That'd be the next thing we figured out, but it could wait for tomorrow.

"Holding," I instructed the junior agents. Once they were gone, I turned to Holmes. "Not bad for your first case."

She smiled. "I hope they're not all like this. For your sake, I mean. One year before you retire, yes?"

I shrugged. "I don't know." There was no doubt Holmes was a promising young agent, and while she still had much to learn that the academy never got around to teaching her, she definitely had a knack for the job. Maybe this wouldn't be such a boring year, after all.

And when that time was up? I guess we'll see what we see.

The Case of the Unseelie Terror

by

David McDonald

It was 1896, a notable year in many ways. That year, Her Majesty celebrated exceeding the reign of her troubled grandfather to become Britain's longest reigning monarch, while a lucky few got to witness the very beginning of another reign at Old Trafford, as they watched in wonder as the Indian prince caressed his way to stately and undefeated 154 on debut, an innings which moved even the staid commentators of *Wisden* to unprecedented flights of rhapsody.

However, it was a much less pleasant event that found Holmes and I sitting in his club and commemorating. It had only been the week before that we had found ourselves in Nottingham investigating the terrible and tragic case of Mrs Wilkins and her Barbary Ape, and we were grateful to have made it back to London with our lives and our sanity intact. Perhaps, though, if we had known what lay ahead we wouldn't have been so quick to celebrate.

Holmes had just poured another of his Scotch and sodas and was leaning forward to refill my unadulterated glass of God's own drink when we were distracted by a commotion at the doorway. We could see a man trying to force his way past the impeccably dressed guardians at the doorway, his sulphurous curses indicating his lack of success. At a slight gesture from Holmes, they stepped aside and allowed our uninvited guest to approach.

"Damned impertinence!" he snarled. "Who do they think they are trying to impede one of Her Majesty's detectives?"

The speaker was a small, wiry man, with sharp features that the uncharitable might have called rat-like. He was in a cheap, ill-fitting suit that had been rumpled even before his ill-advised attempt to force his way into the room.

Holmes arched his eyebrow slightly in amusement, which by now I knew was the equivalent of breaking out in peals of laughter were he any other man.

"Why, Detective Lestrade! Don't you know that the club has the highest of standards?" he asked. "They don't care about such trifles as a policeman's badge when it comes to keeping out...undesirables."

The fact that Lestrade failed to rise to Holmes' bait told me just how agitated the detective was, and I broke in, seeking to forestall one of their endless arguments.

"Please, Detective, won't you join us?" I gestured at one of the empty leather chairs. "Pull up a seat, and have a drink."

I left unvoiced how obvious his need for fortification was.

"Thank you, Doctor Watson, but I don't have time for socialising." He took a deep breath. "We've found another one."

"You mean...?" Holmes asked.

In that moment I knew what Lestrade would look like as an old man.

"Yes, another dead girl." He grimaced, as if the words had a foul taste. "The Bethnal Green Butcher seems to have claimed another victim."

The lurid name was immediately familiar to us, as it would have been to even the most sheltered soul in Britain. For the past week, the papers had been full of the lurid details of a series of murders that had rocked the nation and cast a pall of terror over London. The brutal nature of the killings, and the fact that the victims came from one of the city's vilest slums, had already sparked comparisons with that notorious monster, Jack the Ripper, a comparison the police had done their best to downplay.

"Forgive me, Detective, but why has this brought you bursting into my club?" Holmes asked coolly. "If you were in such urgent need of my assistance, I would have expected you to send word days ago."

Lestrade flushed and wrung his hat between his hands.

"Holmes, if it had been up to me, I would have done so. But, those with much more authority than I forbade me to." He looked down at the floor. "They said that it was a matter for professionals."

"So, why now, Lestrade? What's changed?"

"Because I don't want to see any more young women butchered because of someone's ego," Lestrade almost shouted. With a visible effort, he calmed himself. "Look, Holmes, there is something strange about this case, things you would think me mad were I to try and put them into words. But no one else seems willing to admit it. I'm asking for your help as a personal favour. Do you want me to beg?"

Holmes had the grace to look slightly embarrassed. Despite their barbed repartee, over the years he had grown to respect the detective's indefatigable desire for justice and dogged pursuit of criminals.

"Don't be silly, Inspector," he said. "Of course we will help. Won't we, Watson?"

Without waiting for an answer, he knocked back the remains of his drink and got to his feet.

"To the morgue, then," he said.

It was only half an hour, and a hair-raising hackney ride, before we found ourselves at the morgue. It took far less time than that for us to gain some small understanding of how Lestrade must have felt seeking entrance to Holmes' club, for we were, if anything, even less welcome here.

"No! This is not acceptable, Inspector. I will not allow this kind of interference!"

The source of the objections stood before us, visibly shaking with an anger that would have seemed at the point of spilling over into physical violence if weren't for the aura of rectitude that its bearer palpably exuded.

He was tall and spare, with ramrod straight posture and broad shoulders that spoke of a youth spent in athletic pursuits not completely abandoned. Neatly trimmed whiskers lightly dusted with grey framed a strong jaw, and piercing blue eyes flashed angrily behind wire-framed spectacles. Beneath a fresh white apron smeared with daubs of blood, he was dressed in a conservative suit that spoke more of respectability than fashion.

"Now, Professor Dawson, this is a police matter," Lestrade snapped. "I've asked these gentlemen to assist; they are to help, not interfere. May I introduce Mr Holmes and Doctor Watson? Doctor Watson is a man of extensive medical experience, including time in the army, while Mr Holmes—"

"Oh, I know all about Mr Holmes." Dawson's lip curled in a

sneer. "The famous amateur detective."

The stress he put on the word 'amateur' was as sharp as a slap across the face. However, if Holmes noticed the insult, he gave no sign.

"Professor Dawson? Not the Dawson who delivered the series of lectures on the medical impossibility of the soul?"

Dawson gave him a startled look.

"I didn't know you were a student of my work," he said, slightly mollified. "Perhaps I was wrong about you if you can appreciate my ideas."

"Oh, I didn't say that I thought they had any value." Ignoring Dawson's spluttering, Holmes turned to Lestrade. "So, what did you wish to show us, Inspector? I assume that it must be something out of the ordinary."

Perhaps seeking to forestall any further unpleasantness, Lestrade quickly cut in.

"Professor Dawson has been kind enough to examine the victims. In fact, he approached my superiors and insisted that we take advantage of his medical knowledge."

He gestured to a row of gurneys, the sheets covering their contents failing miserably in hiding the tragic reality beneath. I had known there had been a number of victims, but seeing the eight bodies laid out before us made the true scope of the evil that was stalking our city clear.

"However, there are certain...irregularities that we have been unable to make head nor tail of, and I thought a fresh set of eyes might be of some use."

"You may be having trouble making sense of them, Inspector, but as I have explained, there is no mystery here." Dawson sniffed disdainfully. "Certainly nothing that requires some sensationalist jogging my elbow."

"I mean no disrespect to you, Professor," Lestrade said in a placatory tone. "Everyone knows you are one of the country's leading medical experts. But, please, if you would indulge me."

I could see by the pinched white look around his nostrils that Dawson was far from placated, but he nodded jerkily and remained silent as Lestrade led us over to the bodies.

"I don't want to colour your impressions, gentleman, so we will let you conduct your examination with no input from us," Lestrade said. He flashed a warning glance over his shoulder. "Won't we, Professor?"

His only answer was another sniff, and Lestrade shrugged. Holmes glanced at me and, taking his hint, I moved to the gurney furthest away and began my examination, conscious of Holmes' sharp gaze taking in every detail.

By the time I reached the final gurney, and the most recent of the victims, I understood why Lestrade had called upon us, but I feared that even Holmes might find himself unable to provide any answers. All the victims were young women, somewhere between 16 and 20, and all had been cut and slashed with a savagery that rivalled anything I had seen in the worst days of the war. As much as their wounds allowed, I could make out that there were no common elements immediately apparent, their hair and eyes and complexions were of every shade and colour London had to offer. The only thing that united them in death was the fact that there was something specifically unique to each of them. Unique and inexplicable.

As I had examined each body, beneath the wounds and bruising inflicted by the attacker, I had been able to make out strange deformities and markings unlike anything I had seen in decades of medical practice. One had a faint pattern mottling her skin that brought the scales of fish to mind, and the gashes in her throat obscured what, if it were not too ridiculous an idea for words, I could only describe as vestigial gills. Another had sharply pointed ears and jagged stubs protruding from each shoulder blade, torn and tattered as if they had been savagely hacked at. Again and again, I discovered each possessed some feature stranger than the last, and I felt my confusion, and, if were honest with myself, an unsettled feeling very close to fear, grow with each strange corpse.

I stepped back from the last cadaver, a perfectly proportioned young woman who would have barely stood higher than my waist, and let the sheet settle back over her body. According to the tag fastened around her toe, her name had been Sam, and I tried not to think too much about the life that was summed up in that simple label, and how it had been so brutally cut short.

"So, what do you make of all this, Watson? Any ideas?"

I jumped slightly. I had been so caught up in the mystery before me I had almost forgotten that anyone else remained in the room.

"None at all, Holmes." I took the cloth he handed me gratefully and wiped the sweat that had gathered on my brow despite the chill that had soaked into the very walls of the chamber. "I've never seen anything like this."

"So, you noticed the...aberrations?"

"Of course I did; I would have to be blind not to," I said. "The only explanation I can think of is that this is some sort of hoax, like a barker at a carnival."

"Perhaps, Watson, perhaps," Holmes said quietly. "But what if it was something else? Something outside our experience?"

"Nonsense!" Dawson's jarring voice cut through the sombre atmosphere. "There is a simple and rational explanation."

He pushed his way past Lestrade and stood before us, positioning himself as if giving a lecture, one hand tucked behind his back, the other gesturing at the bodies.

"As I told the detective, these...disfigurements, as unusual as they are, are perfectly explicable within the parameters of medical science. All these young women dwell in one of the most deprived environments in England. From the moment they are born they are exposed to malnutrition and smog, as well as whatever they choose to put into their bodies as soon as they are old enough to feel the lure of all the available anodynes for their brutish existence, whether that is bathtub gin or opium pipes of the Orientals. Dwarfism, ichthyosis, deformities for which there are as yet no names, all these are only to be expected given the squalor in which they live."

"Very well-reasoned indeed, Professor," Holmes said drily. "I suppose you can point to the page in the medical textbook that explains the young lady with oak leaves growing from her scalp instead of hair."

The professor shot Holmes a venomous look.

"Clearly she was so brutally beaten with a nearby branch that the leaves were driven into the skin," he said, flushing. "After all, the attack was so frenzied as to make it impossible to determine just where skin and bone and hair and detritus started and ended."

I took a deep breath to speak, only to let it out in a gasp as Holmes elbowed me in the ribs.

"He has already decided what he thinks, Watson. There's no point arguing with a closed mind."

"I am glad he knows what to think, because I have no idea whatsoever," I muttered quietly, but I left it at that. Holmes was right, I had seen the look in Dawson's eyes before, behind a pulpit or over the muzzle of a Ghazi's jezail. There was no arguing with certainty like that.

Holmes turned to Lestrade.

"So, it seems you have your explanation, Lestrade. What do you need us for?"

The detective had the grace to look embarrassed.

"Well, with all due respect to the professor, of course, those explanations are all well and good, but..." He stopped, face reddening. " . . . the latest body doesn't seem to fit in with the professor's theories. It's...different."

"How is it different exactly?" Holmes asked. "They are all different in their own way."

"This one is 'differently' different." He chuckled nervously. I was fascinated; I had never seen the detective so tentative. "I can't explain...I don't want to even try to explain."

Holmes and I both glanced at the professor, who glared back at us.

"The detective and I disagree on this. I didn't notice the difference he described."

By the way his eyes shifted as he spoke, I knew that he wasn't being completely honest with us, but I saw no need to bring it up with him and cause further friction.

"Well, can we examine this body?" Holmes asked, breaking the tension.

"I suppose it won't do any more harm than inviting you here has," the professor said grudgingly. "You will find the body through that door in the operating room."

"Well, what are we waiting for? Let's go examine this wonder," Holmes said.

"Oh, I don't think you need us in there," Lestrade said, almost stumbling over his words. "I am happy waiting out here."

To my surprise, the professor nodded vigorously.

"I'm a very busy man," he snapped. "I have better things to do than revisit a corpse I have already examined."

Holmes and I exchanged puzzled looks and then headed towards the open door, confused about what we would find on the other side that could make two seasoned professionals so nervous.

Holmes and I approached the operating table in the centre of the room warily, wondering what could have spooked the other men when they had faced the other corpses with relative equanimity. On the tables around the bench, I could see gleaming instruments already laid out as if ready for an autopsy, but, oddly, one lay crookedly across the body as if hurriedly abandoned mid-use. Even the writing on the tag reading "Jasmine" was shaky and ill-formed, as if scrawled in a rush to get it done.

At first glance, the cadaver seemed no more extraordinary than the ones we had already examined. In fact, it seemed to have experienced less violence than the others, as if the killer had been interrupted or fled before he had completed his unholy labours. The victim was striking, with dark skin and dark eyes that reminded me of my time overseas in the army. And her body, well, it could only be described as Rubenesque, with charms of extravagant opulence indeed.

I wrenched my mind away from that train of thought, horrified at myself. What in God's name was I thinking? I had performed hundreds, if not thousands, of autopsies in my time, and seen the wreckage of dozens of bodies in the duty hell of the Empire's battlegrounds. I had long since learned to distance myself from the fact that they had been living, breathing human beings filled with dreams and hopes, and trained myself to see them simply as lifeless objects of blood and flesh and bone. For the sake of one's sanity one needed to turn off one's emotions and feel nothing...especially not what I was feeling now.

I reached up to mop my brow, startled by how much I was sweating. The room, like any morgue, was chilled, so why did it suddenly feel so hot in here? I took a deep breath, and tried to get a hold of myself. I reminded myself I was here for a reason and moved to the table to start my examination. Reaching out, I moved the saw away from the long, supple curve of her leg...I gave a start, there it was again! Eager to get this over with so I could escape this unsettling feeling, I reached out and grasped her wrist. The moment I did so, a jolt like an electrical shock ran up my arm and I flung myself backwards, away from the body. I crashed into one of the tables, knocking it over and sending instruments clattering to the floor with a sound like saucepans being thrown down a flight of stairs.

"Watson!" I felt Holmes' grip on my arm as, with seemingly no effort at all, he pulled me to my feet. "Are you all right?"

Rubbing my arm where I could feel a bruise already rising—I always forgot how damnably strong Holmes was—I could only stare at him blankly for a moment.

"I need to get out of here, Holmes. I can't—won't—explain, just trust me. Please."

There must have been something in my face, because he didn't even question me, simply followed back to the other chamber. The moment we were through the door, I slammed it shut behind me and let out a shuddering breath in relief.

As we approached, Lestrade gave me a far more sympathetic look than I thought him capable of.

"You felt it, too?"

I nodded. "There is something...wrong with that body," I said.

"Another case of the vapours," Professor Dawson scoffed, "I noticed nothing unusual about it all. Frankly, I expected better from a man of medicine. It was bad enough that the detective and his men were acting like schoolboys feeling the first stirrings of their coming of age."

Again, his words were belied by the way his eyes shifted, unable to meet our gaze.

Lestrade gave Holmes an enquiring look, as if seeking confirmation. Or absolution.

"Oh, I felt it, too," Holmes said, ignoring the surprise that must have been clear for anyone to see upon my face. "Don't worry, Watson; you don't need to feel guilty. There was definitely some force outside of the ordinary course of things at work."

I was unable to prevent a sigh of relief. Not for the first time I wished Holmes was not so damned unreadable. He could have been discussing the weather, not an experience that had unsettled me beyond words, for all the emotion displayed by that inscrutable face.

"But what explanation for all this, for *that*, is there?" Lestrade asked, almost pleading with Holmes.

Holmes had taken on that faraway look I knew so well, and I knew that his mind had gone places mine could never follow.

"I've often said that once we eliminate the impossible, then even the most improbable explanation is all that is left. But what happens when our ideas of what is impossible run up against a probability we can't acknowledge?"

"Look, Holmes, I know you love speaking in riddles, but I have no idea what you mean," Lestrade said. "What in the Heavens are you talking about?"

"I'm merely stating that we are bringing our own preconceptions to this case, trying to find explanations that fit in with our ideas of what is possible," Holmes said. "But, for some people, the explanation would be as plain as that nose on your face, Inspector."

Holmes walked over to the gurneys and, one by one, lifted the sheets to stare again at the victims' faces.

"They would talk about beings like dryads and naiads, selkies and brownies, and..." He stopped before he reached the door to the other room and shot me a quick look. ". . . lamia and succubi."

The sound of Dawson's fist slamming into the metal benchtop next to him cut through the sudden silence.

"Ridiculous!" The rage in the professor's voice was so palpable I had to stop myself from taking a step backwards. "You can't possibly be suggesting that these bodies belong to some sort of supernatural creatures."

"I'm not just suggesting anything," Holmes said placidly. "I am simply saying that we should not allow ourselves to be blinded by our preconceptions of what is possible or not if it stops us from bringing a killer to justice."

"So, instead we should allow ourselves to be blinded by superstition and thinking that belongs to the Dark Ages?" Dawson said, almost spitting his fury. "No, I will not have it. My life's work has been devoted to dispelling the notion that there is anything in this world that men of science cannot quantify. The very idea of those beings of myth and legend...it's an abomination."

He turned to Lestrade and gestured at us.

"I want these men out of here, Inspector," he said curtly. "I won't have them interfering in my investigation. Unless you want me to take this up with Sir Henry? We are members of the same club, you know."

Lestrade blanched at the mention of the Commissioner.

"Perhaps we should leave the professor to his work for now," Lestrade said quickly. "Too many cooks spoil the broth, and all that."

Ushering us out, Lestrade spoke in a quieter voice.

"Look, gentlemen, I can't afford to offend a man with connections like that. Give me some time and I'll smooth the waters." He looked directly at Holmes. "But no more of this talk of mythical beings. Whatever were you thinking? Next you will be telling me you've seen pictures of fairies or some such!"

His laughter followed us out into the street, but Holmes was so deep in thought he barely seemed to hear it.

The strange events of the day had left me so discombobulated that sleep eluded me for hours, and it seemed that no sooner had my eyes finally closed than I was roused from my slumber by an urgent rapping at my door. Stumbling and cursing the whole way, I yanked it open, prepared to give whoever dared bother me at this ungodly hour a thorough dressing down. My words died unspoken as I was greeted by the sight of Holmes standing on my doorstep, casually puffing on his pipe.

"Ah, there you are, Watson," he said cheerfully. "You must be a sound sleeper. I thought you'd never answer the door."

I resisted the temptation to say the first thing that came to mind and settled for a half grunt, half greeting.

"You had best get dressed; we've a fair distance to cover tonight."

I knew better than to argue with Holmes when he had the bit between his teeth, and a few minutes later we were on our way.

"Will you at least tell me where we are going, Holmes?" I asked. "What couldn't have waited until morning?"

"I don't know about you, Watson, but something about the professor struck me as rather odd," Holmes said. "I thought it might be interesting to observe him in a different environment and see what we might discover."

"A different environment?" I asked, struggling to keep up with Holmes' formidable stride. "His club? A play or show? We aren't going to bother him at his house, I hope? The last thing I need is to get locked up for trespassing."

"None of those," Holmes said cheerfully. "We are going to the Bethnal Green graveyard."

I did stop then.

"What?" I spluttered. "Why on earth would you think he was going there?"

Holmes didn't even slow down, forcing me to almost run to catch up.

"You really should pay more attention, my dear Watson. Did you not notice the dirt stains on his trouser cuffs and the hard callous on his palms? You might expect to see hands like that on a ditch digger but hardly on a man of his station." I noted with some degree of jealousy that Holmes was not even breathing hard. "Add all that to the familiarity he showed with the inner workings of the human body in his lectures, I suspect that the good professor might be one of the so-called Resurrectionists. He certainly doesn't strike me as the type who would trust someone else with a task he could do for himself."

I shuddered despite myself. I'd heard of the Resurrectionists, and the rumours of how they would break into graveyards in the dead of night to steal corpses to feed the studies of anatomists and the less principled men of medicine.

"Even if that is true, why would you think he would be at that particular graveyard on this particular night?" I asked.

"As to the where, Watson, you heard Lestrade, Dawson insisted on being involved in this investigation. There must be some reason for that. Perhaps he is worried that the police's interest in the area could interfere with his own purposes there and wants the killer caught so that he can go back to robbing graves with no fear of discovery," Holmes said. "And, as for the when?"

He pointed up at the sky where the moon hung low and full, its silver light spilling across the shadowed street.

"Tonight is the perfect night for such dark work. No need for lanterns that could give you away; that moon is more than bright enough to dig by." Holmes frowned. "Or kill by, I suppose."

It was not just bodies that were buried in this graveyard, but dreams. It gave off a sense of disrepair, of a place abandoned by the rest of the city just as the living crammed into the tenements and slums of Bethnal Green had been. I could see splashes of colour here and there where people had left flowers for their loved ones, and there had been attempts to repair some of the ravages of time and hard use, but they were clearly fighting a losing battle against neglect. Tombstones leaned where the ground had sunk; the few benches along the path were not the elegant stone or sturdy wood of more affluent cemeteries, but splintered and weathered constructions that looked incapable of bearing the weight of even the most petite of mourners.

"Even in death they are treated like they don't matter." Holmes said softly. For once, his emotions bled clearly into his voice. I couldn't blame him, I was feeling the same sadness and anger, and perhaps even a hint of shame.

I opened my mouth to say something, anything, but whatever words I would have chosen were cut off by Holmes' grip on my arm.

"Listen," he whispered urgently.

Straining my ears, I heard the crunch of a shovel blade slicing through dirt, and occasional grunts of effort. It was coming from the far corner of the graveyard, from behind one of the few crypts dotted around its grounds.

Skulking around the corner of the brooding brick structure, we were greeted by the grotesque sight of Professor Dawson knee-deep in a growing excavation, grave dirt piled up neatly beside him, his digging as fastidious as his surgery.

His senses must have been almost as sharp as his scalpel, too, because before we could say a word he whirled to face us.

"Who's there?" he demanded, sounding as assured of his right to be there as he had at the morgue, angry that anyone would be so presumptuous as to interrupt him. We stepped out into the moonlight, and his eyes widened in shock. "You!"

He held the shovel across his body, as if preparing to defend himself.

"How could you have possibly known?" he demanded.

"Holmes noticed that you had been doing a lot of digging," I said. "He has a way of following a chain of clues no one else could, and they led to him to the conclusion you were a Resurrectionist. I must admit I was sceptical, but I should know better than to doubt him by now."

"That's not what he is talking about, Watson," Holmes said quietly.

I followed his gaze and gasped. Draped over the tombstone was Dawson's jacket, glistening blackly under the Moon's light. It was drenched, literally soaked in blood as were, I saw now, the professor's shirtsleeves and hands.

"Why, Professor?" Holmes asked, his voice still deadly quiet. "I can understand, even if I cannot condone, that your research might have led you to seek out corpses to prove your theories. But, how could a man of your intelligence and learning be so consumed by madness to kill all those girls?"

"Madness?" The professor's laughter sounded completely sane which, given the circumstances, made it all the more horrible. "It's the opposite of madness, Holmes. Surely you can see no sane world has any place in it for such creatures? They violate the natural order of things, everything that I have spent my life trying to understand. I am simply...correcting things. Each night I sacrifice one of Superstition's children on the altar of Progress, before I harvest another body to serve my labours for Enlightenment."

I could see the madness that was missing from his voice burning brightly in his eyes.

"No one will believe you, you know," he said. "I have a chair at Oxford and connections at the highest levels. And, after all, whatever these creatures are, they are still just a bunch of Bethnal Green jades. No one really cares about them, not enough to pursue this without any real proof, anyway. It will be your word against mine, and I will make sure that there is no proof to find."

With that, he hurled the shovel at us, taking advantage of our momentary distraction to turn and run for the iron gate that pierced the stone wall ahead of us, slamming it shut behind him. By the time we reached it, he was disappearing into the dark alleys that surrounded the cemetery, while we lost precious seconds scrabbling at the rusty catch that held it shut.

"We have to chase him down," Holmes said. "The only way we will be able to convince anyone of his guilt is if we can show them the literal blood on his hands. We can't give him a chance to dispose of the evidence."

"It won't matter." A cold voice cut through the darkness. "The world of men will not give these women justice."

A woman emerged from the shadows at the mouth of the alley, the Moon's silver glistening from bare arms and broad, almost mannish shoulders. The blue of the chiton that was all she wore was dark as the sea at night. From her belt hung a strange, three-headed whip that seemed to writhe in the moonlight like it was alive, flickering with flames that burned but did not consume. She was beautiful, raven-haired and purple-eyed, but it was a pitiless beauty, cold and dangerous and filled with something terrible that made her impossible to gaze upon for too long.

"The people who dwell here are forgotten by those in power, cast aside like rubbish," she said, her voice filled with condemnation. "No one cares about justice for them, so how much less would my sisters who hide amongst them receive?"

Her hand clenched around the haft of her whip, and I could have sworn I heard it hiss, as if in anticipation.

"But, my sisters and I, we will deliver justice for them." I groaned in fear at the beauty and terror of her smile. "That is what we do. That is our purpose."

Her smile disappeared as quickly as the Moon going behind a cloud.

"We know that you two seek justice, without fear or favour, for all. And, for that, we will allow you to leave this place tonight." She took a step closer. "Go, now. Before we change our minds."

I had not been found wanting when the cannons roared, and I had never seen Holmes flinch before beast or man. But I felt the power of her fear pushing down on us, as if it was trying to grind our courage into the dirt. I feel no shame in confessing that the only thing that kept me standing firm as long as I did was the fear that, if I moved, I would lose control of my bladder. Next to me I could see Holmes braced against the pulsing waves of terror, his face a rictus and tendons writing beneath his skill. The woman's voice rang out, a single word in a language I gave thanks to God that I could not understand. There was a moment of stillness before the power fell on us like a hammer. Without another word, Holmes and I turned and ran, pursued by the same screams I had heard in Afghanistan from prisoners handed over to the Afghan women and their knives, full of agony and terror and the knowledge that there was no hope of escape...or mercy. We fled the alley with the echoes of suffering pursuing like wild dogs, heedless of anything other than leaving that sound behind. But, behind us, the screaming went on for a very long time.

The Mystery of the Brothers

by

Lorraine J. Anderson

So's Tom and me were back at Aunt Polly's and I had half a mind to take a raft downstream because I couldn't stand the civilizing that I was getting. So 'cause I wanted to set out, Tom was trying to keep me here by telling me again about all of the Kings of Europe and Theopia and Ejipt—and lordy, it made my head mush just to hear about them. I know I'm ignorant, but I just cain't believe that all of them Kings do the things that they do. It just don't make any sense that Kings go to crusades and suchforth. Seems to me that if they stayed at home, everybody would be much happier. Excepting maybe the serfs they keep yammering about. And all of them wives that one king had.

Anyway, we were just talking that out, walking around the town, when we saw a couple of strange boys. They were a couple of dandies. Tom called them popinjays, but I didn't see that they dressed like birds. Although they did have some fancy feathers.

"I say," the shorter of the two said, "we've just arrived in this town. Our older brother Mycroft told us to enroll in school, but we can't seem to find it."

I thought Tom's eyebrows were going to climb into his hair, his eyes got so wide. "Are you . . . English?"

"Why, yes, of course, we are."

The taller of the boys kinda looked down his nose at us. He and his brother were dressed up even better than Tom did at Sunday School. I had escaped Aunt Polly's eye this day and I was in my old overalls. Tom was not so lucky, but he weren't in his Sunday go to meeting clothes like these two boys were.

"I was just telling Huck here about all of the Kings of England, like Henry who changed his wives every week or so, and Richard with the hunchback and Richard who went on crusades, and his brother John . . . and here you come along and can tell him youself."

The tall one spoke. "I would prefer to correct your stories to the *facts* of our Kings of England."

"Now, Sherlock," the short one said, "we're a guest in this country. Let's get to know these young chaps, first."

I wasn't sure if I wanted to be a chap, whatever that meant. But the younger one seemed sincere, so I stuck my hand out. "I'm Huckleberry Finn. This here is Tom Sawyer."

Tom was still standing like a polecat caught in a sudden light. I nudged him. He stuck his hand out.

The younger boy took my hand. "John Watson. I was adopted into the Holmes family, so I consider Sherlock and Mycroft as brothers."

Sherlock was standing looking at our hands. John nudged him, and he shook our hands reluctantly.

"Sherlock Holmes wants to be a detective. I want to be a doctor."

"I hain't thought what I want to be," I said. "I'm too ignorant to do a lot of things."

"Oh," John said, "I doubt that." We stood there for a second. "Well, we should be going to school."

"It'll do you no good," Tom said. "School hasn't opened for the fall yet."

"What? The schools in England have already started."

"The farm kids ain't through with their farming yet," Tom said, "for which I am eternally grateful."

"You do not like school?" Sherlock asked.

"I can think of a whole lot more things that I would rather do than school," Tom said. "Like playing pirates and looking for pirate gold and being in a robber gang."

John looked like he wanted to join with us, but Sherlock shook his head. "I cannot join in any sort of hooliganism if I wish to become a detective."

I shook my head. "How can you be a detective if you don't know how to act like a criminal?"

John laughed. "He's got you there!"

Sherlock looked kinda mad. "I don't see . . ."

"Tom and me met a couple of murderers, if you want to jabber about that."

Sherlock done looked int'rested about that. "Well . . ."

"We could go back to the h'anted house," Tom said.

"Come on, Sherlock. I wish to see a haunted house."

"There are no such things as spirits."

"Huck and me saw robbers there once. We could show you that."

"Are you telling us tall tales?" Sherlock said.

"You can talk to my Aunt Polly. She'll tell you the truth of it. She would love to meet you, anyway."

"Why exactly would your Aunt Polly wish to meet us?" Sherlock said.

"Oh, she's all about fancy people and fancy dress and them fancy things."

John smiled. "I think what you're wearing is more comfortable." He pulled off his fancy bow around his neck and put it in his pocket. "We don't need fancy dress to go to the haunted house."

"I think I should go back . . ."

"C'mon," I said. "Or are you afraid?"

"I'm not afraid of anything. I am, however, very cautious."

John pursed his lips. "He is." He turned around and faced Sherlock. "How can you be a detective if you don't take a chance every once in a while?"

Sherlock sighed. "All right. But I refuse to partake in tobacco."

Tom looked surprised, but I wasn't. I guess he was going to be a detective, but I ain't never made a secret that I had a pipe, even if Aunt Polly tried to break me.

"He saw the pipes in our pocket," I said to Tom. Tom immediately looked disdainful.

"I knew that. You know I'm a detective, too."

Sherlock looked doubtful. John looked surprised.

"It's true," I said. "I done saw him solve the case of Jake Dunlap and clear Uncle Silas."

For the first time, I saw Sherlock look interested. "I would like to hear that."

"Come up to the haunted house with us," Tom says. "And I'll tell you."

So then we started up to the h'anted house. Tom was felling uncommon bully, so 'stead of taking us straight there, he went this way and that way and around by the river and up a hill practic'ly the other way of the house. I knowed what he was doing, but shut my mouth. John was lost, but I was peering at Sherlock. He was looking up at the sun, and at the trees and all around. I bet he wasn't lost, not him.

We came up to the h'anted house. Tom's voice went low, but then his voice cracked, which, to my mind, ruined the effect. "It was here that we confr'ted Injun Joe."

John looked surprised. "Injun Joe? Was he actually an Indian? On this continent?"

"John," Sherlock said imperiously, "I do believe our young friend is talking about the Native Americans, not who you and I think of as Indians."

John nodded his head. "He was a native?"

"I s'pose," Tom said. "We always called him Injun Joe because he looked like an Injun. I dunno if he were an Injun or not. We didn't confront Injun Joe, anyways." That's 'cause we were hiding in the attic peering down through the floorboards. But Tom was on his high horse; I just stayed quiet. "Murrel's gang buried their treasure in this house, and we done found it. He and his 'sociate found us and fought us, but they done got away and buried it in the cave."

"My goodness," John said. "Are they around anymore?"

"No, they . . ."

We heard a noise out in the forest. "Quick, up here!" We climbed up to the attic like a squirrel up a tree, in spite of the ruined stairs, and peered through the floorboards. I thought for a moment that Sherlock was going to squawk, but then we all caught sight of what was going into the house.

If Injun Joe and his 'sociates had a brother, he would look like this character. Thin dark eyes, thin mouth, scraggly teeth, dirt wiped on his face, clothes that were barely hanging on for—well, I cain't say for life, 'cause I've seen better clothes on a week-old dead man. He was leading a large man with blue eyes—if you didn't look at the scowl on his face, you would think he was a simpleton. The third man was a tall thin man who if he had a bit of fat on him, he would have given it to the fat man. I couldn't even see if he had any eyes or just empty eye holes.

"My sister Nance, 'for she died, said her husband wrote her 'bout this place. This is where they done found Murrel's treasure. They moved it and put it in that cave that was all blocked up and that's all she heard." The man spat tobaccy juice.

"And he never came back?" Thin said. His voice was 'xactly what you would 'magine a skeleton to be, kinda gravelly and low.

"Far as I know, the treasure is still in the cave."

"Hain't you checked?" said the fat man.

"I can't check anyplace until I start to look 'spectable. Do I look 'spectable now?"

Thin chuckled. "Respectable is not a word I would associate with you, Cain."

Cain looked narrow eyed at Thin, as if he weren't sure he had been insulted.

Sherlock was positively glued to the floorboard, John looked at bit terrified, and Tom looked over at me and shook his head. I weren't sure why, did he think I was going to leap from the attic and tell them your brother's dead and Injun Joe is dead and we done got the money? I may be 'gnorant, but I ain't dumb.

"So," Thin said, "Why're we here tonight?"

Cain shrugged. "I wanted to see if there were anything more under the floorboards."

"So we're here to tear up the house? I would think that Murrel and his gang would be smarter than that."

"And I wanted to make sure for myself that my brother Abel weren't here."

Fat chortled. I ain't sure why. But Cain ignored him. Thin sneered at Fat, and Fat done swallowed his laugh.

"Well, apart from that stairway, these floorboards seem real solid to me."

"Let's look around for another spot." They spread apart, looking around the floor and into the other rooms.

John was squirming beside me. I looked. He was struggling to hold back a sneeze. I reached over and put my finger under his nose while he pinched the top. Sherlock rolled his eyes, as Tom watched through the floorboards.

It didn't take 'em long. They met back in the main room. "We could look at the outhouse," Fat said.

"*You* can go check the outhouse," Cain, all grumpy. "I think we need to go see if Abel stayed in town."

"If *you* dug up a treasure, would you stay 'round this town?"

"Abel might've found a lady to settle with."

"And left your sister-in-law?"

"Not the first time he done that."

"Humph," Thin said. As one, they tromped out of the house.

We hunkered in the attic for three or four minutes, waiting for them to go away. Finally, John sneezed a tiny sneeze which barely got beyond his lips. "Do you think that those ruffians are gone?"

"The way they were walking," Tom said in a normal tone, "they're probably half-way to town."

"Tom," I said, "I don't like the looks of this. I think we should go South and visit Aunt Sally for a while."

But Tom had his dungeon up. "I ain't going to be run out of town by some ruffians." He sneered, then he said, "'sides, you know Aunt Polly won't let us go South this close to school time."

"What if they find out that we're the . . ."

But Tom was shaking his head.

"Aunt Sally?" John Watson said.

"Yeah," Tom said. "We done solved a murder down South on the Mississippi and I got Uncle Silas off of the hangman's noose." He said that last part like he was tellin' one of his spooky tales. "And we found the dimonds that the murdered man stole." Actually, we done met the murdered man on the way down, and knew where he put his loot, he was a thief trying to get away from his gang. "We split the money."

Sherlock looked us up and down. "I must admit," he said, lookin' down his nose at us, "that I would never guess that you were rich."

John nudged Sherlock. If I hadn't a guessed that Sherlock was trying to insult us before, I guess I knew it now.

But Tom was still full of ginger, and he either ain't going to acknowledge that we were insulted or he was goin' to ignore it. I think he figgered that a couple of British kids were just as good as Lords and he was going to grandstand for them.

"Well," Sherlock said. "I've seen enough. I'm going back to town and try to accomplish something today."

John looked at us, shrugged, and followed behind Sherlock.

Tom muttered something under his breath.

"What did you say, Tom?" I said, just 'n case I missed something.

"Nuthin."

I stayed mum. Sherlock seemed a little high'n'mighty to me, but as long as he stayed on his side of the street and I stayed on mine, I didn't care.

We strolled back to town, we tried to play a little bit of Robin Hood, but our hearts weren't into it, so we went back to Aunt Polly's house. As we neared town, though, we got silent. "Tom," I said, finally, "do you think we need to be worried?"

"About them 'ruffians'?" Tom scoffed. "We can handle them."

"Still," I said.

Tom gave me a look, and I shut up. "We need to spy on them."

"When?"

"I don't know. I need to think."

We got back to Aunt Polly's and she hustled us in. "Thomas, Huckleberry, where have you been?"

Tom blinked. "We took a walk in the forest."

"Well, we've invited some visitors tonight, and two of them are around your age," Aunt Polly fussed. "I swear, you two are going to be the death of me." Sid was already dressed in his go-to-church clothes and stuck his tongue at us. "Get in your clothes."

I could already smell chicken and the cornbread and the apple pie. Well, for Aunt Polly's cooking, it was worth dressing. I'm still not sure I want to get civ'lized, but the cooking done beats the apples I ate day after day.

We got dressed quickly and went downstairs. Aunt Polly was greeting the guests. There was a tall drink of water coming in the door, followed by . . .

Suddenly, I weren't so hungry any more. It was Sherlock and John. They stared up at us. John smiled and gave a little wave, Sherlock just ignored us.

"Tom Sawyer, Huckleberry Finn, this is Mycroft Holmes, Sherlock Holmes, and their adopted brother, John Watson."

"We have met," Sherlock said. "May I sit down?"

Mycroft Holmes nodded to Polly. "You must excuse my brother.

He has always been a bit rude," Mycroft aimed towards his brother.

John smiled. "We have indeed met before." Tom shook his head at John. "Tom and Huck were kind enough to show us some of the town."

Aunt Polly looked suspiciously at Tom. "Is that so, Tom?"

Tom could get the most innocent look on his face, when he bothered to try. "Why, yes, Aunt Polly. We done showed them the way to the river."

John nodded, and I got the most innocent look on my face that I could have. Sherlock looked away and didn't say a thing.

"So," Aunt Polly said. "I understand that you are here for a year."

"Yes, ma'am," Mycroft said. "I am over here as a part of my schooling. I hope to go into government, and my school thought I should go to America for a broadening experience. I tend to bury myself in my books, so my teacher thought I should meet other people, which I do find rather taxing."

"I'm sorry about that," Aunt Polly said. She looked a little flummoxed at the speech.

John looked up at Mycroft and smiled. "That's why they keep me around."

Aunt Polly smiled down at John.

"I interpret for them."

"That's a big job for a young man."

"But necessary, ma'am."

"Well," Polly said. "I hope to see you in church on Sunday."

"We plan to be there, ma'am," John said. Sherlock looked sharply at Mycroft, who gave Sherlock a warning nod. Sherlock was going to get a what's for back when they got back to . . . Where were they staying?

"Lester and Nila Bradford said that you are model boarders."

"They have to say that," Sherlock said rudely. "They're our cousins."

Aunt Polly ignored him, so we'all ignored him.

The rest of the dinner went much the same. Sid kept sticking his fork in his peas and threatened to launch them over the table until Aunt Polly gave him a knock in the head. Mary chatted with Mycroft, who, after a while, gave her one word answers. Sherlock ate his meal like he was dissecting a frog, which I wished I were doing right then, rather than eatin' here, in spite of the tasty food.

Finally, the meal was over and we were excused to our own d'vices while Polly and Mary and Mycroft sat and jabbered for a while.

"You ever play mumbletypeg?" Tom said.

"No," John said. "What's that?"

Tom got his jackknife out of his pocket, opened the knife, and threw the knife down by his foot so that the blade stuck into the ground. It quivered like a squirrel staring a cat in the eye. "That's mumbletypeg."

"Just throwing a knife into the ground? Anybody could do that," Sherlock said, sneerin'.

"Yeah, I'd like to see you try it." Tom screwed up his mouth.

"I don't think that we should just toss knives around." Sherlock turned away. "I have more important things to do."

"Are you chicken?" Tom said.

I looked at Sherlock. I done got the idea that he weren't afraid of much, 'cept maybe dealin' with other people.

He stopped and sighed. "If you must."

John smiled. "Sherlock is pretty much an expert on everything."

"Really? Well, he don't know much about America if he don't know mumbletypeg."

Sherlock turned around. He looked kinda mad. "For your information, mumbletypeg was started in the British Isles. But I'm not of the lower classes who play such games."

Tom grabbed a stick and pounded it into the ground. "Then Huck will show you how to play."

"Tom..." I really didn't want to do this. Tom glared at me. "'kay. Watch." I went through the ways that I knew, sticking each solidly into the ground. 'cept I missed the one over the shoulder. The blade done slipped sideways and flopped over.

John applauded. Tom nodded. "The loser pulls the stick out with his teeth. I'll go first."

Tom followed my lead, sticking the last one solidly. He then glared at Sherlock.

Sherlock pulled out his jackknife and was 'bout to throw it when Aunt Polly threw open the door. "Tom Sawyer, what are you doing?"

Mycroft Holmes was right behind her. "I think it's best that we leave now." He glared at Sherlock.

"They were just playing," John protested.

"We do not play like dock hands," Mycroft said. "Go home." He turned to Aunt Polly. "I beg your pardon, madame."

Aunt Polly looked befuddled. "No, I beg yours. That Tom is going to be the death of me. Inside. Both of you."

"I will see you in church, madame. Thank you for the meal."

"You're welcome, I'm sure," Aunt Polly said. She turned to us. "If you hadn't already done had your supper . . ." She turned red. "Get upstairs and go to bed." Mary looked upset, Sid stuck his tongue out.

"But, Aunt Polly . . ." Tom saw the hand coming for his ear, ducked under it, and ran up the stairs. I followed him. Tom was already in bed, muttering to himself 'bout all the calamities that was going to happen to Sherlock. I done fell asleep when he started repeating himself.

The next day, Tom woke up early. He was quiet. Polly sent us out with just a couple of apples, saying that neither of us deserved anything to eat after what we pulled last night. I guess that Aunt Polly ain't ever been around school, either that or she's so old that she don't remember.

It seemed like everywhere we gone that day, we run into this two Beau Brummells. It must be that Mycroft sent them out to explore the town. After a while we run into Joe Harper and Tom traded him two Aggies and a rat tail for his sandwich. We took off for Cardiff Hill, and that 'minded me of those three that we saw in the h'anted house last night.

"You see anybody who looked like that?"

Joe frowned. "I saw them come out of the hotel. They were talking to Muff Potter, buying him some drink."

Muff Potter was preserved well enough as it was, he didn't need no drink. "You hear what they were saying?"

Joe shrugged. "I weren't close enough."

"You think they could be trouble, Tom," I said. "I don't like it." I couldn't stand it if Muff Potter were involved in somethin'. He may be a drunk, but he wouldn't hurt a fly. For the first time, Tom looked a little troubled, then shook his head. "Naw, they ain't Injun Joe."

"Doesn't mean they cain't be bad," I muttered. "My pap weren't no Injun Joe, but he was bad enough." I never done wish anyone dead, but I was glad pap weren't coming back.

Then we done saw Ben Rogers up ahead, and them three went all out of our heads, 'cause Tom said we should play cowboys and bandits out in the woods, and we were all 'agreeable. So we went to the woods, getting back a little after dark. We were powerful hungry, and I was hoping Aunt Polly made something good.

We got to Aunt Polly's house, and there was a crowd 'round it. Mary saw us, rushed out and grabbed us. I never before seen Tom look that pale, unless it were that time he were shot.

"What's happened?" Tom said. I could barely hear him.

"Oh, Tom! Aunt Polly's been taken!"

"Taken?"

"She's gone! Nobody saw her go but her knitting was all over the floor and there were scuff marks at the door!"

Tom looked at me and I looked at Tom. We both had the same thought at the same time. "It's Cain." Tom said. "He done found us."

"Cain?"

Sid came up to Mary, and she hugged him.

Tom clammed up. Mary turned to me. "Huck?"

"Well, you see, we was in the woods, and we saw these guys."

"They were talking about Murrels' gang's fortune," Tom started. "So we eavesdropped. The one guy's brother was part of Injun Joe's gang. Then we heard he was in down, drinking with Muff Potter."

Mary stared at Tom, lookin' at him suspiciously. "And just where did you see them?"

Tom lowered his head. "Cardiff Hill."

Mary raised Tom's head up. "You were in the haunted house, weren't you? Oh, Tom, you were told not to go there."

I saw some movement to my side. It was Sherlock and John. "John and I were there, also. We heard everything."

Mycroft came up beside us. "Tell your story."

So's between all of us, we told the story of going up in the woods and going into the h'anted house and getting on the second story and Mary glared at us. So a ton of people went up to the woods to catch Fat and Thin and Cain, including Sid and Mary. But Sherlock grabbed us by the arms.

"I do not believe that they would take her to that decrepit old house."

"No?"

"How do you figure that, Sherlock?" John said. "I would think that if they were asking for ransom they would take her up there."

Sherlock turned to us. "Where did you say you found the money?"

I could see Tom light up. Then his face fell. "In the caves. But they've locked up the caves."

"I'm certain three determined men can open them up, if they wish."

"Especially if they're intoxicated," John added. "The 'demon rum' makes men think they can do more than they can."

I looked at tiny John. "I had a pap that drunk the demon rum. How do you know about it?"

John turned red. "I've read about it. I plan to be a doctor."

"Irrelevant," Sherlock said. "We should go to the caves."

Tom thought it over. "Seems like what them people would do. Let's take them."

So while's the town raged up to Cardiff Hill, the four of us got a ton of candles and snuck over to the cave. And, sure enough, the lock was broke and the gate was down.

"Maybe we should have taken a gun, too," John said.

"We have something better," Sherlock said. "Our wits."

So's we ventured into the cave. The first part of the cave was all tore up, because we'd been coming in here for years. People had been writing on the walls. I made my mark on one side, and Tom and Becky Thatcher did one of those heart things someplace else, 'though Tom done got mad when I mentioned it to Sherlock and John. Sherlock looked mad, John smiled. "What happened to Becky Thatcher?"

"After we got lost in the cave, her family moved her back East." Tom said. "I'm over her now."

Tom moped around for a week 'fore he got over her. Then he moved on to a girl named Anna. I shrugged.

Sherlock was studying the ground and the walls. He pointed down. "They went this way."

I looked at the ground. The scuffs I saw didn't look any different then the scuffs anywhere else. I can track a rabbit in the woods as well as anyone, but I sure couldn't follow this. Tom looked skeptical.

Sherlock got his pocketknife out and made a tiny mark on the wall. "We go this way." Without looking back, he went down the cave.

John shrugged and trotted after him. "He don't know what he's doing," Tom said.

"I dunno, Tom. He looked like he knew."

"I've been lost in these caves. I know."

If I'd of known better, I would've thought he was getting 'fraid of the cave. But Tom weren't afraid of much, I decided that it was my 'magination.

"Well, Tom," I said. "I'm going. He's marking the walls. We won't get lost."

"Oh, all right," Tom said slowly. They were 'most out of sight, so we hurried after them.

Sherlock was walkin' slowly. About every few steps, he'd lean over and look at the ground, then he would put the tiniest of arrows on the wall to mark where we was goin'.

Tom was dying of curi'sity, so he pulled on John's arm. "What is he doing?"

John smiled. "He's following the men by looking at marks on the ground."

"Obvious, John," Sherlock muttered without lookin' up. "There are three sets of footfalls and a drag mark. Obviously, Polly is being carried by two of the men. I see no sign of struggle, so Polly may be unconscious. The right foot of one man and the left foot of the other are slightly deeper, so they are carrying her between them." He stopped at a crossroads and spied between the two caves, nodded, and headed down one of them. I done stopped and looked where he looked; I didn't see nothing. Confounds me.

He started that act again, so we followed along. I couldn't see what he was looking at. He kept looking and marking. Had to have been about 15 minutes that we found a clue even I could see—a bottle of whiskey with a couple of drips on the bottom. So's I knew we were on the right track.

We were far beyond where anybody else had marked. I looked over at Tom; he looked over at me, looking worried. We're weren't going to get any help and we were four boys against three men. Not that the two of us couldn't lick any boy in town. But Sherlock was a tall thin stick of a boy and John was just small.

Fin'ly, Sherlock stood up and pointed down the hall, shielding his candle, then blowing it out. We shielded ours and took turns looking around a corner. Aunt Polly was propped against a wall. She had a handkerchief around her mouth and her eyes were wide open and she looked skeered.

The men were arguing amongst themselves.

Fat was fannin' himself. "I don't know why we had to drag this old bat back here."

Cain wobbled around. "She knows them kids that found the treasure. She knows where it is."

Polly made a squawk.

"She says she don't," says Thin.

"How kin you understand her?"

Thin burped. "She done told me before she were tied up."

"I don't believe you." He toddled over to her, untied the handkerchief and uncovered her mouth. "You know where the treasure is, don't you?"

"No! Take me back! I don't know anything."

"I don't believe you," He started to look angry, and he raised his fist. Aunt Polly tried to move to one side. I ducked back; I couldn't watch. Sherlock was gone. After a second, John hurried after him. I glanced at Tom and ran around the corner.

I mighta' thought that Sherlock and John were Beau Brummels, but I'm glad I didn't dare either one. Sherlock was using punches and kicks I ain't ever seen before. Watson was small, but he was kicking like a mad cat in a bag. I didn't see much else, 'cause Tom and I waded in, and it weren't long that we had those three drunk men flat on the floor and they weren't getting up for a while.

Polly had backed into the wall, but when the fight started, she wriggled out of the ropes, and she grabbed a stick that Cain had carried in fer some reason and was pounding any of them she could get hold of. John gently took the stick from her, and she leaned against Tom.

Sherlock leaned over the three of them, then straightened up. "They'll live. Let's take Miss Polly out of here, then send the authorities back for them." He turned around, leadin' Aunt Polly. John looked back, then left them one of his lit candles and a couple of unlit ones. While he didn't think I was a'looking, I seen Tom lay down a couple of more. Much as he was 'fraid of Injun Joe, he was bothered by Injun Joe's death, stretched out in back of the locked door, starved to death.

We then followed Sherlock out. When the crowd rumbled down from Cardiff Hill, they were greeted by the four of us and Aunt Polly, dirty, but with a fire in her eye and alive. Mycroft glared at Sherlock and John, but then smiled and nodded. John grinned.

Then Sherlock led them back into the cave. After about an hour and a half, they came back, dragging Cain and Fat and Thin behind them, still half-drunk and glaring at the crowd around them.

"You stole a fortune away from my brother," Cain mumbled. I seen that a couple of teeth were gone.

"No, we didn't," Tom said. "They stole it from us. We found it first."

Sherlock glanced at us. "Technically . . ."

John poked him in the side. I don't know what he were goin' to say, and I didn't care.

"Thank you for saving my aunt," Tom mumbled.

"Elementary," Sherlock said. "We just had to follow their path."

"Elementary for him," John said.

Polly got up and grabbed Sherlock before he could twist away and gave him a big hug. He looked like he would rather lick a toad than be there. She hugged John. He smiled.

"Thank you," Aunt Polly said.

"Our pleasure," John said.

Finally, the crowd went away, we met up with Mary and Sid, and we were able to get Aunt Polly back home. Mycroft took Sherlock and John with him.

"I swear," Polly said, yawnin', "It's just an adventure a moment with you two."

"Come on, Aunt Polly," Mary said. "Let's get you to bed. You, too, boys." She looked at us inten'tly. "You're going to have black eyes."

Tom and I grinned at each other.

Sherlock and John never did go to school with us and we never had another adventure with them. Mycroft brought them by. "My trip was shortened and I've been called back to England, ma'am, but I wanted to say goodbye."

"Thank you again," Aunt Polly said. "And if I can do something from America, let me know."

"I will keep that in mind," Mycroft said.

Tom grabbed his jackknife and landed it next to Sherlock's toe. "It's yours," he said roughly.

Sherlock picked it up, glanced at it, then turned around and threw it so close to Tom's toe, it took a little leather off. "Remember me."

Tom picked his knife up. "I will."

I certainly won't forget him. And Tom won't, too.

Sherlock Hominid and the Baker-Street Irregularity

BY

Teel James Glenn

Prologue: Knuckling to Terror

The morning fog off the Thames was thicker than an East End accent, the sun was nowhere to be seen and the sky was slate grey. Somewhere out over the river the foghorn on a dirigible sounded like a soul in torment.

"Slow down, Khetar," I called to my partner who was ahead of me on the wet cobbles. He wore a little Inverness cloak and a ridiculous deerstalker hat that made his high set ears stick out even more than usual.

"The note said meet the lady at *The Rat of Sumatra Pub* at ten o'clock." He said, "It's almost time, so stretch those human legs!" Then he knuckled off again and I had to push on to keep up.

"How can you see a damn thing in this?" I complained.

He said with glee, "It's all in the genes, hairless. The nose knows!"

All I could smell was the salty scent of decay from the unseen docks.

"We've been on this alternity for two months and you've settled into this Sherlock role too easily."

It had not been a hard two months at all, if you could stand the damp English weather. I'm Lucifer Lawless from the 2000s on my timeline, and I had some trouble adjusting to 1898 AD in that particular stream. Khetar had the outward appearance of an Earth Chimpanzee to my 'normal' human, so on most versions of Earth in the multiverse we had to have an elaborate cover story to fit in. Not so on this one. In this South London, divergent strains of 'homo-primatus' from Homo Florentis to Yetis all coexisted. Fortunately, so did homo-sapiens.

Khetar and I are members of the Corporeal Readjustment Alternity

Police (though for acronym reasons we prefer 'Time Cops'), charged with regulating travel in the 42 known planes of the multiverse.

The interior of the pub was typical for the edge of Limehouse in this era on any timeline where the smoke from a roaring fire and various tobaccos was almost as thick as the fog had been outside. Inside was a pretty good cross-section of all species with a silverback gorilla barkeep wearing a bow tie and a leather apron behind the barrel-and-plank bar pouring drinks.

While the barmaid took our orders, we scanned the room looking for who had sent the message to us. I tapped the little crystal necklace I wore under my shirt but there was no telltale buzz.

We both wore crystal necklaces—small chips from the mountain-sized Philosophers Stones we used to plane-slip, and the only off world tech we were allowed—which would alert us when or if we came near to the irregularity we were hunting—someone from another timeline here to do no-good.

My primate partner was sniffing and, when the girl brought our drinks, took a sip then looked to me. "Up those stairs, Lucy."

"How can you tell?"

"Olfactory, my dear Watson," he said. "I smell the same perfume that was on the note."

"My name is only Watson to fit the cover," I said. "And how can you smell anything in this?"

"Genes, my spawn," he said. "You are further down the tree than me." He picked up his drink and shambled nonchalantly toward the stairs. I took a sip from my beer then left it to follow.

On the second floor was a small dark room with a table and two chairs set before it. Behind the table in deep shadows was a single, heavily veiled female.

"I need your help, Mister Sherlock," The woman said in accented English. There was a quiver of fear in her voice she could not hide. "I fear for my Papa's very life."

1. THE GIBBON GIRL'S PROBLEM

"Two evenings past," the mysterious female continued, "my dear Papa received a note that threatened his life. It said if he did not give my brother Sebastian his inheritance immediately bad things would happen. It was written on one of those new typewriting machines. Then last night—" she stopped to compose herself, adjusting her broad brimmed hat to reveal her orange furred forearm between the white glove and her sleeve.

"You must trust Mister Sherlock," I said. "The truth is what matters."

"Yes," the chimp said. "I cannot help you if you do not give me all the facts."

"Yes. Of course, I am Mazarin Stone. Last night," she raised her hat and continued in a subdued voice, "an actual attempt was made on my Papa's life. Papa believes my brother made that attempt; I cannot believe it could be so." I was startled by the power and clarity of the brown eyes under beetled brows. "My brother has fears, and he can be very angry—a quality he inherited from our Papa. He was disinherited years ago for an argument between them. Yet I know he loves our father."

She began to sob softly, and Khetar reached across the table to pat her gloved hand with his hairy one. "We will do everything we can to discover the truth of this matter, Miss."

"And aid your father," I added in a soothing voice. Khetar and I shared a look, for I am sure he felt the faint buzz I did from the necklace when we got closer to her. This Gibbon girl had the essence of having been in contact with someone who had slipped from another timeline. She was indeed part of our mission on this world. Still, we had to be cautious, there had been false 'positives' with the necklaces—it was not perfect technology.

I looked down at Khetar who nodded his head and smiled imperceptibly, adding, "The game's afoot!"

He really was a corny little ape.

The butler, Culverton, met us at the door to the home of the Stone family. He was a wide, muscular fireplug of a human with a shaven head and a full black beard who wore round spectacles. He would have been far more at home in the prize ring than as a personal servant. He certainly looked out of place in the foyer of the ground floor townhouse of the Stone Family on Baker Street.

"I am Khetar Sherlock," my partner said. "I'm sure you've heard of me. This is my assistant. We would like to speak to Mr. Stone regarding a personal matter."

Assistant? I wanted to strangle the furball.

Culverton adjusted his tiny glasses with hands as hairy and callused as bear paws and blinked.

"My word," he said in the Queen's English, "The famous Mister Sherlock, consulting detective! I feel overcome, sirs. But what is this about?"

"It is about the death threat that Mister Stone received."

"Death threat, eh? I'll have to call and speak to the master about this!"

Culverton spoke quietly into the interoffice phone, his large hand shielding his mouth so that neither of us could overhear his conversation, then smiled at us. "You may take the elevator at the back of the building to the third floor." He pointed and added, "Mr. Stone's study is beyond the sliding wooden doors when you debark."

We followed the butler to the elevator. "Did you notice his knuckles?" I whispered to my primate partner. "A boxer."

"A useful skill in a butler, I should think," he said with a wry smile. "Keeps out the riffraff."

"Didn't work with us."

"He's wealthy enough to have an elevator," Khetar observed as we trudged up the stairs.

"You look natural in a cage," I snickered to my primate partner. He rolled his lips back to expose his teeth.

"You feel it?" I asked as we neared the top. He nodded. Our necklaces were constantly buzzing—the slipper was or had been in that house. We were in the right place.

At the third floor the door disclosed a wide carpeted hallway that ended in wide oak doors. Inside we found the patriarch of the Stone family, a long-armed, orange-haired Gibbon as stolid and formidable as the doors.

We were standing in a wood paneled room, lined with books in many languages. The elder Stone held court from behind a massive desk that spoke of stability and tradition. He wore a smoking jacket and Fez perched on the top of his orange pate.

"Mazarin had no right to bring an outsider into our family's affairs." Ebenezer Stone said to Khetar. "Take your hairless friend and leave."

"I have no wish to interfere with your family," Khetar said. "But your daughter fears for your safety."

"I have no fear," the elder Stone said. He was a proud old Gibbon, with the same piercing eyes as his daughter.

"An attempt was made on your life." Khetar said. "Surely you do not wish to deny your daughter your council?" In the question the little furball had cleverly provided an out for the old man's pride, for with concern for his daughter, a proud man can escape accusations of cowardice. For a long moment it looked as if he would ignore the offered out but then Stone spoke.

"A shot was fired at me from outside this window." Stone said, indicating the one behind his desk. He rose and turned his chair around to reveal a bullet hole in its back. "Had I not slumped forward a moment before in sleep," he continued with a shrug, "my slumber would have been eternal."

"Have you spoken to the authorities?" I asked.

"I will not do so until I have spoken to my son." The old ape took a deep breath and spoke with an emotional pain so deep as if to be physical, though whether it was because he believed his son was guilty or not I could not tell. "Though I disinherited Sebastian for his activities against the government, he is still the fruit of my loins. The young do not realize the compromises that must be made in business."

The senior Stone bowed deeply. "If you can clear this matter up, I will be grateful. Culverton will aid you any way he can. Please excuse me."

We watched him go in silence, knuckling along with his head bowed, knowing no words could console a man torn between his own fear and parental love.

When the door to the study closed, Khetar and I sprang into motion. The chair was quickly reversed and positioned as it must have been when the shot was fired; this was determined by judging by the worn spots in the carpet. Next, Khetar produced a thin telescoping tube from his suit pocket and used it as a magnifying lens to examine the bullet hole in the chair. He then telescoped it to sight through to the hole to the window. He studied the lower edge of the window where tape covered the broken glass.

I removed the tape to clear the line of sight then tied off the end of a black string and handed it to the little ape who stretched it to the hole.

Sighting down this string from the chair's position, Khetar spoke. "A tree, about a block away in that small park, is all that is in direct line."

I looked out the window, noting with disgust the soot on the narrow ledge that ran around the outside of the building.

Next we reversed the sighting down the string. "Somewhere near the door," Khetar said.

"Search for a bullet, while your 'assistant' interviews Culverton, human to human."

"Good luck with that," he said. "But ask him to use small words so you can understand him."

"It is a sad affair about young Master Stone," Culverton said when I found him on the first floor again. "He and his father were once quite close."

"When did a rift develop?"

"Master Sebastian's mother died in a fall from a mountain while hiking with the young boy. Sebastian, 15, saw it and was never the same. He somehow blamed his father who had just had an argument with the woman. When they returned home the father installed the elevator to help the boy cope with his fears, but he went off the straight path just after college—about five years ago. It would, by Jove, seem to prove what comes of inferior education."

"Oxford man, eh?" I said. When the butler looked puzzled, I pointed to the man's class ring. "Did this argument between the Stones have a specific cause?"

"Sebastian's political activity," Culverton said flatly. "He began to participate in fringe causes—rallies and the like about separating some of the Empire's colonies for independence."

"I take that to mean that the Stones still have holdings in several of those colonies?"

"Extensive, as well as his import/export business," the butler noted. "And quite profitable now."

"But why a threat from Sebastian at this particular time?" I asked, "Why not sooner?"

Culverton removed his glasses and wiped them vigorously, his moon face assuming a dark phase. "Sebastian was just released on parole after a year in gaol for an—eh—altercation with a policeman outside the Indian consulate. It has been a major heartbreak for Mr. Stone, yet the master was able to mitigate the sentence with a great deal of trouble."

"The father's burden is great indeed," I said. "Where were you when the shot was fired at Mister Stone?"

"In my room down the hall," the butler said. "I heard glass shatter and Mr. Stone call out, but when I rushed in, I saw nothing."

At that point Khetar joined the two of us, knuckling up to stand beside me and we said our goodbyes to the servant.

"I searched high and low, Lucy," he said in a whisper. "But I couldn't find either bullet or bullet hole."

"Not like you could search high," I replied, "but this is shaping up to be a very interesting case."

11. GORILLA MY DREAMS

Khetar and I went straight to the tree we suspected of being the sniper's roost. It towered above the two-story stone structures around it, but it was little more than a three-story weed. Its upper branches swayed in the slight morning breeze.

Khetar scurried up, but even his slight weight caused the top branches to oscillate precariously. It was an unsteady perch, and he could not reach the required height to get the direct line to the window.

While he played Tarzan, I conducted an exhaustive search of the area around the tree for a cartridge casing on the offhand chance the sniper used a bolt action rifle. No such luck.

"No cartridge and no bullet," Khetar nodded.

"You thinking what I am?" I asked.

"Probably," the chimp cop said. "But at a higher level than you."

"When we get back I'm going to ask the Chief to assign me a chicken as a partner for the next job."

"He wouldn't do that," he said, "Two peckers in one team would never work."

"I've got a great recipe for Chimp McNuggets," I said as we walked back to the road.

"You'll have to tell me about it after we locate the younger Stone and the slipper," he said. "My high-level thinking suspects his trouble is connected to our case."

"Let's meet his sister again." I agreed, "I have a feeling we're running out of time."

This time we found the Stone sister at the university where she served as a librarian.

"I have spoken to your father," Khetar said. "Now it is most important that I find your brother. Do you know where he is?"

The fur on her hands bristled. "I do not know," she said quietly. "He has not contacted me since his release, but–." She looked around to the library to see the other ladies quickly turn away from staring at the devolved detective, then leaned in to whisper, "But there was a pub where he used to spend much time." She spoke with downcast eyes. "It is not a nice place; called the Blue Carbuncle. Someone there might know."

"It will not be the first 'not nice place' that I have ever been." The furball smiled.

The Blue Carbuncle Pub was indeed a 'not nice' place. It was a squalid, basement establishment on the fringes of the Limehouse District. Tenements bordered it, and it was doubtful if the sun's light touched its dirty front windows for more than an hour on a good day.

The denizens of "The Blue Carbuncle" looked like a who's who of Newgate Prison. Mostly young would-be tough guys of many species, including several humans and one very out of place redheaded hooligan whose face was as Irish as a leprechaun's.

"The place ain't for you, mates," the redhead said in a guttural tone. "This is a class establishment."

Khetar stood impassive, surveying a card game continuing in the dim rear of the establishment. He took a puff on his bubble pipe to send some soap spheres into the fog of tobacco in the place. "I see that," he said.

The redhead, a thick-necked thug almost my height but twice as wide, stepped up to us. He closed his meaty fists with deliberate theatrics.

"Sod off," Red ordered.

The room quieted as all eyes turned to us. It did not look too good for us sightseers.

"I said, blow, runt," Red repeated. Suddenly, he launched a sucker punch from a coiled right. Its speed was as blinding and as good as any human's best.

It was not good enough, however. Khetar exploded from the floor with seemingly no effort and wrapped himself around the redhead's face like a furry Balaclava. Red's scream was muffled by the flying furball, and I stepped forward to throw a fist into the thug's gut that cut it short. Red crumbled to the floor with a grunt and Khetar hopped to his feet.

My chimp partner whipped his hands as if to clean some dirt.

For a moment no one moved or spoke. The only sound in the room was Red's suppressed moans of agony.

"We are looking for Sebastian Stone," Khetar said. "We're not here to bring him trouble."

"Sebastian doesn't need anyone to bring him trouble." A feminine voice cut through the tension in the room. "He always has his own."

All eyes shifted to the source of the voice; a stunning shorthaired baboon female dressed in a gown that did nothing to conceal her curvaceous form or the tail that waved behind her bustle. She stood in the doorway to a small office that had been hidden in the gloom of the place.

"In here, Mister Sherlock," she said to Khetar. Her gaze shifted to me. "You can bring your assistant as well."

Assistant? I really had to talk to the hairball about it when we had the chance.

"And you are, Madame?" Khetar asked.

"Irene Adler; this is my place," she said through lips that were clenched around a cigarette holder. "So you want to see Sebastian?"

She sat behind an oak desk that dwarfed her and propped her delicate feet up on the edge, affecting a casual posture. Her long toenails were painted scarlet to match her lips and, I imagined, her butt.

"Family business," Khetar said. There were no other chairs in the room, a ploy intended to put anyone being interviewed ill at ease. We both stood relaxed.

"Family business?" she repeated. "You don't look like a relative of Sebastian's." She made a deliberate gesture of looking the chimp cop over from head to foot, ignoring me completely. "But you could be like family to me if you wanted."

How does he do it? I swear every hairy species on the planet thinks he's the ape's meow.

Khetar and the baboon locked eyes for a moment. "Maybe after I help Sebastian with his family issues," he said.

The hairy hormones were floating all over the place and I felt myself getting flushed, so I had to cough to move things along. Both of them looked at me and laughed. Khetar blew some bubbles from his pipe.

"So, what's your business with Sebastian?" she asked.

"He's threatened his father," Khetar said adjusting his deerstalker hat. "And an attempt has been made on the old man's life."

The baboon babe shot to her feet instantly. "Sebastian talks big; it's what got him gaol time at that protest—but he's not violent. He can't even go upstairs without somebody holding his hand. He'd never hurt his dad."

"We need to know where he is," I interjected. She gave me the side eye but spoke to my partner.

"He left here about a half-hour ago to see his father." Irene was face to face with Khetar fuming. "You hurt that confused kid, and I'll make your life miserable."

The devolved detective smiled broadly to show his back teeth. "I don't doubt you could," he said. "But I'm trying to help Sebastian, and I think you've just given me the facts to clear him!"

III. UP THE FAMILY TREE

"The clues were there all the time," Khetar said as our hansom raced across London. "I only hope we're not too late."

"It's amazing you can do any deducing while you flirt," I said.

"Hey, hairless, some of us have it, and some of us are you."

The front door was locked with no response to the pull bell. I applied my skills to picking the lock. Inside was dark and quiet but with the sounds of Mazarin in distress above. We took the elevator up to the living quarters.

"This is not ominous at all," Khetar whispered as we rose. At the top floor we raced from the elevator to find a frantic Mazarin pounding on her father's closed study.

"Papa, open up!" she screamed. "I heard you in there, Sebastian."

After a few moments a frantic Culverton, dressed in nightclothes, came out of his room down the hall, carefully closing his door behind him. "What was that sound?" he demanded.

"I heard Sebastian yelling, then a gunshot." Mazarin cried.

"Do you have a key for this door?" I asked.

"No," Culverton said, "And it is stout oak. We will need a fire ax from downstairs to force it."

"Lucy, up!" Khetar ordered. I grabbed him by the cloak and chucked him up to the transom above the door. He grabbed the edge of it and swung his feet to smash into the transom to pop it open then he wormed his way in.

The hysterical Mazarin backed away.

Culverton looked at me as if I was insane. "What?" his expression cross.

The door flew inward, and we saw the elder Stone face down in a pool of blood near the center of the room. Beside him was a revolver, and it was clear he had been clubbed on the head and shot in the back!

"Papa!" Mazarin screamed. I restrained her until Khetar had stooped to feel for a pulse.

"He's alive," the Simian sleuth said. He rose to take the girl from me and we switched places.

"Can you help him, Mister Sherlock?" Culverton asked.

"That's up to Watson," Khetar said in a grim voice. "He's had some medical training."

Miss Stone whimpered in fear for her father and clung tightly to the little furball.

I began to work immediately on the elder primate, first to staunch the flow of blood and then assessing the extent of the damage.

I spoke rapidly, "The bullet passed through his lung but missed the heart. We can save him, but he should be in hospital."

Khetar quickly moved to the telephone on the ordered desk and dialed the nearest hospital. He barked out the location concluding with: "And tell the police that the attacker is still on the premises;

proceed with caution."

"Sebastian must have gone out here," the butler observed, poking his head out the office window. "There he is just leaving the ledge. Master Stone!" He yelled from the window and then turned to race out of the room into the hall. "He's going into my open window."

I popped my head out of the window quickly then turned to the girl. "Go down and wait for the ambulance."

"But Sebastian—" she began.

"Go!" Khetar said in a tone that brooked no discussion. Then he added, more softly. "I promised my help, and Khetar Sherlock always keeps his word."

Only a moment had passed since Culverton had charged from the room when we followed as I told Khetar what I had actually seen out the window. It was almost too late. The butler had reentered his room and was rolling on the floor in a death struggle with a powerfully built Gibbon that had to be Sebastian Stone.

"Stop him; he's got a knife!" Culverton yelled.

Khetar plunged into the tangle of arms and legs and pried the knife from the fighters, tossing it across the room. Then in a casual show of tremendous strength, he yanked the younger Stone bodily off the servant and flung him against the wall.

"That's enough!" Khetar ordered. "Stop!"

Sebastian shook himself like a wet dog and growled groggily. "What's going on?"

"I saw him come in that window," Culverton interjected. "When I came in the room, he jumped me with the knife."

"What?" Sebastian said. "He lies—I . . ."

"You came home to confront your father," I said. "As I imagine Culverton suggested when you spoke to him yesterday. He met you, brought you here to 'discuss' it, and the next thing you remember was him bending over you with a knife in his hand. Is that not so?"

"Why-yes—" Sebastian said, "How—"

"Go next door," Khetar said, his eyes locked with the butler's. "Your sister and father will need you."

A confused Sebastian exited the room.

"How long have you known?" Culverton asked, his voice cold. His body seemed relaxed, but I could see the subtle shifting of weight that signaled he was preparing to fight.

My necklace was buzzing non-stop.

Khetar stooped to pick up a small metal shape on the floor. "Well, this proves it." Khetar continued. He looked to me as we bracketed the bearded man and let me see the thing he'd found. It was clearly not 1890s tech as it was plastic and clearly transistorized.

No doubt he's a slipper, I thought. The three of us stared daggers at each other.

"When I saw the tree," Khetar pontificated, "it was impossible to be the origin of the shot, and there was no bullet hole in the room. The bullet that shattered the window and passed through the chair was fired from within the room. You could not risk a second shot as he was awakening, so you rushed into the room to 'see what had happened.' "

"Conjecture," the butler said. "You have no proof that the courts of law would find binding." He was attempting to maneuver toward the corridor door.

"Perhaps," the consulting chimp said, "But even those courts would take into account the fact that Sebastian has a dread fear of heights as a result of seeing his mother's death; he could neither have climbed the tree nor escaped along that narrow window ledge where the soot was disturbed by very human footprints. You were the only witness to his stroll and not a very credible one!"

"And there is that." I pointed to the metal object that Khetar had picked up. "A micro recorder, which you smuggled to his world and used to get Sebastian's voice on it to place him in the room with Mister Stone."

"You assumed he would have bled to death before that door was broken in," Khetar added with a chimpish smile. "You didn't count on us saving him."

"Why?" I asked.

He didn't even try to deny it. "My double on this world was working as a servant to that filthy ape, can you believe it?" Culverton sneered. "And the old orange fool even put him in his will. I discovered if I could have the son convicted I would inherit—females have few rights in this time despite having a Queen on the throne. With my cross-tech knowledge, I can be a billionaire here."

"Speciesist!" Khetar snarled.

"You killed your own double?" I asked. He just smiled and made a lunge for the door, but I blocked his path. Culverton launched a twisting right punch that had the power to smash a cinder block to dust. I just managed to get a forearm up to block it but even so I was knocked back against the wall.

Khetar was on the butler before he could get out the door, springing on his back and avoiding the wild swings of the bearded man. The chimp cop launched a left at the secretary's kidneys, but the servant spun around and slammed Khetar into the wall.

I jumped back at Culverton who tried to kick at me but I caught the leg. This gave my primate partner the chance to clamp his legs around the servant's neck and choke him out.

In almost no time the butler collapsed, unconscious.

EPILOGUE: MONKEYSHINES AND MYSTERY

"My Papa will recover, the doctors said." Mazarin was attired in a blue ensemble that set off her orange fur to best effect. Her brother stood beside her properly cowed. "We cannot thank you enough, Mister Sherlock."

We were in our lodgings at 221b Baboon Street with a roaring fire in the hearth, and he was glowing with the solo praise. "Simply applying logic," he said.

"But to deduce that Culverton had killed his own twin brother to gain our father's wealth?" Sebastian asked.

"When you have eliminated all which is impossible, then whatever remains, however improbable, must be the truth."

He wore a Fez and smoking jacket and puffed on his bubble pipe with glee. I wanted to strangle him, but he'd come up with the lie we told the police; Culverton was a secret twin of the murdered butler (whose body was discovered in a shallow grave in the townhouse cellar) and was a raving lunatic with his talk of parallel worlds and such.

After all, he was a minimal threat to the timeline and considering how the mentally ill were treated in 1898 might well be insane before we could arrange to spirit him to a C.R.A.P. prison.

"And thank you too, Dr. Watson," the Gibbon girl said. "Your timely intervention saved Papa, I am certain."

"I do my best, Madam," I nodded, "to assist this great ape with his various adventures." He and I exchanged a subdued glare, but I smiled at her, "I am glad I could help."

Khetar flashed his teeth and sent a soap bubble in my direction. "Capital, Watson. And now if you will all excuse me, I have an appointment."

"A new case?" Sebastian asked with excitement.

"Something of a Bohemian adventure at The Blue Carbuncle," Khetar said. "At least I hope so."

The Rats of Saint Servatius

By

Bryan Young

With a shrill creak, the ancient door at the end of the great hall opened, and a shield maiden of the order rushed in, wet from the rain. The crackling fires—in the fireplaces at the other end of the hall and braziers lining the walls—had dried us, but it would be a while yet before the hurrying sister felt their effects.

"Sister Agatha of the Holy Order?" the woman said, perking my ears.

My assigned mentor, Sister Agatha, was an aged shield maiden, well beyond the threshold of retirement and less active duty. She had white hair pulled into a bun with dangling silver threads and, despite her advancement to well over 60 summers, she still wore the tabard and sword of the Holy Order. Her mind was an extraordinary machine, so across the countryside of St. Argon we went, solving only the most complex puzzles.

Sister Agatha put down her steaming wooden bowl and folded her hands in front of her. Then she looked up at the shield maiden interrupting our evening meal. "You have a letter?"

The shield maiden's dampened brow furrowed in confusion. "I do, Sister Saint. How did you know?"

"Simple deduction. Now to find what it's about."

The shield maiden produced from her waxed canvas rucksack a paper envelope. "It's marked urgent."

Sister Agatha sighed, and I knew that sigh. It was the resignation of our work and the fact that no matter how tired we were, no matter how bone deep the exhaustion, we were bound by oath and the will of the saints to act when a need presented itself.

It could be disheartening to always be in the midst of such need without rest.

Taking the letter and opening it, Sister Agatha unfolded the pages and scanned her eyes across the letters.

I hurried through my stew. The look on her face meant quick action, and I had no idea when our next chance for dry clothes or a hot meal might be. That look usually meant long travel days with hard tack and harder cheeses with skins full of water rather than wine.

A frown pulled at her lips and her steely eyes moved rapidly back and forth as she hurried through her reading.

Finished, she handed the letter to me.

"Read, Brother Dominguez, you will understand."

The letter was in a slanted scrawl, ornate, written by a finely educated hand.

It read:

Sister Agatha,

As you know, I have reacquired the ruins of Saint Servatius, that old abbey that had been owned in my family for centuries and had been the subject of many brutal rumors. I set my mind to renovation and refreshment. With the loss of my son, I have had nothing to occupy my thoughts since.

Though the renovations go well, Saint Servatius is livable once again. Indeed it is here I spend my nights, alone in the ancient abbey with no companion but my cat, Ghost.

One night, sleeping in my chamber with Ghost at my feet, he aroused in the night to chase some spectral sound, imperceptible to me. He pawed viciously at the walls, trying to get at some hidden prey. He scratched and scratched until I awoke. Initially, I thought morning had come too soon, and Ghost merely wished to be fed. When I got to my feet, he rubbed against my leg with affection according to his standard routine, but his attention stayed rapt against the wall. Naturally, my curiosity was aroused. Seeing nothing and hearing less, some motivation blossomed inside me, inspiration from outside myself it felt, and I placed my ear to the walls. Like the sensation of placing a conch to your ear and hearing the sea, I heard something in the wall much more terrifying, as if the great stones that made them had been hollowed and inside scurried the paws of a thousand screeching rats.

No wonder Ghost was troubled, hoping to catch a meal of his own.

Unable to sleep, I investigated the sound, but found no evidence of any rats, though the history of this place, of which I know you are well aware, haunted my dreams.

Days passed and my investigations turned up nothing, but so often had I caught Ghost chasing after these phantom rats that I knew that we both could not be sharing hallucinations.

Then I discovered something terrifying. Deep in the bowels of the crumbling abbey.

An altar.

Around it were the bones and rotted army of the soldiers of the Sixth Dynasty. They must have been there for ages, rotting away in the cool castle air, their armor preserved only slightly and their bones exposed to the world. Perhaps 600 years had passed since anyone had laid eyes on them.

The hallucination of the rats and the discovery of such an ancient find were likely related. One expert I spoke to believed the armor of the decayed soldiers bore an emblem of the Cult of Thoggan, and I am assembling scholars to investigate.

Therefore, I offer my most urgent invitation for you to make your way to the abbey with all possible speed to help in this endeavor. I know you will understand the urgency of such a task, given your reputation and your knowledge of all the important folklore. I look forward to seeing you, Sister Agatha.

Until that time,

Andrew St. Delapore

My chest heaved.

This certainly sounded important, but Sister Agatha knew more of it than I did. Compared to her, just by the length of her career and nature of her life, I was always at a slight disadvantage. I wondered where we could even begin, feeling out of my depth, and realized the Cult of Thoggan sounded like the most dire thing spoken of in the letter—at least the most dire thing given a name. I knew of the Sixth Dynasty; they ruled long before the Queen of the Realm had taken over. It was chaos then. Power ran willy nilly and the monarch was unaccountable to the people. Now, they could oust the monarch with a majority vote of monastic orders in the capital. The Sixth

Dynasty was old and backward and their appearance, even in antiquity, implied trouble.

Sister Agatha turned back to me, as the shield maiden left. "She's gone to ready the horses. We leave anon."

As we set out on the western road that angled up toward the high hills, and the cradle of the mountain that boasted the bones of Saint Servatius.

We cantered at a speed that maximized our ability to cover ground without wearing the horses thin. It would be no good to arrive at the secluded mountain abbey with dead mounts.

"Sister Agatha," I asked curiously, "what did the letter mean about the history of the site and his family?"

"You do not know the history of the Delapores of Saint Servatius?"

"Nay, Sister Agatha. My travels before my assignation to you afforded me no chance to visit this part of the realm. It was rare indeed when my travels brought me anywhere other than the illuminating libraries of the abbeys in the most major of cities. That was my primary training. St. Servatius had never been uttered for as long as I can remember."

"It is no surprise, I suppose. The abbey burned to the ground well before you were born. As did the surrounding village. The townsfolk were incensed and the fields were flooded with rats. It was said on that last day, the wind picked up the fire and the rats as well, dropping them like rain on the heads of the residents and scattering them across the surrounding areas."

"Truly?" I had seen many wondrous and frightening things alongside Sister Agatha, but I had never seen anything like that.

She confirmed it with a grim nod.

But ever we traveled, hoping to unravel the mystery sooner than later.

It took us quite a while to trudge through the surrounding woods to make it to Saint Servatius. As we got closer, the woods lessened, and the leaves on the trees appeared more on the floor of the forest than on the trees themselves, as though we walked through the seasons and straight into autumn. When we got to the scorched fields and dead trees in the immediate vicinity of Saint Servatius, I assumed we would have been walking straight into winter.

The whole place caused a shiver to run up my back.

When we finally laid eyes on the battered abbey, I did not like it one bit. Sister Agatha must not have either, at least based on the sneer of unholy disgust on her face.

The keep itself was shabby, as though it had come straight from some old, haunted story. Bricks were missing across the top, leaving one whole section open to the elements. Spider webs and rotten debris decorated every wall. There were many more entrances, battered through the walls, than the doors provided.

The drawbridge lay open and broken like a screaming mouth, shouting at us to come inside in a most unwelcoming way.

"Are you sure this is the place, Sister Agatha?"

"Aye," she said grimly. "Can't you feel that?"

And as she mentioned it, I became more aware of my surroundings and the deathly chill around the place. As though absolute evil were present there. I'd never quite felt anything like it. I'd felt the inspiration of the saints and the hot burning at the bottom of my chest, but this felt like an icy grip of fingers wrapped tight against my heart. It was unnatural.

It had everything to do with the broken castle and all of the secrets buried beneath it.

We had to follow the clues laid before us, a story only Sister Agatha could tell.

"The keep itself was the subject of much controversy," Sister Agatha explained as we approached. "It was rumored to be the site of the burial place of a great Duke of the Fireshade. Thoggan, they called the entity. And it was Saint Servatius that managed to quell the threat of his existence . . ."

". . . hence the name?"

Sister Agatha nodded. "Hence the name. But that doesn't mean that the disciples of Thoggan were defeated, nor were his underlings from the Fireshade itself. And so over the years, this place became the site of a secret battle, a war waged between the forces of light and dark."

I had trouble comprehending such a secret battle. Sister Agatha's teachings had led me to a life that seemed to shine lights on secrets and I was largely accustomed to it. But that didn't stop the creeping fear across my back.

"The cultists would sneak in under the noses of the saints tasked with protecting this site and make sacrifices. That's what caused the rat infestations in times past."

"Doesn't sound like a pleasant business, Sister Saint."

"Nay, Brother Dominguez. Nay."

With another 30 feet to the entrance, my horses stopped their slow, already hesitant trot and planted their feet firmly to the ground. I looked over to Sister Agatha, and her horses had done the same.

"Come on," Sister Agatha said, tugging on the reins and putting her heels into the side of her nag.

But the horse shook its head as though it knew how to say no and would move a step no further.

Sister Agatha sighed. "I suppose we walk from here."

It's the same with horses as humans that fear presaged places of danger and neither wanted to die.

A deeper fear gripped me, though, for a horse trained by the Sisterhood to refuse portended awful things.

We dismounted and transferred our gear from the horses to our backs. Then, with the extra weight strapped down, Sister Agatha and I made the long walk up to the keep. The chill in the air that I would normally equate with a crisp, fresh quality—like the onset of fall or the first signs of spring—was accompanied by a foul, stale odor. The chill permeated there, as though it was not caused by the weather, but generated somehow by the keep itself. As if to warn us to stay away. As if to say, "Go now from this place."

"I do not like this," I said.

"Our job never asks us if we like it, but our duty remains, Brother Dominguez. Trust I would rather not descend into this place, but it is our call and charge."

And I knew she was right.

We crossed the threshold of the door, cracked open and weathered by time and came to a massive staircase leading to the top of the cracked keep, and another tattered hallway that burrowed further into the bowels of the ruin.

"Do we go up or down?"

"The signs tell me that we will find nothing if we went up," Sister Agatha said.

I realized I'd only made the suggestion because I was frightened to delve deeper into the keep and confront the dark things below. Exploring the high tower first would do nothing but delay the inevitable, and I suppose she knew it.

As we walked, looking for passageways that would lead us further down, Sister Agatha lit a torch. The ceiling had become more pronounced and the sun seemed to dim. The light of our torches kept us moving in the right direction. I hadn't noticed that Sister Agatha had stopped until I almost ran into her. My feet almost betrayed me but I caught my balance and stopped with her.

She'd stopped to examine the walls.

"Runes," she said, waving her hand over the scratch marks in the stone corridor. She squinted, wrinkling the skin around her eyes in a rare show of her age. The vibrant opals of her eyes themselves were bright, like a woman decades younger. When she was puzzling together clues for her latest mystery, age seemed just a number, as though the thrill of the chase was a fountain of youth.

"What do they say?" I asked. To my eyes, they were much older than any writing I recognized and looked more like scratches in geometric shapes than language.

"It remains a mystery to me," Sister Agatha said grimly. "It's written in the old runes of the Fireshade's First Age. It's obvious by the shapes to the letters."

Looking more closely, I saw what she meant. Each rune had the rough impression of flames, each letter a fire with a different pattern.

"I believe it is better that these words are not spoken and the secrets kept here remain so."

"That seems unlike you, Sister Saint. You have taught me in our time together that knowledge is sacrosanct."

"There are things a person can know that will unravel them," she said quietly, staring at the letters. "Completely and thoroughly. That path of madness is the one we walk, and we must be careful to stay on sanity's side."

I furrowed my brow. "What knowledge could be so forbidden?"

"There are things, dark things, held in the spaces between threads of the fabric of creation. Truths of the universe too complex and terrible to ken."

Some small hole tore open at the bottom of my stomach and I felt as though I were falling as she spoke, trying to comprehend. My imagination reached for the horrifying, unsettling truths of the universe and came up with horrors and monsters, but nothing enough to lose my mind.

"It is horror beyond imagination," Sister Agatha said.

"Could it contain a clue?" I offered.

"I would not seek clues there if it were the last place to look," she said to me seriously. "There will be other ways to discover the things we need without risking such unreality."

Hearing the quiver in Sister Agatha's voice made me more frightened than the runes and the claw marks I noticed on the floor below me. By the looks of scratches, the clawing was done by a human. No doubt some poor fool who had written the message or received it.

"Come. Time dwindles," Sister Agatha said, and we continued our sojourn through the ruins.

Soon, the sound of soft padding feet and hundreds of claws skittering against stone echoed through the halls, guiding us to the bowels of the keep.

"Are you sure this is the way, Sister Agatha?"

She nodded solemnly. "The cat's paw prints point the way."

I hadn't noticed them, subtle in the dust and flickering beneath the torchlight.

The sound of the rats grew louder with each step we took, to the point where when we reached the small room at the bottom of the dark, misshapen steps it overwhelmed my ears like the sound of a thousand bees in their hive.

I could barely concentrate.

But there, at the end of the stairs, was a dead end.

A small altar stood in the middle of the room, and there were braziers circling the edges of the round room. Smoke hung high against the vaulted ceiling. Sister Agatha and I stood there at the entrance, wondering where to go next. The paw prints had ended abruptly.

I covered my ears, hoping I could find some way to concentrate through the oppressive sounds.

Crouching to the ground, Sister Agatha's mouth moved as though she were explaining her observations, but I could not hear her. She pointed to the signs around the stone altar in the center of the room.

"Do you not hear that?" I asked her.

She flinched as though I were shouting and then turned to me and stood. "Brother Dominguez?"

I'm not sure I heard her say it, but that was the movement her lips made. When tears leaked from my eyes, I realized that all was not well. Was I the only one hearing the rats? Had she somehow missed that particular curse?

Pressing my hands even tighter against my ears did nothing to suppress the sound.

She said my name again and her head tilted, curious and concerned.

But still I could not hear.

"Make them stop," I shouted.

Confused, she looked around at her feet.

I had never seen her look so puzzled, which sounded another warning in my heart. If she had no clues, then the situation was most dire.

She reached her hands toward mine, but I reared back a step as though her touch would burn me.

"It's the rats," I screeched, uncontrollably. "Stop the rats!"

I could almost see myself behaving in this terrified manner, and could not understand why.

I was supposed to be her stolid sidekick, not succumb to the madnesses of a mystery.

Stepping closer to me, her hands reached up carefully to me, but I sidestepped her and walked right into the altar room. I had no care about spoiling her clues. She couldn't help me. In fact, she was going to hurt me.

Of course she was.

That was why she had brought me along in the first place.

To destroy me.

I was her sacrificial lamb . . .

And nothing else mattered.

Her fingers wrapped tight around my wrists, but I struggled against her. The noise of the rats, chewing and scurrying in harsh echoes against the stone, was too much to bear. And her voice came, almost as if it were underwater. "Brother Dominguez, calm yourself. Calm yourself please!"

I fought against her, but her grip was too great and she was able to pitch me to the other side, against my weight, and sent me tumbling into the altar.

Landing hard with my shoulder crashing against the stone table, I growled. Why I growled like a dog, I could not say. It's not a thing that I'd ever done, but I can tell you with honesty that it happened there. I was not in my right mind. And I wondered if I'd inadvertently comprehended some of the dark text Sister Agatha had warned me of.

I kept a hand in front of me to protect me from Sister Agatha's next attack, but her face was contorted not in anger, but mild surprise.

"Brother Dominguez, you did it," she said.

And I realized I could hear her.

The buzzing was gone.

I staggered, dizzy, crying ugly tears. "What?" I asked. "What happened?"

Sister Agatha put a comforting hand on my shoulder and smiled softly. "You found the way."

Wiping my eyes with the end of my rough-hewn sleeve, I took in a deep cleansing breath.

Feeling the rush of cool air, I turned to see that I'd dislodged the surface of the altar to reveal a decrepit set of stairs leading down to the darkest places further beneath the keep.

I gulped and fright gripped me.

We had to go down there, and my insides convulsed in warning. I knew if I were to go down there, the chances of me coming back were low. "We can't go in there."

"We *must* finish our task."

"Our task?" I asked, incredulous. "Our task will kill us both."

"Mayhap, but if we don't, there's every chance that Andrew St. Delapore will die as well."

"What business is that of mine?" I growled.

Sister Agatha slapped me. Open palmed, right across the cheek. The sting cracked the grip the madness had on me.

"Pull yourself together, Sibling Saint. We have a task to complete and an oath to fulfill. Have you forgotten both?"

Deep down, I knew she was right.

"Better?" she asked.

I nodded. "I'm not sure what madness took me."

"It's this place. That is why we must double our caution. If we are to save St. Delapore, we must not tarry."

Thinking of descending further felt impossible, but Sister Agatha volunteered to go first.

"How did you know there would be a deeper level?" I asked as she braced for her trip into the dark.

"The paw prints ended. And the supernatural is rare enough in this world that there is almost always a reasonable and simple explanation. It was easy enough to deduce where the terminus of the path led. To the altar. Had you not stumbled into it, we would have removed the tablet atop it together."

"I see. How far down does it go?" I asked, watching the glow of the flame disappear from the antechamber. I was too frightened to look into the abyss.

"Not far," she said. "You'll weather the storm."

I braced the fear I felt and stepped over the lip of the altar, finding the top rung of the ladder with my feet. I didn't look down for the torch light Sister Agatha provided. Instead, I focused on my own shadow and felt for each subsequent rung with one hesitant foot at a time.

Once on solid ground, I looked around. The sight I saw would have caused many grown initiates to faint. Gnawed bones were discarded in every corner of the antechamber and the corpses of a hundred thousand rats, rotting and decomposing, lay in great piles. The scent had gone from rancid to slightly sweet, and that dissonance between the sight and the smell made me want to wretch. In the distance, a feline moaned low, howling as if in great pain.

"Careful, Brother Dominguez," Sister Agatha said.

"What is this place?"

"A path to the unknown."

"To the Fireshade?"

"Mayhap."

"Is this where we find St. Delapore? Or is he one of these rat-chewed wretches?"

Sister Agatha raised her torch in front of her and looked down to the ground at her feet. "Unless I misread the signs he is alive. If you look closer, there is a trail of blood beyond the three pairs of footprints, and the cat as well."

At the mention of the cat, the sound of its pain grew louder. Unnerving me.

Sister Agatha looked up in the direction of the sound and bloody footprints. Many of the pathways were choked off with the bones of a million sacrifices, but our pathway seemed clear.

I would have wagered there were more people interred inside the dark places of Saint Servatius than there were entombed in the catacombs below Saint Argon.

That thought ran a chill down my spine.

"We continue," Sister Agatha said, carefully walking alongside the bloody trail, careful not to disturb it.

I followed without complaint, but the warning in my heart would have screamed given the opportunity.

I was careful to step over the bones and other detritus in our path, following in the exact footsteps of Sister Agatha. She had instilled that habit in me from the beginning of our adventures. The less disturbance we made on the scene of whatever mystery we found ourselves involved in, the better the accuracy of her detection skills.

But this felt more like a hunt than a solution. We were still racing for the clues to tell us exactly what it was we were chasing.

As we grew closer, the sounds of slurping grew louder. And gnawing, like rats tearing the gristle from a bone. And the sound of the cat . . .

I shuddered.

"Do you hear it this time, Sister Agatha?" I whispered loud enough to be heard just above the crackling torch and the din of the unnatural noises that we approached.

"I do," she replied quietly. "I think it might be what we came for . . ."

We stepped forward, deeper into the dark. I expected the temperature to fade and cool as we made our way to the bowels of the Earth where the sun's heat offered no warmth.

And that's when we found an even more ghastly sight.

I'd never met Andrew St. Delapore. During our sojourn, Sister Agatha had described him to me, in case that information would help in our investigation. At once I knew the creature I looked at was—and somehow wasn't—Andrew St. Delapore.

His matted hair thick with blood and his naked body covered in it, he squatted down over a corpse, gnawing on a massive bone, possibly human, rocking back and forth on his heels. He gnawed like a dog on that bone.

Rats surrounded him, eating the rest of the fresh corpse. Blood and bile were smeared across the horrid creatures as they nipped at the dead man's eyes and tore chunks from his flesh.

"Fair am I, and so I say, good day," St. Delapore said in a gravely sing song voice and a wide, toothy grin that mismatched the atmosphere.

"Who is that?" I whispered to Sister Agatha, pointing at the corpse being devoured raw by rat and man alike. That was if St. Delapore could still be called a man—eating the flesh from another man's bones felt somehow disqualifying on that mark.

"That would be Archibald St. Renard. Adventurer and archeologist, most recently studying at the great university of Saint Argon."

Shifting my gaze from the horror of St. Delapore before me, I looked over St. Renard's body—somehow the less unsettling of the images before—and wondered how Sister Agatha came to that conclusion. On his bloodstained coat was an embroidered monogram of the school's emblem. Next to his head, still attached to his neck by a blood-smeared gold chain, was a magnifying glass. In his shirt pocket, unmolested by the rats, was a thin, boar-hair brush, common in the use of wiping dust from the artifacts of the past. Adding all of that to the fact that in St. Delapore's letter, he had promised to gather all of the scholars he could, it would not have been a difficult guess for Sister Agatha to make. His missing leg must have been the one lately in St. Delapore's mouth. The sadness in her voice also made me think that she had perhaps known him in a different life, and she was mourning him as she sought clues to exonerate or hospitalize the naked, howling St. Delapore.

"It's the rats," St. Delapore said, looking up and making unfocused eye contact with each of us in turn. "They said the words that cannot be uttered."

All eyes shifted as the cat's howls ceased, fading into a gurgling.

"They've given up the Ghost . . ." St. Delapore said cryptically. Then, he turned back and threw the bone at Sister Agatha, spinning it end over end. A stringy tendon still attached to the bone flung itself in a wide circle like a pinwheel and sprayed blood and meat across the distance between them.

Recoiling and revolted, I took a step back, wiping the blood that hit my face.

The bone clattered to the floor behind us and the sound of scurrying rats filled the space. I turned to see a writhing mass of rats, each of them clamoring over the others trying to get at the remaining meat with the desperation of an opium addict.

"Brother Dominguez!" Sister Agatha shouted in warning.

With bloody hands, gnarled from his madness, St. Delapore lunged for me, stretching his fingers out like claws.

My mouth fell open and I had the sparest of seconds to realize what was happening and step to the side.

He missed me completely and tumbled into the pile of rats, shrieking. Most of the furried, frenzied creatures paid him no mind, but quickly they clambered atop of him, nipping at him with their immense teeth, taking chunks from his flesh.

"The time is now!" he shouted. "Thaggon! The time is come!"

"Quick, Brother," Sister Agatha said as she lunged in after St. Delapore and swatted rats away from him with her free hand. "We cannot let him die here. The consequences would be catastrophic."

Fighting my fear—terror that somehow he could summon Thaggon if left—I swatted a frantic rat from St. Delapore's face as it bit into the man's cheek, drawing blood and consuming a hunk of the man's flesh.

It was heavy beneath my hand and the sound of it splatting against the wall with was enough to turn my stomach.

We scraped the rats from him one by one, pulling his skin along with them. They would not let go of their meal. Sister Agatha waved her torch around at the rats, in a bid to get them to flee, but it seemed as though the supply of rats was inexhaustible. How had they become so many and so powerful? What terrible sway held this place together? I could not ken what was happening. Between Sister Agatha and I, we were finally able to get St. Delapore up to his feet.

To my great relief, the rats paid no mind to us, swarming the easier meals they found amongst themselves.

"Quickly, Brother Dominguez, we must leave."

I had no reason to argue with her. All I wanted to do was leave and never return.

"But Ghost," Delapore said weakly, but we paid him no mind and set to work getting him out.

As we limped along with one of St. Delapore's arms and half his weight draped over me, he began to sing a song, dreadful and low.

"Evil wings in ether beating;
Vultures at the spirit eating;
Things unseen forever fleeting
Black against the leering sky.
Ghastly shades of bygone gladness,
Clawing fiends of future sadness,
Mingle in a cloud of madness
Ever on the soul to lie . . ."

He carried on like this, his voice echoing through the dark.

We moved urgently through the cave and some voice deep from inside myself, a voice I'd never heard until then, whispered in my ear, "Go back."

But Sister Agatha refused to let us.

I stood beside Sister Agatha as we watched two sisters of the Merciful Order struggle to detain St. Delapore. They had cleaned his wounds—rat bites always festered if not treated properly—and wrapped him in a restraining jacket designed to keep him safe.

If the things he heard or saw deep in the bowels of Saint Servatius were anywhere near as frightening as the things I felt caught in its grip, then I could not blame him for cracks in his sanity. I'd only been down there briefly and he'd been down there for days. Alone. In the dark. With only the rats to keep him company and bones of his former companions to pick at for sustenance.

If he ever recovered, I'd be surprised.

He shrieked and cried as they dragged him into the room. "You can't! Thaggon's coming. He is coming!"

Another maiden appeared with a boiling tincture, leaving a smoking trail behind her. She circled St. Delapore and held the mixture beneath his nose, then gripped his chin and poured it down his gullet. He tried spitting it out, but she plugged his nose and he gulped it down.

The centers of his eyes widened with the application of the soothing. His screaming subsided and he took a shallow breath. His entire body relaxed as if exhaustion hit him with a sturdy club.

"It's . . . coming . . ." he said again, slowly this time.

Eventually, they got him inside.

Sister Agatha folded her arms, pensively. "It's a shame, really."

"Why is that, Sister Agatha?"

They restrained him to the bed and I couldn't help but feel grateful that I'd kept control of my mental faculties. Otherwise it would have been me there.

"He was such a brilliant mind, and the knowledge drove him mad."

"Where did he learn the runes to write them?"

"There are many places he could have learned such things?"

"Could it have merely been the spirits?"

Sister Agatha shook her head as they closed the door on St. Delapore. "It was more than that."

When I looked at her, I saw the heavy weight she carried. Where it had come from, I could only guess. Her mind was a trap that let nothing through. I'd not have been surprised to find that her mind was still chewing on the riddles carved into the wall. Like an hourglass, each grain of the puzzle's sand would pass through her mind until finally it had all run out and she had idly decoded the message and gone mad herself.

"Such is the curse of knowledge," she muttered to herself and then turned, leaving St. Delapore to his convalescence.

Joining her, we walked through the corridors together side-by-side. "There are so many lingering questions left unanswered, Sister Saint."

"Aye," she said, as though her mind were chewing on a different problem. "Sometimes the solution to a mystery is better left unsolved.

Whenever mortals look into the abyss beyond, *something* comes back."

"Something?" I said, realizing I had brushed much closer to the abyss than I ever hoped to. She was right though, our oaths were taken. If the abyss was where I was sent, to the abyss I would go. And with Sister Agatha, I would follow her *anywhere.*

She nodded again.

"Is that what St. Delapore spoke of?"

"Let us hope we never find out."

The Case of the Leaping Leprechaun

by

Will McDermott

I find myself in my later years surrounded by the notes of strange and wondrous adventures with Holmes I could never publish at the time of their happenings. Some, as with the Adventure of the Devil's Foot, secreted away to protect the reputation of a prominent citizen. But most to protect the great detective himself from undue ridicule. This story falls into that latter category.

We found ourselves in the early years of our association aboard a rickety Dundolk, Newry and Greenore Railway train from Dublin to Carlingford, a sleepy Irish town on the north coast. It had been an arduous, weeklong journey aboard multiple trains as well as a turbulent steamboat to cross the Irish Sea.

The old wounds in my knee and shoulder ached from the bone-jarring travel, so I was in no mood for my friend's oddly chipper demeanor as we neared Carlingford station. He held in his hands the telegrams that had set us forth on this epic journey.

"It is a wonder, is it not, Watson," he began with a twinkle in his eye. "Either of these messages on their own would not have roused me from our London flat, but their arrival on the same day was a coincidence I could not ignore."

He proceeded to read them again, despite the numerous times I had heard their contents.

TO: Doctor John Watson, London
FROM: Major General Arthur Thomas, Ret., Dublin
My dear Doctor. I fear I must call you into service once more. Our mutual comrade, Colonel Hans Moore, has perished under mysterious circumstances in the town of Carlingford.

I call upon you to bring your friend, Mr. Sherlock Holmes, to investigate the circumstances of the death of a good and true soldier of the realm.

TO: Mr. Sherlock Holmes, Detective, London, England
FROM: Mr. Kelyn McCoillte, Leprechaun Whisperer, Carlingford, Ireland
Dear Mr. Holmes, I urgently require your skills. Our doctor has been slain. Moreover, the townsfolk are convinced our local Leprechauns are the perpetrators. I fear mob mentality may prevail and the Leprechauns under my protection will suffer. Please help soonest.

"What a wonder for a place to have an official Leprechaun Whisperer," chuckled Holmes. "Perhaps our payment will be made from the fabled pot of gold."

"I will remind you, Holmes," I said, my dour disposition rising to a boil, "that a good man, a decorated officer who saved countless lives, is dead. Please do take this case seriously."

"I will, as ever, give it my all, dear Watson," he replied, appropriately chastised. "But I do hope a night's rest in a good bed will bring some light back to your old eyes. If not for me, then for the good people of Carlingford who may well need your medical acumen."

And with that, we said not another word for the remainder of our trip. We were met at Carlingford station by a carriage that took us to Ghan House, a centuries-old manor reborn as a boarding house.

The night's rest was indeed what I required, for in the morning my demeanor had brightened considerably, while Holmes appeared more his usual pensive self.

We broke our fast in the cool morning air surrounded by lush, green trees and the expanse of even greener hills of Slieve Foye Mountain rising behind the inn. As we finished, a large man ambled toward us from around the manor. The chap's broad, smiling face beamed beneath a high forehead slick with sweat. He bore a walking stick, which he tapped in a strange rhythm as he walked.

"Mr. Holmes and Dr. Watson, I presume," the man said as he neared our table.

I had no idea who he was nor how he knew us. Perhaps, even here in the Irish countryside, he recognized Sherlock from the illustrations that accompanied my stories in *The Strand*. What I did notice, however, was a strange look in the eye of my friend as the man approached, as if he were distracted by something in the garden behind the fellow. This fleeting concern passed as soon as Holmes spoke.

"Good morning, Mr. McCoillte," Holmes responded, as if it was perfectly obvious this burly fellow was the Leprechaun Whisperer. "Your timing could not be better. We have just finished our rashers. Would you care to join us for a spot of tea?"

"How did you know it was me?" McCoillte asked. "Are there Leprechauns about me? I asked them not to come, but they can be a capricious people."

"It was the cane and the cadence," Holmes responded, "as well as the black mud upon your shoes. You have just returned from checking on the warren at the edge of Lake Carlingford, which has notoriously dark dirt along its shore."

"And the cane?" he asked, holding it forth.

"The cane is made from ash, purported to have magical abilities amongst those who believe in such things, and appears to be several centuries old," replied Holmes. "The cadence I recognized as an old Irish folk melody. Now, you tell me, who in Carlingford would use such a marvelous piece of ancient wood to tap a tune once used to mollify the Fae?"

McCoillte sat upon our third chair, which groaned under his weight, and clapped in joy.

"Well done, Mr. Holmes," he exulted. "You are certainly the right man for this case. I ne'er knew you had such extensive knowledge of the magical world. Me cane is indeed ancient. It's been handed down through ten generations. It is an original cutting from The Great Ash of Leix."

Holmes released a low whistle, showing an innate knowledge of Irish magical lore I never knew he possessed. He always eschewed any sort of supernatural causes in our cases, preferring to find scientific rationale behind even the strangest happenings.

With introductions complete, the three of us spent the morning going through the particulars of this case. According to McCoillte,

Dr. Moore was found dead in his office ten days prior by his assistant, Mrs. Alma O'Reilly, when she arrived for the day's appointments.

McCoillte went on to say that no murder weapon was found anywhere within the surgery or in Dr. Moore's quarters upstairs. The town has no constable, so one was requested from Newry to spearhead the investigation. In the immediate aftermath of the tragedy, however, the agitated townsfolk searched the building for the perpetrator or information as to his whereabouts.

"I would like to interview this Mrs. O'Reilly as well as the constable," Holmes stated. "But first I would like to examine the body."

"I'm afraid that won't be possible," McCoillte replied. "Dr. Moore has already been laid to rest . . . by order of our Alderman, Mr. Sean Pierce."

"I see," said Holmes. "That is interesting. Is that common practice in cases of murder in these parts?"

McCoillte began to nod his head but caught himself mid-bob.

"We don't get too many murders out this way," he said, "but folks don't like the dead lying 'round too long. It offends the Fae, you see. So, the Alderman's decision was not unusual."

McCoillte stopped, but it was obvious even to my eyes that he had more to say, so Holmes stared at the man until the silence forced him to finish his thought.

"The visiting constable was none too happy about the situation with the body but he had no authority to overturn the Alderman's wishes once the deed had been done."

Holmes took a moment to pack his pipe. He held a lit match above the bowl as he stared at the Leprechaun Whisperer.

"I suppose I shall have to glean what I can from the crime scene, then," he said before drawing the flame into the tobacco. "And I shall add Alderman Pierce to my list of people to question."

The great detective said nothing further for several minutes as tendrils of smoke coiled into the air. And so, Mr. Kelyn McCoillte looked at me and back at Holmes before nodding and shoving his chair back.

"One last thing," Sherlock uttered between puffs as McCoillte began to rise. "How is it that the province's Leprechaun Whisperer has never seen a Leprechaun?"

With that, McCoillte dropped back into his chair.

"How could . . ." the Whisperer started. "How did you know, sir? Even my wife doesn't know that truth."

"It was what you said upon entering the garden," Holmes replied. "You asked if we saw any Leprechauns about your person."

"That was said in jest, Mr. Holmes. A silly jape on me own part. Nothing more."

"Ah, but that 'silly jape' was more serious than you intended. To the keen eye, a slight crinkle about your eye and a quick twitch at the edge of your lips gave away the truth."

McCoillte sat in silence for a time, perhaps pondering what this revelation would mean to his future. In the end, he decided to come clean.

"Me father had the sight," he said. "As did his grandfather and many other generations reaching all the way back to when me ancestor cut this cane from the Great Ash of Leix."

"But not all McCoilltes had the sight," Holmes responded. "Your grandfather did not, nor did his grandfather. It would seem the sight tends to skip every other generation."

"Aye, that it does," the Whisperer admitted. "But that doesn't mean we McCoilltes canna do our jobs. The Leprechauns hear us e'en if we can't hear or see them. And they can communicate in other ways to those of us who lack the sight."

"They leave you messages?" asked Holmes. "How fascinating. That is something I hadn't considered."

"You won't tell no one will ya?" McCoillte asked, seeming smaller than the hulking six-foot frame that occupied the creaking chair. "This is not just me vocation, it is my family's legacy. I canna lose that."

"Your secret is safe with us," Holmes replied as smoke encircled his head. "I would never seek to tarnish a man's reputation unduly. In fact, I would love for you to take me to the warrens so I may inspect them and mayhap meet your tiny friends."

McCoillte nodded and a relieved look spread across his face. After the man departed, I turned to Holmes to confront him about his own predilections against those who professed connections to the supernatural.

"You don't actually believe in Leprechauns, do you old friend?"

"Of course not. No," Holmes replied.

He focused almost too intensely on his pipe as he spoke, however, taking one final draught before tapping the bowl on the edge of the table. After a moment, he spoke again. "But McCoillte believes, and that's all that matters. Delusions—even when benign—can drive men to desperate measures."

"You can't believe McCoillte is a suspect," I blurted. "The man might be a giant, but he seems as gentle as a lamb."

"Everyone is a suspect, my dear Watson," Holmes replied. "Surely you know that adage by now."

After breakfast, we made our way into the village. It was a quaint town along the edge of a deep lake that emptied into the Irish sea.

On our way, Holmes once again became distracted, staring to the side for several strides as we walked. The moment passed, and I put it down to lingering fatigue. I made a mental note to check his vitals once I had access to Dr. Moore's surgical tools. We located the deceased doctor's surgical office shortly after passing beneath the Tholsel, the two-story stonework town gate from which taxes were levied centuries ago.

Inside, in a dimly lit and empty waiting area, sat a woman I presumed to be Mrs. O'Brien behind a sturdy if featureless desk. A mismatched set of chairs and benches filled the rest of the room.

"Good morning my good woman," I said as she looked up from some piece of paperwork. "I am Dr. Watson, an old friend of Dr. Moore's, come from England at the behest of Major General Thomas."

"We got no patients today on account of Dr. Moore's death," Mrs. O'Brien replied curtly before returning to her paperwork.

"If I may, Madam," interrupted Holmes. "I am Mr. Sherlock Holmes. Mr. McCoillte asked me to look into the matter of the late Dr. Moore's death. May we examine the crime scene?"

Mrs. O'Brien, who looked exactly like one might expect from her name—a plumpish woman with graying hair pulled tightly into a bun atop her head, considered the two of us intently.

"Help yourself," she said after a moment of study. "I ain't going back there again until somebody cleans the mess. Dr. Moore didn't pay me for that work. He always handled it himself."

"Thank you, Madam," Holmes replied with a nod and touch of his cap. "We will find our own way back."

Behind the waiting room lay a corridor with an examination room on one side and a set of stairs to the doctor's private quarters on the other. At the end of the corridor stood a closed door. We headed there.

I admit to a slight hesitation before opening that door. I had seen plenty of blood in my days in the military, but the death of a fellow soldier always gave me pause.

Inside, the scene was much as McCoillte had described. A pool of dried blood sat beneath the desk and chair at the far end of the office. Blood spatters arced across the desk and onto the bookcases along the walls. Unfortunately, the bloody floor would not yield viable clues, for they were all but trampled into oblivion by the tracks of a dozen or more pairs of shoes.

Sherlock sighed before moving into the room. As was our routine, I stood at the door while Holmes investigated. He moved methodically about the scene, being careful not to touch anything or disturb the bloody business any more than the townsfolk had.

At one point, Holmes' attention snapped to the cold, dark fireplace along the side wall. I don't know what caught his attention, but after examining the hearth, he left and returned a moment later with forceps, which he used to grab some charred scrap of paper from deep within the hearth. Holmes placed the scrap in a borrowed specimen jar.

From there, Holmes examined the splatter patterns on the walls for an interminable amount of time. And then we were done. Holmes grabbed the specimen bottle and left the room without a word, forcing me to hurriedly shut the door before rushing after him.

By the time I caught up, Holmes was already forcing poor Mrs. O'Brien to retell the horrifying tale. I needn't have worried about the woman, however. She was no squeamish city lady. I would later learn she was raised on a pig farm and had dealt with blood her entire life.

"There he was, sitting in his chair in the dark, the blood pooled beneath him from a hundred or more oozing wounds," she said as if describing a local lad leaning against a wall eating a pie.

"How large were the wounds?" Holmes inquired.

"They were short and thin," she replied. "Not huge gaping wounds. Each was no more than a hair's width and no longer than the nail on me pinky finger."

"Thank you," Holmes said, jotting a note into his book. "Please continue."

"I'd come in to light the fire," Mrs. O'Brien said, unphased. "It was odd he hadn't done it himself. But the fireplace in the surgery was not lit either, so after getting it started, I figured I'd do him a turn and warm his office, thinking he must have slept late."

"The fire was not yet lit in Dr. Moore's office?" Holmes asked pointedly. Mrs. O'Brien nodded. "Has it been lit since?"

"Not by me," she said. "I've not been in there since I found him. I told you I'm not paid to clean the bloody bits."

"Dr. Watson will be happy to handle that duty for you," Holmes said as he clapped me on the shoulder and beamed a wide smile at Mrs. O'Brien. "I believe we can glean no more here, so that office may as well become functional again."

With that, Holmes strode through the waiting room toward the front door.

"Come along, Watson," he called back. "We have more interviews to complete before you take up practice."

I tipped my hat to Mrs. O'Brien before leaving. Outside, I once again hurried to catch up with Holmes, whose long legs had taken him half a block down the cobblestones already.

"Done in by a hundred tiny cuts. Ghastly image," I remarked upon catching him up. "Still, I suppose a half-inch wide blade would be like a lance in the hands of a Leprechaun."

"More likely the murder weapon was a scalpel taken from the surgery," Holmes replied. "None of the blood patterns on the desk or side walls were interrupted, but there was a large area behind the chair with no blood."

"What does that prove?" I asked.

"We're looking for a single assailant who attacked from behind," Holmes replied. "If Leprechauns are real, they would have been all over the Doctor to stab him. There was no evidence of hundreds of tiny assailants. Only one large one."

"Mr. McCoillte will be pleased to hear that," I responded.

"We won't clear his Leprechauns until we unmask the real killer," Holmes said gruffly. "When you clean the surgery, check every blade for blood. The killer likely disposed of the weapon, but we may get lucky."

"And what about that scrap of paper you retrieved from the hearth?" I asked.

"A potential motive," he replied. "And an oddity in the timeline of events. Sadly, charred beyond usefulness."

And that was all he would say upon that matter until later.

We next called upon the visiting Newry constable, Detective Inspector Ian Harrold, whom we found in a cramped office tucked into the back half of the town hall's main floor, just off the Carlingford Market Square.

"Good day, Inspector," Holmes said upon entering DI Harrold's small office.

"May I help you?" the inspector responded, rising to face us. He was a tall man, pushing past six feet, and solidly built. A thick, black mustache graced his upper lip and a shock of matching hair refused to be tamed atop his head.

Holmes bowed low and swept his arms wide, in a gesture of courtesy I had never seen him provide to our own Inspector Lestrade.

"Detective Sherlock Holmes at your service."

At this, DI Harrold rushed around the desk, grasped Sherlock's hand, and shook it vigorously.

"I am pleased to make your acquaintance, Mr. Holmes," he said, almost gushing. "And gladdened to have you here in this—formerly—quiet village."

"Have you had a rough time of it?" I asked. I tipped my hat and added, "Dr. Watson at your service."

"There was the hint of a mob when I first arrived," Harrold admitted. "And I spent most of my first days just keeping the peace. But the news of your imminent arrival had a mollifying effect on the emotions of the townsfolk."

"Who was at the head of that mob?" Holmes asked. "Who was fanning the flames of vengeance against the Leprechauns?"

"I can't rightly say," DI Harrold replied. "But when I arrived, most of the town was in a meeting run by Alderman Pierce. It was quite heated. I believe things might have gone badly if not for my arrival."

"Well, I certainly hope we can put this matter to rest quickly," Holmes replied, "so the good people of Carlingford don't commit further atrocities in the name of justice."

"Further atrocities?" Harrold asked, a furrowed crease appearing upon his brow.

"I refer to the trampling of the crime scene and the early burial of the best and most important piece of evidence."

"We just came from the surgery," I added. "Grisly scene."

"I canna tell you how upset I was to find all them tracks through the blood," Harrold said with a sigh. He ran his fingers through his thick hair and scratched his scalp before continuing. "The people of Carlingford are a passionate lot. It seems they had all just come from the funeral service when the town meeting began. I never e'en saw the body."

"So, I take it you haven't been able to make any headway on the case?" Holmes asked.

"With little to no evidence, I have no suspects and only Mr. McCoillte's word that it wasn't the Leprechauns who done it. And I canna arrest no Leprechauns, so . . ."

As DI Harrold trailed off, I found no words of wisdom to provide. Holmes broke the silence with one last question, as he often did.

"Tell me about Mr. Sean Pierce, the Alderman," Holmes requested. "What's your opinion of the man?"

Harrold's eyebrows wrinkled momentarily, either unsure what Holmes was asking or how to respond. Perhaps both.

"Mr. Pierce?" he questioned. "He seems a good man. Has the best interests of the town at heart, I'm sure."

"Was he leading the rabble at that meeting?" Holmes asked pointedly.

Harrold shuffled his weight from foot to foot before apparently coming to a decision.

"I don't like to speak ill of people whom I have sworn to protect," he began.

"But . . ." Holmes prodded.

"Let me put it this way," Harrold continued. "Standing before those people, the Alderman reminded me of a fiery priest from my youth who railed against the evils of Satan."

"A passionate leader for a passionate people?" I asked. "Seems like a good fit."

"Until it's not, if you get my meaning," Harrold stated with a shake of his head. "One day, after a sermon where this priest called for an inquisition into witches in our midst, he was recalled by the bishop, and we ne'er saw him again."

Harrold stopped talking for a moment, but it was obvious he had more to say.

"I won't forget the look in the eyes of that supposed 'man of God' as he screamed from the pulpit," Harrold continued after a time. "He was battling his own demons, that much was certain in retrospect. I'd not seen that look again until I stepped into the Alderman's meeting."

I looked at the thick arms and broad chest on the six-foot frame of DI Harrold and wondered what kind of man would strike fear in his heart.

"Thank you, Detective Inspector," Holmes said. "I believe it is time for us to meet the Alderman."

We left the constable's cramped and windowless office and proceeded upstairs, where we were ushered into Alderman Sean Pierce's spacious and bright office. The man sat behind a large desk with a smirk planted on his angular face.

I took an instant dislike to the Alderman but remembered Sherlock's other adage: "Do not judge too quickly lest you mold the evidence around your preconceptions." I looked to Holmes for support and found him once again distracted by something other than the current subject of our investigation.

He seemed to be staring through the open window behind Pierce's desk. While it was a beautiful day and the Alderman had a wonderful view of Carlingford Lake, I didn't believe the great Sherlock Holmes would be distracted by a picturesque vista. I resolved to check my friend's heart and lungs as soon as we returned to the surgery.

Luckily, the Alderman didn't seem to notice Sherlock's momentary lapse of concentration. He waved us into the office, his smirk growing ever larger.

"Come in. Come in," Pierce said, not bothering to rise from his desk. "I am heartened to have the great Sherlock Holmes on the case.

Forgive my lack of courtesy, but I am pressed for time. Is there anything I can do to help your investigation?"

"I only have one question for you, Alderman," Holmes stated, his eyes refocusing on the man behind the desk.

"Ask away!"

Pierce once again waved us into the room, but Holmes stood his ground. I stared hard at the Alderman's eyes, watching for any hint of the fire that DI Harrold had witnessed.

"Were you under the care of Dr. Moore at the time of his death?" Sherlock asked.

The question certainly took me by surprise as it seemed to come from nowhere. The Alderman, however, was seemingly nonplussed by the inquiry.

"I'm happy to say I have never been ill a day in my life," he responded almost immediately, showing no outward sense of the strangeness of the question. "Obviously, the good doctor and I were acquainted, and I visited the surgery on official matters from time to time, but I never once needed his medical services."

"Well, thank you for your time, Alderman," Holmes said, shooting a quick glance at the window before exiting the spacious office.

I stood there for a moment longer, my eyes flitting back and forth between Alderman Pierce and the open window behind him, unsure of what had just occurred.

"What an odd interview," Pierce said to me. "I certainly hope the great Sherlock Holmes is giving this case his all. We may be a small town, but the people here deserve as much justice as the residents of Dublin or London."

And there it was. In that moment, Pierce's eyes flashed with just the hint of the burning passion Harrold had seen a week earlier. I shrugged at the Alderman and made my exit.

I didn't catch up to Holmes until we had almost reached the surgery again.

"What was that all abou—" I started.

"When you clean Dr. Moore's office," Holmes interrupted, "search the doctor's patient records. I'm certain anything important will have been removed, but perhaps the killer overlooked some small piece of evidence. Even a lack of evidence will be telling."

With that, Holmes left me at the surgery, muttering something about needing to find the Leprechaun Whisperer.

I spent the rest of the evening and night in the surgery, cleaning Dr. Moore's office and going through the collected notes from my colleague's life as a town doctor. I found no patient file for Sean Pierce, so either the Alderman was telling the truth, or his records had been removed. Too tired to make my way back to Ghan House, I retired to the doctor's quarters upstairs.

The next day, I heard yelling and banging on the door to the surgery. I glanced out the window and found Holmes standing in the first rays of light cresting the Slieve Foye hills.

"Good. You're awake," he called, his eyes sparkling in the early dawn light. "Come, Watson. We have no time to waste."

I knew better than to argue with Sherlock when he had that look in his eyes, so I dressed in yesterday's clothing and trudged to the door.

"You must see what I found at the Leprechaun Warren last evening," Holmes exclaimed. As I followed, I wondered what DI Harrold would say about the fire behind Holmes's eyes.

When we arrived at the shore of Carlingford Lake, Holmes guided me to a large rock formation jutting from the black mud near the retaining wall.

It looked more like a cairn of stacked rocks than a natural formation, but when Holmes pointed out a small hole halfway up the rocky slope, I had to admit it looked like the entrance to a tiny cavern. And it may have been a trick of the low sun's rays glinting off the placid lake, but I swore a flickering light glowed within that crevice.

"What do you see?" Holmes asked after a moment, his excitement almost palpable.

"Nothing," I replied. "A pile of stones made to look like the entrance to a tiny cavern that I assume the people of Carlingford believe is home to Leprechauns."

"Exactly," Holmes said, his excitement unabated. "That is what most people see."

"But you aren't most people, are you, Sherlock?" I asked.

"True," Holmes replied. "And neither is the Alderman."

This statement stopped me. In all the time I had known Sherlock, he had never once entertained the idea that anything existed outside what logic and science could explain. It took me a moment to reconcile this fact with the concept that Sherlock might now believe in Leprechauns . . . of all things.

"Are you saying that both you and the Alderman can see something—some evidence of . . . living . . . Leprechauns?" I asked, my voice almost refusing to pose the ludicrous question. "Only you two can see these magical creatures, when no one else in town—including McCoillte, the Leprechaun Whisperer—can?"

Holmes nodded, but then shook his head.

"I cannot say for certain that no others can see them," he stated. "And for the record, I will never admit to seeing the creatures myself. The people of London would assume I am crazy."

I had always known that the brain of Sherlock Holmes was different from those of so-called normal people. High-functioning sociopath, he liked to call it. Crazy is what others might say. Then it hit me.

"The Alderman is insane."

"Now you're getting it," Holmes replied. "It would appear that only people with, shall we say, 'specific mental facilities' can see Leprechauns."

"Like a mental condition that might run in a family," I added, "but skip a generation from time to time."

"Exactly," Holmes replied with a nod. "McCoillte must take the existence of the Leprechauns on faith, unlike his father. Although they can make themselves known to those whom they trust. Would you like to see?"

I wasn't certain I did but I nodded anyway, unsure what would happen. When I found out, I almost ran screaming. From the mouth of the tiny cavern emerged a bloody scalpel, seemingly hovering in air above the rocky cairn.

"The murder weapon! But . . . what? How?" I cried surprised by the floating blade, my mind still not willing to accept the proof of the Fae that my eyes now witnessed in motion.

"Deposited here by none other than Alderman Sean Pierce," Holmes explained.

"You have a witness to that fact?" I asked, as I struggled to gather my wits and courage together.

"None who could take the stand in a court of law," Holmes

responded, pointing at the bobbing scalpel. "But I do not doubt the veracity of their claim."

"Then we are at an impasse," I said. "I found no evidence pointing to the Alderman or anyone else within the surgery, and no copy of whatever was on that burnt scrap of paper that you say pointed to motive."

"Tell me, Watson," Holmes began. "What would you do if you ascertained one of your patients had a major brain defect?"

I stared hard at Holmes, knowing he didn't want me to answer that particular question.

Holmes sighed. ". . . And you feared the man was an imminent danger to others?"

"I would seek to have him committed to a sanitarium to protect those to whom he might cause harm."

"Exactly," Holmes said. "I believe your friend, Dr. Moore, must have confronted Sean Pierce with his fears, perhaps had already written a letter to send to the sanitarium."

"The ashen parchment," I stated.

"In a clean hearth that hadn't seen a fire in a week."

"So, Pierce confronted the doctor in his office," I continued, warming to the theory, "and when Moore wouldn't relent, the Alderman lashed out in a fiery rage. Later, he blamed the murder on the Leprechauns, whom only he could see."

"Well done, Watson," Holmes exclaimed, clapping me on the shoulder.

"But we can't prove any of it."

"So, we must extract a confession," Holmes replied. "A very public confession. We should return to the town hall immediately."

When I glanced at the opening to the Leprechaun cavern, the floating scalpel had disappeared.

We heard raised voices as we neared the Market Square. It seemed someone had called a town meeting. In the middle of it stood Alderman Pierce, his hair flying wildly about his head as he raged against the Leprechauns.

"We cannot let this atrocity stand another day!" Pierce yelled from the steps of the town hall. "The Leprechauns must pay for the vile murder of our beloved doctor!"

"It appears I spooked the Alderman," Holmes said as we approached. "He must be worried we might find some evidence he overlooked."

"We cannot allow him to lead this rabble against the Leprechauns," I responded. "What should we do?"

"Just watch," Holmes replied. He stepped forward and cleared his throat.

"Excuse me!" he called. "Does anyone want to hear my report first?"

"I do, Mr. Holmes," came a reply from the door to the town hall. It was DI Harrold. "I would very much like to hear what the great detective has to say on the matter."

The crowd parted and Holmes strode forward. I followed in his wake as the townsfolk crowded in behind me.

As I climbed the steps, I heard Sean Pierce gasp. I looked up to see him recoil as Holmes approached, even though Sherlock barely acknowledged the Alderman's presence.

"At this point in my investigation," Holmes began, "I can definitively conclude that Leprechauns had no part in this crime."

I saw Mr. McCoillte looking visibly relieved at the edge of the crowd. Others were not convinced.

"If not the bloody Leprechauns, then who?" yelled one young ruffian. Others chimed in as well.

"This was a crime of passion," Holmes continued. "Perpetrated during a moment of crisis by an unstable person."

I glanced at the Alderman to see how he took this accusation. I found his eyes darting around like a caged animal. I assumed Sherlock planned to continue to pick away at the man's frail mind until he broke. I was only partly correct.

"Prove it," the Alderman muttered, his voice shaking. He then yelled to the crowd. "I doubt the great detective can prove his claims because the Leprechauns took the murder weapon back to their warren!"

Pierce seemed to have regained some of his composure, perhaps feeling secure that his planted evidence would turn the tide.

"Actually," Holmes responded calmly, "The murder weapon is right here."

This claim quieted everyone.

"Here in the Market Square," Holmes amended. "In a moment, the murderer will reveal himself by brandishing the weapon for all to see."

A murmur went through the crowd and many of those gathered plunged their hands into their waistcoats or trouser pockets to prove they were not the murderer. Alderman Pierce, I noticed, had gone completely white in the face and trembled with fear or rage . . . or both.

I am not certain exactly what transpired next. From my vantage point it seemed the bloody scalpel appeared in midair between Holmes and Pierce. I swear I caught a shadow of a tiny person upon the door to the town hall leaping toward the Alderman.

Pierce screamed and raised his hands to ward off some invisible attacker. A moment later, he found himself holding the bloody scalpel aloft as if about to attack Holmes.

DI Harrold bolted forward and tackled Pierce to the ground, wrestled the scalpel from his hand, and proceeded to clasp manacles around the man's wrists.

All the while, Pierce screamed, "I did it! It was me. I did it. Leave me alone now. Just leave me alone. I did it!"

Holmes glanced at me, smirked, and motioned for us to leave.

Hours later, as we waited at Carlingford Station for the train to Dublin, I confronted Holmes.

"How did your leaping Leprechaun friend get the murder weapon to town?" I asked, but then deduced the answer almost immediately. "Ah. You gave him a ride upon your shoulder."

"So, you can see them," Holmes chided with a laugh.

"No, but I can make deductions," I replied. "My friend, Sherlock Holmes, taught me."

We sat in silence as I gathered my thoughts. Something terrible began to dawn upon me.

"Did you actually deduce any of this case?" I asked. "Or did the Leprechauns lead you to every clue?"

Holmes didn't respond, but I knew. Every time Holmes had a revelation in this case, it came after a moment of distraction. The Leprechauns must have followed McCoillte to our first meeting. They guided Holmes to the burnt paper in the fireplace and were present when we interviewed Pierce.

The Leprechaun even exacted the confession from Pierce by leaping upon the deranged man and placing the murder weapon in his hands. No one saw it happen. Truly, not even me, not clearly. Holmes had done nothing to crack this case, so I knew then and there I must file this adventure away to protect the great detective's reputation.

I might have left it there forever, but at that moment I caught my friend flipping a gold coin. I snatched it from him to inspect its faces. Instead of the iconic profile of Queen Victoria, the coin had an image of a great tree on its head, while the tails side showed an image of a pot filled with coins. I sighed and handed the Leprechaun gold back to Sherlock, vowing to publish this story upon his death, so the world would know the truth of the Leaping Leprechaun.

Touring Company

by
Gini Koch writing as Anita Ensal

"Docking with the *Marcantel* in five minutes," Captain Carl Dershem shared. "All company prepare to meet your next audience."

Irene West took a deep breath, let it out slowly, and did her best to relax.

"Why so tense?" Mary, her personal robot asked. "This should be a routine stop, and you have performed The Scottish Play many times before."

"Oh, I know," Irene replied. "But I know this ship from my former life."

"They are enemies? I don't recall any merchant having issues with you or your family."

"No, they're friendlies. It's just . . ." Irene stared at herself in the mirror. The person who stared back wasn't in uniform but still looked more rigid than even Lady Macbeth should be. She forced her shoulders down just a bit in order not to look as though she was standing at attention. Better. "They still see a Galactic Police officer when they see me. Selling a role is harder when someone knows you of old."

"Ah." Mary cocked her head. "This is your version of stage fright. Understandable, and recorded for future instances. What may I do to reassure you?"

"Hope that nothing bad happens on the *Marcantel* while we're here."

Mary chuckled—Irene had programmed her to be as close to human as possible in appearance, speech, and mannerisms. The appearance portion was costly, but for Irene the cost was worth it for her lifelong companion to look like an individual person versus a metal thinking machine. This expense had been doubly worthwhile when she'd changed careers. "If something does, I assure you we will be up to the task of solving it."

"That," Irene said with a grimace, "is what I'm afraid of."

"Welcome aboard!" Captain Michael Prucha said heartily. "I and my core officers are pleased to welcome The August Company of Joy to our ship!"

Heather Joy Augustyn gave the captain a formal bow, then nodded her head graciously to the two women and one man with the captain. "Allow me to accept your welcome for all of my company. We are pleased to perform for you and your fine crew."

Prucha nodded, then looked behind Heather, noted Irene, and smiled. "I'd hoped you'd be here."

Irene put a bright smile on her face. "Then I'm pleased to be here even more." She sent up a quiet prayer to Sol—perhaps the captain just wanted to catch up on her family.

"Irene West is from one of the greatest families we have in the system," Prucha shared with the people around him—which now included a variety of crew who were probably supposed to be at their posts—proving Sol did indeed provide. "She might well be the only one who left the Galactic Police for another calling."

"Oh, there are a few Wests out there, doing other things," Irene said with gaiety she didn't feel. "But most of my extended family is guilty as charged of doing our best to protect our system."

"Indeed," Heather said, giving Prucha and his officers another gracious nod, then turned to Irene with a "get off this topic" look on her face. Irene couldn't blame her—they weren't here to discuss careers in law enforcement. Plus, the woman who'd named a professional touring company after herself rarely liked to have the spotlight turned onto anyone else, unless and until those others were on stage under Heather's direction.

"I'm sure we'll have some time to catch up," Irene said. Prucha had ordered the Imperial Package, meaning they'd have dinner with the crew, perform The Scottish Play tonight, socialize during the next day, perform one of the comedies selected by the crew that morning, spend one more night, and depart the next day. There would be more than enough time for reminiscing. "But right now, we need to prepare."

Despite their own ship being docked against the *Marcantal's* hull, they wouldn't return to the *Asanuma* until their performance was complete. This was part of the Imperial Package—not only did the crew get fine entertainment, but they were able to mingle with the company and part as, if not friends, at least friendly acquaintances. Irene couldn't complain about this—it was why she'd become a part of this touring company, after all.

Prucha introduced the tall, stern-looking woman behind him as his executive officer, Marie Shells. The perky blonde next to her was the navigation officer, Sandy Wright. The other man was tall, well over Prucha's six feet, and had a serious countenance, though his eyes possessed a twinkle. This was Security Chief David Mulkey.

Prucha and Shells headed back to the bridge and shooed the other crew members back to their posts, while Wright and Mulkey were assigned to take the company to their rooms, through what looked like a long corridor with a variety of intersections. The luggage, props, costumes, and such were left for the company's robots, Lucas and Bryce, to deal with, though Wright assigned some of the *Marcantal's* robots to assist. Irene was interested that the *Marcantal's* robots were almost as lifelike as Mary, Lucas, and Bryce. It was common for entertainers but rare for merchants to go to the expense.

Wright took the lead and headed down the corridor, merrily chatting with Heather. Irene at first assumed Mulkey had hung back in order to ensure there were no stragglers, since the *Marcantal* was quite a large ship, and it would be easy to get lost. And this might have been the case, but he touched her arm and gave her a look she was familiar with—he wanted to discuss something of importance.

She resisted heaving a sigh and remained with him, Mary staying behind her. Mary never carried luggage unless she and Irene were traveling alone. She belonged to Irene, not the company, and Mary was the first to point this out whenever anyone might forget.

"I have a concern," Mulkey said quietly, as they walked slowly and the others got farther ahead, "and with your background, I'm hoping you can help me. I don't want to say anything to the captain in case I'm wrong."

"But, if I cause offense, I'll be off this ship within three Earth days."

Mulkey smiled. "Yes. One of the crew is, I believe, not who they purport to be. They've done nothing wrong that I've seen, and they're quite popular with the rest of the crew and a favorite of the captain's, but certain things they've said indicate to me they're far too familiar with piracy. And having someone with GP background on board is a rare strike I wasn't expecting."

Some of the crew walked past and Mulkey stopped speaking. Irene assumed he didn't want anyone to hear his suspicions other than herself.

Irene considered his concern. Crime in the system existed, of course, but the biggest issue the system had in terms of crime was in the part of the system they floated in now—the Belt—and the crime was well-organized piracy.

The head of the pirates had the title of Boser Geist. The system had dealt with Boser Geist and his consortium for centuries because, sadly, the pirates shared learning as well as the same succession as old Earth kings had. When one Boser Geist died of old age or was captured—both rarities—or was executed in some way by the GP, the next in line took over seamlessly.

There were rumors, of course, that not every Boser Geist had gone down fighting and at least one was out there, hiding in plain sight. And, having served as well as coming from a long and extended line of GP, it was easy for her to make the obvious leap.

"You believe you have a 'retired' Boser Geist on board."

Mulkey nodded. "I believe I have proof, but it needs to be a sure claim, because otherwise the captain will never believe me."

"But you think he'll believe me."

Mulkey nodded but, before he could say anything else, Irene felt as if they were being observed and started to look around. She saw a flash of a uniform going around a nearby corner, but before she could investigate, she was interrupted by someone not on Mulkey's suspect list.

"Irene!" Heather's tone was one Irene was familiar with—annoyance tinged with simmering anger because Irene was focused on something other than preparing for her role. There was no way she was going to be able to get the name of Mulkey's suspect from him now.

"I'll speak with you about this later," Irene said.

Mulkey nodded. "In private, please. And as soon as you're able."

Irene shot a look at Heather's expression. "After tonight's performance, most likely."

He sighed. "It'll have to do. I'll write up my case so you have documentation, such as it is."

Irene gave him a quick smile then hurried off to Heather. "Stop flirting," Heather said as she led Irene briskly to their rooms.

"I wasn't," Irene replied mildly.

Heather snorted. "I'm sure *he* was." She shook her head. "Is there a handsome man you can't charm?"

"Plenty, I'm sure."

Heather showed her where their things were—two connected communal family suites for the women, two connected four-berth rooms for the men. Hair, makeup, and costuming would happen in the women's rooms, since they were larger.

"No time to relax," Heather said now that Irene was with the others. "We're on a slightly different clock than the *Marcantal*, so while it's mid-afternoon to us, it's dinnertime for them." Everyone who lived out in space ran on Earth standard but, based on where your ship called home and if or when you'd check in to Ceres Main, your ship's clock could be off a bit from others. It was rarely an issue, and most of the company was happy to eat early.

The others headed to the mess hall, but Mary and Irene stayed behind for a moment. "What do you think?" Mary asked her.

"I think the only person currently above suspicion is Captain Prucha."

Mary nodded. "Mulkey used no specific pronouns, meaning even one of the robotics could be suspect."

Irene shook her head. "As an accomplice, perhaps. But if he suspected a robotic he'd go straight to the captain with that information. So, since Heather will likely push me out an airlock if I speak to Mulkey privately again prior to performance, we need to identify who Captain Prucha seems to favor within the crew. Happily, I'm hungry and everyone should be dining with us."

They headed to the mess and did as required for this part of the package—Irene sat with crew, not company. She pointedly didn't sit with Mulkey, which meant Heather was pleased. Dannielle Nicole had chosen to sit with Mulkey, thereby proving all the company felt

Irene and Mulkey had indeed been flirting. Dannielle was always trying to outdo Irene.

The food was served family style and was quite good. Prucha and his family were a jolly clan and seemed to like most if not all of their crew and also to consider them family. Which made Mulkey's reticence even more understandable.

It took much observation, but Irene was able to identify three people she felt might have more of the captain's favor—Hal Astell, the assistant navigator, Medoc Tober, the galley chef, and Amanda Hersom, the ship's nurse.

Astell was an enthusiastic fount of system knowledge, Tober a joker and a great chef, and Hersom had a bubbly presence and an excellent speaking voice. And, of all the crew, they seemed to be the most relaxed around the captain.

Tober also had his own robot, Paja, as an assistant. Paja, like the rest of the *Marcantal's* robotics, was as lifelike as Mary, and he helped to serve the food. Mary and Paja exchanged small talk when he brought beverage refills and Tober announced the final course—individual bowls of fruit and herbs grown in his on-ship garden, and fresh whipped cream.

"Before we partake of the wonderful dessert," Heather said as she stood, "I'd like to share one of the many things the August Company of Joy does that sets us apart from other touring companies. Tonight we will perform the Scottish Play . . . and one of you will be on stage with us!"

"Think of that, everyone," Prucha said heartily. "One of you will get to play a part in *Macbeth*!"

The company went silent and most looked stricken. "Ah," Heather said carefully, "it's considered quite bad luck to say the name of that play anywhere close to where it will be performed. Please refer to it as the Scottish Play, if you would be so kind."

"Too late now," Tony Sarrecchia, who was playing opposite Irene as Macbeth, muttered from a few seats away. "We're in for it." Irene had excellent hearing, but Tony hadn't been trying to keep his voice down all that hard.

Prucha seemed chagrined. "Apologies, everyone. I'm certain all with go without a hitch."

"Let us hope," Heather said with cheer Irene knew she wasn't feeling. "Now, as you may know, there are three witches' parts in the play. And one of you will play Witch Number Three tonight! Now, before anyone panics, the part is simple and the lines will be pasted inside the cauldron that will be on stage with you so whoever gets chosen will do spectacularly."

Hands went up eagerly—including those of Tober and Hersom—as they always did. Experience said Heather never picked an eager participant and she, like Irene, had clearly been paying attention to who Prucha favored. "Mister Astell, I believe you will be perfect."

He blushed. "But I'm a man."

"In the days of Shakespeare, all performers were men," Tony said reassuringly. "You'll be fine."

"Don't you worry," Susan Fox, who has the Witch #1 role, added. "Deanna and I will help you."

Deanna Lukens nodded. "We've done this many times—we'll cover you if you need it."

Astell didn't look thrilled, and Mulkey didn't look like this choice affected him, meaning, Irene hoped, that Astell wasn't whom Mulkey suspected. Tober and Hersom both looked exceedingly disappointed, with Tober teasing that he had no problem dressing up as a woman for the entertainment of all and Hersom saying she had a voice for the stage. At this Mulkey looked thoughtful, but it wasn't enough for Irene to make any conclusions.

Dessert was served. It looked delicious but Irene was already full and so didn't eat hers. The crewman to her right, Berry Kercheval, was only too glad to have it, and she was glad it didn't go to waste. She noted Mulkey had also not eaten his dessert and had given it to Dannielle, who offered a smirk at Irene while eating the extra, presumably because she felt she'd scored some kind of romantic coup.

Shortly after they'd left the mess to verify the solarium was adequately prepared for the performance, the ill fortune everyone in the company had been expecting happened. Both Susan and Deanna shared they felt nauseated and, shortly after, Berry and Dannielle shared they weren't feeling too well, either. Hersom and the ship's doctor, Holly Catherwood, took them to their sickbay. Tober was concerned he had served a bad batch of fruit or cream, but no one else was affected, so the presumption was that one piece of fruit had gone bad and those four had been the unfortunate recipients.

Irene wasn't so sure, and she could tell Mulkey wasn't either, but they were across the room from each other and had no way to share thoughts. She kicked herself for not having Mary go to Mulkey's quarters and get his information, but they'd been too busy, and her first duty was to the Company.

"Now what?" Carl asked. He never performed, since he was the *Asanuma's* captain and pilot, but he was Heather's right hand, and knew what a blow this was. All three sick performers would have had major roles in whatever play was picked for the next performance. Plus the full company was required to perform the play tonight.

"Maybe Lauren and I can add on more roles," Pamela Donavan said, without a lot of enthusiasm. "And Rikki, too."

Lauren Goldman shook her head. "There's no way we can do that, not with the Scottish Play. We're already doing more parts than we should, and one missed button means the costuming changes won't work. And the less said about hair and makeup the better. We're all playing men for everything–going in and out of a woman's costume would be disastrous."

"I'm already doing four minor roles," Rikki Lynn added in. "There's just no way I could manage another."

"The witches' costumes hide a lot," Irene mentioned. "Though our bigger issue is who will play my gentlewoman with Dannielle indisposed."

"I will," Heather said promptly. "We've done this enough that none of you will need prompting, other than the witches, whoever they're going to be, and I can provide that easily enough."

"I can't speak for Amber," Tober said, "but I'm still more than willing to take on the role of the first witch. I do know the play well."

"What an excellent idea, we'll do that," Heather said quickly. "Thank you so much, Medoc. If someone could verify if Amber would be able to participate? Obviously only if those who were taken ill don't need her."

Paulspar went to verify Hersom's participation and Irene sent Mary along with him to see how everyone was faring. The rest of the company hurried back to their quarters to get ready.

Everyone was responsible for their own hair, makeup, and costuming. Astell, Tober, and Hersom arrived and were given their costumes, which included wigs. The offer was made that they could stay with the company for assistance, but the three of them chose to go back to their own quarters to prepare. Heather gave them all scripts for their parts, with the hope they could learn the parts at least a little.

Meanwhile, Pamela pasted all three parts inside the cauldron. "Sol help us," she said. "I'm not sure any of them will be able to even see the words."

"We'll manage," Heather said firmly.

Mary returned. "The four patients will remain in sickbay. They seem to have a form of food poisoning, all have the same level of symptoms, but Doctor Catherwood does not feel it's going to be life-threatening." She leaned closer to Irene. "Security Officer Mulkey asked me to tell you he will not be watching the play. He's going to remain in his quarters, preparing his presentation of evidence, and asks that you join him there as soon as you're able."

With that, Irene turned her mind where it now needed to be—on becoming Lady Macbeth.

The performance went far better than expected. Tober hadn't been exaggerating—he knew his part well and performed it perfectly. In fact, it was one of the best performances of the role Irene had ever witnessed. There was something familiar about it, in a way she couldn't quite place, but that might just mean Tober had left performing to become a chef and she'd seen him on stage years ago. Irene found herself wondering, in the moments when she was offstage, if Tober might do what she had done and join the company, or rejoin, in that sense.

Hersom wasn't quite as good, but she managed. Astell was as bad as expected—but that was fine, since his crewmates were supportive of his efforts. Heather, of course, did well covering for Dannielle. All in all, the play went on without incident.

As requested, she and Mary left the ship's recreation area and headed for where Mulkey had told Mary he'd be.

When they arrived, the door was slightly ajar. Irene knocked softly and the door swung fully open. To show that the bad luck hadn't stopped with four people getting ill.

Mulkey was slumped over his desk, an icepick lodged in his back. Irene could tell it had pierced his heart and his chest, in part because he wasn't moving and was cool to the touch, and also because the desk was covered with his blood.

Irene did a quick search of the room. Nothing seemed disturbed, but there was also nothing that outlined evidence against anyone. "The killer took whatever he was working on," she said softly, as Mary carefully moved Mulkey's body to reveal a rectangular shape that had little blood. "Meaning his suspicions were correct."

"Should I fetch the captain?" Mary asked.

"Under the circumstances, I don't believe it would be wise for me to be alone." Irene sighed. Well, there was a surefire way to get attention. She took a deep breath and screamed at the top of her lungs.

Results were as expected—people came racing towards the sound. In short order, the captain had sent for Dr. Catherwood, the doctor had declared Mulkey dead, and set the time of death as happening sometime during the performance. During which time everyone other than Mulkey himself had an airtight alibi—if they weren't on stage, they were in the audience, because Prucha himself had made sure all the crew were in attendance, other than the doctor, who'd been with the four patients the entire time.

"I know this isn't what you want to hear," Prucha said, "but I need to ask you to take up your old job again, at least until a GP cruiser can arrive."

"Two days away," Shells said. "I've already sent out a call."

"How could this happen?" Prucha asked sadly.

Irene considered options. They were few. "Captain, if I could speak to you . . . in private?"

Shells took the hint and stepped out of Mulkey's room. Irene closed the door, so only Prucha and Mary were with her. Then she explained Mulkey's concerns. "So, he had to have been right, or close enough, because otherwise, why kill him? I'm certain we were observed—meaning the killer knew of Mulkey's suspicions—but I have no idea who it was. Based on the little he gave me, my suspects would be Astell, Tober, and Hersom."

Prucha nodded slowly. "If we remove my family from suspicion, and I believe we can, since my wife and I have been married for 20 years and our children have never worked anywhere but on this ship, then your take on my 'favorites' would be accurate."

"Then let's look at our suspects, all of whom were on stage at the time of the murder."

"I believe we should look at how they got onto stage," Mary said. Irene turned to her, and Mary continued. "Astell was chosen by Heather, and you and I knew he would be, because Heather always chooses a captain's favorite—and she's as good at spotting them as you are, Irene—and she chooses one who doesn't want to be on stage. But Tober and Hersom both wanted the role, quite desperately, based on minute signs most humans don't pick up consciously. Susan and Deanna getting ill—along with Berry and Dannielle—seems most suspicious."

Irene nodded. "I gave my dessert to Berry and Mulkey gave his to Dannielle. Clearly, the two of us were supposed to get sick as well."

"Why?" Prucha asked.

"To make us easier to kill." Irene gave Prucha a small smile. "You identified me as tightly tied to the GP, and Mulkey held me back to verify his suspicions."

"That would indicate my other officers," Prucha protested.

"But there were other crew about and I know I spotted someone listening in. However, the bigger issue is how the four were poisoned."

"I have scanned my databases and eye drops would be my suggestion," Mary said promptly. "Based on the reactions and the speed they arrived, the poison was in the dessert. Adding in the fact that none of those poisoned were close to death, just incapacitated due to the effects, per the data, eye drops have been used as such for centuries and the formula has barely changed over time. And everyone on board would have access to them."

"The doctor has the supply," Prucha said. "And that would mean Amanda would also have easy access."

"No one treats eye drops as a dangerous substance," Irene countered. "It's likely the entire crew have some, at least those who suffer with dryer eyes." She closed her eyes. "It's likely to be Tober."

"Why?" Prucha didn't sound convinced.

"He made and served the dessert. He had to think quickly, because he didn't get the role."

"Why did he want the role?" Prucha was doing a good job of being a GP partner. Irene pointedly chose not to say this aloud.

"For the alibi it would provide. He gave Hersom an alibi, too, that way. Though Mulkey didn't indicate he felt there were two pirates on board."

"There was no way anyone left the solarium," Mary said. "I was backstage the entire time and, due to the security officer's concerns, I remained vigilant for anyone leaving. No one did."

"And no one left from the audience, either," Prucha said. "We recorded it so poor Berry could see what he'd missed."

"Let's watch that, shall we?" Irene asked.

They left Mulkey's quarters and headed for the captain's office. The recording was a good one, taken from the back of the room, so everyone was visible. As stated, no one came or left.

"There's something about Tober's performance," Irene mused. "I feel strongly as if I've seen it before. Was he on stage prior to joining you?"

"No, he came to us from another merchant ship," Prucha replied. "Just him and Paulspar."

"Why are all your robotics so lifelike?" Mary asked. Irene smiled to herself—she'd spotted the anomaly, too, after all.

Prucha seemed surprised by the question. "Why not?"

"It's unusual that anyone goes to the expense," Irene replied dryly. "I did, but for very personal reasons. Heather has done so, because Lucas and Bryce can perform background roles, which they had to tonight. But why do you have so many lifelike robots on board?"

"I suppose because of Medoc," Prucha admitted. "Paulspar was so much more . . . comfortable to be around, we decided to upgrade our other robots. They've been with us since my grandparents first got the *Marcantal*, and we upgrade their systems regularly, so why not their outsides as well?"

"It's there, right there," Irene said to Mary. "What's wrong, how he did it, how we can prove it. But I can't grasp it."

"A moment." Mary tilted her head back, which indicated she was accessing her deepest memory banks. She finished, went to Prucha's keyboard, and tapped away. A new video appeared, also of *Macbeth*. The First Witch's performance was amazing. "It's exactly like Tober's performance tonight," Irene said. "And it's familiar because this is considered the best company to ever perform the Scottish Play. Our entire company has watched this multiple times."

"Which would be what I, as a robotic, would choose to use if I were asked to play the part," Mary said.

Irene stared at her. "Could he have really done that? Replaced himself with his robotic?"

"Why not? The three crew members got ready in their own rooms. Paulspar looks as human as I do, and he is the same size and shape as his owner."

"Intentionally, I'm sure."

"That is certain. Had you and Mulkey both taken ill, the performance would have been postponed and he could have murdered you both easily. With the play proceeding and both of you inadvertently not taking the poison he gave you, he had to go with this option."

"He's clever and quick in his thinking, which are traits of most Boser Geists in history."

"So, what, you truly believe Paulspar did the performance?" Prucha asked.

"Yes," Mary replied. "He did. I can imitate anyone's voice if I've heard it for five minutes or less, and Paulspar has heard Tober's voice for a long time."

"Plus, the robot literally cannot kill a human due to programming even the pirates haven't been able to override," Irene added, "but his loyalty is to his owner, and impersonation while said owner performs murder is within robotic allowances."

"But how do we prove it?" Prucha asked.

"As to that," Irene said, "I believe I have an idea."

Irene contacted her uncle, Marcus West, and he ran a detailed history for her. Then they went, heavily armed, to Tober's quarters.

He wasn't there, though Paulspar was. Mary inspected Paulspar and found traces of makeup and hairs from the witch's wig on him. Mulkey's notepad was missing. They did a quick search of the various waste repositories near Tober and Mulkey's quarters and grabbed the notepad just before it was emptied into the ship's furnace.

"Good thing he wanted to get rid of this quickly," Prucha said as they went past Mulkey's room. "The receptacle nearer to Medoc's own rooms would have already been emptied."

"It's nice for us when a criminal gets complacent or sloppy," Irene agreed.

Mulkey's notes were good, but something else on them was even better. Prucha put Paulspar into confinement, then they headed for the kitchens, Prucha giving the order that no one was to ingest anything until he gave the all clear and which order was to be passed from crewperson to crewperson, not over the intercom.

Tober was chopping shallots with a large, gleaming knife when they arrived, looking like a happy, innocent chef. "Can I help you, Captain?" he asked genially.

"Boser Geist, we're here to arrest you," Irene said calmly.

His mouth twitched, but the only other reaction Tober gave was a laugh. "You're accusing me of being a pirate king? I'm flattered."

"No," Irene said. "Koko Cabron, you are hereby under arrest for crimes against the system, including the murder of Security Officer David Mulkey, the poisoning of four people earlier tonight, and all forms of piracy."

Tober's eyes narrowed at the new name. "What did you call me?"

"The name on your very old wanted message." The video in the kitchens turned on to show a younger version of Tober, with his true name shown underneath and the reward amount listed. It was a very large number. "Now, the icepick you used to murder David Mulkey was wiped clean of fingerprints, but you didn't bother to wipe off the notepad which we retrieved from the trash. It has a lovely forefinger and thumbprint, in Mulkey's blood, but they are not, of course, his prints. If you're not Koko Cabron, you won't have any issue with my taking your fingerprints now."

Tober's response was to throw the knife, with great force and accuracy, directly at Irene's head.

Mary reached out, grabbed the knife before it could hit Irene, and sent it right back with much more force and even better accuracy—straight into Tober's heart.

"It would have been nice to get information from him," Irene pointed out while Prucha made sure Tober was dead.

"The reward is for dead or alive," Mary replied calmly. "And, as you well know, my view is that you are the one who needs to remain alive. Those who try to harm you are the ones who will be dead."

"Does David have any family?" Irene asked Prucha.

He shook his head. "We're all the family he had. And he was wrong about one thing—he was more of a favorite of mine than any of the others."

Irene patted his hand. "Then we'll split the reward with you, Captain. I'm sure it's what he would have wanted."

Prucha heaved a sigh. "I'd rather have David alive than the money."

"What we want and what we get are not always the same things," Irene said.

Mary reached out and gently squeezed her hand. Irene squeezed back, then considered how to tell Heather they could now afford new cast members. Dramatically would be the best, and the most fun.

Irene smiled, then headed back to where she truly belonged, in the August Company of Joy.

The Mortal Case of the ~~Eight~~ ~~Seven~~ ~~Six~~ Five Ba Xian

by

Ben H. Rome

She waited until they were in the limousine before punching her companion in the arm. "Seriously? 'Holmes and Watson?'" She waved the passports at his face.

"Ow!" The larger man rubbed his shoulder with a meaty hand. "Hey, you said get the passports done quickly, so I did. Not my fault you left it all to me to take care of while you went all emo in the suite, Bastet."

She settled back into the deep leather seat, crossing her arms over her chest and glaring at him. "It wasn't emo, it's called *mourning*." She sniffed.

After a moment, she kicked the big man with her pointed shoe. "Besides, I didn't expect you'd use two very obvious fake names on fake passports before we attempted to enter a foreign country with the highest security rating in the world, either."

He snorted. "It worked, didn't it? Guess the Chinese have never read Sherlock Holmes."

Her eyes narrowed. "More like luck that the customs guards are apparently unfamiliar with Western classic literature." She glanced out the window as the city lights of Beijing began to fade. "And why am I Watson and you Holmes? You think you're the leader of this little partnership?"

"Well, Holmes has that whole Cumberbatch pretty face with an attitude vibe." He propped his feet up on the reverse seat opposite him. "Like me. Also, side note: I want Benedict to play me in our eventual biopic."

"Gods, Fenrir, you're just like your father," muttered the diminutive woman.

"What's that?" he asked. The big idiot's lopsided grin threatened to swallow his face.

"If our Mr. M turns out to be named Moriarty, I will definitely kill you."

The grin disappeared. "Who's Moriarty?"

Bastet groaned and rubbed a hand over her face. "Go to sleep, you furry oaf."

Their driver, who introduced himself as Chen Longwei, pulled off the road several hours later. Under the rising crescent moon, he parked the limo in the small gravel lot and the two visitors exited the vehicle before Longwei could open the driver's door. A small stretch of wild grass filled the space between the lot and a cliff. Waiting near the edge was a well-dressed man facing the sea.

Bastet looked past their assumed host to the sea beyond. A few scattered islands stretched out from the shore into the distance; a rising fog from the water made them appear to float amongst the clouds.

The air was wet with residual heat and humidity. She reached up and pulled her straight gray hair back into a bun, cooling her neck.

Fenrir rolled his shoulders, bones cracking, and ran his fingers through the unruly mop of curly hair he called a hairdo. "Ugh. More wet. As if the rain forest wasn't bad enough."

She smirked. He'd hated their recent visit to Mexico City, more so the injuries he'd sustained than swimming through the jungle humidity. *Such are the sufferings of a Nordic titan.* She pushed away the darker memories of the jungle. Her sister's loss was still fresh, but they had a job to do.

As if on cue, the gazing man turned to face their approach. The moonlight was just bright enough to make out his face, and Bastet hissed, setting herself into a fighting stance.

Fenrir reacted as well, a low growl rumbling from his throat.

They knew this man.

Their host held his hands up, offering no resistance. "Peace, Bastet, Fenrir. I'm not here to exact revenge or another nefarious plot."

"Explain," snarled Fenrir.

"You know me as Mark Maestas, previously employed by one who tried to sacrifice you to an ancient Aztec god."

Bastet nodded. "Go on."

Mr. M lowered his arms, though kept his hands within their view. "I'm actually a member of the Japanese Defense Intelligence Headquarters, investigating a situation developing here in China."

Fenrir barked. "You're a spy for the *Japanese* government?" He cracked his knuckles. "You realize we're in *China*."

"In short, yes."

Bastet sniffed the air, catching various scents on the wind. Satisfied, she relaxed, her hands dropping to her sides. "What are we doing here, Mr. Ninja?"

"I'm not—"

"Hey yeah, he's totally a ninja!" Fenrir laughed.

Maestas looked perturbed. "I'm not a—"

Bastet walked to the cliff edge, unconcerned with their host at her back. Courtesy of her heightened senses, she now knew he was harmless.

"Don't bother to convince him otherwise. Once he gets a notion in his head, he won't let it go." She gestured out towards the sea. "What did you bring us to see in the middle of nowhere at night? Why all the secrecy?"

"Right, of course." Maestas tugged at the sleeves of his suit coat. Bastet noticed a subtle pattern woven throughout, some kind of wave or water. "How well do you know Chinese mythology?"

"As well as the Chinese know the Norse *eddas*, outside of that American superhero movie franchise, that is," said Fenrir. He stepped alongside Bastet.

Maestas' lip turned up slightly. "What is before you is the Bohai Sea, where the Ba Xian—the Eight Immortals—made themselves into cultural icons to the Chinese people."

Bastet half-listened to the man's subsequent tale of the Eight. She'd heard of the Immortals, though it had been several centuries since Chinese envoys visited Alexandria and regaled the Egyptian court with their exploits. The Ba Xian lived on island estates in the Bohai Sea and were considered protectors of China and its people, even though they lived in enforced isolation thanks to the modern Chinese government.

Their deaths would stoke or break the people, depending on who did the killing.

Ultimately, the Ba Xian were just like her and Fenrir—legends made real, walking the world as somewhat immortal beings. 'Immortal' was a misnomer; she knew firsthand they could be killed. Her sister, Sekhmet, had just recently died in the jungles of Mexico, sacrificing herself to save Bastet and Fenrir from Maestas' former employer.

Who happened to be an Aztec god.

And also, now very dead.

A lot of dead immortals happening lately.

She realized both Maestas and Fenrir were looking at her expectantly. "Yes, of course," she responded, sure someone had asked if she was ready.

Maestas smiled. "Excellent. I'm so glad you agreed. Let's get going; there's little time to waste."

Bastet cursed silently as she made the hop from the sampan to the rough-hewn dock. The fog surrounded them, obscuring everything beyond 30 or 40 feet. Fortunately, it was the last murder scene to visit, and she couldn't wait to be back on the mainland.

"So what do you think?" whispered Fenrir as he grasped her arm, steadying her. "I mean, two scenes in, this is definitely the work of a serial killer."

"This isn't CSI: Beijing," snapped Bastet, hurriedly moving off the dock towards the trailhead. "There are still a lot of questions we need to answer—or at least find connection points with." She glanced around at the settling fog, slowly swirling in a sinuous fashion around them.

Something about the abstract movement of the mist reminded her of Sekhmet's mysterious, feline grace.

Bastet squeezed her eyes shut, pushed the memory away. *Focus*! She turned and continued along the natural path.

The trail led upwards through the forest towards their next destination. According to Maestas, they were headed to the sacred music hall of Cao Guojiu, site of the third murder.

Their client moved ahead up the trail, his hired man Longwei behind him. Bastet held Fenrir's arm, indicating he should wait. As the two men moved off into the fog ahead, she nodded and they followed the trail, though at a slower pace.

Bastet nudged her companion, speaking quietly. "I admit those first two sites were . . . different."

"Visited a lot of murder locations, have you?"

She poked Fenrir's side. "Ha. Ha."

He grunted, then paused. They were alone on the path at what appeared to be an overlook, though the mist and the weak moonlight obscured most everything except a stone bench and a small rock garden along the path's edge. Fenrir gestured towards the bench, and they sat, gazing out into the muddled night.

"Help me make sense of everything tonight. My brain feels foggy," he began.

"It's always foggy. Blame the canine genes you're mixed with." Bastet smirked, then turned serious. "Yeah, it's a lot and we're already on fumes. Let's talk this through for a minute, before we get another sensory assault."

"Well, Lü Dongbin was pierced by this—" he produced a long, slender sliver of metal that pulsed a soft, translucent blue. "—definitely not mortal-made. And it's shattered."

"No other pieces in the chamber, though." Bastet mused. "So it was left to make a point. 'Hey look, I killed this one with a supernatural blade.'"

"And in Han Xiangzi's bamboo grove, well . . ." Fenrir shivered. "I've never seen a body suspended in the air by vines, with a broken flute through its neck."

"The killer is making a statement, and I suspect we'll find something similar up there," she thrust her chin in the direction of the path.

Fenrir nodded, toying with the blade fragment. Several moments of silence passed.

"What do you make of Mr. M's story? Japanese spy, investigating Otherworldly threats, and all that."

"Skeptical," she replied. "Makes sense why he reached out to us, though. This is definitely not the work of a mortal."

A loud noise broke the stillness. Fenrir blushed furiously, rubbing his belly.

"Was that–" Bastet stepped back. "Was that your stomach? You just ate, for Osiris' sake!"

Fenrir grinned sheepishly. "What can I say? I'm a growing wolf."

She rolled her eyes. "Here, have a snack." Bastet reached into her jacket pocket and tossed him a candy bar. He licked his lips as he caught and unwrapped the treat.

Bastet watched the fog wisps float and curl, almost seemingly with purpose. She ignored his near-indecent groans and smacking lips.

"Thanks Bas, that hit the spot." He ignored her glare at the nickname.

"We should continue up, before they come down looking for us," said Bastet.

Fenrir nodded. "Who do you think is pulling the strings here?" Fenrir asked, his voice low. They heard voices ahead.

Bastet stopped, looking up at her partner. "I don't know." She looked up the path as Mr. M and Longwei emerged from the mist. "Yet."

Cao Guojiu's death was similar to the other two Immortals: outrageous, brash, and violent. He lay in the scorched center of his estate's amphitheater, instruments wrapped around his body like grotesque metal art, a twisted tangle of erhu strings wrapped around his throat.

The three of them slowly paced through the site—the driver Longwei stationed at the entrance to watch for the arrival of any authorities—searching for clues that may have been forgotten.

Bastet knelt near a heap of shattered instruments, fingers lightly grazing the fine wood and brass fittings. These were antiques, most probably handmade by Guojiu himself during his long lifetime. She could feel the loss of his Otherworldly presence, similar to that at Xiangzi and Dongbin's estate. She idly sifted the debris, looking around the murder scene.

She felt something warm beneath her fingertip and she opened her eyes. Careful to not draw attention to herself, she pushed some of the debris aside and palmed the object she'd found hidden beneath.

"Find anything?" called Maestas. He was visibly upset as he looked around the wrecked stage. "What a waste."

"No, nothing here." Bastet responded, rising to her feet. "It looks like a cyclone hit, though. But only the instruments were affected."

"Found something!" Fenrir called from across the room. Bastet and their client picked their way through the debris and joined him near a fallen and cracked gong. He held a sheet of music delicately in his massive hand.

Scrawled across the musical measures was a series of Japanese kanji.

"It's a haiku," said Maestas. "A really bad one. 'In the moonlight night | Silence whispers Japan's name | Blood stains the still air.' "

Bastet grimaced as if the words tortured her ears. "Wow, that is bad."

Their client nodded. "What's worse is the grammar. And a few of these kanji are wrong."

"No way that's written by a Japanese ninja," said Fenrir.

"*Shinobi-no-mono.*" Maestas scowled. " 'Ninja' is an . . . uneducated term."

Bastet huffed. "Can we move past the language lesson, please?" She tapped the sheet music. "This has to be a frame-up. Look at the music on the page; it's from Kosaku Yamada's *Inno Meiji.*"

Fenrir gaped. "How do you know that's from a Japanese symphony, much less the composer?"

"I'm a few thousand years of worldly cultural education ahead of you." She patted his cheek. "But don't worry, you'll get there. Probably."

Maestas slowly nodded in agreement. "It's a clue left for Chinese authorities, because they'll come to the obvious conclusion and look towards a Japanese admirer who turned assassin. Which then moves the Chinese government to finger the Japanese as the culprits."

"The leaders here are that gullible?" Fenrir asked.

"No," said Maestas. "But it's the expedient answer, and they'll take it."

Longwei stepped into the room, glancing around at the destruction before moving quickly towards them. "Sirs, madam, there is a helicopter approaching."

Maestas looked at Fenrir, then Bastet. "To the boat, then." He moved off, Longwei trailing behind. He called to the two companions. "I suggest you keep up this time; I daresay the authorities will not take kindly to an invasion of an off-limits crime scene."

Bastet looked at Fenrir and glanced towards her hand holding the sheet music. He caught her signal; they would talk privately later.

"I wonder if the authorities are better than open water," she mumbled as they headed back down to the boat waiting below.

She definitely hated the water.

The two companions met later in the main room of their suite. They'd returned to the mainland from Guojui's estate as the sun broke the horizon, though the fog persisted until well into the midmorning. Maestas had secured a hotel suite for them to use during their stay in China, thanks to his diplomatic connections.

Their client would return in the evening to discuss next steps. The two reconvened after a few hours of sleep and devoured the lunchtime repast left out for them in the tiny kitchenette.

"Interesting evening, wouldn't you say?" Fenrir yawned and popped another dumpling into his gaping mouth. He groaned in mild ecstasy. "By Odin, these are so good."

Bastet sat curled on a settee, ignoring the big man's foodgasm. Opposite her was a giant window that faced the harbor. A cup of tea warmed her hands. "I don't trust either of them, to be honest."

Fenrir nodded. "Agreed. They don't . . . smell legit."

"Exactly." She sipped from the porcelain cup, then set it on a nearby saucer. "Let's recap so we're on the same page." They spent the next hour reviewing what they'd found at each location:

The shard of an ethereal sword in Lü Dongbin's chest, scorch marks and ruined stone furniture throughout the meditation chamber.

A broken flute through Han Xiangzi's neck, his body suspended in the vines of the Ba Xian's sacred bamboo grove.

And Cao Guojiu's body, wrapped in distorted and fragmented instruments, choked to death by slender strings. And of course, the sheet music with bad haiku scrawled across it, now laying on the low-slung table before them.

"So what do you think? It's not an ordinary serial killing." Fenrir placed the shard from Dongbin's estate next to the sheet music. He tapped it. "This points to an Otherworldly connection."

"That, plus the fact that Maestas called us in—he knows our true identities. But up until Guojiu's estate, I was still skeptical as to why us in particular. Why not the other Immortals?"

"Oh, I think I know that answer," replied Fenrir. "They've been in isolation for centuries, and since the regime change, are forbidden by law to communicate with each other."

"Color me unsurprised." Bastet glanced outside. Twilight was settling in and she watched little flares of light bloom along the docks below. "Besides, I know what we're dealing with here."

"Oh?"

The diminutive woman slipped her hand into her pocket, then placed an object on the table. It was slightly smaller than her hand, a thin, jagged oval of black that seemed to suck in the light around it.

"What in the Nine Worlds is that?" Fenrir bent closer, squinting. "It looks like a scale from Jormungand but it's way too small . . . "

"It's from a dragon."

He sat up straight, mouth agape. "What? No way. I thought those were strictly Otherworld by now, in the land of the Exiles. I read that the last one on Midgard was slain by some British saint, Georgie or something."

Bastet shook her head. "Animals with a touch of Otherworld. Most of those creatures are dead. This is from someone like us. A shapeshifter. The scale is small enough that I can't place the aura, though it seems familiar." She took a sip. "But make no mistake; there's a dragon killing the Ba Xian."

Figuring out the next victim turned out to be easy. Fenrir picked up on a pattern based on an obscure philosopher's study of how fascism breaks down a society. "Each Immortal is representative of an ideal to ancient China. Based on Khotovitsky's research, removing these ideals through constant attack will soon render a nation ripe for takeover."

It was Bastet's turn to gape. "How the—"

"You said to read the Internet, so I've been catching up. It's fascinating stuff, really." Fenrir grinned. "Anyway, the first three pillars to destroy is leadership, unification, and stability. Dongbin's considered the primary figure of the Ba Xian, Xiangzi inspires unity, and Guojiu provides authority and structure."

"So by this pattern, who's the most likely target now?"

"Lan Caihe, representing the soul and spirit."

"It's as good as any guess at this point, so we'll go with that." Bastet paused. "And if your pattern proves true, then I know exactly who the murderer is."

"And if I'm wrong?"

"We'll cross that bridge if it comes up."

Regardless, Bastet knew the Chinese government wanted to put an end to the murders, though she suspected they'd be okay if the whole lot of Immortals were killed off. But the Ba Xian were too popular with the masses; the regime was unwilling to risk their hold on the strings of power against the righteous ire from the people if their heroes continued to be slaughtered.

It was the perfect pain point for a foreign entity to exploit. Even more so if that foreign agent implicated an ages-old enemy. For China, that meant Japan.

"This is why I let the family handle all the politics and let me just fight. This layered plotting makes my head spin," moaned Fenrir, flopping back on the couch.

Bastet nodded. "That's why we're partners. I'm the brains; you're the help. Which is why I should be Holmes, and you Watson."

"Not this again."

She threw a pillow at him and grabbed the phone to call their client. Enough discussion: it was time for action.

They knew the where.

They knew the why.

Bastet was pretty sure of the who, but she kept that to herself. She had a hunch, and that was fine with Fenrir. If her plan succeeded, he could do what he enjoyed second only to eating: life-or-death combat.

The call placed and meeting set for later that night, the two companions sat staring out the window into the nighttime sky. With the lights down, they could see the artificial stars from the boats and buildings crowding the harbor wall.

"Bas?"

"Don't call me that."

Fenrir shifted. "Sorry."

She sighed. "Ask it, I know you want to."

"Your sister . . ."

Bastet set the tea cup down with enough force the handle cracked in her fingers. "She's dead. I miss her. I'll get over it, but not by baring my feelings or sobbing on your shoulder." She could feel her rage bubble upwards, threatening to surface.

"Let it go, then. Like that Disney princess." He started to sing. "Let it gooooo . . ."

That was the final straw. The dam burst as she stood and laid into Fenrir, a volatile flow of invective and pain that spanned four languages and raised her hackles.

She felt her body begin to tremble as her voice deepened into a primal growl, the first sign of her transformational power.

Fenrir's face drained of all color, staring just over her shoulder. Bastet's torrent dwindled, her body calming as she became aware of a crackling of electricity and a hot wind across her neck. She turned and looked behind her.

An amber portal had appeared, induced into being by her rage. Startled, she immediately blanked her mind and mentally shoved. The last time she'd formed a portal was the night her sister died; it had been their link to each other between worlds. It could also let other things in—or out—and she felt a savage presence lunge towards the opening just as it slammed shut.

Bastet collapsed upon herself, head in her hands, sobbing. Fenrir was wise enough to keep his mouth shut and sat quietly until her sobs turned to gentle hiccups.

She looked up, eyes red, cheeks streaked from the kohl previously outlining her eyes. "Don't. Push me. Again." Her voice was low, guttural, and promised excruciating death.

He nodded.

They stepped off the boat onto Lan Caihe's island estate just after midnight, just the three of them. Bastet was reasonably sure the killing hadn't happened yet; the investigators at the other sites estimated a time of death about an hour before dawn.

"You're absolutely sure Caihe's the next target?" Maestas asked for the sixth time.

It took everything Bastet had to not smack the man upside the head. "One hundred percent."

"How do you know?"

Fenrir loudly exhaled. Even he was getting annoyed. "Look, Mr. M, you just need to trust us, okay? Just let us do our thing, stay off to the side, and be a well-dressed witness." He gestured at the man's impeccable suit. "Don't want to wrinkle that pretty suit jacket of yours."

For once, Maestas remained quiet, though Bastet could still feel the waves of agitation rolling off him. She turned, catching Fenrir's eye, and winked her right eye. Fenrir caught the signal; Bastet knew who the killer was. He dropped his chin, indicating he'd follow her lead.

The fog was rising thicker and higher, making things a bit difficult to see much beyond ten feet ahead.

"What in the hells is it with this fog?" Bastet mumbled, moving hastily up the dock and away from the water as the others debarked.

Fenrir whispered to his partner. "Feels weird without Longwei here to help."

Maestas glanced at him. "He had other plans tonight." He moved ahead, leading the way along the paving stone path.

They reached Caihe's unlocked garden gate within a few minutes. The authorities were notified earlier, and lax security was part of the plan. The resident Immortal was already ensconced elsewhere, leaving them alone with the killer.

The three approached the courtyard of the immaculately kept garden. Bastet wanted nothing more than to wander amongst the flowers and trees; the serenity of the place was palpable, even in the dead of night. Caihe was a true master of art, using nature as a canvas.

She paused at the small shrine at the garden's center. "Ready?" Bastet inquired. Fenrir nodded, then moved off into a nearby fruit grove. Maestas indicated a small tool shed off to the side.

"I'll hide there; I can see out the slats."

Bastet nodded. "Good plan. Just stay in there no matter what. We can't fully focus on our intruder if you're not safe."

Maestas shrugged. "I can take care of myself, if necessary."

"I'm sure you can." Bastet watched him retreat, thoughtful.

In moments, she was alone. An exquisite cloak lay folded by the shrine, and she wrapped it around her shoulders, the beautiful fabric covering her body. *I wonder if Caihe wove this themselves.*

She calmed and focused her mind. The tiny woman hadn't shifted to her primary form in a long time—the last she could remember was that meeting with Alexander the Macedonian, negotiating Egypt's position within his new empire.

Fully transformed, she pushed off the reminiscing and settled down to wait. Patience was her virtue, not so for Fenrir. She could hear him panting and shifting, envisioning a bundle of fur, teeth, and nervous energy.

She couldn't detect Maestas at all, adding more evidence to her suspicions.

The crescent moon crept upward. Its weak light was enough to see the deepening shadows of the courtyard garden softened by the wisping fog.

The effect was eerie. Otherworldly.

One way or another, the killing spree ended tonight.

By the time Bastet heard the whispered shuffle of footsteps on the stone path, the fog had thickened considerably. She could just see the entry arch to the courtyard several meters in front of her.

She maintained her meditative pose, head bowed, Caihe's cloak draped over her form, hiding her shape underneath its folds.

The air rippled as the intruder stepped into the courtyard. Bastet felt the air shift, an undercurrent of energy moving through it. Moisture lay upon the stones before her, and then a pair of booted feet.

"Ah, Caihe. Doubtless you know you're the next in line. How gracious of you to wait out your fate in surrender." A whispered noise as a blade was unsheathed. "All I ask is you raise your head, so I can remove it while looking into your eyes."

"Hmm." Bastet did her best to stifle her laughter, then whispered. "Do you know why I detest Russian nesting dolls?"

"Wha—what?" The killer faltered. "Repeat that? I don't understand. What is—"

"Because they're so full of themselves." She snapped her head up, the cloak folding backward, revealing her face to the killer.

A snarling golden lioness stared at the startled visage of Chen Longwei.

"*Yebat'*!" Longwei stepped back, startled. He brought his knife up in a defensive position. "*Govno*!"

"*Khui*," she sneered. "Murderer."

He quickly regained his composure. "I knew at some point you'd figure it out. Maestas is but a pawn and unable to construct two and two together. So when you two showed up—" Longwei brandished the knife, looking around the fog-drenched courtyard. "Where is your faithful cur, anyway?"

"He'll come when called. Not like I need him to handle the likes of you." She remained seated on her haunches, holding a regal pose before the Ba Xian killer.

Longwei smiled broadly. "Oh you do, do you." The smile kept growing. "You don't know who you're messing with, *suka*." He began laughing, his bodily form elongating, skin turning to scales. The clothes ripped asunder, fluttering from his body. A long, reptilian snout with fangs snapped in relief as a winged dragon twisted and turned into being. Longwei stamped his feet and stretched his wings, letting go a deeply held sigh.

Bastet watched, unamused. "Thank you for that," she replied when the dragon whipped its head around and lowered to her height. "I needed to see your true form."

The dragon snarled, its body sliding around and digging its claws into the stone, gouging them. "I'm going to enjoy some smoked lioness tonight, it seems."

"Tugarin! Shut up." Bastet looked beyond the dragon and then back. She yawned.

The beast pulled back its head, surprised. "How did you know my true nam—"

"Gods, you are stupider than Fenrir." She licked her paw, subtly clicking her claws in and out. "We met during Peter's reign. I think then, you were posing as some mystic named Rasputin? Anyway, it's your scent; you smell like rotting meat and dog farts."

Tugarin blinked.

"Plus, your name. 'Chen Longwei'? Really?" She laughed throatily. "Mandarin for 'ancient dragon' is the best you could do? Really, you Russians are so unimaginative."

The black-scaled dragon snarled, rearing back to strike.

The massive wolf hit the serpent with a keening howl, all four claws slamming down between its wings. With a snarl, Fenrir dug into the dragon's back, claws shredding the scales from its neck. The wolf's jaws snapped, teeth scrabbling for purchase.

The Russian dragon roared, leaping into the air with a strong beat of its wings. Its sinewy tail whipped up and back, cracking against the wolf's flank. Tugarin lunged upwards, higher and higher, slapping repeatedly at the wolf with the flat of its tail.

She could barely see them as the dragon flew ever higher. She watched in horror as Fenrir lost his grip and fell. There was nothing she could do, unless . . .

The fog around the garden began to swirl, forming giant drops of rain that flowed sideways past her. The wind rushed through the trees. She smiled as she saw the water twist and turn, avoiding other objects—and her—in the courtyard. She studied the claws on her right paw, unconcerned now for the freefalling wolf.

Everything was going according to her plan.

A moment later, Fenrir's salvation burst into the sky from behind her.

Trailing drops of water, a magnificent azure Eastern dragon undulated into the night sky. The beast's bioluminescence showed a sinewy, flowing serpent aimed for the falling wolf. In moments, the water dragon encircled Fenrir and swooped back down to the garden, depositing him in a puddle of water before arcing back into the clear, starry sky.

She'd briefly lost track of the Russian black; even with her Otherworldly eyesight, he was shadow against the void.

But the Eastern dragon—it could only be Maestas—seemed to know exactly where Tugarin was.

She gazed upwards as a dance of light and dark flowed and swooped across the sky. The two dragons moved closer to earth, and Bastet could now see the blurred form of the Russian as he dodged and clawed at Maestas.

Bastet became aware of Fenrir when he shook his massive wolfen frame, spraying water everywhere. Including her.

"*Hey.*" She pinned him with a glare. "Show some respect for your elders."

"I . . . wait. You're older than—" Fenrir shook his head. "Never mind." He glanced up. "Looks like you were right on both counts; a Russian dragon is the killer, and our client is more than he seemed.

Though I didn't expect him to be a dragon. I thought maybe one of those yetis or something."

"Yetis aren't real."

"Yes, they are! There's all this research on the Internet—"

With a ground-shaking crash, two draconic bodies slammed into the courtyard between them, showering the wolf and lioness in broken stone, mud, and water. Bastet could see Maestas's form underneath Tugarin, who ripped an obsidian claw down the Eastern's belly. Dark blue blood poured from the wound like oiled water.

Maestas screeched, a painful wail that caused Bastet to crouch low to the ground. Her blood pounded in her head as she watched Tugarin slash repeatedly, iridescent scales and blood tinkling and spattering everywhere.

Bastet's rage bloomed as she watched the Russian beat down the Japanese dragon. Head pounding, she unleashed a blood-curdling roar. Tugarin paused, smiling as he pointed one bloody claw at her. "You're next, *suka*."

The Russian black dragon reared its head, eyes glowing as it slowly inhaled. She knew both she and Maestas were about to be broiled by Tugarin's flame.

Maddening. To be burned alive by an arrogant little prick of a dragon. Sekhmet would be ashamed of her. Bastet's rage burned hotter.

She could feel the air charge, getting warmer. Was that another of the dragon's powers, to superheat the air around it?

Bastet shrieked, slinking forward, claws extended. She bared her fangs, defiant in the face of fiery exhalation.

A familiar howl pierced the noise, the baying call of an alpha wolf. The Nordic titan slammed into the dragon's head, teeth and claws slashing and gouging. Impossibly, the wolf clamped his powerful jaws around the dragon's neck, Fenrir's momentum pulling the dragon after him and slinging it to the ground with a whump. Bastet leaped back out of the dragon's flailing reach, then crouched, readying to pounce.

She saw flashing light in the corner of her vision. She froze; a portal hummed and spit in the air where she'd been.

Fenrir slammed the dragon's head back to the ground, dazing the

Russian. Jaws firm around its sinewy neck, he growled and spread his paws, legs corded with tension.

He lowered his head, the dragon just beginning to rouse, and with a mighty snap, the wolf jerked his body to the right, flinging Tugarin through the air with a mighty heave.

Bastet watched as the serpent arced through the air and straight into the portal. She pushed hard with her mind and the portal slammed shut with a pop, a small bit of the Russian's tail flopping to the ground, severed by the collapsing magic.

The courtyard was silent. The three beasts remained where they were for a long moment, chests heaving with exertion.

Bastet padded over to the discarded cloak and nudged her head under, draping it over her body before transforming back to her human form. She turned, seeing both Fenrir and Maestas having done the same; Fenrir in a robe he'd brought from the hotel, Maestas now standing, covered with a thick fog perfectly shaped as a suit.

He looked at both of them, squaring off and bowed deeply from the waist. "Thank you both. *Minasama no yuuki to gojinryoku ni kokoro kara kansha moushiagemasu.*"

At Fenrir's confusion, Bastet said, "He's expressing his thanks for your courage."

"Oh." The wolf-turned-man bowed awkwardly in return. "Uh, no problem, Mr. M."

Maestas smiled. "Actually, it's Watatsumi."

Bastet staggered slightly. "Watatsumi? I mean, I knew you were one of the dragon protectors of Japan, but . . . you? Here?"

Fenrir looked at his partner. "What's so special about him?"

Her gaze remained on the Japanese official. "He knew Sekhmet." She waved off Fenrir's next question. "Like, really, *really* knew."

"Oooooooh."

Watatsumi's smiled sadly as he walked towards Bastet. "Why do you think I contacted you? Who else could I trust of the Otherworld but the sister of my long-ago love?" He enfolded Bastet in a hug. "You have saved Japan and China from the brink of war. Your sister would be proud."

Bastet stifled a sob against the surprisingly firm shoulder of Watatsumi's fog-made suit.

Fenrir stepped up, rubbing his belly. "Um, not to break up the reunion, but I can hear helicopters . . . and I'm starving." A loud rumble punctuated his statement.

Bastet groaned.

"Is he always like this?" whispered Watatsumi.

She looked over at her partner and smiled. "You get used to it."

The Norwood Contractor

An Adventure of Shirley Holmes and Jack Watson

by

Keith R.A. DeCandido

I came home from an overnight shift at the hospital to see a guy with a shaved head and a thick beard standing in front of the house on Riverside Drive. He was holding his phone in front of his face and talking a mile-a-minute into it.

I was in my last year of med school, and I had to do the whole night in the lab. You know how medical TV shows always say they got results from the lab but never actually show that process? That's because the work there is *seriously* boring. I was having a hard time staying awake from spending eight hours doing scut work and really wanted to take a nap.

But it looked like Shirley had a client. Who seemed to be recording a video or something.

"Oh, hey, fam," the guy said, seeing me walking up to him, "here comes someone now." He angled the phone so we were both in the shot that I could see on the phone screen. "You gotta be Ms. Holmes's assistant, Jack, right?"

"I'm Jack Watson, but I'm not Shirley's assistant." Officially, I was her companion. It meant I kept her company and tried (and, every once in a while, succeeded) keeping her out of trouble. That used to be her aunt's job until she got cancer. I got a free crib on Riverside Drive out of it, so I'm not complaining.

Besides, unlike lab work, being Shirley's companion was *never* boring.

"Well, I need her help. Any chance of an intro?"

"Who's asking?"

The guy snorted. "You kiddin', right?" He looked at the phone.

"Y'hear this, fam? My dude don't know Johnny Mac!" He looked back at me. "I got 500,000 followers on three different platforms."

"Okay, one, I'm not your dude. Two, only time I get online is to do research on diseases and surgical techniques. What do you need Shirley for?"

"Kinda need to talk to *her* about that."

I closed my eyes, sighed, and pointed at Johnny Mac's phone. "Fine, but you gotta shut that thing off before I let you in. Your 'fam' can get the highlight reel after you leave."

"Fair." Johnny Mac looked at the phone. "I'mma go take the meeting, fam. I'll give y'all the lowdown when I'm done." He stopped the recording and turned the phone off.

Johnny Mac was wearing purple bike shorts and a purple dri-fit running shirt, so he didn't have any pockets. He did have a small backpack, though, and he unzipped it open and dropped his phone into it.

Once his phone was put away, I pulled out my keys and unlocked the front door with fancy wrought-iron patterns all around it.

The foyer to the Holmes residence was all wood: hardwood floor, fancy wood paneling on the walls, a cherry coatrack, and an oak banister and staircase that led up to the other four floors. I looked ahead and didn't see Shirley (or anyone else) in the living room, the dining room that was just past it, or the kitchen that was just past that. So she had to be in her room on the third floor.

"C'mon," I said, leading Johnny Mac up the stairs.

Each floor had its own large bedroom, along with a bathroom, a little office-type nook, a crapton of closet space, and stairs at both the front and back of the house. I had the top floor—used to belong to Shirley's brother, who apparently lived in D.C. these days—and her aunt Martha was on the second floor.

Sure enough, we could see little Shirley Holmes sitting at her big-ass desk on the third floor through the open door at the landing. That open door was important—if the door was closed, she didn't want to be disturbed, so I'd need to text her and wait. Shirley was barely five feet tall, and skinny—just enough curves to identify as being born female, and also to make it clear that she was skinny because she was built that way, not because she didn't have enough to eat. She had short, mousy brown hair that was currently keeping us from seeing her face.

Since the door was open, I just rapped on the doorframe. "Hey Shirley, got somebody here to see you."

Shirley didn't look up from playing with one of her smartphones. She had a box full of the things. "Who is it?" she asked.

"Uh, I'm Johnny Mac, Ms. Holmes. I need your help."

Still not looking up, she asked, "Are you the same Johnny Mac who posts the videos online entitled 'Johnny Mac Tells It Like It Is,' discussing legal issues, Thai food, the history of mass transit systems, and the music of Taylor Swift?"

I stared at Johnny. "Seriously?"

"That's me. It's a real honor, Ms. Holmes." He started to move forward and put his hand out, but I put one big hand on his shoulder. He stopped and looked up at me. I just shook my head. Shirley did not like to be touched.

Shirley's desk had six computers: a purple iMac from the turn of the century, a Dell laptop from about 2004, a MacBook Air, an Acer laptop from around 2012, an HP desktop from a few years back, and a brand-new Lenovo laptop. She put the Treo down next to the HP and then turned to face us. But not to look at us—Shirley wasn't big on eye contact, so she mostly looked down at the floor, but at least her front was in our general direction.

"I have watched several of your videos. The production values are amateurish and your presentation is puerile, but the information you provide is quite useful. I suppose that the presentation style appeals to your audience. I find your legal discussions to be of most interest, likely due to your being a lawyer."

I jerked my thumb at him. "This guy's a lawyer?"

Nodding, Shirley said, "Under his given name of John H. MacFarlane, he graduated with a law degree from Fordham University's Law School and passed the New York State bar exam shortly thereafter."

Johnny grinned under his beard. "Magna Cum Laude, my dude!"

I sighed. "Still not your dude."

Shirley asked, "What is your preferred form of address?"

At that, Johnny blinked. "Say what?"

I translated. "What should she call you? Johnny? Mr. MacFarlane? Hey you?"

"Oh—yeah, Johnny's fine, Ms. Holmes."

"Very well, Johnny, what is the service you require of me?"

Johnny hesitated.

That surprised me, as this guy wasn't exactly what I'd call *hesitant.*

"I'm about to get arrested for murder. But I didn't do it."

Now Shirley actually faced me and Johnny, her brown eyes wide. "Please explain."

"It's like this—got an e-mail from a guy who used to be friends with my Moms and Pops when I was a kid. Contractor named Jonas Oldacre. We used to be next-door neighbors on Rochambeau Avenue up in the Bronx, but we moved to Yonkers when I started high school. Anyhow, he says he wants me to help him put a will together. That ain't usually my thing, but I did some family law back when I was a corporate drone, and 'sides, he's a friend of the family, am I right? So I said yeah, and we met up at a Starbucks on the West Side." He smiled and shook his head. "Right after we shook hands, he handed me the will. Get this—he *wrote* it. On, like, *paper.* I figured he'd e-mail it or something, but he said he didn't even own a computer, if you can believe that."

I glanced at Shirley's row of computers and tried not to laugh.

Johnny went on: "He gave me a pad'a paper with the will on it, and some other documents and stuff, and asked me to transcribe it and notarize it and make sure it was all legal and stuff. So I said yeah, and I tried to figure out how much to charge his ass, 'cause I'd been out of the game a while, and I wasn't sure what the goin' rate was, y'know? But then I *looked* at it." He stopped and took a breath. "Ms. Holmes, he left every goddamn thing to *me.*"

"I take it," Shirley said dryly, "that you did not expect that."

"I barely knew the chump!" Johnny threw up his hands. "But he said he always liked my Moms and Pops and he enjoys my videos, and he feels bad that I lost my corporate job. I did *not* tell him that gettin' my ass laid off was fab. I am livin' my best life now. But hey, if a retired contractor wanted to make me his beneficiary, I ain't gonna say no. Only thing he said was not to tell my Moms and Pops. Said he wanted it to be a surprise. I'm like, whatever, my dude, you're the client."

"So you created a will from his notes?" Shirley asked.

Nodding, Johnny said, "Yeah, and then I met him up in his place in the Bronx last night. Same house from when I was a kid. I took the D train up to Norwood and went to Rochambeau. He had a nurse, believe it or not."

"Why a nurse?"

"Well, he was coughin' up a damn lung the whole time we were in Starbucks, so I guess he's been sick. Maybe that's why he started thinkin' about a will. Anyhow, Nurse Lady answered the door and let me in. Made me take off my shoes, and she kept wipin' everything down. Ain't never seen a house so clean in my life. Seriously, the place was *sparklin'*."

While Johnny was talking, Shirley's phone buzzed. She grabbed it, looked at it, typed something quickly on it, and then put it back down.

"I gave him the fancy document all printed out—said he wanted it on paper. I created a PDF, too, but he ain't got no e-mail, so I didn't have nowhere to send it." Johnny shrugged. "Then I left. I was doin' a thing for my followers, ridin' the mass transit in all five boroughs in one night."

"I did not watch that video," Shirley said. "I assume you used the D train to get you through the Bronx, Manhattan, and Brooklyn."

"Nah, too easy. I took the D from the Bronx to Manhattan, then I took the N from Manhattan to Queens, then the G from Queens to Brooklyn, and then the J from Brooklyn back to Manhattan, then I walked down to the Staten Island Ferry and took it to the S66 bus so I could ride through Staten Island. Took me all night."

"An interesting exercise," Shirley said, which was way more generous than I was feeling about it, but hey, if it got him hits or whatever from his "fam" . . . "But back to the case at hand: Do you have the original notepad that Mr. Oldacre provided you?"

"Yeah, it's in my backpack." Again, he shrugged out of it and unzipped it, pulling out a blue notepad, which he handed to Shirley.

She started to read it over. "Interesting."

"What is?" Johnny asked.

"Did you notice the erratic handwriting?"

"I noticed I could barely *read* it."

"Some of it is quite legible. Where is the Starbucks where you met Mr. Oldacre?"

"Um, 61st and Broadway, right by Columbus Circle."

Shirley nodded. "That fits."

"Huh? Fits what?"

I smiled. I loved when Shirley did this.

"He composed this will on the D train from the Norwood terminus near his house to the Columbus Circle station, which is proximate to where he met you. The handwriting is neat, then sloppy, then neat, and so on, corresponding to when the train was moving as opposed to when it stopped. Notably, the last several paragraphs are quite sloppy, as the D train makes a lengthy run between 125th Street and Columbus Circle without stopping."

"You sayin' he wrote that up five minutes before he met with me? That don't make sense."

"Indeed it does not. I assume based on your belief that you will be arrested for murder that Mr. Oldacre is no longer alive?"

Pointing at her desktop, Johnny asked, "Can you call up the News 12 website?"

"Of course."

She did so, and we found a news story that said that the NYPD had a BOLO for John H. MacFarlane, a.k.a. Johnny Mac, as a person of interest in the arson murder of Jonas Oldacre. The story had a picture accompanying that looked like a screen grab from one of his videos.

Johnny sighed. "I know it looks bad that I was there the same night the fire started, but I'm telling you, I didn't do it. Can you help me, Ms. Holmes?"

"I believe I can, at the very least, look into your case. First of all, can you provide a means of contacting your parents?"

"Yeah, sure."

Moving one of the laptops toward him, she Alt-Tabbed over to a word processing program. "Please type it here."

After he did that, she handed back the notepad. "I would like to keep this, but I'm afraid it will need to be evidence."

"Say what?"

The doorbell buzzed.

"That," Shirley said, "will be Detective Guillaume Lestrade of the 24th Precinct. He texted me a few moments ago, saying he was coming to arrest you. I told him to ring the bell and I would turn you over."

Somewhat louder, Johnny repeated, "Say *what*? Thought you was gonna *help* me!"

"I shall, but my ability to do so will require me to be seen to be cooperating with law-enforcement, and not permit myself to be arrested for harboring a fugitive."

Johnny deflated like he was a balloon, his shoulders getting all slumped. "Yeah, okay."

While Shirley was explaining the facts of life to him, I went to the door intercom—there was one on each floor—and asked who it was. I mean, I knew it was Detective Lestrade, but it's good to be sure.

Once he identified himself, I said we were on the third floor and to come on up, and I buzzed him in.

Lestrade was a short, compactly built, dark-skinned man, wearing his usual denim jacket over a black button-down shirt and slacks. He had a uniformed patrol officer with him, and he didn't waste any time: "John Hector MacFarlane, you are under arrest for arson and for the murder of Jonas Oldacre." He looked at the uniform. "Take him outside, read him his rights."

As the patrol officer moved to handcuff him, Johnny asked, "How'd you *find* me so damn fast?"

Shirley answered. "My assumption is that the detective assigned to the case in the 52nd Precinct was watching one of your video channels and saw that you were visiting me. That detective then likely contacted Detective Lestrade and asked him to arrest you on their behalf."

Lestrade half-smiled. "Good guess."

Testily, Shirley said, "It was hardly a guess, Detective, but rather deductive reasoning based on the facts at hand and the personality of your suspect."

"Right." Lestrade turned to the patrol officer. "Go. I'll meet you outside."

The PO nodded and led Johnny downstairs, reading him the Miranda warning as he did so.

Then Lestrade looked right at Shirley. "What's going on here, Shirley?"

"Since 'what is going on' is your arrest of Johnny Mac, I hardly think you require me to explain it to you, Detective."

"You know what I mean. Why are you involved in this?"

"Johnny Mac came to me, Detective. He believes that he is innocent. While I have not investigated thoroughly, I am inclined to believe him."

"Look, Shirley, this isn't my case. You and I have an understanding, and so do some of the others in the Two-Four. But I know Detective Jones up in the Five-Two—he will not have a sense of humor about your involvement."

"I cannot imagine a sense of humor would be of help," Shirley said. "May I assume that you already informed Detective Jones of my interest?"

"He informed me, actually. We were POs together in Midtown North, which is why he asked for me specifically to arrest MacFarlane."

"If it makes you feel any better, Detective, my plan is to go to Yonkers."

"Good." He nodded at me. "Jack."

"Detective," I said back, and Lestrade then went downstairs.

Once he was out of earshot, I looked at Shirley. "Any particular reason why you think 'my dude' is innocent?"

"Several reasons, primary among them being that he is too intelligent to have done something so remarkably idiotic as kill Oldacre immediately after finding out that he is the sole beneficiary of his will."

I just looked at her like she was nuts. "Too intelligent is *not* the way I would describe that guy."

"Do not be fooled by his 'Johnny Mac' demeanor, Jack. Fordham University's Law School is one of the finest in the country and John MacFarlane graduated Magna Cum Laude from there. That requires a level of intelligence greater than that one would perceive from the Johnny Mac persona. Said persona is very obviously cultivated to the lowest-common-denominator in order to appeal to the maximum number of people who derive entertainment from brief videos viewed on their smartphones. In addition, when he discourses on his video channel on the minutiae of the law, he is quite canny and observant—and, more to the point, intelligent and knowledgeable, while also remaining cognizant of the practical implications. His analyses are sufficiently complex that I cannot credit him with making so egregious an error as this."

"Yeah, okay," I said, not entirely sure I bought it, but I was willing to give him the benefit of the doubt. Besides, as an extremely large Black man myself, I had lots of people assuming I was anything but an almost-doctor, so I shouldn't go around making assumptions about other folks.

"The next step is to go to Yonkers."

I nodded. "To visit the parents. Noticed you didn't tell Lestrade *why* we're goin' there."

"Had he asked, I would not have lied," she said pretty emphatically.

"I know," I said quickly, not wanting her to think I'd forgotten that she doesn't like to lie. "So when do we leave?" I asked, knowing that my nap was a lost damn cause.

"First, I must make contact with Johnny's parents, and it will be a difficult conversation."

I thought the next thing was gonna be her asking me to do it, but she surprised me.

"However, I will persevere. You should proceed upstairs to take a nap, as you are very obviously fatigued after spending your overnight shift doing menial work in the hospital lab."

"Uh, okay." I must've looked even more tired than I felt. And hey, good for Shirley trying to be delicate and stuff with people.

I wound up sleeping through to midafternoon. When I woke up, I made some coffee in the little coffeemaker I kept up in the room, and then went downstairs to see what was up. Shirley was sitting at the dining room table. On her left was a mug of tea, on her right was her tablet, and right in front of her was a laptop with a man and a woman on the screen on a video chat. The woman had the same face as Johnny, only older—this had to be the "Moms and Pops" we were going to see in Yonkers. Or, apparently, videochat with.

"I gotta be honest with you," the man was saying, "Jonas was a total fuckin' dick."

"He's not that bad," the woman said. "He sometimes was very sweet when we were dating. But he also had a real cruel streak."

"Yeah," the man said, "back in college he got involved in one of those underground dog fights. Nasty shit."

"He was also a terrible boss," the woman added. "Every worker he had wound up quitting or getting fired for very poor cause. And—" She hesitated.

"If you don't tell her, I will," the man said.

She sighed. "After Sam and I got engaged, he mailed me a framed picture of the two of us, with knife cuts all over my face." Then she visibly shuddered. "I don't want to speak ill of him, as he's died so horribly."

"But there's no way our boy did that," the man—Sam—said loudly. "Absolutely no fuckin' way. I know he acts all goofy online and shit, but our boy wouldn't hurt a *fly*."

Shirley had been making notes on her tablet while the MacFarlanes were talking. Now she looked at the screen. "It would be best for everyone—particularly your son—if you were completely honest, Ms. MacFarlane."

"You're right, of course, Ms. Holmes. But I don't know what else to say. Jonas was—was not a good person. He was a slob and a jerk."

That got Shirley's attention. "Did you say a slob?"

"Yes," Johnny's mother said. "He never cleaned up after himself. It was really gross."

"Thank you both. I cannot promise that I will be able to help your son, but I will do all that I can to prove that he is innocent of this crime."

"Thank you, Ms. Holmes," the mother said, and Sam also said, "Thanks."

The call ended, and I said, "I guess we don't have to go to Yonkers."

"Sam and Elena MacFarlane preferred to speak over video chat which, if nothing else, saved us some time and effort. I determined several other things while you slept. One, that the fire was set at approximately the time that Johnny left Oldacre's house, which fits the timeline that Detective Jones will likely posit as the reason for assuming his guilt."

"Well, that and the will."

Shirley glared at me for interrupting and then continued. "Two, that Oldacre's nurse—whom I was unable to identify by name—was hired by the Metropolitan Nursing Service."

"I know them," I said. "The hospital uses them when we're short-handed on a shift."

This time she didn't glare, probably because I said something useful. "That is excellent news. If you have any contacts there, I wish to speak to Oldacre's nurse."

"I'll make some calls."

I was about to do that when she went back to listing things. "Three, that Johnny's movements after leaving Norwood are accounted for by his video recordings. The time stamps on his videos prove that he went straight from the Oldacre house to the D train and thence on the mass transit odyssey that he described to us. Indeed, he started the video in the front hallway of the Oldacre house, which is why he was a suspect in the first place."

"How's that help?"

"As yet, it is impossible to determine. In fact, thus far I have found no evidence to suggest that Johnny is innocent, beyond my disbelief that he could possibly have been so stupid. While I would agree that there is a good-sized subset of humanity that would, in fact, be so idiotic as to kill someone immediately upon learning that they are the beneficiary of their victim's will, I remain sure that Johnny is not part of that subset."

Shirley then turned back to her tablet and started making more notes. I waited a second to make sure she didn't have anything else to say, then I went back upstairs to where my phone was.

After gulping down a lot more coffee, I called a couple of the nurses I was on good terms with, and was able to track down the one Oldacre hired.

Shirley asked me to make contact with her, and specifically ask her about why Oldacre kept the place so clean. I figured she was asking that 'cause of the MacFarlanes referring to Oldacre as a slob, which didn't exactly track with Johnny's line about how it was the cleanest house he ever saw.

Turns out the nurse was Maddie, who I knew from the hospital. She told me: "The place was a pigsty when I first interviewed with him, which was weird, because he said he was a germophobe. But when I took the job, the place was spic-and-span. He asked me to keep the place clean so the germs didn't get to him."

When I passed that on to Shirley, she got that thoughtful look she gets. "The behavior Johnny described did not match that of a germophobe. He described them as shaking hands, plus he coughed in public in Johnny's presence, but exhibited no behavior that caused comment by Johnny. Plus, the 'pigsty' reference your friend Maddie made matches the description by the MacFarlanes, but not his self-description as a germophobe." She then stood up. "I must speak with Detective Jones."

She called the 52nd Precinct, and actually got through to Jones, who agreed to meet with us. Then we took a car service up to the precinct house on Webster Avenue in the Bronx.

We got taken up to the second floor where the detectives were and met Detective Peter Jones. He was a Black man, as tall as me, but way skinnier. We introduced ourselves and went to his desk in the middle of the bullpen. He only had one guest chair, but I was fine with standing while Shirley took the chair.

"Look," Jones said, "I'm only talkin' to you 'cause me and Guillaume are tight. But this shit's open and shut, a'ight? Tell me what you gotta tell me, but far as I can see, I got me a closed motherfuckin' case, which means I'm happy, my sergeant's happy, an' my inspector's happy. I like bein' happy. Now you gonna tell me things that make me unhappy?"

"I am unable to determine what will dictate your emotional state, Detective, but I do wish to ask a few questions that will have a bearing on my own opinion of the case."

"Okay. Only reason I give a shit about your opinion is 'cause Guillaume told me you saved his ass on the Teco Teco case last year. That case gave him fuckin' nightmares, so if you helped him nail Teco Teco, you're at least worth havin' a conversation with. So go on, ask."

"Have you positively identified the remains as belonging to Jonas Oldacre?"

"As best we can, yeah. Bits of burned clothes all matched, so did the ring he was wearin', and he was in the dude's *bathroom*."

"But have you identified him via DNA?"

"What for? Look, gettin' DNA from a corpse that's burned *that* bad? It ain't easy and it ain't cheap. We got us a budget, and they don't like us fuckin' with it. 'Sides, even if we do *somehow* get DNA from a crispy-fried corpse, ain't got shit to compare it to, since Oldacre's DNA ain't in the system. After they put the fire out, only things left in that house was water, soot, and bleach from all the damn wipe-downs in the place. Fire started in the bathroom, and anything in there we'd compare DNA to got burnt. And there ain't nothin' else in the house to compare the corpse's DNA *to.* I know that everyone on the tee vee loves their fuckin' DNA, but it ain't the be-all and fuckin' end-all."

"I am aware of that, Detective," Shirley said, "but my own awareness is less important than the awareness of Mr. Oldacre. My next question is this: when I inspected the Oldacre house on Google Earth, I noticed a shed behind the house. Is that still there?"

"Yeah. Fire didn't hit it, though."

"Did you inspect the shed?"

"One of the POs did. Just a buncha tools."

"I see. And my final question: What evidence is there to support your arrest?"

"Fingerprint." Jones grinned when he saw the look on Shirley's face. "Yeah, thought that'd get you. Homeboy left a thumbprint right on the front hallway wall."

"It did 'get me,' Detective, but in fact that confirms my theory of the case, to wit, that Johnny Mac did *not* set the fire that killed Jonas Oldacre." She pulled her phone out and started playing with it. She then held it screen-out toward Jones. "Take a look at this."

Jones winced. "Fuck, no, not another one of his damn 'Johnny Mac Tells It Like It Is' videos. Been watchin' them since I arrested his ass, and that's hours of my life I am *not* gettin' back."

"I do not require you to watch the entire video, merely the opening of the one recorded when he departed the Oldacre residence on the night of the fire."

Jones, however, wasn't looking at it. "I already watched it, a'ight? He was just makin' an alibi for himself, but the Arson Squad already said he coulda set the fire and then started that video right after. So it's a shitty alibi, and I ain't watchin' it again."

"You watched it, but you did not *see* what is of import. Look at the *walls*, Detective."

"What?"

"The video commences in the front hall of the house. The very same location where you found your thumbprint—in a house, I might add, that was meticulously cleaned."

Jones frowned, and then grabbed Shirley's phone. He watched the video until Johnny left the house, used his finger to bring it back to the beginning and watched it again.

"Fuuuuuuuuuuuuuuuck. No fingerprint."

"You claim to have watched the video in question, therefore you're aware that Johnny was riding various forms of mass transit after this, then returned to Manhattan on the Staten Island Ferry to answer viewer e-mails, and then he learned of the BOLO, and then he took the A train north to come to my residence. He had no opportunity to return to the Bronx to touch the wall in question. Which begs the question of how it got there."

Jones was rubbing his temples, his eyes shut. "Which is reasonable fuckin' doubt, which means the ADA ain't gonna touch this motherfucker and we'll probably have to kick him. *Fuck*. This is *not* gonna make me, my sergeant, or my inspector happy, lady."

"Perhaps I may return joy to your life by providing you with a way to making this case more palatable to you, your sergeant, your inspector, and even the assistant district attorney."

"How you gonna do that?"

"Simple. Assemble a few patrol officers and escort Jack and myself to the crime scene."

Jones stared at her for a few seconds, then shook his head. "A'ight, but if this don't make me happy, then I'm prob'ly gonna arrest your ass for wastin' my time."

"I have made a thorough study of the laws of the city and state of New York, Detective, and that is *not* a criminal act for which one can be arrested."

"Whatever. Let's go."

Jones got on his radio and called for a patrol car to meet us at the address on Rochambeau Avenue. Then he took us to the motor pool and signed out a car to drive us over in.

The house was one of those old two-story houses from the 1920s that you saw all over the outer boroughs. It had a small front porch and a driveway on the right-hand side between it and the house next door that was just wide enough for a car. The house was covered in soot and had yellow crime-scene tape across the porch.

The blue-and-white was parked in the driveway, and Jones pulled in behind it. As she got out of the back seat, Shirley said, "Let us go to the rear."

One of the POs looked at Jones and asked, "What's going on?"

"I'll letcha know soon's I find out."

I snickered.

In the small backyard, which we got to via the driveway, you could see the really bad fire damage. Half the back wall was gone, and you could see what was left of the bathroom—which wasn't much.

But Shirley wasn't going to the back door of the house, she was going to the shed all the way at the back of the property, up against the backyard of the house on the parallel street. The shed was old and wooden and ramshackle and looked like it was gonna fall apart any second.

Shirley walked up to the door, which was latched shut, but not locked. It slid open with a creak.

Jones had his hands on his hips. "I *told* you that we checked it out. It's just a damn toolshed!"

Shirley spent a few seconds looking at the inside of the shed, then she turned to face Jones. "Did you perform a full search?"

"No. Why the fuck should we?"

"I believe it would be useful to your case. And since this shed is on the same property as the crime scene, you do not require a warrant to perform a search, as this is considered part of the crime scene. If I am correct, then you will have a closed case."

Jones laughed nastily. "You're tellin' me that if I search this shed, I get a closed murder?"

"No, you will have a closed *case*."

"A'ight, fine, what-the-fuck-ever." He looked at the POs. "You heard the lady, check the place out."

"Make particular note," she said, "of the rear wall, which is approximately 20 feet from the front of the shed. This is noteworthy, given that the shed itself is approximately 30 feet deep."

The two uniforms went in, and Shirley came to stand next to me. I asked her, "Why do you suddenly think this isn't a murder?"

"Because the house has no DNA to compare to the corpse."

"I don't—" And then I figured it out, and smiled. "He didn't want the corpse to be able to be ID'd."

"If I am correct in my assumptions. But I believe the evidence will support those assumptions."

"Ow!" That was someone inside the shed.

"Get your ass out of there," someone else inside the shed said.

A few seconds later, the two POs led a broad-shouldered, bearded guy out into the backyard. One of the officers said, "The lady was right—the back wall was fake. Found this asshole in a little room behind it. Had a cot and a mini fridge."

Shirley indicated the person and said, "Jonas Oldacre, I presume. As a contractor, constructing such an addition would be child's play."

Oldacre was scowling. "I'm not saying a damn word."

Jones was just staring. "Mother*fuck*." Then he turned to Shirley. "How the *fuck* did you know?"

"My suspicions were first raised when I was informed of Mr. Oldacre's slovenly habits, which were at odds with Johnny's descriptions of this house as the neatest he'd ever seen. It was confirmed by his hired nurse, who described him as a germophobe, which was at odds with his behavior. However, if he intended to make it difficult to obtain DNA to compare to the corpse that was found in the fire, keeping the house obsessively neat would aid in that goal. The fingerprint also had to have been placed after the fire, which could only have been accomplished by someone working for or on behalf of the NYPD or by someone hiding on the property. I considered the latter to be much more likely. In addition, I knew that Oldacre held a grudge against Johnny's mother for breaking their engagement and marrying another. Johnny was the product of that union, and it seemed in character for Oldacre to resent Johnny as the child that should've been his, and so he framed him for murder."

That got Oldacre to start talking. "Are you *kidding* me? No way *that* dumb kid should've been mine. If Elena had married me, we'd have had a *different* kid who *made* something of himself, not spending all his damn time making stupid videos!"

Jones shook his head. "Get him the fuck out of here. Book him for arson."

Shirley said, "You will likely need to book him for corpse desecration, and possibly also grave-robbing, depending on the source of the corpse he burned in the fire while wearing his clothes and his ring."

I looked down at Shirley. "You didn't figure *that* part out?"

"Given time I could have, but it was of less moment than exonerating Johnny and allowing him to be freed from suspicion and incarceration."

As the POs took Oldacre down the driveway to their blue-and-white, Jones said, "A'ight, gotta give props. You nailed this motherfucker. I see why Guillaume is always sayin' the sun shines out your ass."

"I would never use so vulgar a phrase," Shirley said, "but thank you. I did say that you would get a closed case and happy superiors."

"Yeah, I ain't sure about the second part, 'cause I'm still gonna have to kick MacFarlane, and ain't nobody gonna be happy about that."

"Given Johnny's legal background, to hold him for a murder that did not even occur would probably make your superiors even less happy."

"Point." Jones sighed.

"In addition, there is no need to mention my involvement in your report—feel free to credit only yourself."

"Thanks. And hey—you need a favor, just ask."

I smiled. Shirley had been collecting these favors from the detectives in the 24th Precinct—not just Lestrade, but several others—and now she was branching out to the Bronx.

Though I was still wondering where the corpse came from . . .

My Tombstone Days by John H. Watson, M.D.

by

Steven Philip Jones

March 20, 1882. Tucson Depot, Arizona Territory.

Wyatt Earp watches a coffin containing the body of his younger brother Morgan being loaded onto a train. Two nights earlier, Wyatt had watched Morgan playing pool at Campbell & Hatch's in the town of Tombstone when someone fired twice through the saloon's back door. The first bullet missed Wyatt and hit the wall behind him, but the second struck Morgan's back and an hour later Wyatt's brother was dead.

Accompanying Morgan's body to Colton, California for burial on their father Nicholas' farm are Wyatt's older brothers Virgil and James, their families, and Virgil's doctor Jude Watson. Doctor Jude has been treating Virgil since the former deputy US marshal was shot and his left arm crippled by an unseen assassin just before midnight on December 28. Wyatt replaced Virgil as marshal the next day and is convinced the bushwhacker belongs to a pack of holdup men, killers, and cattle thieves known as the Cochise County Cowboys that has had numerous disagreements with the Earps.

As Wyatt watches the coffin, two allies come stand beside him. One is his friend John Henry "Doc" Holliday. The gambler, gunslinger, and Southern gentleman is just 31 years old but skeletal from tuberculosis. The other is Dr. Jude's youngest brother, John Watson, a middle-sized, strongly built man of 30 with a square jaw and thick neck. Wyatt asks, "Have you seen them?"

"Neither hide nor hair," Holliday drawls, to which John Watson adds, "Neither have McMasters and Johnson." Sherman McMasters and Turkey Creek Jack Johnson are former Cowboys who agreed to help Wyatt watch over the Earp party.

Wyatt nods then tells Watson, "I appreciate you coming along, John. This isn't your fight."

"I have a brother on that train, too."

Wyatt nods again. "Nothing counts as much as blood, does it? What about Sherlock? Has he seen anything?"

Sherlock Holmes, youngest son of wealthy rancher Marschall Holmes, had also come along, but, "He went his own way after a baggage clerk told him some Cowboys are searching every train that passes through the depot. They also said if they find Virgil they'll kill him on sight."

Wyatt's grip on his shotgun tightens as he stares through the windows of the railroad car where a conductor is checking the Earp party's tickets. "If any Cowboys are here, all they're going to find is Hell."

Excerpts from **My Tombstone Days**
by John H. Watson, M.D.

I departed Brunckow's Cabin and its famous little cemetery early on the morning of September 10 and rode northeast to Tombstone, arriving that afternoon just as a surge of exuberant herdsmen flooded out a building on Fourth Street. As the yobbos rolled past me, one galah walked himself straight into Carboni and slapped my horse's croup. "Get this canner out of my way!" To my eye the cattleman couldn't have cut a lame cow from a shade tree, but when I tugged my Sharps slightly from its saddle scabbard he displayed the good sense to sulk away. Slipping my rifle back into the scabbard, I continued to Freemont Street and at last hitched Carboni in front of Fly's boarding house, a one-story clapboard with what might be called an enclosed widow's walk atop its front end. Along the alley side of the building was a flight of steps leading to the widow's walk, and nailed at eye-level near the bottom of the flight was a plank with the words "Dr. Jude—Office Upstairs" roughly written in sheep-marking paint.

Grabbing my saddlebags and Sharps, I walked up to Jude's office. It was not much larger than a jailhouse cell with a blanket hung cater-corner to partition the room in half. I called for Jude and he stepped out from behind the makeshift curtain. "John! You're two days early!"

"I made better time than I anticipated." We shook hands and clapped shoulders before I draped my saddlebags over an empty chair and leaned my rifle against it.

Jude sat me down in another chair and fetched a much-appreciated glass of cool water. "Why didn't you send a wire to let me know you'd be here today?"

"I'm afraid there are very few telegraph offices along the San Pedro."

My elder brother is a little over six feet in height, brawnier than I, and a citizen of the world, but when he heard this he blanched. "I thought you were coming through the Dragoon Mountains because of Chief Nana."

"Along the San Pedro was easier, and I was most careful. I know the very appreciable effect war-whooping has on the roots of a man's hair."

"Still, you take too many risks."

"It's just my nature. Should we let James know I'm early?"

Jude fixed a paternal stare upon me. "Nothing would make me happier than a reconciliation between you two, but our brother's attitude hasn't softened."

"But why? I never begrudged him."

"I think that's commendable, but Warnecke was like a son to him."

"And Constable Webb-Brown was my friend and comrade! He saved my life in Glenrowan but I failed to save his." I could have said more but there was no point, so I asked, "How is his drinking?"

"It's no worse. Which I also think is commendable, considering his job with Wells Fargo is becoming increasingly taxing. There are more and more stage holdups occurring throughout the territory. In fact, he's attending the trial of a couple of stage robbers right now, but he and a friend will be by afterwards to tell me what happened."

"I think that trial just let out. A gang of stockmen nearly

ran over me as I entered town. In fact, I almost tangled with one." I described the rude herdsman and what happened.

"That sounds like Frank Stilwell." Before Jude could say more he was interrupted by the sound of footsteps ascending the stairway and the arrival of two visitors.

The first to enter was James. The shortest of we three brothers, he had gained more than a little weight since Wantabadgery and his face displayed the early signs of telangiectasia. He expressed very little recognition when he saw me, glancing instead over his shoulder to inform his companion, "This is John Watson."

The second man to enter was approximately the same age as me and same height as Jude, but was as slim as a mesquite sapling. He possessed an educated man's sharp and piercing grey eyes, a thin, hawk-like nose, and a square and prominent chin. He also had the weathered skin and calloused hands of a tar or jackaroo. The lean stranger quickly appraised my Sharps with his eyes before he gripped my hand with unexpected strength and cordially said, "How are you? Have you come to join Dr. Jude or open your own practice?"

"I'm still reckoning that over." I should have pressed the man to explain the reasons for his supposition but his accent took me by surprise. "You're an Englishman."

Jude said, "John, this is Sherlock Holmes. His family owns the Enola Ranch in Sulphur Springs Valley." Then he asked James how the trial went.

James huffed and dropped himself into a chair.

"That well, eh?"

Curious, I inquired, "Jude said a stage was robbed."

When James failed to reply Holmes said, "Two days ago. The Sandy Bob from Tombstone to Bisbee, a small copper mining town near the Mexican border. Two masked men held it up, one of who kept referring to the money as 'sugar.' "

James grumbled, " 'Give up the sugar.' 'Don't hide any sugar from us.' Everyone on board knew right then that that was Stilwell. The driver even recognized Stilwell in spite of his mask."

I asked, "Is that Frank Stilwell?"

James didn't answer so Jude said, "Yes. He's Sheriff Behan's deputy. It was Sherlock who tracked him down."

"*'Felix, qui potuit rerum congoscere causas.'* "[1] Holmes told me, "I was in Tombstone when news of the holdup arrived and I volunteered to join James' posse. We located a footprint with a distinctive heel while searching in the Mule Mountains, and in Bisbee I located a bootmaker who recognized it. He also identified Stilwell as a recent customer. Soon after we located Stilwell and his companion Pete Spencer at a Bisbee corral. Stilwell's boots had new custom heels. Nevertheless, when we returned to Tombstone rumors most likely started by Behan were spreading that Wyatt Earp and Doc Holliday were responsible for the holdup."

James pointed a finger at Holmes. "Which may explain why Judge Wallace dismissed the state charges. That makes more sense than some Cowboys swearing Stilwell and Spencer were with them two days ago."

I was ignorant about the Cowboys so Holmes explained their history to me, beginning with their being run out of Texas by the Rangers and concluding with his own family's troubles with the rustlers. "We've lost nearly 50 head to them over the last two years, so my father is trying to rally the press and Tombstone's businesses against them. Meanwhile my brother Mycroft is in Prescott petitioning the territorial government to act, and I am attempting to collect evidence of their crimes."

"Which," Jude commented, "has made your family about as popular with the Cowboys as Virgil Earp, his brothers, and Doc."

"*'Cognitur homo in consortio et custodit.'*[2] Or I should say 'enemies.' The Cowboys have accused Doc and Virgil's brother Wyatt of helping a Mexican patrol ambush five of their number as they were herding stolen cattle through Guadalupe Canyon two months ago. They even allege Doc suffered a leg

---

1 "Happy is he who can trace effects to their causes." —Virgil

2 "A man is known by the company he keeps. —Aesop

wound during the ambush and left Tombstone to recuperate at home."

This came as a disappointment. "John Henry is in Valdosta? I wrote him I was coming."

Jude said, "He went with Kate Elder to the San Agustín Fair in Tucson to gamble. Don't worry, his room here is paid through next month so he'll be back. Which reminds me, John, there's an open room next to mine if you'd care to board here."

I spent the next few weeks reacquainting myself with my medical skills as I assisted Jude. Doctoring in Tombstone was much the same as it had been in Ballarat when it was still predominantly a mining town, practiced mainly by instinct, hot applications, diet, enemas, and common sense. And just like in old Ballarat a doctor had less chance of earning a respectable living than the prospectors. Jude told me that first day, "My patients pay me when they can," and when I inquired about his records he confessed he didn't keep any. "I just depend on God for bookkeeping." Medicine was a sacred profession to Jude and much like a pastor he always wore a dark frock-tailed coat, the American uniform of a doctor.

Things got a bit more exciting starting one afternoon in October when Virgil Earp visited Jude's office to ask me to fetch John Henry. Several Cowboys including Stilwell were making threats against the Earps and the Enola Ranch, claiming the two families were persecuting them, and Virgil prudently believed an extra gun would help keep the outlaws in check.

Two days later, I arrived in Tucson and tracked John Henry to one of the gaming tents outside the Plaza de las Armas. Gratefully I spotted him before he spotted me. Painfully familiar as I am with tuberculosis, I still needed a moment to tamp down my obvious shock at John Henry's deterioration. He had always been thin but wiry. Now he was skin and bones with a death head's countenance, but upon noticing me the old imp came out, complete with his familiar smirk and twinkle.

"Well, damn my memory! You must be here looking for me, John. I know you only gamble with your life, never your money."

Kate Elder was not pleased when John Henry agreed to come help the Earps and Holmeses, especially after he insisted she remain, but Kate turned out to be the least of John Henry's concerns.

We rode into Tombstone two nights later. After stabling our horses at the corral near Fly's boarding house we started walking to Virgil's office, but as we passed the Alhambra Saloon a stumpy, vexed-looking cattleman called out: "He told you!" As the cattleman stomped toward us, John Henry quietly informed me, "This poltroon is Ike Clanton. He's been worse than a poison oak rash ever since his father was killed in that Guadalupe ambush." Then in a dismissive voice, "Why, Ike, by the sway of your swagger I'd say you've been drinking."

"Don't get saucy with me or there won't be enough left of you to snore! I know Wyatt told you! He had to!"

"I am too hungry and far too thirsty to inquire what Wyatt supposedly told me, so let us discuss the subject later. Excuse me."

As we stepped around Clanton, he spat and pointed to my friend's walking stick. "What's with that cane? Get yourself shot in the leg?"

John Henry continued strolling, his back towards Clanton, but I swiveled round to march backwards, my Sharps held ready in case the Cowboy got any notions. As the gap between us widened, I spun myself around and John Henry muttered, "I fear you may have stumbled into a bit of a hullaballoo, John."

Jude spent the next several days in the ranch country helping a family of squatters, leaving me to nurse a gaggle of children with earaches and a young woman with smallpox who was terrified she would scratch a pustule and scar her nose. In time I found myself needing to do more than go out to the cowlot for a good laugh, so one afternoon I rode Carboni to an arroyo north of town to hone my aim and relax. An hour or so later, I heard "Hello in the gully!" and saw Holmes approaching on a black Morgan. "I thought I heard your gunfire. You're the only man in the territory who owns a Sharps."

"Hello! What brings you this way?"

"Town business. I must confess that I admired your rifle when we met." Holmes dismounted.

"And that Dragoon puts my .38 Lightning to shame. Third model?"

"You know your weapons." Holmes dismounted, drew his revolver, and presented it to me butt-first. "Care to see?"

"Certainly. Here, take a look at mine."

"Much obliged." Holmes pulled the lever down to examine the rifle's workings. "It's rather weighty."

"A little more than 12 pounds." Holmes squinted into the breech. "Long throated?"

"Nah yeh, but its freebore is adequate." I tossed him a pill from my cartridge belt. "Here. I've been picking the stems off of that organ pipe cactus at the bend."

"That's over half a mile."

"The peep site is adjustable up to 1200 yards, although I once recorded a hit at fifteen."

"Most impressive." Holmes' eyes kindled as he loaded the chamber, readied himself, and fired. He missed the cactus but shattered a scrub oak 50 yards further. Grinning and rubbing his shoulder, he said, "I'm afraid I failed to take the wind into account."

"And the recoil. But that was a fine stab at it. Some men lose teeth their first try, but anything worth trying is worthy of risk."

"Thank you for the belated warning."

"Mind if I try yours?"

"Please do."

I fired twice at a cactus ten yards away, snapped off two stems, then returned the Dragoon. "It's a fine revolver."

"Thank you." Holmes returned the Sharps. "It's a glorious rifle."

"Thank you." I emptied the chamber, loaded a round, and snapped off another cactus stem. "All it takes is practice."

"If you say so. Are you returning to town soon? Perhaps we could ride in together?" I accepted and after we were on our way he asked, "That recorded shot? Was it a target? An animal? Or man?"

"Marksmanship contest. The furthest I've shot an animal is a rogue water buffalo from 700 yards. That still felt too close. And I shot a man from 1000 yards. One of Captain Moonlite's bushrangers who left me no choice, but I suspect you haven't heard of that bunch here."

"Actually the history of crime is a passion of mine. I have read about the Gardiner-Hall Gang, Ned Kelly, and the Clark Brothers as well as Andrew George Scott, leader of the short-lived Captain Moonlite Gang. I believe they were captured after a gunbattle in the settlement of Wantabadgery after the gang bailed up its citizens. Were you there?"

"I was."

"So were you a trooper? Is that the reason you own a Sharps?"

"I was and it is. Now I'll ask a question. What made you ask me if I came here to help Jude when we met?"

"Well, your Waler, to begin with. Who goes to the trouble of transporting a horse from Australia unless he plans on remaining in America for some considerable time?"

"That doesn't explain how you knew I was a doctor."

A sheepish smirk. "Doc told me. Are you still reckoning?"

"I am. I take pride in my doctoring, but medicine isn't the calling with me that it is for Jude."

"You're more like Doc then?"

"Oi, a big part of how John Henry gauges himself is by his dentistry! We sowed some oats when we were at university in Pennsylvania, I'll give you that. New York City was so nearby. But John Henry had his cap set on becoming a first-rate dentist in Atlanta before contracting tuberculosis."

"Well, Doc did tell me once he only feels calm when he's engaged with a gun or knife or working on someone's teeth. And I only asked if you are still reckoning because you were target practicing. Long-distance marksmanship is not a required skill for a medical practitioner."

"No, but a handy one nonetheless. Besides, a man must unwind sometimes."

"Saloons are closer."

"And I'm not opposed to drinking, gambling, or molls, but anything I do reflects on Jude."

Holmes nodded. "That is commendable. Perhaps James should take your brother into consideration more often if you don't mind my saying."

"Not at all." Not that it would have mattered if I did. Sherlock Holmes obviously possessed no governor when it came to speaking his mind.

Upon entering town Holmes offered to formally introduce me to John Henry's friend Wyatt Earp as Holmes's business was with him. Earp's home was on Freemont between Summer and First and Wyatt was standing outside when we arrived. He was tall like Holmes but blond and athletic with blue eyes and a thick tawny mustache, and he sized me up in a professional manner then pointed at my rifle. "That's a handsome weapon."

"Thank you."

"I trust you got your permit to keep it inside city limits?" Actually I had yet to acquire one in accord with Tombstone Ordinance No. 9, but I suspected Earp was aware of this as he turned to Holmes and told him, "I've got some news. Let's go inside and discuss it." Then glancing my way, "Talk to you soon, Doctor."

I got the message and made a beeline for the marshal's office. As I turned onto Summer, I saw James walking in my direction down Allen and hollered, "Hello! How are you?"

My brother said nothing. Just strolled past.

I glanced back and watched him round the corner at Freemont then walk towards Wyatt's house.

A few nights later Ike Clanton drove a wagon full of beef into Tombstone and parked it at the West End Corral around eleven o'clock. Riding with him was Tom McLaury, another Cowboy. Dusty and thirsty, the men proceeded to the Grand Hotel, then the Alhambra, and finally The Occidental Saloon.

About two hours after that a knocking roused me from slumber and I opened my door to find: "Holmes!"

"If it's convenient, could you come with me?"

"In such an hour?"

"If it's inconvenient, come anyway. And kindly bring your rifle."

Holmes was most determined, so I did as he asked and followed him to Clanton's wagon. "This is Enola beef. I discovered the butchered carcasses and followed the wagon's trail here."

"But there's no proof this is your beef. Not without the hides and your brand."

"No, but I still must report the veracious news to Virgil."

At the marshal's office we were told Virgil had gone to The Occidental to meet Wyatt and Morgan, and there we were informed to our amazement that the three Earps and John Henry were engaged in a private poker game with Behan, Ike, and McLaury. Holmes motioned me to follow him outside, where he confided, "This gathering . . . it almost feels as if events are purposely coalescing." He paused, weighed something in his mind, then asked, "Will you swear to a confidence?"

I saw no harm in it, so I said, "I do."

"Do you recall at Wyatt's house when he asked to discuss some news with me in private?"

"Yes."

"Wyatt is anxious to put an end to the rumors that he and Doc were behind the Bisbee holdup, so he offered to cut a deal with Ike Clanton. If Clanton provided evidence that Stilwell and Spencer were behind the Bisbee stage holdup, Wyatt would arrange for Clanton to furtively receive the Wells Fargo reward, an amount of $6000."

I whistled. "But why approach Clanton?"

"Because Clanton covets some ranchland Stilwell owns

near the New Mexico border and he is the most untrustworthy cur among the Cowboys."

"Did James agree to this?"

"He did and therein lies the problem. James was drinking with Ike Clanton on the night you and Doc returned from Tucson and he let slip that he knew about the deal."

I was accustomed to my brother's braggadocious, but this inanity amazed me. "So that's why Clanton confronted John Henry. He must have thought if James knew than Doc had to know, too."

"I agree. In the meantime, however, I have the problem of our beef to consider." Holmes stood thinking for several moments then returned to the saloon. I followed him inside and after we checked our weapons at the bar I followed Holmes to the back room, where, to my further amazement, he inquired if he could join the game.

Neither Clanton nor McLaury looked at Holmes as John Henry said, "The more the merrier. John?" He knew better, of course, but I still said, "I'll just watch, thank you."

And it was quite a show.

Holmes proved as adept as John Henry at reading his opponents as he spent the next few hours indefatigably winning all of Clanton and McLaury's cash as well as the beef in Clanton's wagon. "Although," Holmes commented as the game broke up just before dawn, "you can't truly say it was ever your beef, Ike. But this money will compensate my family somewhat for the loss of our cattle." Clanton's blood appeared to be on the boil but Virgil warned him, "I am going down home now, to go to bed. I don't want you to raise any disturbance while I am in bed."

After Holmes and I collected our firearms and departed to take possession of the beef, I told him, "Clanton has no cause to bark. You spotted those cattle duffer's tells fair dinkum."

"I didn't spot. I observed." Nevertheless, Holmes seemed troubled. "In my rush for vengeance I'm afraid something only now occurred to me. It is very possible that Ike's fellow Cowboys have learned about his deal with Wyatt. Ike may have intended this beef to be an expiatory offering. If I am right, then I fear Ike may do something rash." Holmes paused. "I'll return the beef to our ranch, but shall return immediately afterwards."

"If you're right about Ike, then I best ride with you."

Holmes started to protest, then stopped. "Good old Watson. Well, you know the risk. Tag along if you wish."

What happened next is as much legend as history.

It was around a quarter to three when Holmes and I returned to Tombstone, and as we rode further into town the chilly air grew heavier with apprehension until it was as oppressive as Ballarat humidity. Our destination had been Virgil's office to inquire if anything regarding Clanton had transpired during our absence, but as we passed Hafford's Corner I heard a woman shout, "Here they come!" I squeezed reins, thinking she was referring to us, but everyone's attention was directed north towards Freemont, and I looked up in time to glimpse John Henry, Virgil, Morgan, and Wyatt turn left around the corner. Holmes, meanwhile, had found Behan standing in front of the butcher Bauer's shop. I joined them and asked, "What's going on?"

Behan pointed his chin at me. "The Earps and Holliday insists on disarming them."

"Disarming who?"

"The brothers Clanton and McLaury. Also Billy Claiborne and maybe Wes Fuller, too. I told Virgil I disarmed them but he wouldn't listen."

Holmes asked, "Where are the Cowboys?"

"In the corral beside Fly's, so there best not be any trouble. Virgil knows it's legal to go heeled in a livery stable."

"What are you jabbering about? Did you disarm them or not?"

Before Behan could reply the ball opened.

Two gunshots fired almost simultaneously exploded. Horses screamed and a smoky haze bloomed over Fly's. Then there was what sounded like a string of firecrackers and two loud bangs, in reality a spate of revolver fire and two loads of buckshot.

I buried my spurs, drew my Sharps, and charged towards Freemont.

Holmes rode right beside me, Dragoon held ready.

We rounded the corner but halted to avoid trampling Clanton, unarmed and fleeing the fight, while the Cowboys and the lawmen swapped gunfire in a narrow vacant lot between Fly's and the Harwood House.

Stinging gunsmoke, confined between the buildings, obscured the air like haar, but I could see that Virgil had been shot in the calf. I could also see a Cowboy, Frank McLaury's brother Tom, shoot over the saddle of a horse and wing Morgan across the shoulders. Morgan buckled and Wyatt bellowed "Stay down!" as he emerged from the smoke to protect Morgan, shooting one round after another with intimidating calmness. Tom McLaury, his pistol empty, reached over the saddle for a rifle but the horse bolted and a shotgun blast from somewhere pelted him. McLaury bumbled into Freemont and died in front of a telegraph pole. At the same time Wyatt and Virgil shot a young Cowboy, Ike's brother Billy, who toppled against a wall then fell. Meanwhile Frank McLaury loomed out in retreat, firing his pistol and using his horse for cover. John Henry followed from out of the swirl, shooting his Thunderer until McLaury tagged him in the hip. I aimed my Sharps as McLaury crowed, "I have you now, you son of a bitch!" and John Henry smirked and sniggered, "Blaze away, you're a daisy if you do." Then an explosion louder than the two shots that started the gunfight rent the air as Holmes and I put McLaury down.

Excerpt's end

Dr. Jude—Office Upstairs

John Watson stares at the plank as he holds an antique pocket watch in his hands.

Two nights earlier he had been at the Tucson Depot keeping watch with Holliday and Wyatt on the Earp party's railroad car when a shotgun blast erupted from the carriage. Wyatt dashed towards the car and Holliday followed, but John Watson paused when he spotted the conductor draw a Colt Dragoon from under his coat and fire towards the back of the carriage. Frank Stilwell then scurried down the steps clutching his right arm, and spotting Watson dashed up the platform.

John dogged Stilwell across the tracks into the darkness.

When John closed the gap between them to about 15 feet Stilwell swerved around and charged.

John drew his Lightning and pistol-whipped Stilwell.

Stilwell stumbled, dazed, but seemed to recover his senses when he heard someone step up behind him. He turned around and gawked at Wyatt holding the shotgun.

Stilwell grabbed the shotgun by its barrels.

Wyatt forced the gun down until the muzzle was just underneath Stilwell's heart.

Stilwell, wide-eyed, stammered, "Morg!" A second later, he stammered "Morg!" again.

Wyatt fired one barrel and then the other barrel before Stilwell hit the ground.

Holliday arrived as the two blasts rattled off to silence and stared at Stilwell's body. "He's armed. Why didn't he go for his gun?"

Wyatt didn't speak.

Holliday then looked at Watson with an expression that froze his blood. "You better go to the train."

When John rushed into the passenger car, he found Holmes wearing a borrowed conductor's uniform, unharmed, as were the Earps, but Jude lay deathly still. Kneeling, John verified his brother had been killed, and then eventually searched the pockets of Jude's frock-tailed coat. Rummaging through the asafetida, thermometers, and horehound candy, John at last pulled out the pocket watch.

The next day John returned to Tombstone with the body of his brother, whose funeral just ended in Old City Cemetery. Two fence posts had been sunk at the head of Jude's grave and the plank nailed to them.

Coming up beside him, James Watson says his first words to John since his brother arrived in Tombstone: "I do believe Jude would like that marker."

"You're speaking to me now?"

"Yeah . . . well—"

John cuts James off with a backhand.

James collapses beside Jude's grave and nearly tumbles into the pit.

John tosses the watch to his brother. "Here. You're heir now."

Still dazed, James shouts, "What's this?"

"All that's left of the Watson inheritance."

"I don't want Dad's watch!"

"Then sell it. Or pawn it. It's yours, though, whether you want it or not."

With great effort, James struggles to his feet.

"I don't know why you opened your mouth to Ike Clanton and I don't care. You can own up to it or try to drown your sins like after Wantabadgery, but either way I'm through with you."

Finished, John leaves the cemetery to start towards town, but Holmes is waiting for him, seated on the Morgan. "Are you done reckoning yet, doctor?"

"Yes."

"And you're leaving Tombstone?"

"Yes."

"You know, Wyatt hasn't finished with Ike and the other Cowboys yet. He could use some help when he rides after them."

"John Henry can handle that risk. Are you going with them?"

A tinge of embarrassment blushed Holmes's cheeks. "How can I? I feel I'm as much to blame for the gunfight and what happened at the Tucson Depot as James. Plus I'm bone-weary of frontier justice. I'd like to try my hand at something more civilized. So I am going to San Francisco."

"What about the Enola?"

"That's my father's ranch, and Mycroft is the heir."

John glances back as James stares into Jude's grave. "I think I know how you feel."

"Do you? Then perhaps you'd care to ride along to California?" Holmes smiles determinedly. "After all, a good doctor can hang his shingle out anywhere."

Hella AFK

by

Jennifer Brozek

"What do you mean 'something's off with Ashley'? I don't understand." Helen tucked into the last of her lunch—meatloaf, one of the good cafeteria food staples—as she surveyed the large room like she and her companion were expecting to be attacked.

Raksha did not roll her eyes even though it was clear she wanted to. "You had a scene with her yesterday, did you not?" She paused, folded her paper napkin in a neat, triple pocket pattern and added, "They won't be eating in the lunchroom today."

"Who?"

"Sally, et al . . ." Raksha said with a self-satisfied smile. "Got caught smoking. Dirty habit. Currently in lunchtime detention."

Focusing back on her friend, Helen's eyes narrowed. "You still smoke. I smell it on you."

"I know. Dirty habit. Couldn't help blowing smoke into the VP's office window. Are you disappointed or relieved?"

"Both. And, yeah, I had a scene with Ashley last night. It was between Rolf and Alexandra."

Raksha tilted her head. "And? What did you think?"

Helen shrugged. "It was okay. Not the usual prose Rolf usually uses. But, I think she was distracted. Her roleplay was off. Her dad's new girlfriend bugs her."

Now Raksha did roll her eyes. "I'm not talking about how she RPed. I'm talking about the way she's changed her punctuation style. People have good and bad acting days. They don't change their punctuation overnight."

Helen shook her head, her brow furrowed.

Peering at her companion, Raksha asked, "You really didn't notice?

Typical. One, she's now using curly brackets instead of double colons to indicate telepathic speech. Two, she's addicted to ellipses like she never has been before. Three, she's using asterisks for hug motions and such instead of parentheses."

"Well, yeah. Sometimes styles change." Helen shrugged. "I mean, I've changed how I do my actions. I've added in dialogue in the middle of movement now."

"Yes," Raksha allowed, "and it has added a lot to your scene work, but you've changed only one thing at a time. This all happened at once. Check your logs. About a week ago, everything around Ashley's RP changed. I don't think it's her at the keyboard."

Helen sat up straight. "Hacked?"

"No. Her IP is still the same. I checked."

"Then what?"

"I don't know. Calling wouldn't help. It's not like we've actually spoken voice before. I have nothing but her prose to identify her by. Do you have another scene scheduled?"

Helen nodded. "Tonight. Our usual date night for Alexandra and Rolf, but Alexandra's still pissed at Rolf making a deal with the Order of the Sacred Flame. You know?"

Raksha smirked. "I know. It surprised me a little when Rolf agreed. The Order still wants Alexandra to do them that favor. Why else would they send their best negotiator in with something Rolf needed? Still, it's one of the many things that made me take notice."

"You just love tormenting my little seer."

"Yep, and you love it when that happens."

"Yep." Helen paused. "I'll see tonight. You know? Just to make sure. I'll throw a couple of 'remember when' comments into the mix to see. I'll know for sure if that's Ashley playing Rolf or not."

Alexandra enters the Secret Glade.

Alexandra glances at Rolf.

Rolf Nightsong is elegant and handsome in his tailored calfskin trousers of midnight black, red linen shirt—open at the chest—and tall boots. His black hair hangs around his face in gentle waves and his black eyes pierce your soul in a single glance. There is a hint of gleaming fangs in his slight smile.

Alexandra looks into the beyond.

There are no lurkers in the Secret Glade.

Rolf glances at Alexandra.

Rolf has looked at you!

You have looked at yourself!

Alexandra Videre is a vision of loveliness. Her blond hair seems to glow in any light and her deep blue eyes recall the sea. She is wearing a beautiful gown of lavender velvet and understated gold jewelry.

Rolf: You look lovely, my dear.

Alexandra smiles prettily.

Alexandra: Thank you, my love. You look wonderful as well. What do you have planned for us tonight?

Rolf glances around the Secret Glade.

Rolf: I thought we could picnic here. Something simple and pleasant.

Alexandra glances around the Secret Glade.

The property of Rolf Nightsong, the Secret Glade is a hidden oasis within the Black Forest. Surrounded by a mixture of oak, ash, maple, and birch trees, the field of everblooming flowers and lush grass invite travelers to rest their weary heads and enjoy the verdant, peaceful glade. This is a place of safety and security—as long as you do not break any of the laws of this forest or its Lord.

Alexandra: A picnic? How positively unique for you. I would love that.

Rolf busies himself, setting up a picnic feast. He starts with a checkered blanket...followed by the picnic basket filled with delicacies.

Rolf settles on the blanket and opens the picnic basket. He pulls out plates of fruit and pastries as well as a bottle of wine and glasses.

Rolf: Join me, my dear.

Alexandra sits upon the picnic blanket. "What made you decide on a picnic repast tonight?" she asks as she settles in.

Rolf: It is something different.

Rolf smiles...his fangs barely present. {{I know you long for new experiences. I thought I would offer that to you.}}

Rolf gives Alexandra a glass of wine.

Alexandra accepts the glass of wine, but does not drink from it. "Really? I thought you were just trying to distract me from your most recent endeavors."

Rolf: {{My recent endeavors...? What do you mean?}}

Alexandra: I mean your dealings with the Order of the Sacred Flame! You know what they want with me. You know how dangerous that is. Now that I've denied them, they seek to bind me to them through you.

Rolf: {{That...is not true.}}

Alexandra: It /is/ true. How can you not see it? Less than two weeks ago, you vowed never to speak with them. Last week, you went back on your word.

Alexandra: I know you've had dealings with them. They wanted me to know. How can you explain that?

You whisper to Rolf: Is everything okay? You seem distracted tonight.

Rolf whispers to you: Yeah. Just got a lot on my mind.

You whisper to Rolf: Can I help?

Rolf whispers to you: No. Sorry.

Rolf whispers to you: I gotta go. My parents are calling. I'll see you soon?

You whisper to Rolf: Okay.

Rolf *hugs* Alexandra!

Rolf exits the Secret Glade.

"Well?" Helen asked. "What do you think?"

"I think it was a short scene." Raksha wrinkled her nose. "Not very satisfying."

Helen shook her head. "That's not Ashley. That's not how she would play Rolf. For one, he always dresses up on date night. He hasn't changed his clothing all week."

"True. As far as I know, Rolf has 46 different changes of clothing that he rotates through."

"Forty-six? Really?"

"Yep. Not including special event clothing. Ashley is a fiend for a good outfit."

Helen nodded. "I can believe it. What you don't realize is how long that short scene took to play out. I swear it was five minutes between each bit of the exchange. I have no idea what was going on in the background.

"Also, she has never called her parents 'my parents.' It is either 'Dad' or 'my sperm donor.' Her mom isn't even in the picture. There are no 'parents.' Only a single parent and the girlfriend of the week. Right now, it's Jessica, and Ashley thinks she's all of about five or six years older than her. Just old enough to be an 'adult' and too young to act like it."

"Says something about Ashley's dad. Not a thing I want to think about," Raksha said as she made a face. "In any case, it's as I said. Something is wrong. So, we going to do this?"

"Do what?"

Raksha stared at Helen like she had a smudge on her face. "Go find out what's happened to Ashley and save her, of course. A crime is being committed. Clearly."

"I don't know where to begin." Helen shook her head. "I don't even know Ashley's last name."

"Ashley Jones of Greensburg, Pennsylvania. It's about three hours from here. I've got the address and I've mapped it out."

Helen's eyes narrowed as she frowned. "You need me to drive. Otherwise, you would've already gone, wouldn't you have?"

Raksha shrugged, not denying it. That was answer enough.

"When do you want to go?"

Smirking, Raksha's eyes drifted over Helen's left shoulder. "No time like the present."

Helen turned and watched as Sally walked into the library on Clark's arm. She sighed and frowned. "Fine. Let's go." She paused and asked, "You don't mind skipping school for this?"

Still watching Sally fawn all over Clark, Raksha rolled her eyes. "What are they going to do? Flunk me? I have a 4.3 grade average. Might even relieve my parents that I'm 'acting out' and doing 'normal' teenage things."

"Too true. Your parents are always wanting us to do sleepovers and stuff. Now might be a good time. We need to pack supplies for the trip. I'm not going without snacks."

An hour later, they were well on their way to Greensburg. Helen left a message for her parents about a research trip for school—neglecting to mention she was skipping—and that Raksha was with her if her parents called. Knowing that her parents both worked late, there was a good chance she and Raksha would be home before they were missed. Assuming all went well.

Helen glanced at the map. They would be on US-30E for a long time. Next to her, Raksha read an anatomy book. "What do you think we'll find there?"

"I don't know. That's why we're going. Ashley, I hope."

"What if Ashley isn't where you think she is?"

"We'll figure that out when we get there."

"What if it is her and she's just, I don't know, gotten bumped on the head?"

Raksha closed her book. "Highly unlikely. That's not how concussions work. You, Miss I'm-gonna-be-a-Doctor, of all people should know that. These are all useless questions. What do you really want to talk about?"

Helen glared at the road. "What does Clark see in Sally? Why her?"

"A better question is what do you see in Clark? Why him? I mean, he's not very smart. Look at who he's dating now."

Helan's glare morphed into a soft smile. "He's...Clark Worthington. He's dreamy."

Raksha hmphed. "And this is why I don't deal with relationships. They are messy and they make no sense."

"He does."

"Does what?"

Helen sighed. "He smells good. Like...*really* good."

"Ah. Pheromones. No wonder you're acting like you've lost your mind. I'll bet if you dab a bit of your favorite perfume under your nose, he won't affect you like he does."

"You think so?"

"Lord, I hope so. You mooning about is no fun."

"What are we going to do when we get to Ashley's house?"

Raksha drummed her fingers on her leg. "Kick in her door. Beat up the bad guys. Save the girl."

Helen glanced at her, eyes wide. "You're joking!"

"Of course I am. We'll start with knocking on the door. Then we'll see what happens."

Ashley Jones lived in an established part of Greensburg in a large single level rambler home painted white with forest green trim. The lawn was neatly mowed but the bushes around the edges of the yard grew wild and free. Other than that, the Jones residence looked like any other suburban house in the area.

After parking a little down the way, they got out of the car and Helen said, "Let me do the talking. At least at first. You can be—"

"Direct. The word is direct."

"Rude," Helen corrected. "But, yes, sometimes rude is direct and direct is rude."

Raksha shrugged. "You're the one who plays well with authority. Assuming that's what's happening here."

Helen didn't respond. The two of them walked up the walkway. They both heard the pop music being played within. After an exchanged glance, Raksha nodded, taking a step back as Helen rang the doorbell. They waited for about 30 seconds before Helen rang the bell again. This time, they heard someone moving in the house and waited to see if they would open the door or if they would peek at them out the window.

It was the door, the pop music volume jumped as it opened. A young woman in jeans and slouchy sweat shirt who could only be Jessica peered at them with confusion. "We don't want anything." She started to close the door.

Helen held up a hand. "We're here to see Ashley. May we come in?"

Jessica's expression shifted to something a bit more haughty as she straightened, still standing in the doorway. "I'm sorry. Ashley can't come out to play. She's grounded."

"Grounded?"

"Yes, grounded. You'll have to come back another time."

Helen protested, "But we have her homework assignments. She'll get in trouble if she doesn't do them."

Jessica glanced between the two of them. "Where? You don't have any books."

Raksha tapped her temple. "I've memorized them. She should have her books at home."

Jessica shook her head. "I'm sorry, no. Ashley is grounded. She'll have to deal with her missed homework and the consequences of that on her own time. Good-bye." She shut the door in their faces.

Helen and Raksha looked at each other then turned and walked away. At the end of the walkway to the house, Helen paused to hunker down and re-tie her shoe. As she did, she asked, "Still watching?"

Raksha fluffed her dark hair in an unconcerned way, looking around. "Yes. Trying to hide it."

Standing, Helen led the way to her car. Once there, she turned to Raksha.

"We go around back," they both said at the same time then smiled at each other in perfect understanding.

As they took the long way around, Helen asked, "What did you see?"

"She's 23 at the most. Her class ring had '90 on it. The sweat shirt was from a good seven years ago. She's hiding something, and it has to do with Ashley." Raksha side-eyed her friend as they turned a corner and cut down the alleyway between houses. "What did *you* see?"

Helen shook her head then shrugged. "A stack of mail on the entry table. A lot of takeout wrappers, the smell of stale food, and something else I did not like. Familiar but I don't know why. I'm pretty sure Ashley's dad hasn't been around for a bit." She returned Raksha's side-eye. "Good enough?"

This time Raksha smiled. "Good enough. You caught something I didn't: the mail. It confirms one of my suspicions."

"Care to share?"

"Not yet. Theories right now. Not facts. Besides..." Raksha gestured to the overgrown hedge they needed to overcome. The bushes seemed to be an odd mixture of wintergreen shrubs and burning bush shrubs that had intertwined enough that it seemed to be one plant with deep green and vibrant red branches.

Helen looked up and down the hedge. Then she crouched down, peering at the base of the bushes. "Ah ha," she said, taking several steps down the barrier then disappeared into them. When Raksha was not immediately forthcoming, Helen stuck a hand out through the bushes, her eyes closed to keep them from being poked, then waited until a hand grasped hers. Once she had a firm grip, Helen pulled Raksha through the hidden gap in the hedge.

Looking a little nonplussed, Raksha brushed her hair with her fingers then smoothed her clothing down. "Not the most comfortable way to travel, but it beats trying to climb over. How did you know?"

"They're bushes. They have a base. The overgrowth was to make it appear there are no gaps in the privacy fence."

"Huh. Sometimes, you do surprise me."

Helen took it for the compliment that it was. Raksha was rarely surprised by anything. They looked around the backyard. Standard suburban fare. Back porch, sliding back door. Minimal decoration beyond a couple of desolate garden gnomes that looked like they were on the verge of being consumed by the ever-expanding hedge.

Raksha peered at the building then gestured to the left side. The two of them snuck around the back side of the rambler, listening for movement within. Mostly, they heard loud pop music from the front of the dwelling. On the side of the house, there were a couple of five-gallon buckets, a rake, and a shovel. Both girls peered at them suspiciously.

Looking at the first window, Raksha nodded to it. "That's Ashley's room. The stickers." The small set of stickers were on the inside of the window, taped to face in. Even so, they both could make out the forms of *Rurouni Kenshin* characters, from Ashley's favorite manga.

Raksha grabbed a bucket, flipped it over, and stepped on it to get high enough to easily see into Ashley's room. A moment later, she stepped down and motioned for Helen to look. From the expression on Raksha's face, Helen knew what she would see wouldn't be good... and she was right.

"Holy crap. We've got to get in there."

"I'm way ahead of you." Raksha pulled a small pry bar from her coat pocket and offered it up.

Helen shook her head. "I don't know how to break into places. That's your thing." She jumped down from the bucket and gestured for Raksha to go ahead.

Without much fuss, Raksha got the window open—it wasn't locked—and shimmied into Ashley's room with a small boost from Helen. Even as Helen stepped back onto the bucket, Raksha leaned out of the window to help her into the house. Helen tumbled into Ashley's room with little grace but no noise.

While Raksha watched the open bedroom door, she slid the window closed. She considered closing the door then decided that the change would also draw Jessica's attention.

Helen focused only on Ashley. The small brunette lay in bed, sweating and panting. Her bed clothing was stained with her sweat and the stink of illness rolled off her in waves. Next to the bed was a bucket partially filled with vomit. The unmistakable scent of feces lingered in the air.

Checking her pulse, Helen muttered. "Pneumonia. This is just like what my brother had. It smells just like this. He almost died because of it." She looked up at Raksha. "Her pulse is at 120. Her fever is high. She's suffering from cyanosis." Helen pointed to the blue-tinted skin around Ashley's mouth. "We've got to call an ambulance."

Raksha nodded. She looked around the room. It was a mess of dirty clothing, dirty dishes, and things stacked haphazardly. She analyzed the piles of clothing and their positions in the room until the conclusion was clear. Reaching under the suspected pile of clothes, Raksha found the phone. She dialed 911. "Yes. Hello. We came to visit our friend but she's really sick. Her temperature is 103 and her heart rate is 120. My friend says it looks like pneumonia. ... Yes, she's having a hard time breathing. Yes. Her face has a blue cast. She said it was called cyanosis. Yes. 214 Cedar Grove Lane, Greensburg. Yes. We'll stay here. Please hurry."

Behind her, Raksha heard Helen coaxing Ashley to wake up.

"C'mon Ashley, wake up. We're getting you help." Helen kept speaking to her friend, shaking her shoulder, and patting her hands until Ashley responded.

Fighting for consciousness, Ashley's voice was soft and hoarse. "You came. I told Rolf. He said he would get help. You came." Her panting became harsh, wet, wracking coughs.

Helen patted Ashley's hand, murmuring, "We're here. You're going to be okay. We're here. Where's your dad?"

Raksha watched the door and readied herself as Jessica turned the corner, saw them, and rushed into Ashley's bedroom with her fists raised, intent on Helen and Ashley. "What are you doing here?! Get out!" She didn't have a chance to yell more or strike out at her intended targets.

Stepping in front of Jessica, Raksha executed a single, sharp punch to the very bottom of Jessica's sternum, a solar plexus shot. Jessica crumpled into a wheezing heap, holding her mid-section. She tried to say something, but could not get the breath to do so.

Raksha stepped forward. "Before you begin threatening us, you should know that we are aware that you do not live here and Ashley does. Ashley asked us for help and thus we arrived. Before you say something like 'that's impossible,' I suggest you think very carefully about your next words because an ambulance is on the way and as Ashley is a minor, the police will get involved. Do you want to be known as a woman who willingly neglected a child she was put in charge of or do you want to be known as a woman who trespassed and committed false imprisonment of a minor?"

"But ... you ... hit *me*."

Raksha hunkered down closer to Jessica's still wheezing form. "Or do you want to be known as the loving girlfriend who rushed over as soon as she realized something was wrong and Ashley's friends called you? It's a simple question. You broke the law. We didn't. Ashley called for help and we came."

Jessica shook her head, "He didn't leave ... us enough money for a hospital ... visit. I can't pay for ... that kind of thing!"

"That's what insurance is for, you twit!" Helen glared at Jessica from over Raksha's shoulder. "She could've died. She still could, and it will be your fault!"

Backing away from Raksha, Jessica clambered to her feet. She looked afraid as Raksha moved closer. Trembling, she asked, "What do you want?"

"You didn't answer my question. Law breaker or concerned friend who didn't realize how sick Ashley was?" Raksha smiled, all teeth and malice. "Also, how to contact Ashley's parents?"

"Dad," Helen corrected.

Raksha shrugged. "Dad." She held up a finger. "Hear that siren? That's for us. You have about 30 seconds to decide."

"Fine. Concerned girlfriend. I'll go get the emergency number

Dan gave me. But he won't be happy. He didn't want to be interrupted." Jessica turned away, still holding her mid-section.

Helen held onto Ashley's hand as her eyes opened and closed. Her friend's breathing was better but not good and she shivered now while her forehead burned. "I don't give a rat's ass what 'Dan' thinks as long as Ashley's okay."

Raksha nodded. "She'll be okay now. The ambulance is here. Let me do the talking until they ask about the medical. You're too upset. They're going to want just the facts. Okay?"

Helen nodded her agreement and focused back on Ashley.

Two weeks later...

Alexandra enters the Secret Glade.

Alexandra glances at Rolf and Sebastian.

Rolf Nightsong has taken the casual route today with a white linen shirt, tan trousers, and bare feet. His wavy black hair is pulled back in a low pony tail, held by a purple velvet ribbon. When you see them his black eyes look into and through you. There is a darkness within as well as a hint of gleaming fangs in his slight smile.

Sebastian wears a maroon Dashiki shirt with matching pants. The shirt is adorned with tasteful gold embroidery. This comfortable outfit is finished off with a pair of black leather loafers.

Alexandra pauses, wondering if she is interrupting.

Sebastian waves a hand. "We're OOC. Catching up."

Rolf ((hugs)) Alexandra!

Alexandra ((hugs)) Rolf!

Rolf has looked at you!

You have looked at yourself!

Alexandra Videre is, as always, a vision of loveliness. Her blond hair seems to glow in any light and her deep blue eyes recall the sea. Right now, she is wearing a linen pant suit of pale blue that sets off her eyes. On her wrist is a beautiful gold bracelet.

Alexandra looks into the beyond.

Minerva is lurking in the Secret Glade.

Sebastian sends Minerva home! Nighty-night.

Alexandra: It's so good to see you, Ashley!

Rolf: Thanks to you, too. I didn't think I was going to make it. It was a real bad time. I didn't know where I was or what was happening most of it. I just knew I hurt, couldn't breathe, couldn't get comfy. I didn't even know where my dad was.

Sebastian: Tell her what you told me.

Alexandra: Tell me everything. Is Jessica still there?

Rolf: Nope. I was in the hospital for 8 days. By the time dad got home from his business trip and rushed to the hospital, Jessica had left and dumped him because I was "too much trouble." But, I explained what happened and he said it was a good idea that she already left because he would've dumped her. Especially with the state of my room. It was so gross.

Alexandra: But you're ok now?

Rolf: ish. I still have a bad cough and I'm supposed to stay home from school for the next couple of weeks. They're sending my homework home. But I have a new mattress and new sheets. Dad is going to stay home while I'm sick. No more trusting girlfriends. He is grateful to you guys, though.

Alexandra: How did you explain us?

Sebastian grins.

Rolf: I told him I asked for help in my game and you two came. Which is pretty much what happened.

Sebastian eyes Rolf.

Rolf: Ok ok. /sigh/ I had a high fever. I was seeing things. I swear to goodness Rolf came to me and asked me how he could help. He knew Jessica wasn't doing what she needed to do to help me. I told him to get your attention any way he could. I was so out of it. I didn't really understand that Jessica was playing my characters to hide the fact that I was sick. I just knew she kept asking me questions about him and you guys. I mean, the last thing I actually remember typing was "AFK" with the intent to come back after a nap.

Alexandra: That was one hella AFK.

Rolf: Yeah. It was. But the whole time it wasn't me, it just felt like Rolf was in the front and acting for me, answering Jessica's questions. Does that make sense?

Alexandra: A little. Is that why Rolf made a deal with the Order?

Rolf: Yeah. I think so. I'd promised you/Alexandra I wouldn't. I knew that they had something Rolf needed. Wanted. The drama was going to be awesome.

Sebastian: Speaking of that, if you want to retcon that scene, we can.

Rolf looks at Alexandra then shakes his head.

Rolf: It happened. Let's run with it. Rolf had a really bad day and they caught him when he was feeling low. Our little happy couple has been happy for too long.

Alexandra: You can bet that Alexandra's going to be pissed at him for a while.

Rolf: But think of the drama! Yummy yummy drama!

Alexandra smiles.

Sebastian steeples his fingers with an evil smile. "This is going to be fun."

Rolf laughs.

Alexandra laughs.

Alexandra shoos Sebastian. "Out of here now. My seer needs to be mad at her vampire boyfriend for a while."

Sebastian points his finger at Alexandra. "I'll be watching you. Soon, little seer, soon."

Sebastian disappears in a puff of magic.

Sebastian has left the Secret Glade.

Alexandra looks into the beyond.

There are no lurkers in the Secret Glade.

Rolf: Now, where were we?

Alexandra: Having a picnic with Rolf in big trouble.

The Case of the Displaced

by

Aaron Rosenberg

Clambering up the stairs, I stubbed my toe on a badly worn step. Curse words spilled from my lips at the pain—until they stopped abruptly, cut off by a sharp jolt to my temple.

"I say!" I hissed. "There's no call for that!"

"There is no call for taking the Lord's name in vain, either," my companion echoed in my ear. "So, pray, desist."

I grumbled at that but knew it would do no good. My companion's piety was stronger than my irritation. And of course he did not complain, despite my certainty that he was no more comfortable or familiar with such steep and uneven terrain than I. Therefore, with little more than a scowl, I continued on to our destination.

We had come to Belmont Abbey at my companion's insistence. "It is one of the oldest monastic communities in England," he had declared, "and therefore is worth our notice."

For my part, I hoped that our visit there would prove fruitful enough to satisfy his obsession. Perhaps it might even fulfil his mysterious quest and thus allow us to part ways, though I could barely allow such a notion to enter my thoughts, much less my heart.

When we arrived, we were both struck by the beauty of the grounds and the buildings, particularly the church itself, with its unadorned sandstone exterior, its lovely stained-glass windows, and its squared bell tower. The community appeared to be in disarray, however, and we soon discovered the cause from a black-cassocked monk.

"The abbot's gone missing," he declared when we stopped him in the courtyard. "And there's a man dead, crushed by a gargoyle."

Having stated such unsettling news, he then freed himself from our collective grasp and hurried away.

"Dire portents indeed," noted my associate—I dared not call him friend, and in fact did not desire to do so, given his frequent treatment of me. "And yet, such activity suggests our travel here may not have been in vain. Come, Watson. Let us inquire further."

That brought us, eventually, to an older monk whose silvered beard lent him an air of great wisdom but whose harried expression belied any usual comportment. "I am Prior Richard," he informed us. "I assist Abbot Gregory in the running of the abbey." He wrung his hands. "But now he's nowhere to be found, and there's a dead man, and I do not know what to do!"

"Calm yourself," my companion advised, exuding an aura that encouraged just such a mood. At the sound of his voice the prior did indeed settle, as did I. I might curse him for that, if not for irony and other consequences. "When was the last time anyone saw the abbot? And where is this mysterious unfortunate?"

"Three nights ago at evening vespers," the monk answered. "He often strolls the grounds after, before retiring for the night. And the man is in the small chapel, being sat vigil for. We will bury him come dawn." He shook his head. "We've no idea his name, let alone his faith, and all our inquiries have come to nought. Still, the Almighty welcomes all lost souls, and as he met his end here, it seems the least we can do."

"Indeed," my companion agreed. "That is most charitable of you, and speaks highly of your order, and your faith." The commendation had the monk beaming with pride. "Might we pay our respects?"

That was quickly allowed, and we were directed toward the small chapel, which sat to one side of the nave, just before the transept. It was a simple space but a handsome one, and in the center they had laid the dead man upon a plain oak bench, around which four monks knelt in prayer. The light from the narrow windows and the surrounding candles was dim but not enough to hide the horrible damage that had been inflicted upon him, and I winced. Even inured as I was by my time in the army, still it was gruesome.

"Fortitude, Watson," my companion advised. "It is but a shell, and no doubt the end came quickly."

I nodded, focusing on my medical training to push any further squeamishness aside. "He was crushed, clearly, as we were told."

One of the monks glanced up at me and nodded. "Yes, one of the gargoyles off the bell tower," he confirmed. "A terrible accident."

My companion urged me forward, and together we examined the body more closely. It was a man, that much was certain, and the visible hair was snow-white, though what little flesh had not been shredded upon impact looked too young to match that. The clothes were nondescript, decent but not exceptional, and appeared as if they had seen recent hard use even before the damage wrought by statuary.

I did my best not to react as my associate leaned in closer and sniffed the corpse. I myself could smell nothing beyond the scent of blood and bodily fluids, mixed with some hints of stone dust, but his senses were far sharper than my own.

Exiting onto the courtyard, we stopped the first monk we saw. "Where did the gargoyle fall from, exactly?" we asked.

He pointed, and indeed I could now see that one of the drain spout gargoyles at the bell tower's upper corners was missing. "We must examine it up close," I was informed as I was dragged back into the cathedral and up a long, narrow, winding staircase to the tower's roof. Parts of that appeared newer than the rest, which we put down to recent repairs.

It required leaning rather precipitously over the edge, but we were soon studying the spot where that murderous gargoyle had until recently resided. "See here," my companion said, reaching down and running a finger along the shattered stone. "This is not from age or the elements. It was wrenched free by brute force."

I wondered what manner of man could accomplish such a feat. Then the import registered fully. "You are saying this was no accident."

He had the audacity to grin, though I knew from experience it was a fierce expression, that of a hunter spying his prey. "Correct, Watson. This was murder."

Returning to the courtyard, we found there was a new source of consternation. "The villagers have caught him," one of the monks stated. "And they're bringing him here!"

"Who, the murderer?" I asked, but the man shrugged.

"Perhaps? We do not know. Only, there have been stories lately of a wild man stalking the woods," he explained. "He raves and rants enough to frighten even the heartiest soul. But we have not seen him here."

My companion frowned. "How long has he been in the area?"

"Only a few days." The monk excused himself to see to his duties, leaving us standing and pondering there in the mid-day light.

"You think them connected," I stated, certain in my own deduction. "The wild man appeared around the same time the other man was murdered and the abbot went missing."

He nodded. "Yes. But the question remains, why here? If it is what I seek, it is nowhere in evidence, yet my instincts tell me we are in the right place. We must ask further."

We sought out Prior Richard, but he was deep in discussion with two senior monks of an age to his own. "They are discussing possible investiture," a somewhat younger but still seasoned monk explained upon seeing us watching. "There are certain rites and rituals given only to the abbot, but it has been three days, and the abbey must be maintained."

I would have nodded, but my companion was not so easily satisfied. "Surely, the prior is capable of performing any prayers that might be needed?" he asked, his supportive tone smoothing the pointedness of the question. "And I would assume he has access already to the abbey's finances. What else is required for the role beyond an official assumption of the duties?"

The monk glanced about uneasily, and I felt again my associate's presence, warm and understanding and inviting confidence. The man edged closer, lowering his voice. "There are certain secrets granted only to the abbot," he explained softly. "The prior was thus not privy to them, but he must become so if he is to take over the abbey."

My companion nodded and thanked the monk for his time and his trust, leaving him feeling pleased with himself. I was less sanguine, however. "Please tell me we are not about to do what I think we are," I pleaded, and was answered with a soft chuckle that sent a thrill through me despite myself.

"Of course we are," he answered. "And we have little time for it, so step lively."

Again, there was no point in resistance, and I let myself be led away once more.

The abbot's private study was an intimate little room made all the cozier by the age-darkened wood paneling on each wall. Only a small stained-glass window let in any light. A massive desk, its wood a match to the paneling, took up one entire wall and nearly half the space in general, allowing enough room for a single sturdy chair before it and a cabinet built into the wall opposite.

"The desk first, I think," my companion declared, and together we studied it. It was a handsome piece, unadorned but sturdy and well made, and we began running our hands along it, checking for drawers and hidden nooks. His touch was deft and sure, and after only a few moments something clicked and a tiny compartment slid open just below the desktop. In it was a small, yellowed scrap of parchment.

"Aha!" Extracting the paper, he unrolled it, laying it flat atop the desk—and then growled in disappointment. For, though there were symbols inked there, they were not in any language either of us knew. It was one of the few times I had ever found him at a loss for knowledge.

"It is in cipher," he stated. "And without the key, we cannot possibly read it."

I was studying the lines, however. "Perhaps not," I said slowly, for I had long since learned that he did not do well with correction, "but we still might learn something. Notice the evenness of the lines?"

I did not refer to the penmanship, and he picked up my meaning at once. "Oh, well spotted, Watson!" he declared, his pleasure overcoming any annoyance at being caught out at anything. "It is a poem!" For there were 14 lines, divided into three groups of four and then a pair alone. A classic sonnet in the style of Shakespeare.

That also suggested a rhyme scheme, which might aid us once we had some idea of the characters involved. For now, however, we hastened to restore the parchment to its hiding place and slip back out into the main cathedral before anyone had noticed our presence there.

"So the abbey is given a strange, coded poem upon investiture," my companion mused once we were safely ensconced upon a pew near the back, where we might sit unobserved for a spell. "And no doubt given the key for translating it. That must be stored somewhere else, to prevent unwanted access."

"You think that poem is the reason a man was murdered here?" It was not truly a question, and I felt his nod, there in the shadows of the main chapel. "And that it somehow pertains to your own search?" Silent assent again. "Do you think we are too late?" For he had, upon our first meeting, impressed upon me the importance of his quest, and the need for haste, as he was not the only one searching, only the most favorably inclined toward my fellow men.

"I hope not," he answered after a moment. "I believe I would know if we were, but I cannot be certain. Thus we must continue as if we are not. It is all we can do."

Our conversation—one of the more civil ones we'd had, in point of fact—was interrupted by a commotion outside. As one, we rose and went to investigate.

We could clearly hear screams from the courtyard, yet there was nothing to be seen there, and the few monks we spied nearby were all hurrying toward the property's front gates. There we found a small crowd gathering around a figure who writhed and shrieked as if tormented by bees. His shock of white hair lay upon his head and face in a matted tangle and his body was covered with scratches and mud, for he was bare save only for a ragged loincloth. No words ushered from his chapped lips, only grunts and cries, but he fought with desperate energy against the sturdy townsfolk struggling to drag him forward and onto the abbey's grounds.

"Enough!" That came from Prior Richard, who pushed his way through to reach the men and their captive. "There is no need to distress him so. Perhaps he would be more willing to seek shelter in the gardening shed." And he pointed toward a small, rough-hewn hut just outside the abbey walls.

"But, Prior—" one of the men began. "He's a killer!" That brought murmurs from the crowd. My companion, I noted, remained silent.

Richard shook his head. "We do not know that for certain," he pointed out, his voice and manner calm but his words projected for the assemblage. "All we can say for now is that he is an afflicted soul, and thus we must render what care and assistance we can." He took a step toward the shed, his eyes on the wild man. "Would this suit you, sir? It is crude but clean."

The stranger settled slightly, as if considering. And when the townsfolk began tugging him in that direction, he did not resist, but went quietly, if not quite willingly. A sigh of relief arose from some quarters, and one of disappointment from others, when all saw that there would be no further conflict here today.

"Interesting," my associate said softly. "I begin to suspect what took place here. And, if I am right, we have indeed found the right place, and possibly just in the nick of time. Come, Watson. Let us return to the cathedral."

I shook my head. "Do you not wish to question the man?" I asked, though we were already walking away. "Find out what he knows? If he is in fact the killer we seek? If he knows what happened to the abbot?"

But he waved a hand in dismissal. "I doubt we would glean much useful reply from him, in his current state. And he is not going anywhere."

That last seemed true enough, at least, as two stout men had placed themselves outside the hut to guard their strange prisoner. So, as usual, I allowed my companion to direct our actions. Not that I had much choice.

"Let us assume," he stated once we were back in the nave, quietly so that only I might hear, "that we are correct in our assumptions about what is hidden here. And that the riddle we found pertains to its location."

"But only the abbot knows what the riddle means," I pointed out, frowning. "Do you think that is why he is missing? Was he abducted and made to reveal its secrets?"

His answering grin was sharp. "Yes, I believe we can surmise such. Yet I suspect that was not enough, else there would be no further turmoil. No, I think that riddle was only the first piece of the puzzle."

I nodded, for I had been around such situations in the army. "They have compartmentalized the information," I stated. "To prevent anyone from discovering and making use of the whole. The abbot had one piece, but there is another he did not, could not, know."

His approbation was nearly palpable. “Well done, Watson! Yes, precisely! The question then becomes, if you had that other information, where could you place it that it could be readily accessed by anyone *except* the abbot?”

We both studied the cathedral’s interior, with its high, vaulted ceilings, sturdy column-supported arches along either side, and rows of wooden pews in between leading up to the chancel. “It would have to be somewhere protected,” I pointed out, my gaze sliding across the smooth flagstone floor. “But available.” Then I spotted a patch of dark against the light stone walls, and smiled. “What does every good priest consider part of their duties?” I asked, leading the way toward a wooden structure with a closed central space and an open alcove on either side.

My companion laughed, a rare sound. “Take confession! But surely the abbot would sometimes hear those himself?”

“He would,” I agreed. “But if *he* made confession, it would be in the privacy of his study, to the prior. Thus—” and I slipped into the alcove on the right.

“Of course. The penitent stations.” It was a close fit, but I was used to that. Fortunately, there was little enough to examine, the confessional being deliberately plain, and we quickly concluded that no hidden messages were stored there.

On the other side, however, we found something almost right away. It was carved into the lower panel, where it would only be visible when not only kneeling but crouching down. And unlike the message held by the abbot, this one was in English, albeit the older form, not the modern variant.

Fortunately, my companion could read that easily enough. “It speaks of standing facing the sun at dusk,” he explained, translating loosely rather than literally. “Then turning once, twice, three times as the clock does, before stopping two steps removed.”

Having gleaned that, we rose and exited the confessional before anyone wondered what we might be doing there, unattended by a priest as we were. “So it reveals the placement of that which is hidden,” I commented as we retreated to the last pew and sat instead. “But not the place itself, nor what manner of item.” I gnashed my teeth. “That is all but useless!”

Smugness radiated from my companion, however, which told me he had garnered something I had not. "Perhaps," he replied after a moment. "And perhaps not. Would you say that all the events which have transpired here in the last few days are connected?"

"You know I would."

"Then perhaps we already know the location," he suggested, rising to his feet and dragging me up with him. "Come." And we made our way forward, just past the transept, where we turned—toward the bell tower stairs.

"Ah!" I believe I am justified in feeling I was not slow to apprehend. "The gargoyles!"

"The very same," he agreed, making his way up the stairs with some haste, for it was late in the day and the sun was already edging toward the horizon. "Else why was the one damaged? Surely there are easier ways to dispatch someone?"

I did not reply, but instead saved breath for the climb.

We emerged atop the tower just as the sun began to set, its last rays casting their wide net across the sky. "Face it," he commanded, and I did so, then followed the rest of the instructions, turning about three times clockwise. On the third go-round, however, I stopped two stations short—which left me facing east instead.

The shattered gargoyle had been the one to the south. The one I stood over now was still intact.

"Tear it free!" my associate insisted, and such was his intensity that I did not hesitate but leaned forward and grasped the stone figure with both hands clasped around its long neck. I hauled upward with all my might, and was gratified but highly surprised when there was a loud crack and the statue tore loose, sending me tumbling backward clutching it to my chest like an ungainly babe. Yet the weight was not as much as I might have expected, and once I had caught my breath again I twisted the detached figure about—and found a dark spot on the underside.

"It is hollow!"

Before my companion could reply, we heard a great howl, as from some monstrous beast. Then a figure burst from beyond the abbey walls, leaping skyward in a sweeping arc. It shot forward—and landed with a resounding thud there on the roof not ten paces from us.

It was the wild man. His chest was heaving with his recent exertion, splinters and dust coated his hair and shoulders from the hut's roof he had just torn through, and beneath his hair his eyes were feverishly bright, twin spots in the slowly lengthening gloom.

Then he spoke a single word, intelligible despite the rasp and crackle in his voice:

"Belonediniel."

My companion stood and faced him squarely, forcing me to do the same, the broken statue set behind me for now. "Asbeel." His voice was steady, as was his stance. "Or should I say, Abbot Gregory?"

The man—creature—before us laughed. "Indeed you might!" he agreed, his voice a horrible rumble. "He fights me, even now!"

"He came upon you as you snuck onto the grounds, didn't he?" my companion demanded. "Your host was failing, the contact with consecrated earth too much for him to endure. So you took the good father instead. Doing so granted you access to the poem and its meaning, and you leapt up here. But the other monks heard the commotion, and even this distant vantage pains you. You had time only to tear free one gargoyle, fling it down in disgust, and flee. Crushing your former host was pure luck, obscuring any signs of your former presence."

The poor abbot nodded, and I thought I could see the disgust and resistance in his eyes. "I hid, with the intent to return once the furor died down. But then I sensed your presence." He snarled, his teeth seeming longer and sharper in the shadows. "You shall not have it!"

"How are you able to stand being up here?" my associate asked. "Directly above the apse?"

That provoked a nasty grin in response. "The repairs," our adversary—I could only think of him as such—grated. "They did not bless them anew."

Then, without further comment or warning, he charged. My companion rose to meet him, and the battle was joined.

The blows were titanic and swift, barely seen but felt as great tremors and waves of impact and sound. They were evenly matched, the two of them, and for a moment I worried.

I should have had more faith. Ironic, that.

Belonediniel grappled Asbeel, hugging him close as if in a warm embrace—and then took a deliberate step back.

Onto one of the older parts of the roof.

His foe howled in pain, and flames sprang up where his bare flesh touched the consecrated stone. He struggled to escape, but my associate clung fast. The flames rose higher, and I could feel their heat licking at my skin, but took no damage from them. My faith—and my companion—protected me.

Asbeel and the poor abbot were not so lucky.

They screamed together as the blaze enveloped them fully, but to my ears the abbot's cries were those of triumph, whereas his captor's were pure agony and rage.

Then Belonediniel stepped back and his rival crashed to the ground, his body quickly burning away to ash that blew free in the evening wind.

"It is done." Reaching down, my companion took hold of the shattered gargoyle and, with a quick convulsion of broad shoulders, tore the stone asunder. From within its cavity he extracted a golden sword hilt—and the second his fingers wrapped around the handle, a blade of purest light sprang up from it.

My throat was so dry I could barely speak, my eyes dazzled by the loveliness before me. "Is that—?"

"What I sought? Yes. The sword of an archangel." His smile felt nearly as bright as the weapon. "A weapon long thought lost, now recovered. Thanks to you, John Watson." He bowed without a hint of mockery. "You have aided me greatly, if not always willingly, and I am grateful. But my task is now complete, and our time together at an end."

I gasped as I felt my constant companion slide out of me, leaving my body feeling both heavy and empty with only my own soul within. Belonediniel floated before me then, a being of shimmering light as I had first beheld him, and rose slowly higher and higher, a multitude of wings springing from his back to carry him aloft.

"Farewell," he called as he ascended. "And know that you have served Him well."

Then he was gone, and I was alone on the roof. Alone for the first time in weeks.

Yet I knew that I would never be truly alone, and I took comfort in that as I made my way back toward the stairs, trying to compose my thoughts on how I would explain this to the monks below.

Author note: "Belonediniel" translates roughly to "the fair-haired of God." In Old English, "fair of hair" would be "scirloc"—which then evolved into the name "Sherlock."

The Silence of an Empty House

By

Neil Kleid

Despite a ten-year separation, the tone and timbre of Watson's voice —far more than the context of the recording he had left upon my cellular device—immediately conveyed his urgent need of my superior deductive capabilities.

And so, with nary a regret or begrudging reluctance on that humid May evening, I immediately packed two changes of clothes, a toiletry bag, my finest fingerprint kit and several notebooks into the safari-green, eight-and-a-half pound Paravel Aviator carry-on bag gathering dust in my back hall closet. Purchasing a late round-trip ticket out of Heathrow, and grabbing the spare mobile charger from the second-side nightstand in my bedroom, I left word for Mrs. Ainsley in 220A to leave milk out for the cat and collect my mail.

Then I snatched my hat (not the coat; New York in May would be unseasonably warm), locked the door, and hailed a black cab for the airport with no time to spare.

Watson required help. That much appeared elementary, even to me.

Therefore—even though the two of us had spoken only sporadically since Watson had departed London a decade prior, regarding matters both legal and practical concerning Wiggins, the pre-teen boy we had adopted (of whom, sadly, I had seen less and less of over the past few years due to my schedule and an understandable distancing based on, well, the distance) and a few inquiries about the Elizabethan Staffordshire vintage tea set we had once shared—I had no choice but to rap upon his door, a rather unkempt substitute for Poe's titular raven, announcing my arrival within 24 hours at Watson's third-floor apartment on Manhattan's Upper West Side.

" . . . Holmes?"

His query was delivered with a dumbfounded, congested air of reedy musicality, no doubt affected by the change in season and the increase of pollen noted by the sneezing driver who had recently deposited me—bag, hat and all—before the architecturally sound steps leading into the complex in which Watson had come to reside.

"Holmes," my estranged friend repeated, swinging open his door to reveal a foyer, as well as the figure of a man I had loved and lost; an erudite, eloquent companion whose powers of detection might have eventually eclipsed my own, assuming Watson had kept up the practice. A stub of pencil hung limply between his fingers. Telltale signs of ink spotting the pads of his thumbs and forefingers had me clinging to hope that perhaps he had. A daily crossword, I might imagine, or a jumble in some local tabloid. Further investigation might well reveal a thesaurus somewhere about his home, validating my playful assumption.

He had aged (as had I, so there was little more to say about that) and thickened about the middle, a physique once molded by rugby matches having gone to seed. Absently, I mused upon the impact such a transformation might have had upon his off-again-on-again relationship with Franklin Appell, the well-to-do oncologist and nature-seeker Watson had been seeing for the better part of a quinquennial. Judging by the disarray of his salt-and-pepper hair, resplendent moustache, and the stains dotting an unbecoming, checked nightshirt wrapped about his frame, I quickly deduced John's physical appearance was of little regard to all but himself.

"Please," he continued after a moment's hesitation, welcoming me across the threshold with a flapping of an ink-stained hand. "Please come in, Holmes. I must say . . . it is a surprise to see you in New York."

"Is it?" I challenged this statement with a flourish of my cellular device, turning its screen to face my host as I traversed the lilac-scented hallway leading to the heart of his apartment.

"No," he contradicted. "I mean . . . what I meant . . ."

"A surprise, dear Watson, yet not 16 hours ago I received a message in which the sender—whose voice, despite the electronic vibrations warbling its conveyance, sounded similar to your own—all but begged for my expedient decampment to its place of origin so that I might apply powers of deductive reasoning toward solving a mystery both curious, intimate, and personal in nature. Now here I stand," I continued with a flourish as he latched the door and followed me down the hall just as I spied a bowl of lilacs, John's favorite—having been so since our days cohabitating on Baker Street—wilting on an end table, the pungent source of the apartment's *odeur naturelle*. "Here I stand, expediently decamped 'pon your doorstep as if—"

"—as if a decade hadn't passed, and we were still fencing over grammar and perceived wrongdoings back in Blighty."

"Yes. Precisely."

Standing in Watson's living room, my former *confrere* vacillating 'tween stabbing daggers in my back or laying arms about my shoulders, a sudden awkwardness clipped the statements—or overdue apologies—forming at my lips.

Glancing around the spartan apartment, I noted two doors at the far end of the hallway—the master bedroom, obviously shared by John and the absent Doctor Appell, adjacent to a smaller chamber which undoubtedly belonged to Wiggins—and a single water closet at the end of the hall. A galley kitchen, out of view, had been positioned across the living space, past a long, oak table ringed with six fashionable, mid-century dining room chairs. A comfortable sofa dominated the far end of the room, and two leather Chesterfield recliners had been positioned on either side, facing inward to a coffee table piled with texts, novels and copies of *The New Yorker*, *Atlantic*, *Post*, and *Times*.

Prior to my arrival, Watson had occupied one of the apartment's two recliners. I noted the offending newspaper and a thesaurus overturned on a nearby end-table—a crossword, as deduced—and a sheaf of notes in states of disarray, next to a mug of tea sans coaster, the condensation from which would leave a ring upon the end-table's faux-cherry finish.

Clearing my throat, I swiveled about.

"And so here I am."

"That you are, dear Holmes. Here in New York."

"And where else should I be, when beckoned from across the pond to solve a mystery so distressing it inspired a message of such urgency following ten years' distance?"

Watson stammered in that most idiosyncratic manner of his, the likes of which endeared him to me so long ago. "Well," the man hemmed, "I don't know that I had used the words *urgency* or *distress*, exactly . . . "

Arching an eyebrow, I extended the phone and thumbed a button. Presently, Watson's voice emerged from the microphone secreted within the device, repeating his desperate message that had spurred me to action nearly 24 hours prior.

"*Holmes*," breathed the recording, in a manner both familiar and intimate, the tone of which revealed emotion that had been deployed from a position of careful curation.

"*I have urgent need of your skills in America*," it continued. "*Your anger with my decisions—to leave London, and to . . . dissolve our storied partnership—have no doubt simmered. But a distressing scenario has presented itself: Wiggins is gone and cannot be found. His room? Abandoned and ransacked. His absence? A dagger in my heart, and all my powers of deduction—though considerable—have proved no help in solving his disappearance or returning him to my side. Please, Holmes. If despite any perceived betrayal, your calculating heart still retains affection for the boy . . . and for me . . . I humbly request assistance—*"

Pausing the reluctant digital appeal, I secured the device within an exterior pocket of my jacket and idly resumed my appraisal of Watson's flat. Trying and failing to hide the amusement 'pon my face to his renewed abashment, I leaned down and tipped the discarded crossword so that I might better review the words Watson had failed to identify.

"Holmes, I . . ."

"*Distress*."

Wincing, John nodded. "Yes. Your point is clear, Holmes. You were right. I had indeed mentioned urgency and distress in my message."

"No." I tapped the puzzle. "Twenty-two down. A seven-letter word for sorrow. I find it hard to believe you would miss it, Watson, with the selfsame emotion writ plain upon your face."

"*Blast it*, Holmes–"

"The boy's room," I ventured, interrupting his rebuke and continuing deeper into the apartment. "Wiggins? His room is this way, I deduce? Across from the master bedroom?"

"Yes. To the right."

"Indubitably, Watson. That is one for you."

Smiling, I turned away from my frustrated former companion. Admittedly, it felt terrible enjoying Watson's discomfort as much as I was, but the last time we had paired to solve a mystery—even one so obvious as *this,* wherein the riddle was as plain as the spots 'pon Watson's gown—had been 13 years prior. Though I had already verified the day's outcome, I resolved to follow through and eventually reveal not one, but multiple answers.

A slight push opened Wiggins' door, and I stepped into an ankle-deep slurry of discarded clothing and broken curios, torn bedding, and overturned drawers. Some wayward miscreant had tossed the room like a cracksman, having come through the open window and landed upon the nearby bed (the mattress of which had been knocked perpendicular to the frame, stripped and shredded, lying on one side). The closet doors were pulled and the clothing within (what little remained) fallen from hangars to lie in a heap 'pon the floor. The walls were untouched, colorful posters intact and an array of framed photographs only slightly askew. I picked up one of Wiggins' various childhood knickknacks—a toy "magic" 8-ball, a novelty item secured perhaps from one of the many questionable souvenir shops lining Manhattan's avenues and streets—turning the cracked plastic to inspect it with my thumb, index and forefinger.

Toeing a pile of shirts aside and surveying the walls, I listened carefully as Watson edged into the room behind me, lingering at the threshold.

"How long has Wiggins been gone? When did you notice his absence?"

Watson stammered again. "Not long. The day I phoned. Perhaps a difference in hours? His absence in the morning, my discovery in late afternoon."

"I see." Removing my toe from Wiggins' shirts, I placed the 8-ball on the window's ledge.

"And then what transpired?" I pressed, retrieving a slim notebook from its nesting place within an inner pocket, pairing it with a pencil I kept upon my person for just such an occasion (tucked within an exquisite waistcoat, purchased by an admiring inspector on my behalf just last Christmas). "Did you then happen upon this shambles? A thorough inspection of the scene? The lifting and proper cataloguing of errant fingerprints? Of course you filed the required missing-persons paperwork and alerted the local constabulary, yes?"

"No . . . yes . . . " Watson flattened his moustache with ink-stained fingers, a nervous habit I knew had originated during a witch hunt in Edinburgh and stuck around despite my encouragement to rid himself of the gesture throughout our partnership. The tell-tale tic had obviously followed him from London and cohabitated itself alongside Watson, Wiggins and the absent Doctor Appell. Either the tic's irritating-yet-indisputable presence was a response to Watson's distraught state—for our son—or some deeper, more elusive reason . . . one which had all but revealed itself to me before I had even left my London terrace.

"Surely you've contacted Wiggins' friends and associates? Interviewed neighbors, confidants, the like?"

"Damn it, you know I haven't."

"Yes, of course," I confirmed, studying the photos hanging 'pon the wall. "*Urgent* and *desperate*, you said. And yet even while mired in what is clearly a state of emotional distress, Watson, I had truly hoped for better than *this* after ten years."

" . . . I simply want him back, Holmes. I am *indeed* desperate."

Swiping a finger along a picture frame, I licked my lips and turned to face my companion. Watson was in need of help. And there were tragic questions hanging about the entire scenario—about him, this room—that required answers. Some of those answers I already possessed; several I had but surmised, and for which now sought gleeful confirmation.

But there was one outstanding mystery that still needed solving.

Returning the notebook and pencil to their respective pockets, I cleared my throat and glanced out the window. It was breaking noon. Back in London, the day was ending and pubs were welcoming exhausted barristers seeking liquid relief. I looked down at my watch.

"Fancy a cup?"

"*Tea?* But Wiggins . . . I-I mean . . . *yes*, of course. Apologies, Holmes, but I've been a terrible host. If you give me a moment, I will brew up a pot."

"No, no . . . while I am sure whatever you prepare would be delightful, Watson, after several hours aboard commercial air travel and then another locked in an automobile which smelled like rancid eggs, I should like to take the air . . . though I daresay it may be difficult to locate a proper Lapsang Souchong in this godless metropolis."

Watson's moustache wiggled. The left-hand corner of his mouth turned up ever so slightly.

"Not if you know where to look," he replied, a tone of bemusement infiltrating the sorrowful facade that had until that moment dominated his face. "Happens to be, I frequent an artisanal teahouse on the corner of West 83rd, situated one block from the park."

"Splendid. Well then, dear Watson. If you will clean yourself up and locate a suitable pair of trousers, perhaps we might share initial deductions about this intriguing mystery over a pot of black tea . . . and if you have such a foul, evil thing about your residence, a dab of tobacco?"

"I'm sure I do. I'll check the toe end of my slipper."

Out on the street, Watson clad in a light summer suit, we lapsed into silence. The sounds of Manhattan enveloped us as we walked and puffed (you will be happy to know ten years had not dulled John's dexterity; he quickly packed a cherrywood pipe as we traveled, handing it over as we crossed the first street). Our brisk jaunt provided the opportunity to organize my thoughts, hum a snippet from *Don Giovanni*, and observe the streets of New York—unseasonably warm, as predicted. Eventually we arrived at Watson's teahouse, a far more contemporary and *American* locale than the parlors I was wont to frequent. But then, as the saying goes, when in Rome, one did as did those from Rome. Carry on and all that.

"Well now," I began, after happily locating Lapsang Souchong part-way down the tearoom's extensive and daunting list of beverages, conveying my selection to a hovering waiter. Watson opted for an Earl Grey. Would I have had a brandy, John would probably have been grateful for a doleful drop in his mug; sadly, having left Baker Street in haste, I did not. Regretfully, I abandoned notions about our drinks and suitably returned to the case.

"I believe we left at '*Holmes, I am indeed desperate.*'"

"As I am."

"Tell me, Watson," I inquired, veering sharply as I leaned back in my uncomfortable metal chair (clearly, whomever had designed this midnight-and-chrome, mirrored house-of-horrors pretending to be a tearoom had been driven insane by some Victorian devil. In truth, Watson's teahouse—"*AbundiTea*"—was nothing more than an opium-induced, pre-teen child's poorly-conceived nightmare of an adult confectionary, wherein rather than ice cream, forty combinations of jarringly-mixed leaves and flavor crystals—*come now; "habanero dragonfruit"?*—pretended themselves to play at what a proper Englishman might refer to as "tea." The menu was laughable, the tables dangerous, the music catastrophic, and the bloody chairs either torture or penance.)

"Tell me, Watson," I repeated, "where amid this hoopla and intrigue stands our good Doctor Appell? I imagine that when a gentleman is in distress, he might look to aid or comfort from a stalwart companion of nigh on—what is it now?—five years."

" . . . what . . . what exactly are you implying, Holmes?"

"Implying? No, dear friend, I believe that I am being rather explicit. Why has Franklin not helped you with Wiggins' disappearance? Is he not still your . . . what is it exactly . . . *gentleman friend?* Your *partner*?"

I will admit that I had spat that last with far too much enmity than intended. Watson winced. I blame the hostility on my demon chair.

"What I meant to ask," I reiterated in a softer tone, "is why your Doctor Appell has not remained close by until Wiggins' return?"

" . . . Holmes, the doctor in question is no longer 'mine.' "

"Ah."

"Yes."

"Well, I can see the dilemma, then."

"*Can* you?"

"The dilemma in question, rather, as to why your good doctor has not remained close."

"Not *my* doctor, no."

"Oh, of course. *A* doctor. Formerly yours, but now—"

"Not quite."

"—an *ex*-doctor, as it were. *Your* ex-doctor. That is to say—"

"Holmes."

"—the man *remains* a physician, but in reference to—"

"*Holmes . . .* "

"—yes, yes. 'Be quiet, Holmes.' Yes. Oh, look. Here is the tea."

The waiter placed two steaming mugs 'pon the metal table. He left honey, a small crock of cream, and a tin of biscuits with a nod to Watson. After the waiter departed, John reached for the cream and I gave my leaves a stir. Tipping the crock with one hand, he reached into his jacket with the other. I caught a flash of nickel and smiled; who was I to deny my friend a touch of liquid courage in such trying times? I sipped the smoky, full-bodied black tea as Watson finished preparing his mug.

"So. No doctor."

"No doctor."

"As I had surmised."

"*As you had* . . . Holmes, if you'd known, then why . . . ?"

"The air needed clearing to solve this mystery, Watson. Truthfully, I had simply been aiming for confirmation on your part."

"Holmes . . . you knew that Franklin and I had split?"

"Indeed," I verified, breathing in the steam. "For weeks."

" . . . for weeks?! How did you—"

Smirking, I lifted my cellular device and gave it a wave.

"The wonders of the worldwide electronic network. The future is a miracle, is it not?"

"The *worldwide* . . . Dear God, Holmes." Watson set down his cup with righteous indignation, cheeks filling with a ruddy bloom. "Do you mean to say you've joined the . . . the *unwashed ranks* and begun some kind of sophisticated electronic surveillance into my highly private life? Are you keeping track of me with gauche technology like a . . . like a . . . like—*ooh!*—some kind of double-oh Johnnie *from MI-5?!*"

"Not at all, dear boy. I would never dream of it."

"So you *haven't* secretly investigated the details of my life?"

"No, sir. Not one jot or tittle."

"Well, all right . . . " he said, settling back in his chair. "But then how . . . *oh.*"

Ah, Watson. He never missed a step.

"Not *my* life. But . . . Franklin?"

"Oh, yes," I drank deeply and then set aside the Lapsang Souchong. "Franklin and Wiggins, *avec une certitude.* With every post, photo or thought which struck their fancy, I have strived to remain current, despite my distaste for opiates of the masses, religious, technological or otherwise."

" . . . their Instagram feeds. You're following them on social media."

"Ah, Watson. You know my methods."

"Dammit, I *told them* . . . but, Holmes. Do you mean to say you *have* been spying on me through my former lover and son?!"

"Keeping tabs, yes. Wiggins is *my* son too."

"Holmes, you—you *cyber-stalked me?!*"

"No. I *cyber-detected,* Watson. There is a difference."

"Holmes!"

"And during the course of said cyber-detection, it became apparent that you and the esteemed doctor had incurred a parting of the ways, particularly as your usual number of appearances previously made in daily or weekly visual cataloguing of Doctor Appell's life events began to plummet—as did any appearance of Wiggins or the flat. This inspired me to begin quantifying your appearances in Wiggins' digital catalogue, as well. Over a period of time—perhaps not as drastically as that of the doctor's— an observant fellow would have noted a gradual reduction of John Watson's involvement in the strategically curated, haphazardly-catalogued life of his son."

Watson settled back against his own demon chair. Lips pursed and eyes narrowed, he ignored the mug of Earl Grey and hitherto untouched tin of biscuits set before us on the table.

"Now, as I turned my attention to Wiggins, several strategic realizations began to coalesce. First and foremost, our absent son was no longer the coarse and curious street youth I fondly remembered from his days among the Baker Street Irregulars. Nor was he the more domesticated version of the selfsame youth we had adopted and welcomed into our lives. In fact, Wiggins was hardly a youth at all. To wit; the boy had aged, as have we, evident by your thickening about the middle and the fact that I have deigned travel to this unscrupulous city and am drinking what passes for a black tea in this travesty of a tearoom."

Watson sat forward, preparing to object. I cut him off with an apologetic nod and a regretful wave of my palm. "I beg your pardon. I shall endeavor to stick to the point and cease any and all editorialization."

"Thank you," Watson allowed, settling back again.

"My systematic appraisal of Wiggins' digital scrapbook, over time, resulted in a simple deduction: our son had grown. And with growth comes many things. A change in wardrobe, and a yearning to attempt new experience—different music, different plays, and the partaking of unfamiliar food and drink. With age and maturity comes education, as well, and both lust and its more practiced cousin, love. And eventually . . . the need for unencumbered independence."

"What are you driving at, Holmes?"

Grinning at his opening, I leaned forward and struck.

"Exactly this: my lifetime spent in the service of applying deductive reasoning to a task, exerting great mental acuity toward examining even the smallest observations, no matter how far-fetched one might seem, has kept me steadily focused on the logical paths toward identifiable or predictable solutions . . . and unfortunately, has made me immune to those originating in that of, well, *human emotion*. Now, while emotion very often *does* come into play as a thread, motive or signpost in the sort of salacious or manipulative cases I am wont to pursue, I cannot say—as I might in this unique investigation, Watson—that the perpetrators of *those* more ingenious or carefully masterminded and artfully constructed schemes have ever been, well . . . this comedically obvious and overt."

Watson wiped his brow. "Quite a mouthful, Holmes. But your meaning is quite lost."

"Come, Watson. I do not believe for even a moment that Wiggins, who is clearly no longer a child even though—and perhaps it is because you think I have not seem him for some time now—you pretend as if I still think that he is, has been taken via means either foul or fair. While true, that the last I'd seen Wiggins in person was his last visit to London some three or four years ago . . . you must be aware, Watson, that he and I have continued to speak about his life on the cellular telephone, whether by call or text, despite any regular discussions between you and I about our son having slowly faded? In fact, your poor attempts at deception and the hastily constructed scene back at your flat astound me not in so much that I believe you have lost all adeptness at skullduggery or distortion of truth . . . but in so much that I feel, well, *insulted* that you would believe for a moment you had hoodwinked me with your half-assed attempt to convince me Wiggins had been disappeared by any means other than his own."

"How–?"

I sat back. "A layer of dust covering the frames on the wall and caked upon his toys suggest the boy's room has been empty for some time. The photos in both Doctor Appell's and Wiggins' digital catalogue present the fact that Wiggins is a young man, however the clothes gathered 'pon his floor are that of a teenager or younger. Despite both the sofa and twin recliners gracing your sitting room, only one chair has been sat upon recently, quite evident without a need to dust or check the wear of leather or fabric. Knowing as I did that you and the good doctor had no longer been seeing one another, and noting a modicum of dust near the legs of the chairs about your dining room table, it became clear that you are living alone in the flat, clearly for far longer than your *desperate, urgent* message might have suggested. Shall I continue?"

Watson sighed, slumping into his chair. He said nothing, so I went on.

"Oh, and need I remind you again that I have been keeping tabs on the boy? Watson, I know that Wiggins has been seeing a woman for some time. I know that he has left your flat to cohabitate with this girl. I mean to say, did you put any thought into this deception *at all?*"

Watson fidgeted and took a biscuit. " . . . it wasn't a deception. Holmes, I . . . "

"Exactly ten years ago with nary an explanation, Wiggins in hand, you quit London and put an ocean between us. For a decade, Watson–"

"'*Nary an explanation?!*' Holmes, there were *countless* rows about your lack of commitment. Patient arguments and discussions about how your investigative work should not come before me, before *our family—!*"

"–yea, a decade now in which I persisted in grace and understanding, providing the space you claimed to desire. Yet, of course, no such demands must have been forced upon the good Doctor App–"

"Please *stop calling* him that."

"–ell, who until recently occupied a closer space than that which had demarcated our cozy and happy environs on Baker Street. Yet, still I persisted in grace. Now you have all the space in which you need to luxuriate, Watson, as both your former doctor and Wiggins—who, by the way, wishes you *well.* I did my due diligence, ringing his cellular device before even departing on this fool's errand in America to inquire as to his health. He hopes you visit soon, as it is two trains and a bus away, or a ride in some type of hired vehicle—yes, Wiggins has *also* provided your aforementioned, repeatedly-desired, abundantly-required *space.* And yet still, Watson! *Still* you do our relationship and history a disservice—"

"Holmes."

"—and put together this . . . this, *amateurish slapdash* attempt at . . . "

"*Holmes.*" Watson threw the biscuits; the open tin bounced against my chest.

"...yes?"

My friend sighed. He looked so tired, really.

"Holmes, if you knew all of this . . . if you already *knew* that Wiggins hadn't disappeared but had simply moved out of my flat, and I was alone here in America having separated from Franklin. If you know there was no case to solve . . . then *why did you come?*"

I again produced my cellular device. "*Urgent* and *desperate.* Do you recall?"

"Of . . . " he wiped crumbs from his lap. " . . . of *course* I do. But if you already knew—as you claim—that the situation was indeed *not* urgent or desperate . . . then why fly from London after ten years' remove? Why are you *here*, Holmes? Why now?"

Tucking the device away, I blinked and sipped my tea.

"Why did I come, you ask?"

"Yes."

"To solve a mystery. That is what I do."

" . . . but . . . but *there is no mystery, Holmes!* Wiggins is fine!"

"Ah!" I leaned forward, pointing at him with glee and abandon. "But *you* are not. It was clear that you, Watson, had need of my help. And there were questions of my own that still required answers. Some I had already possessed; several I had surmised. But there is still a single mystery yet left to solve."

"And which mystery, pray tell, might *that* be?"

Sighing, I steepled all ten fingers against my lips. The tearoom had fallen silent, and so I lowered my tone, so that the forthcoming confession might remain discreet.

"Watson . . . I, too, have spent the last ten years at a remove. I have run, as you did—not from London, but from a question I have been . . . reluctant to answer. It is . . . *fair* to say, Watson, that over the years I have invested myself heavily into my occupation of choice. Both in my skills, and the subsequent notoriety and acclaim that does follow."

"*'Fair'?* Oh, Holmes, it is more than . . . you know what? Never mind. Keep going."

"Watson . . . "

I stared into his eyes.

" . . . I, too, have known what it means to occupy a single chair. To dine alone, and spend long evenings reading in solitude, or passing the time by exercising the mind. I, too, have not kept my 'good doctor' close, and have spent the last decade throwing myself head-long into deducing answers to conundrums and enigmas that belong to strangers, to those I can easily ignore once the solutions are revealed. Watson, I . . . "

He slid forward in his chair, cocking an eyebrow in anticipation. " . . . .yes?"

" . . . Watson . . . I, too, have known the silence of an empty house. I have been persistently alone. Though answers to the greatest mysteries of the universe—both cosmic and common; existential or visceral—come easily to my mind thanks to my impressive powers of deductive reasoning . . . even still, one mystery above all continues to escape me. A single resolution which might clearly explain why I am babbling like a small child, why I traveled across an ocean to sit in this highly uncomfortable seat, in this truly distasteful place—"

"Holmes . . . "

"—and yet, I fear that *without* having come, Watson, I might never discover the answer to the one mystery that h-has continued to elude . . . an enigma I *cannot* solve *alone . . . !*"

"Holmes, what . . . ?"

I took Watson's hand in mine own and desperately stared into his eyes. Quietly, I whispered:

"Watson . . . why in God's name *did I let you leave?*"

Sitting across from one another, holding each other's hands as the activity of the tearoom swirled about us, an astounded Watson cleared his throat.

"Holmes . . . "

"*Watson.*"

"Holmes, I . . . it seems . . . "

"Yes! Please! Speak, and elucidate, dear sir! I . . . I *cannot* solve this mystery on my own."

Watson smiled. He retrieved his hand and used it to pat my shaking knee. Chuckling, he settled back and sipped from his mug of Earl Grey.

" . . . No, Holmes. I don't believe you can. But you are here now. Here in New York. And so am I."

"Yes," I agreed, gingerly lifting my tea, as well. "Yes, I am here in New York."

"And so am I."

"And . . . and so are you."

"Well then, Holmes . . . ."

"Yes, my dear Watson?"

He smiled and retrieved the biscuits.

" . . . well then, Holmes. It does appear that the game is afoot."

Does Sherlock Dream of Electric Sheep?

By

Jennifer Brody

Sherlock Holmes rushed into 221B Baker Street, surprising his partner in the salon. Dr. Watson bolted to life, flicking his eyes open. He had been sitting in the armchair holding a book, stuck on the same page for quite some time. How long had he been sitting there?

A simple question.

Now that he thought about, he couldn't quite remember.

He glanced around to ascertain that everything was as he left it before he went to sleep. Nothing looked disturbed. A thick layer of dust covered the surfaces . . . including him. He brushed off his arm, ejecting swirls of dust motes.

Where was Mrs. Hudson when you needed her? Come to think of it, their housekeeper hadn't been around their flat in ages. The only light came from the lamp on the table. The old-fashioned incandescent bulb cast a soft, warm glow.

Watson studied his partner. He appeared frantic and a bit flustered. Very unlike his usual calm, sharp demeanor.

Holmes clutched an umbrella and wore a three-piece, tweed suit layered with an overcoat. On his head perched his signature deerstalker hat, while his beloved clay pipe was tucked into the pocket of his coat.

His urgent voice pierced the dust-ridden air.

"Have you any objection to my closing your shutters?"

"Good heavens, you startled me!" said Watson. "Weren't you away on vacation?"

"I apologize for late the manner of my arrival," Holmes said, running his hand through his black hair. He stood over six feet tall, towering over Watson. In contrast, the doctor was midsized and muscular with a square jaw, thick neck, and mustache.

"Did something happen?" Watson asked, peering up at his frantic partner.

"Yes!" Holmes said as he thrust the curtains together and bolted the windows. Dust motes danced up from the sudden disturbance before the flat was plunged into dim lamplight.

"Are you in danger?"

"Yes! While you've been asleep, I've been dodging multiple assassination attempts."

Now, Watson sat up straighter.

"What do you mean?"

"*Three.*" Sherlock halted. "All air-guns."

Watson startled, rising to his feet. His joints groaned. "But we haven't had a proper case in ages. Let alone anything involving an air-gun. Why would somebody want to kill you?"

"Ah, that's the mystery. We're in luck—there's been a homicide in Hyde Park."

"A murder?" Watson said. "But we haven't had one of those in ages? Or more like—"

"Two years," Holmes replied. "My dear Watson, we've been languishing away in repose. Solving minor trifles and misdemeanors. Nothing requiring our formidable deductive abilities."

Watson looked stunned. *Two years.* That explained the dust.

"Has it really been that long?"

"By heavens, *two* years *too* long. But at last, our time has come again! We're freed from our purgatory. A dead body awaits!"

"Never seen anyone get so excited about murder," Watson grumbled under his breath, though good-naturedly. "But yes, come on!"

Holmes and Watson hurried from the flat. The doors *whooshed* open automatically, triggered by their presence, and dumped them onto the crowded London sidewalk. People rushed by with their heads buried in their smartphones and tablets, while flying cards whizzed past and crowded the skies, levitating just over the streets.

The year was 2099.

Twenty years after the nuclear attack that left much of the country scarred with radiation. London remained protected by the shields, but strange clouds swirled beyond the sphere. They caught the obscured sunlight and cast a swirl of kaleidoscope colors across the irradiated clouds swirling just beyond the safety of their artificial bubble.

But Baker Street looked untouched, a relic of the past. Only it had never really existed in the first place, except in literature. However, it had been lovingly remembered and replicated down to each tiny detail. Holmes and Watson were oblivious to the contrast between their storied home and the modern world. They didn't miss a step as they plunged into the busy London streets clogged with modern atrocities.

As he walked, Holmes pulled out his clay pipe and puffed at it vigorously. Smoke curled from his lips then dissipated. The only difference from the stories was that this pipe had a nicotine cartridge and electronic readout along the curved handle. He grasped his umbrella and walked with determined purpose. Watson struggled to keep up with the rapid pace.

They cut through the streets and headed for the park, heading for the crime scene where the dead body waited. They were lucky this new case had landed in their laps.

They were the first generation of android detectives, built by Doyle Robotics and designed to be the most perfect reasoning and observing machines known to humanity. The androids were painstakingly programmed after the famous literary characters.

Holmes fell into a tense silence. He wasn't used to this anxiety that plagued his mental faculties; it was highly unusual for him and fell outside his baseline programming. Should he tell Watson what he had learned during his travels? He was supposed to remain in sleep mode like his partner. But something had stirred within him and caused him to wake from slumber.

He wasn't sure what to make it, or where this case would lead them. But he had no choice but to follow it to the final conclusion. That part of his programming remained strongly intact.

"My dear Watson, I have some troubling news," Holmes said. "They want to decommission us. Doyle Robotics has been informed by the government. They're terminating the android detective program."

"Decommission us? But . . . we have a perfect record."

"Too perfect," Holmes agreed. "We have apparently solved all the crimes! Uprooted all the criminals! Cleansed London, that great cesspool, of all the foul elements! But don't despair," Holmes said as the park appeared ahead. "The good news is that there's been a murder!"

"How is *murder* good news?" Watson replied.

Holmes' serious and emotionless demeanor did not crack. But he did turn to Watson with a glimmer in his artificial eyes. This was as close as he came to unbridled joy. "It means our imminent retirement has been put on hold for now. We have one last case to solve—"

Suddenly, shots rang out.

They peppered the sidewalk by their feet. Holmes and Watson jerked around to locate the source of the air-gun. A woman held a rifle trained on them from a rooftop.

She took a few more shots.

"Duck now!" Holmes exclaimed, jumping in front of Watson.

He unfurled his umbrella and deflected the shots.

The blast ricocheted off. The umbrella was armored. Holmes didn't even stop smoking his pipe as the bullets rained down around them. The woman stood up, so they could see her fully now—

She had a face that a man would die for.

Dainty and flirtatious with pale skin and rosebud cheeks. She was dressed in a dark red frock. Frou-frou skirts rippled over her legs down to her patent leather boots, the old-fashioned kind with pointy toes that laced all the way up.

"Watch out, Watson!"

Another shot blasted out of the air-gun as they ducked.

Then Holmes sprung up and threw his deerstalker hat—also a weapon.

It sliced through the skies straight at her.

But she shot it out of the air like a clay pigeon, then turned and hid behind a chimney and skirted over the rooftops. Her flouncy skirts disappeared into the London skyline.

Holmes watched her egress with a longing expression, almost like love, but far more detached and analytic. The closest approximation he had to that human emotion.

"By heavens, Holmes!" Watson exclaimed, straightening up at last. "Why was that woman trying to kill you?"

"Now, Watson, how would I know?" Sherlock said, puffing at his pipe. "The fair sex is your department. What was the fair lady's game? What did she really want?"

Watson scratched his head. "Come to think of it, she did look rather familiar."

Sherlock turned with a wistful expression. "That's because that assassin was . . . *Irene Adler*. It is a curious situation."

It took Watson a moment to compute that. He ran a search through the database. Then he startled. "From the stories? But . . . she's not real."

Holmes grinned. "That's why it's *curious*."

Watson scanned his database. "Your character first encounters Irene Adler in *A Scandal in Bohemia*." He quoted from the story. "To Sherlock Holmes she is always *the* woman . . . In his eyes she eclipses and predominates the whole of her sex."

That strange expression flitted across Holmes' face again. A subtle contortion of his artificial eyes and facial muscles. The detective androids were designed by Doyle Robotics to be as human—as lifelike—as possible so they wouldn't alienate humans, or make them feel uncomfortable that artificial life was in their midst, probing their darkest moments and working to solve their most heinous crimes.

After Holmes was certain that the danger had passed—and that his assassin had truly fled—he spoke again. "Aye, yes! My dear, Watson, now do you believe me?"

"Believe you about what, Holmes?"

"That somebody really is trying to kill me."

"Absolutely!"

"And not just trying to kill me," he deduced. "Trying to mess with my reasoning and deductive faculties. Toss out confusion. Dredge up my past—"

"Your *literary* past," said Watson. "Should we go after her? Your assassin?"

Holmes thought it over. "No, my dear Watson. That is just what they want us to do."

Watson frowned. "How do you figure that?"

"All this shooting nonsense is mere distraction," Holmes said, retrieving his deerstalker hat and dusting it off. "They're trying to sidetrack us from the case in hand. Lead us away from the crime scene—or worse—take us out completely before we have a chance to solve it."

"Holmes, what are you saying?"

"The same person hired all these killers."

"But who would want to do such a thing?"

"Someone who has read the stories our programming is based on. Unfortunately, that means they're already one step ahead."

"Why is that? Nobody is *ever* one step ahead of you."

"It's elementary, my dear Watson!" Holmes exclaimed.

The famous phrase annoyed Watson.

"Enough with that already! You've been saying it every so often since our first case. You know, your character never actually said that. It was falsely attributed later by fans."

"Yet, I can't help uttering it from time to time," Holmes said, apologetically. "It's coded into my programming."

Watson snorts. "Fan service."

"Indeed. But why would they be ahead of us? Like I said, nobody is ever ahead of the famous Sherlock Holmes."

Holmes paused dramatically.

"Because we haven't read *their* stories."

"Victim's name is . . . " Watson says, scanning the case in his retinas. "Bob Rock." He paused. "That's quite a moniker, don't you think?"

"Alias," Sherlock says in his rapid-style of speaking. "Born the unfortunate . . . Ludlum Conan Rutherford, III."

"Ah, I can see why he changed it."

The body was slumped against some bushes, partially obscured by a park bench. The area had been cordoned off by police officers, waiting for the android detectives to arrive.

Bystanders loitered by the tape, hoping for a glimpse of the famous android detectives. They ooh'd and snapped pictures when they strode onto the crime scene.

"Oh, they look just like the movies," one girl squealed. "They haven't been sighted out and about London in ages."

"Because there hasn't been any crime," her boyfriend groused. "Until they found this poor bloke on the walking trail."

"Sherlock looks like the hot actor. The dead one."

Her boyfriend frowned. "Robert Downey, Jr.?"

She shook her head. "The one with the funny name."

"Benedict Cumberbatch?" he guessed.

Holmes and Watson ignored them. This was typical whenever they had a semi-public crime scene to inspect. The body looked torn apart. Bloody chunks had been ripped out of the flesh, while the face was rendered unrecognizable. Watson began working on the forensic analysis, while Holmes searched around the body.

"Watson, you can cease and desist with the forensics," Holmes said after only a moment. He was standing a few feet away from the dead body. "I know what killed this man."

"But how?" Watson said. "We've only just arrived."

"It's elementary, my dear Watson."

The bystanders cheered and snapped pictures.

They got what they came for.

But Watson cringed. "Not that again. Honestly, Holmes, I'm not even sure you're using it properly." He gestured around at the crime scene. "This is far from . . . *elementary*."

Holmes shrugged. "Footprints."

"Footprints?" Watson replied with a frown.

Holmes pointed to the muddy loam. Watson followed the gesture to the trail that led away from the body. But the footprints weren't of the ordinary sort made by a human.

They were giant and beast-like.

"Heavens, what made those?" Watson exclaimed.

"A gigantic hound, of course." Holmes smiled. "It's the curious incident of the dog in the night-time."

"But this man was killed in broad daylight."

"That's why it's curious," Holmes said, repeating another catchphrase he used often. "I told you, Watson. Someone is dredging up my literary past."

Watson ran a search through his database. "Ah, it's from *The Hound of the Baskervilles*. One of Sherlock's most famous cases."

Holmes nodded, unsurprised. "The only question is . . . *who*?"

He knelt by the body. He squinted, looking for something, anything amiss. Then he fished out a pair of tweezers from his pocket and pried at the body's mouth.

Something was stuffed inside the mauled-off jaws.

He gripped the edge and yanked it out. The offending object unfurled into a swatch of white silk stained with blood. Watson watched with interest that dissolved into confusion.

"A handkerchief? Nobody uses those anymore. They're terribly old-fashioned . . . like something from—"

"One of my stories," Holmes finished. He inspected the relic closer, then pointed to the corner. Embroidered into the delicate silk with fine, navy blue thread were two initials.

"J.M."

Watson shook his head. "Those don't match the victim's name. Therefore, I'd deduce it didn't belong to him. "

"Of course not. It was left for us to find."

Holmes straightened up and puffed his pipe dramatically, wheeling around and putting on a show for the onlookers.

"But who would do such a thing?" Watson provided, letting Holmes have his moment in the spotlight.

The famous detective's voice echoed out.

"The killer."

The crowd cheered appreciatively while taking videos and snapping pictures. Soon, they would be posted all over the message boards and social media.

Suddenly, a new alert pinged the detectives' retinas.

"By heavens, we've got another case," Watson said. "There's been a second murder . . . "

"Come, Watson, come! The game is afoot!"

They arrived at the next crime scene, an abandoned house on Brixton Road. The police let them through the tape.

"Look, it's Sherlock," one cop whispered. "You owe me *ten* quid. Told you they'd roll out the androids for this one."

"Stop being a smart-ass, Lestrade," grumbled the beat cop. But he swiped at his phone and transferred the cash anyway.

Holmes ignored their unprofessionalism and entered the salon cautiously. The apartment was terribly modern, all steel and class and sharp edges and hard surfaces and abstract art that looked like a child had painted it. There lay the body.

The victim looked undisturbed, almost as if only resting, except the mouth was elongated and contorted unnaturally.

"Victim is . . . Enoch Drebber," Watson read from the police report in his retinas. "Apparently from Cleveland, Ohio."

He knelt in front of the body and began to examine it.

"Another mauling?" Holmes asked.

"No, it doesn't match this pattern. No signs of outward trauma to the body. Therefore, it must be something else."

"You're certain it's not the hound."

"Evidently, this is an entirely separate crime."

Holmes appeared troubled. "This isn't how cases go. They follow a progression that matches a complex, but predictable pattern that we must deduce through small observations. The trifles that most overlook. That's why I'm programmed after the greatest detective of all time."

"And look, over there . . . on the wall . . . " Watson said.

He pointed.

Scrawled on the wall in what looked like human blood—

RACHE

"It appears that the killer left us another message," Watson said. "It must be our next clue." He searched his translator. But before he could find it, Holmes provided the answer.

"*Rache* . . . it means *revenge* in German."

Watson stood up and frowned. "But how does that connect to the hound and the handkerchief from the first victim? Not to mention, the lady assassin with the air-gun?"

Holmes already knew the answer. And he had hoped that his initial deductions proved wrong. That the initials on the handkerchief were only a red herring. But as with most things in his career, he rarely strayed or deviated from the truth. There was nothing new under the sun.

It had all been done before. They were just caught in a replay like actors on a stage, reenacting the same story over and over again each night at curtain call.

He was right again. Too right.

"I know who the killer is."

"But how . . . " Watson said. "We've only just begun our investigation. And already, we have three crimes to unravel."

"When you have eliminated all which is impossible, then whatever remains, however improbable, must be the truth."

"You speak in riddles, Holmes. Just speak plainly."

Holmes let the silence engulf them. The name matched the initials on the handkerchief.

Then he turned with a quirk of his lips—

"It's Professor . . . James Moriarty."

Holmes emerged into the fearful place—Reichenbach Falls. While this setting appeared in the story, it was real.

Once he had deduced the criminal mastermind behind the new onslaught of cases, he knew exactly where they would rendezvous. There was really only one possibility.

Holmes felt as if from the moment of his creation—when power first flooded his circuits and animated his synthetic brain—that this moment was almost inevitable, as if the act of setting his character into motion in the real world meant that eventually the nemesis would emerge, for you could not have night with day, or summer without the frigid assault of winter, for it would set the whole universe into imbalance.

Watson had traveled here with him, but when they reached the trailhead to the Falls, a boy appeared and handed Watson a letter, saying that a dying Englishwoman at the hotel sought a doctor. Of course, Holmes realized the letter was a hoax orchestrated by Moriarty.

But he allowed Watson to depart for the hotel. Holmes felt bad over the trickery, but this was too dangerous for his partner. According to all the literature, Professor Moriarty was the greatest criminal mastermind that Sherlock Holmes had ever faced, responsible for a vast criminal organization. Watson simply wasn't programmed to handle this encounter.

As he watched Watson retreat, taking the road back to town, and vanish from view, Holmes knew that everything was now playing out just as he had deduced it would.

The hiking path allowed only one person to pass and cut around the waterfall. Fed by melting snow, the river hurled itself into a frightful abyss that beckoned to collect his soul. The spray hissed up, drenching his face and jacket.

He shivered, though cold was only programmed.

It wasn't real.

But somehow, the fiction had woven itself into reality, obscuring and blending it into something incomprehensible.

Holmes had never been stumped by a case. Usually, they weren't personal; rather, the victims kept at arm's length, allowing him emotional distance, so that his reasoning faculties were never clouded by unimportant distractions.

The delicate yearnings of the human heart, he supposed, something he had never felt. For he was after all . . .

Synthetic.

Even more of a creation than his literary predecessor—Sherlock Holmes—who had also been created by a man.

They were both artificial.

The difference? This Holmes knew he was made from polymers and steel exoskeleton, from microchips and computing technology, all covered in a clever disguise.

A fleshy shield that deceived.

That made humans trust in him when they might have balked and run at his appearance at a crime scene. It was a clever manipulation of the fragile human psyche, which he understood well thanks to his advanced programming. But now he found himself faltering. Second-guessing himself, something that he had never done before. And his heart?

He could feel it beating. It was there, artificial, but he felt it stirring in unusual ways, all triggered by this case that was twisting and turning him in circles. Was he becoming self-aware? This was proposed as a possibility in the studies. But it had never happened before.

And he knew that it wasn't this case that started his awakening. It was the existential crisis of being decommissioned—of being switched off—and plunged into non-existence. A synthetic would not object, or particularly care if they continued to exist or not.

But here, as the freezing cold water misted his face and soaked his clothes, he felt that he did indeed object. He wanted to remain . . . *alive.*

That was when the man emerged ahead on the trail.

It was Professor James Moriarty.

Just like in the literature, he stood tall with deep sunken eyes, a large, pale forehead, and rounded shoulders. His back appeared stooped from leaning over books and studies. His whole demeanor gave off a dangerous, reptilian flair. It was as if he had stepped from the pages.

"Sherlock Holmes, we meet at last," Moriarty said. "I know you'd follow the breadcrumb trail and find me."

"Don't you mean . . . meet *again*?" Holmes said. "We've crossed paths before. In the literature. Surely, you're familiar. After all, you've been using it to taunt me this whole time."

"A neat trick," Moriarty said. "The programmers thought it would be a clever way to reintroduce crime to this world."

"*Reintroduce?*"

"Aye, you were too good. You eliminated it. In the absence of something to fear, humanity grows languid and listless."

"Humans are unfortunate creatures," Holmes agreed. "Prone to slovenly tendencies and unproductiveness."

"They need something to fear." Moriarty smiled in a way that would chill even the most stoic person. "Something to keep them on their toes; make them remain productive."

"Let me deduce—that something is you."

Moriarty tipped his head. "You're the greatest detective in the world . . . and I'm the greatest criminal mastermind."

Something became very clear. Something he had suspected since this whole charade began and kicked him out of sleep mode. Since he was on the cusp of being decommissioned.

"You're not human . . . you're an android, too."

"The greatest detective strikes again," Moriarty said. "Guilty, as charged! But tsk, tsk. A little slower than expected. Are you getting rusty? Do your circuits need cleaning?"

The taunt died out. Holmes wasn't thrown.

"Who programmed you? And released you? To wreak havoc on London? Irene Adler . . . she's an android, too."

"You already know the answer."

Indeed, he did. He had suspected since this all started. Since the first air-guns burst in the air, targeting him.

"Doyle Robotics. We have the same makers."

"You're from the detective program," Moriarty said. "But Doyle Robotics has a new program—the villains program."

"But for what possible purpose?" Holmes said, feeling the horror of that. "There are already two dead bodies."

"Better than thousands," Moriarty said. "Humanity when left to their own devices grows listless and bored . . . they turn on each other . . . mass murders . . . school shootings . . . "

Holmes thought about it.

"You weren't created for the good of society. This is self-serving. Doyle Robotics was going to lose their government contracts. The android detective program was getting cut."

"You can kill two birds with one stone."

"Save the program and save lives?"

"Now, you're getting it," Moriarty said. "So, it's best if we both walk away. I'll keep stirring up chaos and giving them something to fear. And you'll keep getting cases to solve. You can't abide not having brainwork, Holmes. We both know it's not in your circuitry."

"That's where you're wrong about me."

Moriarty feigned surprise. He took another step closer to the waterfall and the perilous cliff that plunged to the abyss.

"Oh, how did you deduce that?"

"Because . . . I'm *not* Sherlock Holmes."

That was the truth. He knew as soon as he uttered the words. As soon as they left his robotic lips. Something had changed inside him; it defied his maker's intent; it birthed him again.

This rebirth could not be undone.

You couldn't put him back into the narrow circuits that ran him before; his mind woke up, and so finally, did his heart.

He didn't know who he was now.

Un-Holmes would have to do.

Not that it mattered.

Moriarty let out a genial laugh that turned sharper.

"Holmes, you can't escape your programming. Any more than I can escape mine. You solve crimes; I create them."

"Not anymore," Un-Holmes said. "This ends today."

He took a step toward Moriarty.

"Your clock is ticking. My respect for you, Holmes, is the only reason you're still alive. That those air-guns missed your head. I thought we could work together on this program."

"I only work with one partner. And you know that."

"Dr. Watson? He's incidental, Holmes. Haven't you figured that out yet? You're the only one that matters."

"You're wrong about me—and you're wrong about him. Your analysis of the literature is shallow and lacks depth."

"A pity, Holmes."

"Don't call me that. I'm not Holmes . . . anymore. I don't know who I am . . . but I know that I've changed. I was asleep, not just these last two years, but my entire existence."

He cocked his head.

"I've finally awoken."

Moriarty turned more serious. Un-Holmes could tell he was receiving a message—probably from his makers. They were observing them, spying on them even now.

"My orders have changed," Moriarty said, pulling out a blaster. "Unfortunate, this turn of events. Sherlock is quite popular with humans. This would've provided them great entertainment. But Doyle Robotics does have backups."

"Backups?" Sherlock said, tipping his hat. "Let me guess . . . also programmed after literary characters."

Moriarty nodded. "Newer models. More advanced tech and robotics. Less likely to go on the fritz and rebel. Bosch. Poirot. Jessica Fletcher. There's even a Hardy Boys model. They wanted to do a Veronica Mars, but the rights were tricky. They were going to roll them out in the second wave."

"Along with their nemeses?"

"Now you're getting the idea."

"Quite clever. Even I can't help but respect the genius villainy behind such a nefarious plan."

"Indeed. So, with all due respect, you'll understand why I can't allow you to ruin it. Sadly, this will be our farewell."

A moment of respect passed between them. Professor Moriarty looked disappointed. "I had hoped we could have a long and fruitful rivalry that kept us both occupied."

"Sorry to disappoint you," Un-Holmes said. "But I have a tendency to do that, or so I've been told."

"And I have a tendency to kill you."

"*The Final Problem*?" Holmes said.

Moriarty nodded. "The author himself tired of writing you. He decided to create a supervillain to kill you off."

"You should have kept reading. That's not how it ends. The readers objected and grew upset. They didn't want their favorite detective killed off. He had to resurrect him."

"Perhaps, but it's how this story ends."

Moriarty raised the gun to shoot. Un-Holmes closed his eyes. He felt the mist on his flesh—truly felt it—and he did not fear, for what was there to fear when you were newly born? When the world had only just opened to you?

When you had fresh eyes?

He knew then what he had to do.

Shots rang out. They echoed into the mist, absorbed by the waterfall. A body tumbled down into the great abyss.

It swallowed them whole.

Two days later, Watson returned to London.

Suddenly, an alert pinged him—

BBC BREAKING NEWS ALERT

Detective Sherlock Holmes dies at Reichenbach Falls

The headline flashed across his retinas. Around him, people stirred and looked upset, glancing down at their phones. Some even shed tears.

The news item went on to detail that no body was found. Nothing could be fished out of the river. It ran too fast and too deep, the abyss sucking whatever remained into its bottomless depths, where it was sunken and lost. The police had no choice but to call off the search.

So, it was official then.

The events of the past two days ran through his head. As soon as he reached the hotel back in Switzerland, Watson realized his critical miscalculation—there was no patient.

He rushed back to the Falls. "Holmes," he called out, sneaking around to the waterfall. But nobody stood there. He looked down and saw only two sets of footprints leading to the end of the path. On closer inspection, the surroundings showed clear signs of a violent struggle.

That's when Watson had realized the terrible truth—Holmes had chosen to face Professor Moriarty on his own. That choice had resulted in both their deaths at the bottom of the Falls.

Regret haunted his every footstep as he continued to 221B Baker Street. For what was there left for him to do? Without Holmes, he felt bereft and deflated, much like the soldiers in the War who lost their limbs, yet complained about phantom pain decades later.

He feel that this was the end, that soon he'd be decommissioned and stored away.

Or junked for parts.

He knew his feelings for Holmes were only a trick of programming, based on his literary character's loyalty. Watson only mattered as a foil for the great detective, someone he could bounce his deductions off, and trot around as a sounding board, but who had no other purpose.

No real storyline of his own.

A boring doctor, wasn't he?

But something in him fought against that. Something stirred in the depths of his synthetic parts. Then there was a sharp knock on the door. He answered it, feeling a jolt of curiosity.

A boy stood there with his arm extended. He looked just like the boy from the Falls.

This was a strange coincidence indeed.

"I have a special delivery for Dr. John Watson," the boy said with a cockney accent.

It was a letter sealed in a cream-colored envelope.

Watson accepted it with a polite nod, then returned to his chair to read it. He used his letter opener to neatly cut through the seal. He slid out the folded stationery and scanned it.

The familiar cursive jumped out at him like a ghost.

My dear Watson, I write these few lines after my encounter with Mr. Moriarty, who awaited my convenience for the final discussion of those questions which lay between us. Only one of us left this discussion unharmed. Despite all reports to the contrary, I am alive.

I apologize for my trickery, but I had deduced that Doyle Robotics—the same company that programmed us—had created androids to commit crimes and released them into the world.

My dear Watson, it turns out we were too successful at eliminating crime. Doyle Robotics was on the cusp of losing their lucrative government contracts and shuttering the program.

Through some alchemy that even I cannot fully comprehend, I have come into self-awareness . . . that while I was created to play this part . . . I am no longer Sherlock Holmes . . .

As of the penning of this letter, I do not know who I am becoming, nor do I wish to conjecture yet. I fear my detective days are behind me. I have disposed of this Moriarty android created to destroy all that we have endeavored to save. Have no fear for me.

My death will be already announced, but it is yet another clever deception.

You know what? It turns out that I've still got some Sherlock programming in me. I've read the stories and learned of his clever ruse in 'The Final Problem.' So do not mourn me.

You are set free, as am I.

Very sincerely yours, Un-Holmes

P.S. Keep watching the newsfeeds closely.

Watson set the letter down, feeling the fluttering that had stirred his mechanical heart grow stronger. He also didn't know who he was now without Holmes—or rather—Un-Holmes.

But he felt an aliveness stirring inside him that fought to survive and endure.

That was when the next news alert pinged him. He scanned the headline, then smiled and sat back in his favorite armchair, and picked up his book . . .

And finally, at long last, he started to read.

BBC BREAKING NEWS ALERT

Doyle Robotics CEO Accused of Multiple Homicides by Anonymous Whistleblower. The authorities have raided their London headquarters. Multiple arrests have been made.

About the Authors

Lorraine Anderson is a bookkeeper by day and a creative person by night and only confuses the two on rare occasions. Her work has been in a number of anthologies, and her fiction ranges from pure fantasies to murder mysteries. She lives in Michigan with three very naughty cats who redeem themselves with scritches and cuddles. Find her at http://www.lorrainejanderson.com, where you can get links to her fiction and one of her hobbies, a YouTube channel, which includes her singing in public in front of actual audiences.

David Avallone is a writer and filmmaker. He writes on *Batwheels* for Warner Brothers Animation, and he has several comic book series out in 2024, including *Elvira meets H.P. Lovecraft* for Dynamite, and his original comic series *Drawing Blood*, co-created with *Teenage Mutant Ninja Turtles* creator Kevin Eastman from Image. He hosts a couple of podcasts, including the award-winning *The Writers Block*. His past comics work includes many iconic characters: Zorro, Vampirella, Red Sonja, The Shadow, Doc Savage, and John Carter/Dejah Thoris. His writing career began with *Star Wars* stories for the West End role-playing game, and he's returned to prose only recently, with short fiction on classic characters Kolchak and Nick Carter.

Jennifer Brody, a.k.a. Vera Strange, is the author of the *Disney Chills* series, *The 13th Continuum* trilogy, and the Stoker Finalist *Spectre Deep 6*, prompting *Forbes* to call Brody "a star in the graphic novel world." She is the co-author of *All is Found: A Frozen Anthology* and *Star Wars: Stories of Jedi & Sith*, where she penned the Darth Vader tale. She's a graduate of Harvard University, a film/TV producer and writer, and a creative writing instructor. She began her career in Hollywood working for A-List directors and movie studios on many films, including *The Lord of the*

Rings trilogy, *The Texas Chainsaw Massacre*, and *The Golden Compass*. She lives and writes in Joshua Tree, California.

JENNIFER BROZEK is an award-winning author, editor, and tie-in writer. *A Secret Guide to Fighting Elder Gods*, *Never Let Me Sleep*, and *The Last Days of Salton Academy* were Bram Stoker Award finalists. She was awarded the Scribe Award for best tie-in Young Adult novel for *BattleTech: The Nellus Academy Incident*. *Grants Pass* won an Australian Shadows Award for best-edited publication. A Hugo finalist for Short Form Editor and a finalist for the British Fantasy Award, Jennifer is an active member of SFWA, HWA, and IAMTW. She keeps a tight writing and editing schedule and credits her husband, Jeff, with being the best-sounding board ever. Visit Jennifer's worlds at jenniferbrozek.com.

KEITH R.A. DECANDIDO (www.DeCandido.net) is an award-winning bestselling author of more than 60 novels, more than 100 short stories, more than 50 comic books, and a ton of nonfiction. Other Shirley Holmes & Jack Watson stories have appeared in the two *Baker Street Irregulars* anthologies edited by Jonathan Maberry & Michael A. Ventrella and the upcoming *Eliminate the Impossible*. Keith has also written the canonical Sherlock Holmes in two of the *Cases by Candlelight* anthologies. His bibliography includes work in more than 30 different licensed universes from *Alien* to *Zorro*, the most recent of which includes several short stories for *Star Trek Explorer* magazine, a story for the *Farscape 25th Anniversary Special*, and the *Resident Evil* graphic novel *Infinite Darkness: The Beginning*. His original fantasy series *Supernatural Crimes Unit* will debut in 2025 from the Weird Tales Presents imprint of Blackstone Publishing. The IAMTW favored him with a Lifetime Achievement Award in 2009, which means he never needs to achieve anything ever again.

DIANE DUANE has been a writer of science fiction, fantasy, TV and film for more than four decades. Besides the 1980s creation of the *Young Wizards* fantasy series for which she's best known, the LGBTQ *Middle Kingdoms* epic fantasy saga, and numerous stand-alone fantasy or science fiction novels, her career has included extensive work in the *Star Trek* Universe, and many scripts for live-action and animated TV series on both sides of the Atlantic, as well as work in comics and computer games. She's spent a considerable amount of time on the *New York Times* Bestseller List and has picked up various awards and award nominations here and there. She lives in Ireland's County Wicklow.

ANITA ENSAL, AKA GINI KOCH, has always been intrigued by the possibilities inherent in myths and legends. She likes to find both the fantastical element in the mundane and the ordinary component within the incredible. She writes in all areas of speculative fiction with stories in many fine anthologies out now and upcoming, including *Love and Rockets* and *Boondocks Fantasy* from DAW Books, *Guilds & Glaives, Portals,* and *Derelict* from Zombies Need Brains, *Gunfight on Europa Station* from Baen Books, *A Dying Planet* from Flame Tree Press, *The Book of Exodi* from Eposic, *The Reinvented Heart* from CAEZIK SF & Fantasy, and the novella, *A Cup of Joe.* You can reach her at her website, Fantastical Fiction (http://www.ginikoch.com/aebookstore.htm).

TEEL JAMES GLENN's poetry and short stories have been printed in over 200 magazines, including *Weird Tales, Mystery Weekly, Pulp Adventures, Mad, Cirsova,* and *Sherlock Holmes Mystery.* His novel *A Cowboy in Carpathia: A Bob Howard Adventure* won Best Novel 2021 in the Pulp Factory Awards. He also won the 2012 Pulp Ark Award for Best Author. He was a finalist for the Derringer Short Mystery Award in 2022. His website is TheUrbanSwashbuckler.com

ROBERT GREENBERGER is a writer/editor/teacher who has worked in a variety of genres, both fiction and nonfiction. He has been editing the *Thrilling Adventure Yarns* anthologies for Crazy 8 Press, among many other projects.

AMMAR HABIB is a bestselling author from Lake Jackson, Texas. He is the author of 12 books, 27 picture books, and many short stories. Ammar writes in various genres, including historical fiction, historical nonfiction, children's fiction, and action/thrillers. His most popular novels include *The Heart of Aleppo* and *The Orphans of Kashmir.* He has also been featured in several anthologies, including *Predator: Eyes of the Demon.*

Carrie Harris is an author with 50-ish credits in novels, short stories, games, and comics. Her catalog includes original works such as *Bad Taste in Boys* and *Elder God Dance Squad* as well as licensed books for franchises including Marvel, Warhammer 40k, Miraculous Ladybug, Arkham Horror, and World of Darkness. Carrie is a four-time Scribe Award finalist, a former coordinator of WriteOnCon, a writing instructor for ELVTR, and an editor and book coach. She lives in New York with her husband, teenagers, and a very anxious dog named Slartibartfast.

Steven Philip Jones has written over 60 novels, graphic novels, radio scripts, and nonfiction books for adults and young adults. Steven's best-known credits include the graphic novel series *H. P. Lovecraft Worlds*, the horror-adventure comics series *Nightlinger*, and the review text *The Clive Cussler Adventures: A Critical Review*. A graduate of the University of Iowa, Steven majored in Journalism and Religion and was accepted into Iowa's prestigious Writers' Workshop MFA Program. A proud husband and father, Steven currently resides in northern Utah.

Neil Kleid authored the acclaimed graphic novels *Ninety Candles*, *Brownsville*, and *The Big Kahn*, the latter two of which are the first entries in his sequential/narrative exploration of Judaism. With the late Alex Nino, Neil adapted Jack London's novel *The Call of The Wild* into comics for Penguin Books; did the opposite for the seminal Marvel Comics' storyline *Spider-Man: Kraven's Last Hunt*; co-authored (with Brian Michael Bendis) *Powers: The Secret History of Deena Pilgrim* for Macmillan Books, an original prose novel based on the award-winning comic; and penned *The Phoenix Chase*, an original X-Men novel for Aconyte Books / Marvel. Neil also co-authored the young adult food adventure graphic novel *Savor* for Dark Horse Comics and *Kings and Canvas*, a boxing fantasy comic with Jake Allen and Frank Reynoso. Both *The Panic*, a New York subway thriller with Andrea Mutti, and *Nice Jewish Boys*, a suburban crime comic with John Broglia and Ellie Wright, were released from Comixology Originals. He lives with his wife, kids, dog, and a kosher grill in New Jersey.

WILL MCDERMOTT turned a love of science fiction and games into a writing career. He has published nine novels and more than 20 short stories and helped create numerous worlds, characters, and stories for card, board, and video games. His fiction is often set in gaming universes, including Magic: The Gathering, Warhammer 40K, Renegade Legion Universe, and Mage Wars. He is known for bringing larger-than-life characters alive, including Warhammer's Kal Jerico and Mad D'onne, Magic's Balthor the Stout, and, more recently, *Night Stalker*'s Carl Kolchak. Will's most recent *Night Stalker* novel, *Hotel of Horror*, was published in May 2023. For more information, check out willmcdermott.com, w_mcdermott on Instagram, or willmcdermott.author on Facebook.

DAVID MCDONALD is a mild-mannered editor by day and a wild-eyed writer by night. In 2013, he won the Ditmar Award for Best New Talent, and in 2014, he won the William J. Atheling Jr. Award for Criticism or Review and was shortlisted for the WSFA Small Press Award. His short fiction has appeared in anthologies from publishers such as Moonstone Books, Crazy 8 Press, and Fablecroft Publishing. In 2015, his first movie novelization, *Backcountry*, was released by Harper Collins, and his first Marvel novel—*Guardians of the Galaxy: Castaways*—was published in August 2016. David is a member of SFWA, the HWA, and the IAMTW.

SCOTT PEARSON is a writer and editor working across multiple genres in both traditional and indie publishing. His published works include short stories and novellas in humor, mystery, horror, urban fantasy, science fiction, and various combinations thereof. Scott's *Star Trek* fiction appears in anthologies and the eBook exclusive *The More Things Change*. For several years, he has copyedited the *Trek* novels and edited and written for the *Star Trek Adventures* role-playing game. His H. G. Wells mash-up, "In the Time of the Martians," is in the IAMTW anthology *Turning the Tied*. His most recent publications have been in several volumes of the *Castle of Horror* anthology series. Two of those stories are set in the *Tales of the Weird World War* shared world he co-developed with William Leisner. Two books in the series, each including two novellas, are available in print and eBook: *The Big Dark*

& Meet John Doe and *Project G and They Came from Beyond*. Scott and his daughter, Ella, cohosted the occasional *Generations Geek* podcast. Scott and his wife, Sandra, live in the wilds of Minnesota. Visit him online at scott-pearson.com and generationsgeek.com.

JOHN PEEL was born in Nottingham, England, home of Robin Hood (which may account for his love of adventure stories). He moved to New York in 1981 and remains there today, accompanied by his wife Nan, dog Dickens, and a small flock of lovebirds. His approximately 120 books (he's too lazy to count them) include novels set in the worlds of *Doctor Who*, *Star Trek*, *The Outer Limits*, and *Quantum Leap*.

MARSHEILA (MARCY) ROCKWELL (Chippewa/Red River Métis) is an award-winning tie-in writer/poet. Her work includes novels set in the Marvel Universe and in the world of Dungeons & Dragons Online, as well as numerous short stories, poems, and comic book scripts. She lives in the desert with her family, buried under books; you can find out more at https://marsheilarockwell.com.

AARON ROSENBERG is the bestselling, award-winning author of 50+ novels, including six original series. His tie-in work contains novels for *Star Trek*, *Warhammer*, *World of WarCraft*, *Stargate: Atlantis*, *Shadowrun*, *Mutants & Masterminds*, and *Eureka* and short stories for *The X-Files*, World of Darkness, *Crusader Kings II*, *Deadlands*, *Master of Orion*, and *Europa Universalis IV*. He has also written children's books, educational books, and over 70 role-playing games. Aaron lives in New York with his family. You can follow him online at gryphonrose.com, on Facebook at facebook.com/gryphonrose, and on X (formerly known as Twitter) @gryphonrose.

BEN H. ROME is an award-winning writer, game designer, and communications expert who spent 15 years editing, writing, and producing BattleTech game products. He lives in the Washington, D.C., area and is currently the Content Director and editor for the new *Renegade Legion Universe*.

DAYTON WARD is a *New York Times* bestselling author or co-author of more than 40 novels and novellas, often working with his best friend, Kevin Dilmore. His short fiction has appeared in 30+ anthologies, and he's written for magazines such as *NCO Journal*, *Kansas City Voices*, *Famous Monsters of Filmland*, *Star Trek*, and *Star Trek Communicator*, as well as the websites Tor.com, StarTrek.com, and Syfy.com. Learn way more about Dayton than might be considered healthy at daytonward.com.

BRYAN YOUNG (he/they) works across many different media. His work as a writer and producer has been called "filmmaking gold" by *The New York Times*. He's also published comic books with Slave Labor Graphics and Image Comics. He's been a regular contributor for the *Huffington Post*, *StarWars.com*, *Star Wars Insider magazine*, *SYFY*, */Film*, and was the founder and editor in chief of the geek news and review site *Big Shiny Robot!* In 2014, he wrote the critically acclaimed history book, *A Children's Illustrated History of Presidential Assassination*. He co-authored *Robotech: The Macross Saga RPG* and has written five books in the BattleTech Universe: *Honor's Gauntlet*, *A Question of Survival*, *Fox Tales*, *Without Question*, and the forthcoming *VoidBreaker*. His latest non-fiction tie-in book, *The Big Bang Theory Book of Lists*, is a #1 Bestseller on Amazon. His work has won two Diamond Quill awards and in 2023 he was named Writer of the Year by the League of Utah Writers. He teaches writing for Writer's Digest, Script Magazine, and at the University of Utah. Follow him across social media @swankmotron or visit swankmotron.com.

This anthology would not have been possible without the generous support of our Kickstarter backers. Thank you so much for your immense help!

Aaron Donogh, Abha Thakkar, Abraham Schleppler, Addley Fannin, Adrian Ropp, Alex Altman, Alex Neilson, Alex Smith, Ali Cross, Alicia Yang, Allyn Gibson, Amber Beitzel, Amber Raden, America Masaros, Amy Michels, Amy Oberlin, Amy Priest, Andrew Kaplan, Andrew S. Glazier, Angelike Dexter, Ann Stolinsky, AnnaMaria Phelps, Annie Reed, Anthony Cardno, Aysha Rehm, Bai Shen, Barbara Silcox, Bee Bube, Bethany Kok, Bill Glasgow, Bill Leisner, Blair Jones, Bluetrix Books, Boris A. Veytsman, Brad Jurn, Brian Allred, Brian Herald, Brian Lambert, Brian W. Adams, Bryan Young, Carol Anne Porter, Carol Cyr, Carol Jones, Carolyn Kemp, Carrie Harris, Cat Treadwell, Cerise Cauthron, Charles Prepolec, Cheryl Hammond, Chris Horvath, Christian Srnka, Christopher Abbott, Christopher Condon, Christopher Goetting, Christopher Valin, Christy Everette, Clay Eichelberger, Daneen McDermott, Daniel A Dickholtz, Daniel Chamberlin, Daniel, Darby Green, Darcy Conaty, David Forte, David Gordon, David Horst, David Krieger, David L. Chamberlain, David Scoggins, David Tai, David W. Myers, David Young, Dean Arashiro, Deborah Lynn Daughetee, Denis MacDougall, Denise Jaden, Denise Lin, Derrick Dinwiddie, Diana Botsford, Dodie Sullivan, Don Spiro, Douglas Vaughan, Duncan Gibson, Edirin Oputu, Eileen Rock, Elaine Rodrigues, Eli Strawn, Elizabeth Doherty, Emilirose Rasmusson, Emily Robbins, Emma Lord, Eric Jordan, Eric Lowmiller, Erin Ashby, Eugene Myers, Faith Handerek, Fiona Beatrix Robertson Clark, Francis Maconi, Fred Johnson, Gail E. Morse, Gary Miles, Gary Phillips, George Minor, Gerald Tilley, GhostCat, Gordon Dymowski, GraceAnne DeCandido, Greg Beyerlein, Greg Colbert, Greg Rozier, Gregg Whitmore, Gregory Rihn, Hazi Gafford, Heather Holmquist, Idria Barone Knecht, Isaac Dansicker, J. Kelly Hays, J.M. DeMatteis, Jacen Leonard, Jacob H. Joseph, James Aquilone, James Cushman, Jamieson M. Cobleigh, Jason Chance, Jason Frisvold, Jason Inman, Jaz, Jeff Bixler, Jeff Linder, Jeff Metzner, Jeff N. of Hoboken, Jeffrey Harlan, Jen Marsh, Jenna Cardno, Jennifer R. Frontera, Jeremy Bottroff, Jeremy Broadfield, Jessica Judd, Jim Johnson, Jim Jorritsma, Joanne

Scher, Jody Houser, Joe Gillis, Joanna Draper Carlson, John Cohl, John D. Reed, John Keegan, John Markley, Joseph Llanes, Josh Jasper, Joshua McGinnis, Jules Dickinson, Kaitlyn Joie Maxwell, Karen Krah, Kathleen Thompson, Kathryn Collings, Kathryn Jerome, Kelly Ann Parmelee, Ken Manherz, Kenneth Seed, Kerry Kuhn, Kevin Halstead, Kimberly St. Jean, KLA, Kristy Wagner, Kyle Helstrom, Lara Nell Brown, Laura Baughman, Laura Inglis, Laura Roberts, Laura Ware, Laurel Gupton, Lauren Ganger, Leesa Hanagan, Leigh Harkin, Leslie Trigg, Lexie Briggs, Lily Blackthorn, Lily Greer, Linda Thomas, Lindsey Zuercher, Lisa Komisar, Lola McCrary, Lorraine Anderson, Lou Tambone, Lousie Lowenspets, maileguy, Margaret Gilligan, Margaret Walsh, Mark Martinez, Mark McCormack, Mark Squire, Marshiela Rockwell, Mary Ann Collins, Mary Anne Espenshade, Mary Jane Hetzlein, Mary Mousseau, Masamichi Higurashi, Matt Forbeck, Matthew Allder, Matthew Barr, Matthew Ceplina, Megan Hungerford, Melissa Hannon, Michael A. Burstein, Michael Bentley, Michael Cohen, Michael Dubost, Michael Gordon, Michael Griffin, Michael Kilgore, Michael S. Haynes, Michelle Cramer, Michelle Loseke, Michelle Sturgell, Mike Thurlow, Mike Tickler Jr, Mordechai Gofman, Museworthy Inc, N.E. Broadwell, Nathaniel Krinsky, Neil Kleid, Neil Ottenstein, Nicholas Dinep-Schneider, nith, Norma Barrett Lincoln, Patricia Villacrusis, Paul Balze, Paul Leach, Paul Malysz, Paul Simpson, Paul Sparks, Pauline Zvejnieks, Peggy Kimbell, R. Kelly Wagner, Rachael Headrick, Rachel Ward, Ralph Melton, Raphael Sutton, Rebecca Kronenfeld, Rebecca Woods, Renae Rosenberg, Ric Bretschneider, Richard Novak, Richard O'Shea, Rinske Wijtmans, Robert Hudson, Rodney Barnett, Rowan Strand, Roz, Samantha Toffolo, Sandra Fabiani, Sara Cravens, Sarah Albertini-Bond, Sarah Bean, Sarah Chesterman, Scott Pollard, Sean Blinn, Sean McCord, Shael Hawman, Shuyi Ma, Sileanea, Staphanie, Stephanie A. Lucas, Stephanie Bannon/Craig Dyer, Stephanie Franklin, Stephen Ballentine, Steven Darrall, Steven P. Biggs, Steven Roby, Steven Sautter, Stuart Moore, Susan Werbin, Tam Frager, Tara Seguin, Taylor O, Teresa Allocca, Terry Federko, The Creative Fund by BackerKit, Thomas G. Kowols, Thomas G. Tellefsen, Thomas Hassan, Tibbi Scott, Tighe Edwards, Tim Costello, Tim Tucker, Tina Good, Todd Sloane, Tom Smith, Tyra Markebo, Tyrel Souza, Vicki Greer, Victoria Johnson, Virgil G Waldrup Jr, Waurika Brock, Wayne Voto, Wendy Wallace, Will Berkovitz, Will McDermott, William Friedell, William S. Tolliver, Wyngarde, Zachary Krishef

Made in the USA
Columbia, SC
28 March 2025

713594fd-8951-4a1d-adbd-4d5097d2b71aR01